LANE WHITT

Copyright © 2019 by Lane Whitt

All rights reserved.

No part of this book may be reproduced in any form or by any electronic or mechanical means, including information storage and retrieval systems, without written permission from the author, except for the use of brief quotations in a book review.

Cover Design: 2019 © L.J. Anderson, Mayhem Cover Creations

Dedicated to these two.

"Stop finding excuses for failure!" he said, disappointment in his eyes. My success will always be in spite of you, she thought, determination in her gaze and a knife in her heart.

CONTENTS

Chapter One	1
Chapter Two	11
Chapter Three	28
Chapter Four	60
Chapter Five	83
Chapter Six	105
Chapter Seven	124
Chapter Eight	142
Chapter Nine	159
Chapter Ten	164
Chapter Eleven	178
Chapter Twelve	193
Chapter Thirteen	226
Chapter Fourteen	247
Chapter Fifteen	264
Chapter Sixteen	293
Chapter Seventeen	299
Chapter Eighteen	307
Chapter Nineteen	316
Epilogue	324
Coming Soon	329
About the Author	333

CHAPTER ONE

Pregnant. I can hardly believe the words coming out of my mouth. Me. Pregnant. With a baby. I thought Kellan was losing it when he rushed in and put his ear to my belly, shushing me when I asked what on Earth he was up to. I'll never forget the look in his beautiful grass-green eyes when he raised his head. I don't think I've ever seen so much pure emotion pour out of another being and feel it seep into my own soul such as it had in that moment. Kellan then proceeded to press his face against my belly, occasionally drying happy tears on my shirt, which is where he still remains.

Mere seconds later I'm gathered in Logan's long-armed embrace and spun around until I'm dizzy. "I knew I made the right call in keeping you, you fantastic little creature! Our baby is going to be fucking gorgeous, just you wait and see. Paris and Milan will go to war to have our beautiful pup walk their runways," He tells me dreamily, already picturing it in his head. I toss my head back and laugh at his silly declarations before hugging him harder and accepting the wild kiss he delivers upon me.

When my vision finally catches up with the room, I'm able to take in the rest of my mates as they look on with various expressions. Logan hands me off to Tristan, who is beaming his perfect Tristan smile at me. I receive a hug from him as well, and a promise of a celebratory feast tonight in honor of our "little miracle". Reed and Jace approach me together, both taking kisses of their own, while Reed promises a proper, private celebration with just the two of us later this evening, and Jace informs me that we should name the baby Jace III, his trademark smirk in place. I have to laugh at the reminder of the Big Jace/Little Jace fiasco. While the non-teddy bear Jace took the whole thing in stride, it sure didn't stop his prideful need to remind me just how *big* he truly is. Actually, I think I totally deserve a pat on the back for that one. Who knew a prank would turn out to be so rewarding?

Finn responds just as I knew he would—without words. He lays his emotions, raw and unfiltered, out for my perusal within his minty green eyes. I'm sure his brilliant mind is battling countless thoughts of everything he's ever learned about pregnancy, childbirth, and parenting, but he doesn't voice those things now. I keep quiet, too, and just let him hold me as he inhales deeply at my hair. Both of us just want to *feel* right now, not think. Although I'm sure lessons with Finn will, no doubt, take a turn to all things baby moving forward. That's probably a good thing, as I have yet to excel at any of the social interaction lessons.

At Finn's suggestion, everyone except Remy and Ash head out of the family room and busy themselves to give the three of us a moment alone. Both men before me act as if they are glued to their posts at the entryway. For the first time in what seems like forever, I'm nervous around my mates. Ash stands as tall as ever in his V-neck t-shirt, dark-wash jeans, boots, and black leather jacket. Oh, the things that jacket does for his insanely attractive figure. His big brown eyes are blown wide and staring at me unblinkingly as tanned skin ripples over endless muscles. I know he's fighting the need for his wolf to take over, and a pang of understanding hits me square in the chest. My poor Shadow doesn't do well with emotions, does he? Part of me wishes I knew what he was thinking right now, but the other, more sensible, part of me knows that I'd probably be very scared of the thoughts in my overprotective giant's mind.

Still, Ash's reaction is a whole lot better than Remy's. I think I might have broken Remy. I'm not even sure if he's breathing. His bright copper hair appears even brighter and his already fair skin has taken on a ghostly pale color. The blank expression on his handsome face, and in his intimidating grey eyes that seem to see nothing at all, has me worried. My mates and I haven't exactly spoken of children before. I mean, comments have been made, but this little alien inside of me wasn't planned or anything. Remy may not have been born an alpha like Grandfather speaks about, but he's our family's alpha—he's *my* alpha, and his opinion matters to me very much.

Is he angry with me? Angry that he didn't get a say about this? My heart pounds harder at the thought, and my need to please my alpha mate has me taking a cautious step forward. "Remington?" I breathe out.

The sound of my voice snaps both men out of their strange trance, and they blink their dazzling eyes at me before glancing briefly at each other. I gasp in shock—and somewhat horror—as a glistening tear falls from Ash's eye and Remy erupts in booming, happy laughter. The two very large men move to embrace one another, clapping each other on the back. My head tilts to the side as I watch them curiously, confused by their actions. As adorable as the two of them are right now, I can't but help think how very strange men are.

Ash turns away from Remy to look at me and I feel my whole world stop. There are no words to describe the look he gives me in that moment. The wide smile, the tears, the love that radiates out of this man...it's all too much for me. I rush to Ash, jumping as high as I can so that I can wrap myself around him like a pretzel. I sob with my face buried in his neck, inhaling his fiery scent, and hold on to him like my life depends on it. This man, all of my men, couldn't be more beautiful if they tried, both inside and out. I have no idea why I'm crying. Maybe happiness, maybe because I'm so utterly confused as to what I've done in my life to deserve them, and the very real fear that one day they will ask the same question. But I can't seem to stop.

My mates let me cry out whatever emotions I needed to exorcise for what feels like forever. With Ash glued to my front and Remy plastered to my back, I'm not sure if I ever want to move again. Eventually, though, Remy gently coaxes me down and places me back on my feet. Ash's huge hand rubs at my back as I'm turned to face Remy. His hand shakes a bit as he slowly brushes my hair away from my face, until every strand is tucked behind my ears. His rough fingers continue to caress my face, running under my chin and eventually over my lips with the barest of touches. He kisses me then, soft and sweet and completely devastating to my already too-full heart.

"Kitten..." He whispers my name like a prayer, sinking to his knees in front of me and placing his forehead against my tummy. I take the opportunity to run my hands through his coarse hair that reminds me of the sky at sunset, scratching lightly at his scalp with my nails as he likes me to do. Remy starts to speak a couple of times, but it's as if he can't find the right words to say. I give him time, eventually moving my free arm to hold him to me. I've decided that I very much like this position and I don't want him to move.

"I don't think I can ever explain what this child means to me, Kitten. I've lived for so many years, so many decades and centuries, knowing I could never be a father. Knowing I would never have a son to teach to hunt or fish, or even ride a bike. Or a daughter to look at me in that way only daughters can look upon their fathers. Like the sun rises and sets by my willpower alone, that no harm could ever come to her because I'm her dad and no man will ever be greater. I've watched so many children be born to this world, so many families made and I...this child, this little life growing inside of you, is my deepest desire come true." He raises his head to look at me, even though we're nearly face to face as is.

"You, Kitten, are my greatest love, my deepest joy, and now you're going to be the mother of my child. The words "thank you" will never be enough, but I vow to spend every waking moment of the rest of my life showing you how grateful I am to have you in my life. You brought my family closer together already, in our shared love for you, and now you give us a new member. A new life to cherish, and celebrate, and love."

My mouth opens to speak, but no words come out. Tears of my own spring up and make warm tracks down my cheeks as I try to form a response worthy of such a declaration. "So, you're not mad." I blurt. *So glad I took the time for that lovely thought*, I chastise myself mentally. Both Remy and Ash laugh, each of them hugging me once more before clearing their throats and taking a deep breath.

Remy gets to his feet and smiles down at me, shaking his head. "I could never be angry at you for such a gift, Love."

"I'm not as eloquent as Rem, but what he said holds true for me, too. I'm happy with the family I already have, but this child already means the world to me, Baby," Ash tells me.

I giggle at his use of my nickname. "I don't think you can all me that anymore, Ash. The baby will be Baby, right?"

Ash narrows his eyes roguishly. "I'll call either of you whatever I like, as both of you will always be precious to me and protected by me. You're both mine to care for."

"Oh, really? Does that mean I call you 'Baby', then? You're *mine* to care for," I joke.

"Oh, please do. I insist," Remy prods with a devilish grin. Ash just shakes his head and rolls his eyes at the two of us.

Wow. Feast is an understatement. "Tristan, you have outdone yourself, truly," I tell him with awe. The large conference table in the meeting room is almost completely covered with piled plates of food. Hams, turkeys, and several whole chickens make a line down the center of the table, surrounded by mashed potatoes, ears of corn, salads, baked breads, and even a few things I have no name for. I don't know where to start. Part of me just wants to roll around in it all and take bites of whatever ends up near my face.

"Aww, you broke her, Tris," Logan jokes with an elbow to Tristan's side. When I narrow my eyes at him playfully, he just sticks his tongue out at me.

"I'm not broken, just...awed, I guess. How did you make all of this? And it smells so wonderful!" I make my way to Tristan and wrap my arms around his torso as hard as I can. "Thank you."

"Anything for my girl," he tells me with a peck on my forehead. "And wolf speed does help a bit, though I had plenty of helpers today. Mike, here, was one of them; we may have a budding chef on our hands with that one," he says fondly, looking to Mikey, making him blush in embarrassment.

"Yeah! I helped. I peeled potatoes and carrots and got to smash them, too!" Mikey tells me excitedly.

Jace grunts in amusement. "You put the kid on scut work?"

Tristan shrugs a shoulder. "Every good chef starts out on the bottom."

"I bet you did," Logan mumbles with a wicked grin.

Ash and Remy laugh as Tristan releases me to chase a cackling Logan around the table. There was probably a joke in there somewhere, but it's over my head. All of the guys have been playful and lighthearted today. More smiles and laughter and back-patting have gone on since this morning than I've experienced in a lifetime. I like this. I like seeing them all so happy.

I let Mikey pull me to a seat near the middle and sit beside him as he tells me about his day in the kitchen. I've been thinking all day about how to break the news to him. I'm not sure how much he'll care one way or the other, but it's important to me to go about this the right way with him. I also feel like since bringing him home from the hospital Mikey and I haven't spent much time together, and there's a lot of things left unsaid and undecided between us. I did, however, come to a decision today. I thought about waiting until I spoke with all of my mates, but even then, my own mind is made up. They can choose whatever they wish, but it won't change for me.

A natural lull in conversation in the middle of dinner has me shifting nervously as I look to Mikey, watching him dip bits of his chicken into gravy. "Mikey, I want to talk to you about something."

He drops his chicken, eyes going wide as he sits back and turns to me with his palms out. "It wasn't my fault! Perry started it, and Morris was the one who drove it! I told them they'd get in trouble. I only got in to make sure they didn't get hurt." He nods his little head emphatically.

I blink at him at few times. "Uh...what?" Well, this isn't how I thought this would go.

"He's talking about him and his friends getting a hold of one of my forklifts. They managed to push the right controls to get it work and went for a little joyride," Remy explains, the reproach clear in his voice.

I put my head in my hands and sigh. Clearly this was something we'd have to address, and it only adds to my guilt about not watching him like I should.

I try again. "That isn't what I wanted to talk about, Mikey.

Please just listen for a moment, because I want you to think about this seriously. I don't want to push you into anything, and I want it to be your decision only, okay?"

I can almost see the walls slam down over his emotions. Given everything that has happened to him in his young life I'm not surprised, though it hurts to see it all the same. "O...kay?"

"It's nothing bad," I promise quickly. "It's just that...ever since you to came to live with us there's been an open-ended question about what we are to each other. I think of you as family now, and I think I considered you family for a long time even before. I just didn't know what it really meant. Does that make sense?" I'm rambling and I know it.

"Sort of," he answers warily.

"Well, you see, I left it up to you before, about whether you would see me as more of a sister or aunt or... a mother figure." I pause, trying to read him. He just looks confused.

"Yeah?"

"And, well, it's still up to you, of course, but I'd like to take on more of a mother role for you. I feel like leaving it open before may have made you think I didn't want to. Honestly, I didn't know if I wanted to. I didn't and still don't know what it means really, but I'd like to try." My heart feels like it's beating way too fast and I'm so nervous.

Mikey takes his time answering, pushing food around his plate before looking back to me. "You mean you want to be my mom?"

I, too, take my time answering, but for different reasons. He could say no. "I do. I found out earlier today that I'm going to have a baby. After some thought I realized that, while this might be my first baby, it won't be my first child. Not the first child that I'd die to protect, not the first child that I'd do anything to make happy and safe. I already have a child I'd do those things for. You. You mean the world to me, Mikey. I'm probably a horrible pick for a mom, but you have me if you want me." I try to smile, but I'm near tears for some reason.

To my absolute horror, he laughs. Like really hard, holding his stomach laughing. Then he throws his thin little arms around me in a side hug. Speaking lowly, so he thinks only I can hear, he tells me, "Okay, Mom." Tears sting the back of my eyelids as I feel a hole I wasn't aware of stitch itself back together again in my chest.

"Really?" I pull back so I can see his face. He looks happy, lips turned up in a grin. I awkwardly put my arms around him, too, pulling him closer.

He pulls away first, already nodding up and down. "Yeah. Back at the ice rink, I used to tell new kids that you were my mom. They didn't believe me, but I didn't care." He shrugs like it's nothing. While he goes back to his food, considering the matter over and done with, I finally glance around the table, not knowing what to expect from my men.

Kellan and Finn are seated across from me, so my eyes land on them first. Twin grins greet me and I can tell they aren't angered. Jace's golden eyes shine with something I can't understand, and Logan smirks like he knew this was coming. Ash is hard to read, but he nods once in approval. Remington gives me a look like we'll talk about this later, but his body is relaxed and I get a sense of approval from him as well. Reed mouths, "I love you" with a smile, while Tristan leans around Mikey to kiss the top of my head. No one makes a big deal out of the discussion, simply going back to enjoying their meal, and I'm thankful for it. I really don't want to start crying again. It might give Mikey the wrong idea, and I honestly can't predict how long the crying will take anymore.

I let out a relieved and calming breath. Knowing that, no matter their reactions, I would still feel the same about Mikey didn't mean that I wasn't worried about what they thought. I'll proudly claim the title of mom, but that doesn't mean that they had to stand up and take on the role of Mikey's father. Or, well, fathers. I still don't know if they will, or if they want to, but from this day forward Mikey Ivaskov is my son. I'll have to figure out this whole mom thing as soon as possible, because I want to be a really good one for both him and this baby.

CHAPTER TWO

I watch his black curls bounce around his shoulders as we jump over the cracks on the hard walking space. He was kind enough to warn me earlier that stepping on the cracks would break his mother's back, so I concentrate hard on avoiding them. Friends don't break their friends' mother's backs.

The boy takes my hand as I stop outside of his sleeping place, and he drags me through the door behind him. It smells nice in here, like food and warmness. I hear one of those magic boxes with people trapped inside, like they had in the hospital, but the boy pulls me to a smaller room with a table and a tall person with her back to us.

"Hey, baby, did you have fun at the park?" she asks my friend without turning around. What is she doing? I hear water and splashing, but I can't figure out what she's doing with the eating things. Plates, those are plates.

"Yes!" My friend tells her as he lets go of my hand and walks around the small room. "I made a friend, can we have a sleepover?"

"Hmm, I don't know, honey. Do I know his parents? Do you go to school with him?" she asks.

"She doesn't have parents. I promise I'll feed her and give her a bath. I'll take good care of her, Mom, I swear!" He pleads with Mom, going to her and hugging her leg.

"What on Earth are you going on about, boy? She? And everyone has parents, Tony." Mom admonishes as she dries her hands on a rag. She turns to face me, her eyes going wide and her hand going to her chest.

"E-ever one h-ham parent? E-even smeee?" I ask hopefully, speaking slowly and as clearly as I can.

Mom lets out an ear-piercing scream that scares me, while she grabs my friend and pulls him close to her. "What is that? Oh my God, Tony! What have you done? It's...it's an alien...or...or some kind of beast!" She continues to yell at me, placing my friend Tony on top of the table and grabbing a long stick with something on the end of it.

I look behind me for the beast, scared that it will get me. It's a good thing Mom has a stick. Should I climb up on the table...Oww! Hurt starts on my arm and I look back to Mom. She has the stick raised in the air and she's looking right at me again.

"Get out of here! Git! You leave my son alone, you hear me?" she screams, poking me with the stick, hard. I hiss at her. Mom is mean.

"No, Mommy! She's my friend! She's a nice alien, she eats berries off the tree in the park, not people!" my friend Tony pleads.

She takes a step toward me, the stick raised again to hit me. I back away from her and she lets me turn and run away from their sleeping place. As I run back toward my own sleeping place, I step on every crack along the way. Tears leak down my face as I take time to stomp on some of the bigger ones, wondering if I've broken Mom's back yet. I hope so, because my friend is in danger. I hope she doesn't hit him with the stick, too. And what about the beast?

I end up going to the big warm place that always makes me feel better. Maybe one of the tall people will tell stories again. When I arrive, I notice there's not many people here this time. The tall *person called Librarian is at her table, though, and she frowns down at me.*

Before she asks me her usual questions, I ask her one. "W-what tis awien?"

"Oh, sweetie. Where did you hear that word?" she asks.

I shake my head. "Awien," I repeat for her. "A-wi-eeen. I tis awian?" I sound out, like she's showed me before.

Librarian clears her throat, like she does when I make her sad and she doesn't want me to know. "An alien is science-fiction; they're not real. Some people think they are real, that they're another species from another planet, or outer space, who might one day try to take over the world or enslave humans, and other nonsense like that." She steps slowly around her table to kneel in front of me. "So, Kitten, you can't be an alien, you see?"

I shake my head at her again. "No, I tis awien. I takes world and swace p-pawents come b-back fur smeee. I not Titten, I awien." I stomp my foot and cross my arms to make my point. Everyone has parents, Mom said, so maybe mine are out in space, with the lights in the sky, and they just forgot where they left me. They'll come back for me, I know it, and when they do, we'll take over the world like aliens do.

"Kitten. Sweetie, is everything okay?" Reed's voice is rough with sleep as he gently shakes me awake. It takes me moment to remember where I am, or better yet *when* I am. That's the third time this week that I've dreamed so hard I become disoriented upon waking. Only they aren't really dreams, are they? Scenes from my past seem to haunt me, just waiting until I'm too tired to fight them back.

"Just a dream. Go back to sleep," I tell him quietly, running my fingers through his blonde locks. His breathing evens out in moments, and I can tell he's asleep again. After last night, I'm surprised he could even form words. That man and his tongue...insatiable.

I, on the other hand, don't think I'll be sleeping again. I don't know why these dreams are coming on so strong lately, but I feel like they're happening for a reason. The reason for this memory was pretty clear. I had thought the term 'alien' earlier, about the baby, so I was given the memory of when I was younger and was determined to be an alien.

A baby. I still can't believe it. My life has been a constant whirlwind for months now. I can clearly picture the day I first met Tristan and Ash. Or the Giant and Chocolate-eyes, as I had named them that day. Until that night, that day had gone as most days did for me. I had checked in with my various jobs to see if they had work for me. The diner had let me wash dishes, although it was an odd shift that left me returning home after dark. Skipping over accidentally falling asleep, and the resulting assault, I remember how I had felt running away. I had told myself at the time that I refused to give up, but looking back I realize that I had. I made my body move, but inside I had been dying a slow death; a battle I wasn't aware of. I wanted something more, some connection to this world other than the breath I took into my lungs.

Then, by fate or by chance, *they* had shown up. One as tall and thick as a tree and the other with a voice like silk. They *saw* me. Not just a broken girl, but *me*. They brought me to their home, brought me into their family. I may have started out as a fun project for Logan, but he took care of me that first day without question. He and Kellan both. I smile to myself in the dark, remembering how I also started out as a threat to Jace, and being scared to death of Remy. Tristan had fed me, Reed had smiled shyly at me, and Finn was and forever would be my Mr. Wolf.

Paintballing, carnival rides, Noah, motorcycle rides, and shopping trips with Ash. It's hard not to laugh right now. I loved them even then. Maybe not in the same way as I do now, but it was the start. My love has just grown since then. One of my favorite memories was being on the ice, having them watch me skate from the stands, and finally knowing what it felt like to have people you cared about cheering you on. It happened fast, faster than it probably does for others. I regret being so cold toward Jace. Time is funny that way, isn't it? Looking back, I know he was sorry for the things he said long before I forgave him. And he never should have been sorry in the first place. He was and is protective of his family, in his own way. I love him dearly for that very reason now.

I think it was mere weeks before I was taken from them. Actually, I spent more time away from them than I had *with* them at that point. That's a place in my head I don't want to go right now, or maybe ever. It was too late after that, though. I already loved them. Knowing that at least some of them were still out there was all that kept me going. Becoming a wolf, becoming like them, was just something that had happened along the way. Kind of like finding out my last name, that I had blood family ready to accept me, and that an entire pack of wolves would come to depend on me. All of that was just life happening, but my *reason* for life started the moment Ash and Tristan saved me from giving up at that angel fountain. They were what I was looking for all along. A connection, a place where I belonged.

And here we all are, getting ready to bring new life into our family and accepting another child as our own. We're growing our pack already, and it's only been months. I don't know what my past has to do with any of it, but I as I lay here, thinking over how exactly I *got* here, I know without a doubt that I can face anything. Because I'm not alone anymore, not because of my mate that I feel beside me, or because of the baby growing inside of me, but because there's simply no going back now. Not for any of us. And I think that *this* is what family means. Forming bonds that simply cannot be broken, because we won't allow them to, because we don't want them to.

"What are you thinking so hard about?" Reed asks, pulling me out of my head. I shift around, now noticing that the sun has begun to rise, and my sensitive, multi-color-eyed mate has been watching me.

I smile lazily at him, reaching out to run my fingertips over his jaw, tracing his thin, pink lips. "I was thinking of us. All of us. We've had a crazy ride so far. I keep dreaming of my past, back when I was little. I don't know what it means."

His hand covers my own, placing a kiss in my palm, entwining our fingers and laying them between us. "What was it like when you were little?"

I frown, trying to find the right words. "Confusing, I guess. Everything was kind of a mystery. What things were named, why people went here and did that. Why I wasn't like everyone around me. I wasn't sad or angry most of the time, but confused."

"I can only imagine. I guess you learned a lot of things out of order."

"I wished for words. That's what went through my head the most. I never had the words," I try to explain.

"Words for what?" he prods.

"Imagine standing on the grass in your bare feet, still damp from an overnight rain just as the sun starts to paint the sky in every amazing color there is. A soft wind is blowing through your hair, you can feel it on your fingertips. A bakery across the street has been working for hours by that point and decides to open their doors to let out some of the heat from the kitchen. The smell of fresh baked bread and pastries carries on the wind to you."

Reed's smile turns soft and I know that his artistic mind can paint it all clearly for him.

"Now, imagine not knowing what you're standing on. Why is it softer here than the hard stuff next to it? What makes the water fall from up above sometimes, when other times it doesn't? Where does the ball of light go and why does it come back? You don't know the names of the colors you see, or what presses against your skin. You smell something new in the air that you breathe, but you don't know why you like it or why it makes your mouth water and your stomach hurt. You just recognize the smell as food, something you're supposed to eat, but you know that if you follow the smell the tall people won't let you eat the food."

Reed closes his eyes, the skin right below pinkening in the way that it does when he fights back his emotions. The dreamy smile is now gone from his face, replaced with a crestfallen expression. "I can picture that, and I don't know if I would've been strong enough to endure it." He takes a deep breath, gripping my hands tightly. "Kitten, I know you don't like me to go "*all sad*", but I just don't understand how you made it through your childhood. Babies and young children can't make it on their own. Without someone to provide the basics needed for survival, they die."

"I'm aware of that now. I should have died a million times over. At best, I should be mentally handicapped from malnutrition and neglect. I should've gotten sick from unfiltered water and bacteria. But I didn't, and I think I know why now. Like *right* now, from this conversation." I feel my eyes widen and my heartrate pick up at the realization.

"Tell me," Reed says softly, making me realize it's been a while since I've spoken.

"Because of her...my wolf. I think she was with me this whole time. Everyone keeps saying that I'm different, that I'm not a born wolf but I'm also not a changed wolf. I'm somewhere in between. I think my wolf was always a part of me, waiting to be released. It would explain a lot anyway. The instincts of a human alone wouldn't have kept me alive, but the instincts of a wolf might have."

"Or the instincts of both." He finishes my thought. "If you had the ability to heal yourself, even slightly, that would explain a lot of things."

"Yeah, it's a theory anyway."

He raises himself up, gently placing a kiss on my forehead. "I love that beautiful brain of yours. Whatever the reason, I'm grateful that you survived long enough for me to find you."

"Me, too. Enough about me, though. What was it like when you were little?" I ask, curious to know more about him. I know the him now, as I do the others, but I don't know a whole lot about the *before me* times of their lives.

Reed smiles as his eyes drift off behind me, or maybe into the past. "My mother was an artist. Did I mention that?"

I shake my head no. "That explains you, though," I tease.

He laughs, pulling me to him and throwing his leg over mine. "Probably. From the time that I can remember there were always drawings flung all over the house, and her hands and sometimes face had charcoal all over them. She was a sketch artist. She made money as a seamstress, not in art, but it was her real passion. I was born in New York, but both of my parents were immigrants. I can't for the life of me remember where they came from, but that's probably because as soon as they stepped off that boat, they were Americans. That's what my dad always said, anyway."

I stay quiet, just listening to him talk. I wonder if our child will have memories like these, of him, covered in paint most of the time.

"I remember running around muddy streets filled with people, clothes hanging from lines across buildings, and really hot, stinky summers. What my dad did then, I have no idea. He worked outside of the home. He would bring things home, though, something my mother would chide him about not having space for. Then one day we were packing all of that stuff onto a cart, and we left New York for good."

"Where did you go?" I ask.

"I guess my parents had been longing to head out west for a long time. They were saving up for the trip. I remember hating that damn wagon, though. I slept a lot and I have memories of digging the wheels out of mud with my dad. Also, campfires. Lots and lots of campfires and flat bread. I grew up a lot on that trip, but everyday was basically the same, so my memories are all scattered. I did learn to hunt, and I liked doing that. My mother learned to cook, and she loathed doing that." He chuckles.

"We ended up in what would be California. My dad was going to dig for gold. However, he got sick one day. Not long after that, he died. Our house had already been raised, but to provide for me and herself my mom converted it into a general store of sorts. She served food, too, along with taking side jobs here and there mending and washing miners' clothing. She'd collect the gold dust that got caught inside of pockets and whatnot and use that for money as well. By that time, I was old enough to help her."

"She sounds like an amazing woman. That couldn't have been easy. And I'm sorry about your dad," I tell him honestly.

He kisses me then, just a chaste one. "It was a lifetime ago. My mom had a long life; there weren't many times we went without, and people generally loved her. My only regret is that she gave up art for me, because of what she had to do after my dad died. I should have helped her more, given her more time to do what she loved," he tells me with a hint of sadness in his voice.

"I think she would have loved to know how good an artist you are now, and that you have your own galleries. I think she'd be proud." I smile.

He smiles back. "I think so, too."

He turns then, bringing his lean body over mine and settling himself between my legs. Just the brush of his hardness touching my sensitive skin has my blood on fire. Reed's soft lips brush mine and I open for him, needing to taste him. His tongue dances around mine as one of his hands fists in my hair at the back of my neck, the other lightly tracing my outer thigh. I comb his hair back with my fingers, one hand sliding down his back. The warm, silky skin and feel of his shoulder blades makes me arch up with my hips, wanting to feel him inside me.

At the move, Reed pulls back. He loves to take his time caressing me, both with hands and his mouth. His lips skim over my jaw, moving down the column of my throat before I feel the first lick, sending lightning straight to my core. I moan his name, making him chuckle darkly against my collarbone.

"Not yet, beautiful."

He licks all the way down to my nipple, eliciting another moan from me before pulling the tight bud into his mouth. His hand at my hair slides around to play with the underside of my other breast, driving me crazy. I run the heel of my foot up his thigh, pressing it into his backside, knowing that drives *him* crazy. I smile at his groan of pleasure. Sure enough, he rocks his length into me. Just what I wanted.

"You play dirty," he pants through a smile.

"Only fighting fair, handsome," I tell him as I repeat the move with my other foot. The position leaves my thighs open wide, driving home exactly what I'm wanting. His hips thrust forward harder this time, the full and heavy length of him sliding through my slick core. This time we both moan. He repeats the action a few times with purpose. Once I think I've won, though, he slides his body down mine, giving my inner thigh a teasing bite and nearly making me growl in unexpected pleasure.

Then, he starts. That sinfully amazing tongue of his flicks out to play with my most sensitive flesh, licking and swirling, dipping inside of me over and over again. As sweat forms on my body, and as I'm about to fall over that blissful edge, he repositions himself at my entrance and drives me to ecstasy in one hard thrust of his hips. I call out his name, rocking my hips in time with his as one hand feels his abs flexing and the other holds him to me by his hair. He's all that grounds me now. My body feels like it's floating, chasing the last few moments of electricity pulsing through me and around him. He soon finds his release inside me, my favorite part—when I can feel him pulse and the warmth floods me.

"Only a woman with eight bed partners wakes up looking that tired. Come here, you ravenous little thing." Logan greets me after a much-needed shower and dressing in yoga pants and a one-shouldered sweater.

"Good morning to you, too." I blush even though I roll my eyes at him. He pulls me down on the couch next to him, letting me snuggle into his side. He kind of has a point, though. I *could* use a nap already. Reed, though, looks as if our morning romp has actually *given* him energy. So not fair.

"So, what are the plans for today? Anything interesting?" Reed asks as he picks through a bowl of fruit and some other platters left out on the coffee table. He makes a small plate of strawberries, cheese, and sliced French bread and hands it to me before going back for himself. I thank him with a smile for his thoughtfulness.

Logan shrugs beside me. "Not really. Remy wanted us both to meet up with him and the others at some point today. He took Mikey and headed out to one of the construction sites early. Ash is doing training, and the others are all around here somewhere. Oh, but Marcus did come by a little bit ago to see Kitten." He says the last to me. I nod that I heard him as I take a bite of bread and cheese.

"And you?" Reed asks.

"I'm torn between rounding up some of the wolves and taking them shopping and looking into fabrics to design clothes for our upcoming little one." His foot taps the floor as he ponders.

"You're going to make clothes for the baby?" I gasp, more than a little surprised.

He gives me a look like I'm crazy. "Duh." He almost looks hurt.

I shrug. "I didn't know you made baby clothes."

"I didn't. I don't. But it's a thought. I'd like to at least design a few things for our kid, though."

I beam at him. "That sounds wonderful, Logan."

"Why would you take some of the pack shopping?" Reed asks.

"Ugh! Because this online shopping thing is for the birds! That's why. A lot of the ones who lived in that god-forsaken nightmare out back don't know their own sizes due to only wearing what was available. Now, though, they should be able to have some things that fit them properly…and that I like," he tells us dramatically.

"Remy most likely won't want you to go, though," Reed tells him.

"Oh, yeah. That slipped my mind. Probably best if I don't," Logan agrees.

I tilt my head at the two of them. "Why not?"

Logan's eyes shoot to Reed's. They share a moment before Reed turns to me, a smile on his face, but it looks off. "Because we have to meet up with him and the others today, remember?"

"Right," Logan adds. He jumps up from the couch. "We should go get that out of the way."

Before I can ask why they're acting strange, both of them have their backs to me as they walk toward the stairs. Boys. Weird.

After finishing off my small plate of food, I fell asleep right where I sat. It was nearly noon when I woke back up again, but I was determined to accomplish more than eating and sleeping today. Readjusting my clothes back to rights I'm about to head down the stairs, when I scent Finn close by. He wasn't in his room when I passed by, so, curious, I seek him out. I find him in one of the unused rooms on our floor. The door is shut, so I knock lightly before opening it.

Peeking my head around the door, I see a slightly flustered Finn trying to shove papers into drawers. I tilt my head at him. "Sorry if I interrupted..."

Dazzling green eyes meet mine, instantly losing the mild panic from a split second ago and softening into a different emotion. "Oh, it's just you. You can come in, Kitten. I thought you might be Remington."

I raise a brow at him, a smile tugging at my lips. "And just what are we hiding from Remy?"

Finn's boyish grin lights up his whole face, his pinkening cheeks only adding to his appeal. "I'm not hiding anything. I was just working on something and it isn't ready for him to see yet," he explains.

"Okay." I shrug. As he pulls the crumpled papers back out of the desk, I walk behind his chair and place my arms around his neck. I bury my face in between his shoulder and chin, inhaling his unique scent. The only way to describe it would be that of vast, open spaces of rolling green hills. Closing my eyes for a moment, I bask in the calm strength that only this man can provide me.

"This..." Finn mumbles quietly.

"This?" I question as I open my eyes, letting my hands trail lightly over his narrow chest.

His midnight hair tickles my cheek as he nods. "Yes, this. Little moments like this one...it's what was missing before," he explains. We share a smile of understanding before I kiss his pouty lips and move my hands to his shoulders.

"Can I know what you're working on?" I ask with a glance at the random-looking papers.

"Uh, yeah, I guess. It's just an idea. I don't know if it will work, or if we even want it to." He trails off, seeming to get lost in his thoughts.

I walk around him and hop onto the edge of the desk. "So, what's the idea?"

He takes several minutes to respond, running his long fingers through that inky hair. "On the most basic level, it's a school."

I chew my lip, nodding as I wait for him to add more. When he doesn't, I press further. "A school for wolves like us?"

"Maybe." He sighs. "It's just an idea. I'm trying to figure out a few things long-term for the pack. I feel like the changes we've made since being here are just temporary. Like band-aids. Necessary band-aids, but ones that won't completely solve the problems."

"What problems are we trying to solve, exactly?" I ask, now more interested in this project than just a passing curiosity.

"For starters, it could be a place for pack members to become educated, as any school's purpose is. We are wolves that live as humans, so it stands to reason to be educated on both the wolf world and the human world. The school would solve the issues of pack members being left in the dark when it comes to their own histories. As well as them understanding human society well enough to blend in. Most of the wolves here have never stepped foot off of pack lands; they wouldn't know the difference from a five-star restaurant and a post office."

"I know," I whisper sadly. "The neglect shown to these people is overwhelming. I think I know why no one ever educated them on all things wolf, though."

Finn raises a brow at me. "Oh, really? Why is that?"

"Probably because nobody knows. Which doesn't make sense, I know, because everything I've read makes it seem like there have always been scientists and researchers and those who want to record our history. My guess is that those in charge hide whatever information they don't want brought to light. I mean, how is it that no one can tell me why I exist? I can't be the first of whatever I am."

"I agree with you, in part. Your own grandfather is known as Maksim the Great due to what humans would call an "Enlightenment Age". I have no doubt that the science, research, and history are there. What any of the history books forget to mention is the *why* of how everything changed. It's almost as if wolf society was advanced at one point, only to fall back into the Dark Ages where the answer for everything is magic."

"My guess would be The Suffering. When that took place, it seems as if everything shifted. New rules came forth, and whatever knowledge was common only became known to the few." I shrug. I've read through the few books available here and facts seem to be far and few between, mostly written as opinion pieces. I know Finn had read them, too, probably coming to the same conclusion.

"Your grandfather would know," he hedges.

I nod my head, biting at my lip. "I've thought of that, too. I just don't know how to start that conversation. How does one simply ask, *"You know all that information you're hiding from everyone else? Yeah, I'm gonna need that."*

Finn's startled laughter makes me smile. "There are more subtle ways of beginning an uncomfortable dialogue, Kitten." I just shrug. If there are, I don't know them.

"I still think anything he would tell us would just be more pack propaganda. The only way to get a full wolf history would be to ask all the wolves. Not just ones in our own pack."

Finn nods. "I agree. There needs to be an open information exchange amongst us all. That's what I would want for the school. That wouldn't happen overnight, though."

"No, but if anyone could make it happen it would be you. You could be the first person to map and record the entire wolf history," I say brightly.

"You think too highly of me." He snorts.

"I think you don't think highly enough of yourself. If this is something you want to make happen, then you'll make it happen. And I'll help, if you want. We could start by documenting what we *do* know about wolves now. I think the hardest part of it all will be separating fact from fiction. Or better yet, science from magic. And let's not forget that you and the others carry with you important information that no one has ever cared to document. The history of changed wolves."

Finn stares at me for a long time, his face held in wonder and contentment. I gaze back at him quietly, hoping to convey just how much I believe in him and his dreams. I don't know what makes Finn shy, or why he second-guesses himself, but I decide right here and now to find out and build his confidence in himself.

His cheeks pinken, realizing he's been staring, and he clears his throat to hide unnecessary embarrassment. "We got off topic there."

"Just a bit." I giggle. "Do you want to tell me more about this school you're thinking about?"

CHAPTER THREE

I peek around the corner, scanning the room quickly. No sign of the enemy. I roll my eyes, about ready to give up and start wondering why I'm so bad at this game, when I remember to use my wolf senses. *Duh, Kitten.*

I hate trying to sniff the air, as absolutely everything has a scent and it can be overwhelming, but I've been practicing with my advanced hearing. I listen for the telltale pattering of heartbeats and follow the one I detect hiding behind the curtain. A giggle escapes me as the excitement of the chase is just too much to contain any longer.

A squealing peal of laughter is all the warning I get before Mikey, dressed head to toe in ninja black, shoots out from behind the curtain and high-tails it out of the room. I laugh fully now, giving chase and dashing down the hallway while trying to avoid running into the few people walking about. For a young thing, he sure is agile. It's not until he slows to make the turn into the kitchen that I have the opportunity to catch up with him.

We're both laughing way too hard as I grab him around his waist and start tickling him senseless. We end up falling to the floor in a tangle of limbs, with me trying to find his most ticklish spots and him trying to escape me. I know we've caught the attention of several people, but I'm not ready to give up until Mikey tells me where his accomplices are hiding.

"Just tell me where they are and this can all be over!" I manage through laughter as I aim for the pits.

"Never!" he squeals back.

"I got twenty on Kitten." Tristan's voice floats to my ears.

"Nah, the kid is squirmy. It's like trying to wrestle an alligator." Logan takes his bet.

Their banter gets my attention and I glance over, spotting Logan atop the counter, popping grapes into his mouth as Tristan leans next to him, catching the ones he drops. They both watch with amused grins. Unfortunately for me, Mikey takes advantage of my distraction and hops up faster than a bunny on crack.

"Ha! You'll never take me alive!" he shouts at the top of his lungs as he makes his escape.

"No fair!" I call after him. "They distracted me." Turning back to the guys, I point an accusing finger at them both. "You distracted me. Whose side are you on anyway?" Tristan just shakes his head as Logan makes a face, sticking his tongue out.

I get back to my feet and race down the hallway to where I think Mikey has run off to. As I'm approaching the corner my shoulder bumps into something hard, and I let out a squeak as time slows down in that odd way that only happens when you're falling. Strong arms wrap around me and catch me right before my face makes impact with the floor.

I'm lifted up and set to rights, but before I can say thank you a pair of angry, liquid-silver eyes are right in front of me. "What are you *doing*?" Remy booms at me, making me take a step away from him. "You can't be running around that fast. You could have gotten hurt! The *baby* could have gotten hurt! You can't just..."

He trails off as he closes his eyes on a deep inhale, fists clenching at his sides.

"Ah, so it's been confirmed then. I'll try not to take it personally that none of you have reached out to me to share the news. Or the fact that there was no ceremony for the pack's sake." Grandfather's Russian accent slips out as he makes it known he's none too pleased to be informed of the news in such an informal manner.

I take my eyes off Remy for a split second to see that he was in the company of Maksim and Albert. "I-I was playing hide and go peek," I stutter an explanation.

"Well, don't!" Remy barks at me. He appears to have calmed himself. A little.

I purse my lips at him, hands already sliding to my hips. "I will if I want to. I don't need your permission to play a game."

"Do you realize what could have just happened?" he says in a softer voice, though I can still sense his anger.

"Um, I could have fallen?" I stare at him confusedly. "I was doing fine before you appeared out of nowhere. Maybe I should get you a bell or something." I say with a smirk, remembering the first time I ran into him.

Silver eyes widen as his mouth drops open. "Are...are you blaming *me* for what just happened?"

"Now, now, children. Let's not fuss over what could have been and point fingers. The matter was handled." Grandfather steps between us and slides an arm around my shoulders, ushering me back down the way I came. "Albert, why don't you run ahead and see to it that the sitting room is suitable for a private chat?"

I look back over my shoulder at Remy as Albert moves past us. He looks like he's cooled off now, and I can't help but stick my tongue out at him playfully. His eyes narrow heatedly in response and he mouths the word "Later" at me. I clear my throat and move out of Grandfather's hold as my cheeks turn pink. A satisfied-sounding grunt from behind me reaches my ears, but I choose to ignore it.

We pass by the kitchen. Both Tristan and Logan are singing "Kitten got in trouble" in a sing-song tone before Remy shushes them with a look.

"Hey, can one of you guys go tell the boys I can't play right now?" I ask.

"Sure thing, Pretty Girl," Logan tells me, kissing my forehead and sauntering off.

Tristan chooses to join our little group and it appears as though Jace will be here for it as well, as he's conversing quietly with Albert in the sitting room when we come in. I approach my golden boy with a smile already tilting my lips, but as I near them his golden eyes flash to me and his whole body goes rigid.

Turning to Albert he speaks formally and sharply. "Find me later, Albert. I have to figure this out before it drives me insane."

As Jace passes by me he nods his head but doesn't so much as say hello.

"Of course, Alpha Jace," Albert replies.

Jace stops dead in his tracks in the doorway, his skin rippling as he tries to control his wolf. "Don't call me that! I can't stand this shit!" He throws his hands out to his sides, stomping away from us. I blink at the empty doorframe in shock. What was that about? Now that I'm thinking about it, I realize it has been a while since I've had a real conversation with Jace. He's been sleeping in later than the rest of us and I had just assumed he's been busy. But now…I wonder if he's been avoiding me. I finally turn my eyes to the rest of the room and silver orbs are waiting. Remy shares a look that tells me that we'll figure out what's going on with Jace. Together.

Grandfather clears his throat in an attempt to get us back on track and say whatever he brought us here to say. "Well now, look at you! Already glowing. I had my suspicions, but I was waiting for your mates to catch on," Grandfather jokes.

His powerful arms go around my shoulders as he pulls me into a warm hug. "Congratulations, my dear. With this child, you will secure your mate's place as alpha and ensure the Ivaskov line continues." He beams at me as he pulls away.

"Yes, Princess. The news of an heir and our future, rightful Alpha is most welcome news," Albert adds.

"Uhhh, thanks?" I'm not sure what the right response is here.

"It would be a good move to announce this news to the pack as soon as possible. I'll need to set up a receiving line after the announcement, and correspondence will need to be sent to the other packs. While some may take offense to your mates, none will challenge the legitimacy of an Ivaskov heir." Albert takes out a notepad and pen and starts making a list.

My eyes connect with Remy's as my earlier shock of two minutes ago fades, and a dismaying weight of something unnamable fills my chest.

"Come, Granddaughter, let us sit for a moment." Maksim leads me to the small two-seater couch as everyone else finds somewhere to sit or lean. A moment later, Logan returns and quietly sits next to Tristan.

Maksim takes my hands in his, effectively turning my body towards him. Eyes so much like my own implore me to hear him out. "You might want to take this time to consider young Michael's position within the pack. I know you are fond of the boy, but the wolves won't like their future alpha having competition. Especially from a human child, and one not of royal blood. His title may need a bit of...fine tuning."

And there it is...the reason my blood had turned to ice. I guess I should have seen this coming. "His position in the pack is my son. That's not for anyone to question or challenge. He'll be a brother to any other children I have," I state firmly.

Maksim sighs deeply. "Can you just, for one moment, try to see things from a wolf's perspective?"

"That's hardly fair." Tristan speaks up, offended on my behalf.

Maksim raises a hand to stop any other protests. "I am aware of Kitten's past and the fact that it is not her fault she wasn't raised to be who she has become. I just want you to understand that you now have a child that you are claiming as your own, who will be older than any other children you have. In effect, a first-born son who is now known as Michael Ivaskov. As in, it appears to others you have named him after your father and a beloved Alpha."

"But I didn't name him." I say in a *duh* tone. "He's nine and already had a name. All of us took the Ivaskov name when we came here. *You* told us to," I remind him.

"Yes, and I understand that." Maksim nods slowly. "However, others will not. Do remember that I had two sons once, two brothers. One was born to be Alpha, the other was never considered. Does that sound familiar to you?" His pale green eyes narrow on mine, crinkling in the corners. I can tell this is a hard subject for him, even if I want to hate him for what he's asking me to do.

"It does, and I understand where you're coming from," I say as gently as I can, patting his hand awkwardly. "But I will never abandon Mikey. Not physically, emotionally, or even in title. He's my family now. He's mine in any way that counts. If I'm to be princess, then he's to be my little prince. If and when I have another son, maybe a future Alpha, then the boys will have to work out their issues as all brothers do. I hope what happened to your sons doesn't happen to mine, but I refuse to put such a separation between them for the sake of what *might* happen."

He pulls his hands from mine and stands abruptly, choosing

to pace the carpet in front of me. My eyes widen when he's suddenly in my face. "You are so stubborn! Just like *him*!"

The room explodes in point-two seconds. In a flash Maksim is across the room with a mad-as-hell Remy pinning him to the wall. Albert is holding out his notepad like a shield as he tries to placate the room of angry wolves. Logan stands fully in front of me, shouting expletives, and Tristan sits next to me, mumbling in that calming tone of his to soothe me.

Well, I don't need to be soothed. I stand up, displacing my wall of Logan to move around him. "Enough!" I shout, making the room quiet.

"Remy, you can release him. He wasn't threatening me, and he isn't going to hurt me," I say carefully. Something about telling Remy what to do never sits right with me, but I've learned that if I ask instead it makes it easier. To my relief he releases the older man, but he doesn't allow him to move away from the wall. Good enough.

I move to get closer to them, still staying slightly behind Remy so he doesn't become angered again. "Maksim...Grandfather. I know that, while your words might sound harsh and calculating, you are actually trying to help me. I know you feel guilty for what happened with both of your sons, and are trying to save me from that fate." I pause so that my mates present can let that sink in. I had first thought the same as them, that an old Alpha didn't want a non-Ivaskov on the Ivaskov throne. But the truth was in his eyes. The pain of losing two sons, one in cold-blooded murder and the other to corruption. I'm not even a real mom yet and I can't imagine surviving that.

I looking my grandfather dead in the eye, I continue. "But we won't allow that to happen with my sons, your great-grandsons. We learn from the past so that we may have a better future, right? And I'll be here, and my mates will be here. And you'll be here for the boys, too. If we all work together to make sure that hate and jealousy don't fester and grow between them, then they don't stand a chance, right?" I try to smile and add levity to the situation. It probably comes off as more of a grimace.

Something must have worked because I can almost feel the tension leaving the room. Grandfather wipes under his eyes before clearing his throat in that manly way of his. He comes to me, kissing the top of my head and offering a shaky smile before exiting the room with his shoulders back and his head held high.

"Well, that was impressive. Sometimes I wonder..." Albert trials off with a shake of his head and a curious grin.

"What do mean? You wonder what?" Tristan asks as he stretches out on the small couch comically. His long legs hang off the end, but he seems quite content.

Albert blinks at us, having obviously forgotten we were still in the room or something. He adjusts his glasses and straightens his already-straight tie. "Oh, nothing. It's just a thought I've had for a while."

"Would you care to share this thought?" Remy drawls out, sending a suspicious glance in the Omega's direction.

Albert's eyes meet mine and pin me in place. "I think that's a conversation I should have with our princess first."

My face contorts in confusion. "Uh, I'm just going to tell them what you tell me," I admit with no shame. Surely, he knows that. Albert's eyes flit nervously about the room, traveling from each of my mates.

"How about just the three of us for now? Would that help?" Remy throws out. Albert relaxes slightly, but still doesn't seem happy about it.

Logan snorts in amusement. "I think that's our cue, homie," he says to Tristan. They each offer pecks on my cheeks before making their way out. Remy comes to sit beside me, laying his arm on the back of the couch behind me. I scoot closer, loving the warmth radiating off him.

Albert remains standing, too nervous to sit it seems as he paces back and forth in front of us. "Princess, can I ask you a question first?" I nod my head. "Who is the Alpha?"

"In my family or the pack?" I respond quickly.

Albert instantly stops his pacing to stare hard at me. I can feel Remy staring at the side of my head as well. "Ah, see, they're supposed to be one and the same," he states, like that was his point all along.

"Well, they are the same. Sort of. I mean, Remy is the Alpha in our family. He always has been, way before I came along. And he and my other mates are the Alphas of our pack."

The room stays silent for too long, in my opinion. Thankfully Remy thinks so, too. "What does this have to do with what you wanted to speak to Kitten about?"

"You see, I have this theory. Actually, I've had this theory ever since I officially met the young princess, and I've been seeing evidence of this theory's truth. But none more so than just a few moments ago."

"And what truth is that?" Remy almost growls. I understand his frustration. Sometimes it's like pulling teeth to get information out of Albert. I wonder if it's an Omega thing.

"That which makes Kitten different, or special, also makes her an Alpha." Albert pauses to let that sink in.

"I thought females couldn't be Alphas. Or that natural wolves were born Alphas or something," I state.

Albert nods. "Yes, in every case before you a male has been born with the rank of Alpha. I've been watching you from the beginning. I've seen how the pack responds to you, how I respond to you. Your mate situation is a unique one, which made me think any confusion I had on who was the true leader of this pack was due to that."

"But you're saying that's no longer the case?" Remy asks him.

"I'm saying that Alphas are Alphas, leaders are leaders, and just because rules and laws say one thing doesn't change that fact. Kitten sees you as her Alpha. Whether you were born a wolf or not, it's who you are. My theory is that the two of you are an Alpha pair."

"Is that even a thing?" I ask. I've read the books around here on wolves and wolf history. An Alpha pair was never mentioned.

"It's not, no. Females have never taken on a leadership role in a pack before. But you're different. From the start you've made it your mission to help this pack, and it's no longer because you're the only one in your family to have the Ivaskov name. All of your mates now have the name and power that comes with it. Even now you could sit back and allow them to lead us all, but you won't."

"Ugh!" I groan in frustration. "See? This is what I was talking to Finn about the other day. Your rules change too often, so no one knows what's true and false. You're all operating on hearsay and old wives' tales, but none of you have been told the same things." I wipe a hand down my face. It's pure craziness.

"As I said, it's just a theory of mine."

"What exactly do you expect us to do with this? Wouldn't this pack, and every other, rebel against the thought of a female in charge?" Remy questions.

Albert shrugs a lean shoulder. "I don't expect you to do anything. I just thought you should know what I've noticed. The princess just took an old Alpha with control issues, and not only put him in place but gave him a lifelong purpose. Maksim will now make it his mission to make sure your sons will not end up like his. Also, as the Omega of this pack, my loyalties and wolf stay firmly with the Alpha. I hope it does not displease you to learn that I feel no strong pull towards your other mates, but I do feel equally drawn to you and the princess."

I share a look with Remy, but once again I know we will be talking about this in private. Now's not the time. However, Albert continues. "I realize this is something to think about and talk about with your other mates. I would like the two of you to consider taking on the role of an Alpha pair, and your other mates as Betas. I think it would do well in putting the pack at ease and giving them a very clear chain of command. Something this recovering pack could really use."

Albert bows low to the both of us, but I stop him mid-stride to the doorway. "Albert, if your loyalties lie with us, then why are you always with Grandfather?" I ask him.

To my surprise, he laughs. "Because you will not allow me to be by your side. I'm sure you're not aware of it, Princess, but you isolate yourself from everyone but your mates." I blink a few times in shock at his retreating back.

I frown and turn to Remy. "I do?"

"Pretty much," he answers with a raised eyebrow. "I thought you were doing it on purpose. Like Ash does."

"I'm always around people. When am I *ever* alone anymore?" I bite my lip, trying to figure out the answer to my own question.

"He means the rest of the pack, not us or Mike," he counters.

"I'm around them. I mean...they're around. I say hello to everyone!" I try to defend myself.

"I know you do, Love," Remy says gently as he tucks a strand of my hair behind my ear. "As I said, I thought you were doing it on purpose. I see now that you were just unaware. You're not used to being a part of a pack. Even with just us guys, it's different because you're our mate. You see, most packs are very close to one another. Even this one, with all its issues, is a very tight-knit community. They've looked out for each other as best they could. They were raised together, hunt together, eat together, and even relax with each other."

"But there's so many of them! How am I supposed to do all of that with everyone all of the time?" I question.

Remy shrugs. "I don't think anyone expects you to be best friends with every single wolf here; you're a princess after all. It wouldn't do well to be too close to too many people, but I think they expected you to at least form a small group of close friends by now."

"Have you?" I ask him.

"Have I what?" Remy answers, though the grin on his face lets me know he knows what I'm asking.

I simply stare at him, awaiting his answer. "No, I haven't gotten close to any of the pack members. I have my family as far as I'm concerned. There are many men I've grown to respect, and even a few I trust, but no one expects more than that from me."

I make a face at him. "Why do they expect it of me, then?"

"Because you were meant to be raised with these wolves. These are your people; they always have been and always will be. They look at me and see a changed wolf that doesn't belong, but when they see you, they see a wolf pup they should've been allowed to help raise. A best friend they should've had, a girl to spoil and play with, and a howl that should've joined their midnight melody for the past twenty-one years."

"You belong here," I whisper quietly, buying time to let what he said play out in my head. The thought makes me sad, and I wonder if the other wolves are sad, too, about all we've apparently missed.

Remy leans over to kiss the top of my head. "They accept me and the others because of you. But you've missed the point. My point was that, as much as these wolves belong to you and are yours, you belong to them and are theirs."

I nod my head in acceptance. "I get it. Do you think they're angry with me for not befriending them?" I wonder.

"I don't know, Kitten. Probably not. My guess is that they're just confused. You've already shown yourself to be a champion for them, and they love you for it. I'm guessing they can't understand what it was like to grow up outside of the pack anymore than you can understand them growing up inside of it."

"You're just full of wisdom today, aren't you?" I say half-jokingly to lighten the mood. I don't know what it is about today, but apparently it's deep conversation day and I've been given way too much to think about already.

"Guess what, Kitten?" Remy says after a long pause.

"What?" I ask.

"We're all alone," he says with a devilish grin, eyes filled with heat.

"Hmm... I suppose we are. Just what do you plan to do about that, oh observant Alpha of mine?" I tease with a wide smile gracing my face.

"First and foremost, I plan to get you behind a door that locks and then maybe I'll give you that tongue-lashing you deserve." A giggle escapes me as Remy picks me up in his strong arms, bridal style.

As we enter the hallway and he makes his way briskly toward our floor, I wrap my arms around his neck and whisper in his ear, "Tongue-lashing, huh? I thought I only got those for being good."

A copper-colored eyebrow raises at my question. "Oh? And have we been bad, Kitten?"

I bite my lip and nod slowly. "Very bad." I answer, hoping I don't sound like a dork and that he gets my meaning.

I squeak in shock as Remy seems to miss a step, his arms tightening around me. Before I can react further, though, my legs are released momentarily only to have each thigh grabbed and parted around his waist as my back touches the wall. A deep rumble from within him vibrates my entire front, but it's the intense pool of liquid silver in his eyes that makes me utterly melt inside.

His rough, callused fingers brush my outer thigh, distracting me. "Are you sure? I know you've played to my brand of foreplay before, but you've never asked." His deep, gravel-like voice is more of a purr as he leaves his statement open for an answer. His firm lips trail lightly up the delicate column of my throat, causing my breath to hitch and my nails to dig into his shoulders.

"I like it," I tell him honestly. He grinds his hips into me, hard, before pulling back. Oh, I like that. "I like seeing you dominant, and powerful, and in control." He does it again, making me pause to catch my breath, as it's coming faster now. "Only to lose every ounce of that control at the end...with me... to me...*in* me."

"Fuuuuck," he growls in my ear. "You are exquisite for a man's ego. Last chance, Love. You sure you want to play?"

"More than anything," I respond quickly, meeting his eyes with determination.

Remy keeps me wrapped around him as he pulls us away from the wall, probably to hide his noticeable excitement from the onlookers who were casualties in our very public display. As caught up as I am in my Alpha, my hearing still picks up the comments.

"Do you think she knows she's giving off enough pheromones to knock a dude out?"

"Her? Did you not feel how strong the pull from the Alpha was? Took everything in me not to submit and it wasn't even directed at me."

"Cold showers for the whole house again, huh? We need more damn females around here. If the Alphas insist on putting that much orgy energy into the air, I demand a damn partner."

The last is met with agreement and laughter, and thankfully

we've gone far enough up the stairs to be able to tune them all out. One step onto our floor and Remy's lips attack mine. Hot, demanding, and as hard as the rest of him. His hands slip from my waist to my backside, squeezing pleasurably as he rocks me up and down his covered length. I release a growl of my own into his mouth, feeling frustrated at all these dang clothes between my mate and me.

I gather the fabric of his shirt, ready to tear it open, but I'm stopped by one of his hands grabbing both of my wrists. I break away from the kiss to pout at him.

"*Tsk, tsk*, naughty girl. You said you wanted to play, and when you play with me it's always by my rules," he taunts.

"What game do you think they're playing?" Tristan's voice speaks up from behind me.

"No clue, but it looks pretty fucking fun if you ask me." Logan replies, sounding highly entertained.

Twisting my head around as best I can, I see the two of them leaning against each side of the wall in the hallway where our bedrooms are. "Do you guys just lean on things all day, or what?" I joke, trying to hide my embarrassment. A quick kiss to one of them in front of the others is one thing, but I think it's fairly clear what Remy and I are up to and I've tried not to rub anything in anyone's face so far.

"What do you say, Kitten? Up for a couple more playmates?" Remy asks before nipping at my collarbone. My mouth pops open in shock, surprised my Alpha wants to share. While I'm pretty sure he's joking, I can't help my body's reaction to the thought. Between my nipples tightening painfully hard and squeezing my thighs to alleviate the throbbing of my core, I think I give myself away.

Remy takes a deep breath, those silver orbs of his swirling with lust. "Do you boys smell that? I think our little mate likes the idea."

Loving My Pack 43

"Yeah, I do," Tristan replies huskily while Logan nods, swallowing thickly.

"My room," Remy orders.

My heartrate spikes when I see the two of them following behind us, Logan closing and locking the door, leaning against it.

"Same rules apply to you guys: my game, my rules." He tosses me roughly onto the bed, turning his attention to Logan and Tristan, getting their acknowledgement before continuing. They both seem nervous, clearly never being a part of Remy's "games" before. I think I might pass out. No way is it healthy for one woman to be this excited.

"Kitten, on your knees. There you go, now move closer to the end of the bed. You two stand on either side of me," he instructs us. A small smile plays on my lips as I await my next order.

"I want you to take off our shirts. Slowly, one by one. You can only touch the shirts, though, not us," Remy tells me while smiling wickedly at me. How frustrating! He knows how much I like touching them.

I do as I'm told, shuffling in front of Logan first. I meet his electric-blue eyes as I reach for the top button of his shirt. I pull it slightly away from him so I don't accidentally touch, causing an amused smirk to take over his expression. I undo the buttons at the cuffs of each sleeve, then pull the fabric over his shoulders and down his arms. Goosebumps appear on his arms, making me feel amazingly confident. I have to pull his undershirt out of his pants where he had it tucked in, but I manage to remove that as well without touching his skin. I sigh sadly as my eyes rake over his gloriously smooth and tan chest, lightly defined abs, and slim waist.

"Next," Remy growls out, letting me know my little show is getting to him. In this moment, I feel powerful.

I skip over Remy, moving over to Tristan. Remy's eyes narrow roguishly at me and I stick my tongue out at him. Faster than my eyes can track it his hand snakes out, catching my jaw. He moves his face in front of mine, dancing his tongue along mine in one long stroke. "I've warned you once about that tongue of yours."

"Holy shit," Tristan whispers heatedly.

Remy releases me and I meet Tristan's milk-chocolate eyes as I reach for the hem of his t-shirt. He has to bend down to help me get it over his head, but I manage to get the damn thing off. My fingers twitch with the need to touch his pecs. Oh, how I would love to lick that thin line of hair trailing from his bellybutton down into his jeans. It's barely noticeable, a sandy color, just like the hair on his head.

I hurry back to Remy, becoming impatient with this task and wanting to move onto the touching and being touched parts. I bite my lip hard enough to taste blood as I grab the hem of his shirt with both hands, pulling in different directions. I pull slowly, watching every inch of delectable skin on this mountain of a man as it becomes visible to my eyes. Finally, with a forceful yank, I get the material free from his arms and drop it to the floor.

"Our turn." Remy takes a step back, gesturing for me to stand before him. His hand comes up to cup my jaw. I lean into him, closing my eyes to enjoy the simple touch. "You're such a sweet girl, aren't you? Now, kiss Logan while we divest you of these clothes."

Logan's hot lips close over mine, his tongue sweeping out to taste mine. I open for him, taking him into my mouth for a quick suck before chasing his retreating tongue with mine. At the same time I feel long, slim fingers dip into the waistband of my yoga pants and ease them down my legs. I continue my kiss with Logan as I dutifully step out of my pants.

"*Fuck* me. She's wearing red lace. Can we keep her in these for a while longer, Rem? She looks amazing in candy-apple red, doesn't she?" Tristan asks as one of my feet is placed on his thigh as he kneels before me. I pull back from Logan to see what's happening. Remy takes that moment to pull my sweater up over my head, revealing the matching red lace bra and fixing my hair so it's behind me.

Logan tilts my head to the side to get better access to my neck. "Of course, she does. She looks sexy in everything I put on her," he says through nibbles behind my ear.

Tristan places a kiss on my knee as my eyes track him, those chocolate eyes solely focused on the lace between my legs. His tongue slips out to taste the skin of my inner thigh and my knees nearly buckle. Remy chuckles heatedly as his fingers find my nipple through my bra, pinching just hard enough to make me moan. My eyes close for just a moment, my brain trying to process all the touching at once. However, they snap open quickly when I feel Tristan's lips and nose trailing up my leg to where I want him most. Oh God, please let them touch me soon!

I cry out in pleasure and shock when Tristan nuzzles my core through my panties. With a deep inhale followed by a long, slow lick, I fall back onto the bed like a heap of jelly. Three amused male chuckles meet my ears, making my face heat up.

"Don't ever be embarrassed, Kitten. That was hot to watch. Now, plant your feet on the bed and spread your knees for us. Show your mates how ready you are for us. I want to see how hot and wet that little pussy is getting."

I bite my lip and do as he asks. Even if he tells me not to be embarrassed, I do still feel shy. I think Remy likes making me blush, though.

"I like the way you think, Rem. God damn, this is so fucking hot," Logan pants.

"Her panties are soaked. I think our girl is more than ready for us," Tristan says as he strokes the material over my core.

"Oh, I bet she is. Move those to the side, Tris. I bet a hundred dollars she'll cream harder once she's exposed fully to us. Won't you, Kitten?" Remy challenges me with a smile as Tristan pulls my panties to the side. The weight of three pairs of eyes on my most sensitive skin is almost more than I can bare. I feel my core pulse hard as I whimper in need.

"Please! One of you touch me," I demand. "This isn't fair. I need more," I all but beg. Okay, so maybe I was totally begging.

"Told you," Remy says smugly to the guys. "But that's not how I want to play this game," he says to me. My eyes nearly pop out of my head in disbelief. He motions for Tristan to take a seat in the chair beside his bed as he orders me to my knees again. "Logan, what would you like from Kitten at this very moment?" he asks casually, as if he's stating we might get rain today.

Logan's face shows his confusion as his eyes flit between the other two. "I...uh...I thought we were...*What*?"

I'm so used to seeing Logan extra-confident and sure of himself, it's almost cute seeing him like this. I don't know if it's because of what we're doing or if it's because Remy, his Alpha, is in control and in the room, but I decide to help him out. As lost as he looks right now, I know he's turned on and excited to be playing with us in this way, too.

Composing myself as much as my tightly-strung, jelly body will allow me I crawl my way back to Logan. Placing my arms around his neck I gaze up into his gorgeous face, my fingers brushing lightly at the chestnut strands at the back of his neck. "Remy is asking what you want to do to me next...or what you want me to do to you," I say softly, creating the illusion of our own personal bubble. "This is meant to be fun and playful. You're my king of fun, so I know there are plenty of things going on in that mischievous head of yours. I like doing this; it doesn't feel bad or wrong to be intimate in this way. No one is going to make you feel bad or wrong for saying what you want. You have to trust that I'll tell you if I don't want to do something. And you should know me enough to know that I will," I finish, hoping that the sincerity in my words is clear.

Logan visibly relaxes, his hands coming forward to land on my hips, his thumbs caressing the dips on my sides. "I didn't want to ask what you do with the others…or if it's something you just don't like doing…"

"Tell her," Remy commands. "If she doesn't want to, she'll tell you."

"Right," Logan huffs. His hand reaches out to my face, his long fingers brushing over my parted lips. Instinctively, the tip of my tongue reaches out to taste him. Logan's pupils dilate, a rush of air leaving him. "I want you to put me in your mouth, Pretty Girl. Please."

My eyes flit around the three of them, my face heating as I think I know what he wants me to do. Why couldn't he ask me to do something I was good at! "I…uh. I would love to, Logan. But you see, I, umm…" I trail off. I can see the wall slamming down over his emotions and I panic, rushing to say what I need to before it's too late. "I don't know how," I whisper, biting my lip and looking to the bedspread beneath me.

A finger comes up to lift my chin, forcing my eyes to look at Remy. "As much as that information astonishes me, it also pleases me greatly. What better way to learn than with three of your mates, who probably enjoy different aspects of the act?" He turns to Logan, clapping him on the shoulder. "You'll have to walk her through it. Praise her when she's doing good, tell her to suck, lick, speed up, or slow down. She wants to please you, so tell her how so she learns."

Logan takes a minute to think about something before coming to some sort of internal decision. His hand shakes slightly as he reaches for his belt buckle, unfastening it and his zipper. He slides his jeans and boxer-briefs down, stepping out of them and kicking them free. He climbs up on the bed, shifting a pillow behind him as he spreads out from the top right corner to the bottom left corner. He gestures for my hand so I place mine in his, allowing him to guide me between his long legs. I sit on my knees, my butt resting on my heels. I take a minute to just enjoy the beauty of the man before me. Usually when the guys are intimate with me, we're under blankets or we go from kissing to tearing each other's clothes off. Now, though, I can see every inch of him. From his chestnut hair with the blue stripe slicked back, his blue eyes burning hotly, his pink, parted lips. My hands have a mind of their own as they glide up his strong thighs. I continue my perusal of my playful boy; his slim but defined chest has goosebumps forming, his tapered waist flexing his abs in excitement timed perfectly with the throbbing of his manhood.

I sigh in appreciation. My curiosity gets the better of me as I gaze as his long, hard length. I notice the very top of it is shiny and wet. For some reason I want to touch it, so I do, sliding my thumb over the wetness and enjoying the feel. Logan sucks in a harsh breath.

Remy comes up behind me, his hand rubbing my back. "You should see how it tastes. See if you like it."

I nod my head. That sounds like a good idea. Bringing my hand up to my mouth I cautiously lick at my thumb, my eyes snagging on Logan's as I do so. The first lick has me curious, but there's simply nothing to compare it to. I close my lips over my finger, sucking off the rest of the shiny fluid. Logan closes his eyes on a groan.

"I don't think I'm gonna make it. It's even hotter knowing she doesn't know how fucking sexy she's being," Tristan says from the chair as he stares at my lips, taking in the scene before him.

Remy chuckles. "That's not what I meant when I said you should taste it, you naughty girl, but what do you think?"

I smack my lips together and tilt my head. "I like it. I mean I really like it. As in I want all of it now, but I don't really know why I like it so much. It doesn't taste like anything really, but it has its own taste and I know it's Logan's and I like that," I ramble.

"That's instinct, Love. Now, put that pretty little mouth on your mate before he explodes," Remy teases.

I do as I'm told, placing my hand around the base, aiming it at my face. I lick up all the shiny stuff first, my tongue dancing around the tip. I've held my mates in my hands before, the hard yet impossibly soft skin never ceasing to fascinate me, but I have to say it's a whole new level of amazing on my tongue.

"You're killing me, Pretty Girl," Logan pants out. "Put your lips over me and suck gently." I put him in my mouth, sucking lightly as he said to. Much to my delight, I get more shiny stuff. "Can you move your lips down, Kitten? That's good.... fuck." He trails off as his hand comes up to the side of my head, gently guiding me up and down on him. He keeps his thumb close to my lips, almost as if he wants to feel himself sliding in and out of me.

Behind me Remy's hands guide my body up, my butt now sticking up as he nudges my legs apart as far as Logan's legs allow. He applies pressure to my lower back, making it arch.

"Now that's a fine fucking sight to see," Tristan praises. I continue my slow stroking of Logan with my mouth as hands caress me from my knees up my inner thighs. Without warning, a hand lands harshly on my backside, making me both jump and moan around Logan, which makes him jerk his hips up toward my face. My eyes flare wide, the urge to gag rising up my throat, but I swallow, hard. How utterly embarrassing would it be to throw up right now? An odd thing happens then...instead of my swallowing forcing Logan out of me, it actually makes him slide deeper down my throat.

I pull back immediately, panting for air and wondering what the hell just happened. I hear Remy chuckle as Logan's worried eyes meet mine. "Don't choke yourself, Kitten. Just take what you can. I want you to enjoy this, too."

I scrunch my face in confusion. "You mean that felt good to you?" I ask.

To my horror, Tristan cracks up laughing. "You mean you deep-throating him? Yeah...I think it's safe to say he enjoyed that."

I narrow my eyes at him. How am I supposed to know these things? How dare he laugh at me. I turn back to Logan, deciding to get my revenge on Tristan later. "If you liked it, I can try to do it on purpose. I just don't want to throw up."

"Kitten, just know that it feels good no matter how much you take. If you're determined to take it all, though, then you'll have to learn the right moment to swallow, like you just did. Just don't keep it in your throat for long, as it's impossible to breathe. If you panic, you'll throw up," Remy instructs.

Hmm. Challenge accepted. Time ticks by as I gradually take Logan deeper and deeper into my throat. Remy's right about not being able to hold it there for long, but the pulsing and groans from Logan are worth every second. At first my throat burns, saliva gushing into my mouth at every attempt, but I learn that on the way up if I swallow again it creates that sucking motion that Logan likes so much. So, bonus!

After a while Logan's hips can't seem to stay still, thrusting and twitching spasmodically as his breathing quickens. Remy warns me that Logan is about to come in my mouth and tells me I can either pull away or swallow it. It's my choice. Before I can make up my mind Logan's manhood expands even more, pulsing with his release. I quickly decide to see what it tastes like. If I don't like it I can always spit it out, I guess. His warm cum coats my tongue, flooding my mouth. A sense of pride overcomes me. I did this to him. I made him give me of himself. I feel...powerful.

As Logan begins to deflate, I continue to lick at him, wanting every bit of my prize for doing a good job. Once his breathing returns to normal and he seems to come to, he gently pulls me up his body by my arm, cradling me to his chest, his hand rubbing at the back of my head. "Thank you, Pretty Girl. That was amazing." I lift my head to look at him, a wide smile on my face. "I love you, you know that?" he tells me before lifting his head to kiss at my temple. He falls back, utterly spent.

I sit up to see a beaming Remington. He turns to Tristan, raising an eyebrow. "You're up. What would you like from our sexy mate?" he asks him, reaching around to smack my bottom again. I moan at the contact. Only Remy could make something that's supposed to hurt feel so good.

Tristan leans back in his chair, stretching a leg out to prop one foot up on the bed. His hands go behind his head, his perfect Tristan smile coming out to shine. "Hmm, I think I'll start with Kitten crawling over to me on her hands and knees, unbuckling my pants, and using that amazing mouth on me," he says with a wink. Is Tristan ever *not* confident? I have to admit, I love that about him. His biceps are flexed in that position, leaving his bare chest open for my perusal, that thin trail of hair leading down to his obvious arousal.

"You heard your mate. Go be a good girl and give him what he asks," Remy whispers in my ear, making me shiver. He sucks at my neck for a moment, readjusting himself as he moves to sit on the bed.

My eyes lock onto Tristan's chocolate swirls, a smirk playing on my lips as I slowly crawl off the bed and nuzzle my face into his leg near his knee. I can't wait to try out my new-found power on him. Remy once explained that in his games of dominance, it was I who actually had the power. He only had the power and control that I gave him. What I enjoyed most when we played was testing the level of trust that I gave him to pleasure both me and himself. I can now see how having such control over the situation can affect a person.

Sliding my hands up Tristan's covered thighs I reach up and free him, noting how he, too, has shiny stuff covering the tip of him. I stroke him slowly, letting the slickness cover every inch of him.

"Use your tongue first. Especially right here," he tells me, pointing out a vein on the underside of him where the top meets the rest of him. I run my finger over it, watching him shudder. His smile never leaves his face, clearly enjoying himself. I make it my mission to wipe that smile off of his face, wanting to see him panting for breath, begging for me to help him find his release.

I start with a long, slow lick at his base, moving up to the tip. I purposely avoid where he wanted me. I do it again on the other side, watching in delight as more shiny fluid seeps from the top. I swirl my tongue around in it before lightly pressing a kiss to him. He groans, his hips flexing. I pull back before he can push into my mouth, looking up at him with a devilish smirk of my own. Turning my head to the side I use my lips to create suction on the side of him, moving my head up and down. Every now and again I flick my tongue out, teasing that special, tender spot. After several minutes of this his hips refuse to stay still, and I can see beads of sweat form on his abdomen. He reaches down, replacing my hand at the base of himself, squeezing tightly.

"Please, baby, suck me. I know I said to use your tongue, but a man can only take so much," he tells me as he swallows thickly, his hand guiding my head into position. Mission "Make Tristan beg"? Accomplished!

I form a tight ring with my lips, pushing my head down slowly, creating suction. I swallow as he approaches my throat, sliding down until my lips meet his neatly-trimmed groin. I back up even slower, able to suck harder in this direction. I feel his thighs lose some of their tension in relief. I make a loud popping sound as I pull off of him. I can tell how close he is to finishing, but I have other plans.

With a smile, I sit back and turn my head toward Remy. "Is Logan asleep?" I ask casually, though it takes effort to control my breathing. Tristan swears, his head thumping back onto the chair. I suppress a giggle.

Remy's eyes light up, enjoying my teasing of his friend. "I believe so. He'll most likely wake up soon."

"Hmm, that's interesting. It's usually me who falls asleep first. Logan likes to cuddle before falling asleep," I tell him conversationally.

"Kitten!" Tristan growls impatiently.

"Yes, sweetie?" I inquire brightly, turning back to him.

"Why are you torturing me?" he asks with a frown.

I tap my lip with a finger, looking lost. "I don't know, why were you laughing at me before?"

"Ugh! That? Because it was cute of you, and Logan looked like his head exploded! I wasn't laughing at *you*, just the situation," he explains, clearly frustrated.

I smirk at him again. "I guess you know not to do that anymore, huh?"

I realize my mistake immediately. Those chocolate orbs burn brighter than ever before, his perfect smile tinged with dark intentions. How could I have forgotten that he's Logan's mischief-making partner-in-crime for a reason? And he's not nearly as shy as Logan in the bedroom. Or shy at all, really.

He slowly takes his eyes off me, turning to Remy. "I think it's time for part two of what I want from Kitten. I'll let you get started, Rem. Mind if she's on all fours while you stand at the edge of the bed?"

"Not at all. That position works perfectly for what I want to teach our girl," Remy responds darkly, his time for control of me exciting him further. He gestures for me to hop back onto the bed, making sure my back is arched like how I had it earlier. The height of the bed puts me at just the right level for him as he stands in front of me, lowering his pants and freeing his magnificent manhood. It's already aimed right at my lips, framed by those lovely V shapes of his abdominal muscles. I sigh wantonly. Even his cock is powerful.

Remy lifts my chin, forcing my eyes away from the wonder in front of me. "I'm going to do something a little different. I want you to stay as still as you can, okay? I'm going to fuck your mouth. If I push too far, or hold you down for too long, you let me know. I *do* want you to gag sexily around me, but I don't want you to be too uncomfortable. You understand?" His eyes bore into mine expectantly. He wants both reassurance that I'm up for this and that I'll tell him if I want him to stop.

I take a deep breath, holding his gaze. "I understand, Remington."

He guides himself to my lips, pressing gently in and out as he gathers my hair up in his hand. I suck lightly, waiting for what comes next. "You're such a good girl, Kitten," he praises breathily. My heart warms at the endearment.

He continues his movements for a few minutes, letting my mouth wet his length entirely. I can tell he's about to change it up when the hand at the crown of my head grips my hair tighter, pulling, but not too hard, and his other hand comes to rest under my chin. Both hands work to hold me in place as he pushes slowly, but further than before. I work to swallow him down, his larger size causing a slight burn in my throat. Unlike Logan and Tristan, Remy doesn't immediately pull back out. His hips press forward, my nose buried into the base of him. A few seconds tick by and my throat convulses, seeking air. He pulls my mouth off him quickly. I take a deep breath, my lips coated with my own saliva, a string of it still attached to the tip of him.

"How was that, Love? Think you can handle more?" I nod my head, my hand coming up to wipe away the spit. Remy stops me, though. "Leave it. It's sexy. This time I want you to continuously swallow once I've pushed past your throat. Ready?"

Instead of nodding again I open my mouth, locking my eyes onto his. "Such a good girl," he growls, pushing in again, harder this time. My eyes water and this time I do gag, but nothing comes up. He does it a few more times, always letting me catch my breath before staying in my mouth for a few pumps, then sliding into my throat again—knowing the rhythm helps me know when to swallow, making the whole process easier. It's definitely harder than just licking and sucking but it's nothing I can't handle, and I love the pleasure rolling off my Alpha in waves.

Long, skilled fingers lightly touch my backside, drifting over first one cheek then the other. My body instantly ignites into flames. My mind has been occupied learning new tricks and trying to please my mates, but my body seems to have never lost focus on our own needs.

Tristan plays with the sides of my panties, pulling them down a little then back up again. I groan in frustration around Remy. He sucks in a quick breath, biting his lip as he pushes into me harder. Okay...so the guys like it when I make noise with them in my mouth. Got it. I do it again just to test my theory. Remy holds me down on him, his head rolling back as his mouth goes slack. Yep, they like it.

Tristan trails his lips over my exposed skin, his face nuzzling between my thighs. I hear him inhale deeply, a loud growl of pleasure leaving him on the exhale. Without warning, my panties are pulled tightly against me before tearing sounds in the room, and then they're gone completely. "You won't be needing these anymore," his melodic voice sings smugly.

My thoughts turn into a looping chant at that point. *Please touch me, please touch me, please, for the love of all wolf gods touch me!"*

My mind blanks momentarily as I'm overloaded with sensation at the first touch of Tristan's manhood against me. My hips move back, trying to get him inside me, but he moves away. If it wasn't for Remy holding my head in place as he smoothly takes my throat, I'd yell at him.

Instead of pushing into me Tristan teases by rubbing against my slick center, gently tapping my sensitive core with the head of himself. Now that...that makes me purr around Remy, who takes full advantage of it. After years, or minutes, or something, Tristan finally pushes into me, taking time to make sure I'm properly stretched and ready for him. He sets his rhythm in time with Remy's pushing. Long, hard thrusts followed by a circular grinding against that bundle of nerves as Remy pushes deep, my moans of pleasure vibrating around him. They work together, building all three of us up till we're riding the edge of the wave of pleasure, ready to crash and burn brilliantly.

Remy is the first to peak, his thrusts gaining speed, becoming erratic before he swells in my mouth, pulsing my liquid prize onto my tongue. He thrusts slowly, but doesn't stop until after he stops throbbing. As he pulls away Tristan increases his pace, our bodies pounding together harshly. He reaches up, gripping my shoulder for better leverage with one hand, the other digging into my hip hard enough to bruise. I can't control the sounds I make as he rapidly slams into me. They boarder between a moan and a whimper, giving up all thought as electricity vibrates through my body, heating my blood as I'm pushed over the edge.

Remy's hands sneak under me, his thumbs and forefingers each tugging a nipple, extending my release and eliciting a shout of pleasure from me. Tristan swears under his breath, a continuous growl emitting from his chest as he uses my body to find his own release a few minutes later with a roar of satisfaction. He collapses onto me, pinning me under him. He continues to pulse inside me, flooding me with his heat. Our sweaty bodies stick together, but I love the feel of his weight pressing me into the bed.

Remy lays on his side, facing me, with his head propped up on one hand. He pushes the wet strands of my hair away from my face, his eyes shinning with love and contentment.

After a few minutes Tristan shoves himself up on shaky arms, making me wince as he leaves my body. My eyes close momentarily until I feel his fingers sliding through my wetness. My tender flesh protests as his fingers enter me before he starts a slow, massaging rhythm inside me, his palm laid flat against me, pushing in a light circle pattern.

"Flip over for me, sweetie," he instructs.

"*Mmm*," I respond, feeling too worn out to do anything.

He laughs lightly, his mesmerizing voice washing over me like honey. "Just this one last thing, please. For me?" Damn that alluring voice of his.

Remy helps me turn over, sliding one of my legs between his. Tristan slides my other leg up and out, leaving me completely exposed to the both of them. He continues his slow massage within me, his fingers dipping in and out, pausing to rub a sensitive spot inside me. When my eyes meet his he smiles at me, dipping in one last time then bringing his fingers up to my lips. He smears the slickness across my lips before I open for him. "That's it, baby. Taste us together...damn, that's hotter than I imagined it would be. Do you like it?" he asks huskily. I nod around his fingers, sucking the taste of us mixed together from them. He pulls his fingers away, going back to his massaging as his head lays heavily against my outstretched thigh. I close my eyes. Remy's hand comes up to play with my breast as he, too, starts to become excited again.

Tristan's tongue joins his fingers, working in tandem to build me up once more. Sensation overload wreaks havoc throughout my body, but the guys pause in their ministrations before I can explode again.

"Get that gorgeous ass up on Logan," Remy demands, helping my jelly-body to crawl over to my sleeping mate and mount him. "That's it, Love. Rub that wet pussy over his cock and wake him up," he pants in my ear.

Logan comes to on a growl, his hands gripping my waist tightly as he uses his hips to seat himself inside of me and push all the way in with a single thrust. "Oh, hell yes. This is how I wanna wake up from now on. Ride me, beautiful. Ride it like you fucking own it," he orders through clenched teeth.

Sweat slicks my body as I grind my hips into Logan in a harsh rhythm, chasing yet another orgasm. Tristan's hands guide me to lean forward, taking one nipple into his mouth. His hands help rock my hips harder on his best friend.

Remy opens his nightstand drawer, taking out what I know to be lubricant. He meets us back on the bed with the bottle, using it to coat his fingers before he rubs at my back, making his way down to my rear end.

I suck in a harsh breath, my eyes flashing to his. "Just keep riding Logan. You'll like this, I promise," he tells me with a hot smirk on his face. Easing a finger into my behind, he bites his bottom lip when I arch back into him. He slides in and out, adding a second finger, which elicits a deep growl from my throat. It's pleasure and pain and everything in between.

"Jesus Christ, Remington," Tristan exhales intensely as he watches the scene.

"You'll have to hold yourself back, take it slow. If you hurt her, I'll hurt you," Remy warns.

I'm leaned even closer to Logan as Tristan covers me from behind. Remy pauses my hips momentarily as Tristan prods at my backside. I suck in a sharp breath, my eyes locking with Logan's as we both feel the pressure of Tristan entering me slowly.

"Fucking hell! Impossibly tight," Logan pants, thrusting up into me as if he can't wait any longer.

"Agreed," Tristan breathes on a whisper.

"How do you feel?" Remy asks me, brushing my hair away from my face.

"Full. And really, really needy," I answer him honestly. I can't handle the pressure without some kind of friction. Not waiting on them, I begin to rock my hips slowly. Onto Logan and off of Tristan, then back, just to do it all over again. I can't even process thought right now, only need.

My head sags onto Logan's chest as both men take over, taking from me what they need for their own release. My eyes slide to Remington's as he sits off to the side, his own hand stroking himself slowly as he watches us. He stares back, silver orbs raking my body from head to toe.

I nearly black out when I orgasm, taking the other two with me as I pulse around them. I'm filled to nearly breaking as they swell inside me, filling me to the brim with shouts of male satisfaction.

In a blink Remy removes me from my other mates, laying me on my back as he lifts my legs over his shoulders and shoves into me roughly. He takes me hard and fast, taking his own release quickly, losing control. His triumphant growl is the last thing I remember.

CHAPTER FOUR

"Fly free, little babies. Wherever you land is where you is meant to be!" I giggle as the tiny rocks filter through my hands as I spin round and round. I imagine that the rocks have little families and friends and me throwing them around helps them get back to them. I mean, how else would rocks travel around?

I wince and grab at my tummy as it rolls around painfully. It groans angrily, so with a few pats I try to reassure it that Davis will be back soon. He had asked me to wait in this park while he went to work for a few hours. The sun has come up seven times now, but we're in a new area and I don't know how to find him. I'm afraid to leave, to seek out a restaurant or a grocery store with overflowing trash bins, because he could be back at any minute. Since I first met Davis I've felt a pull towards him, like something inside of me says that we'll survive better if we're with him. Right now, that same thing in me is saying that we should leave here. But I don't want to leave Davis. Davis is sad and he's lonely. Even if he won't admit it.

"Hey there!" a voice calls, startling me and making me

drop my rocks. I dust my hands off, a quick glance showing a middle-aged man approaching me. I start to walk off like I didn't hear him. "Whoa, whoa, slow down there, kiddo," he says with a smile as he jogs, catching up to me.

I take a few steps back, not liking how close he gets to me as he cuts me off. I blink up at him, wondering what he wants. Already, I don't like this man. I don't know why, but it's in his eyes.

Always in the eyes.

"You all alone here?" he asks.

I quickly shake my head, pointing to a random building across the street. "My dad works there, he said I could play. I should get back to check in, though," I repeat what Davis told me to say anytime I was caught alone.

The man's smile suddenly looks different. My plastic bottle of water crunches as I grip it nervously. "How odd. I work in that building, too. What's your dad's name?" he challenges.

"John," I lie.

"You know what? I do know him. He and I are great friends! Why don't I take my great friend John's daughter for some ice cream?" I shake my head, about to protest, when grabs at my arm, jerking me forward and whispers in my ear through his teeth. "If you put up a fight, I will have the cops over here so quick your head will spin. You and I both know you're here by yourself. I've been watching you for days. Just come along with me and nothing bad will happen."

I don't have time to respond as he starts leading me to the woods where running people go in the mornings. I start to cry, not liking this man and afraid. I hate being touched; why hasn't he let go yet?

"None of that now. All you have to do is talk to me, that's all. I'll even give you a whole twenty dollars!" he says excitedly as he leads us away from the main path and through some trees. All I have to do is talk to him? My gut tells me he's lying. Why couldn't he talk to me where we were?

Where we stop isn't much of a clearing, just a small space where a large rock makes it impossible for trees to grow. As I look around, I notice that I can't see or hear any people; there's nothing but us and the trees. He sits down, dragging me down to sit beside him. His hand moves to my wrist, a gentle reminder that he's not going to let me leave.

Bite. Run.

"So, tell me, girl. Why did you run away from home?"

"I-I didn't."

His free hand comes around to rub my hair. "Sure you did. Stop lying. Was it because daddy touched you in bad places?"

"Bad places? No. I didn't..." I respond, confused.

Bite. Him.

"You can tell me. I won't tell anybody."

"I don't want to be here!" I yank my arm away and try to stand. He pulls me back toward him. "No one touched me anywhere, I don't know what you mean!" I yell, now trying to kick him away.

I jolt awake as a shout reaches my ears. My eyes fly open, my heart racing both from the dream and from the feeling of danger at the shout.

"Have you lost your ever-loving mind? What in the actual *fuck* is wrong with you!" a sleep-mussed Logan shouts at a distraught looking Jace.

I calm slightly as I realize that there's no cause for panic. "What's going on?" I ask through a yawn.

"Yeah, Jace. What's going on?" Ash growls from the open doorway. His dark eyes scan the room for danger, his fists clenching at his sides. "I heard you scream Kitten's name like she was about to fall from a cliff."

The three of us stare at Jace, waiting for an explanation. His golden eyes are filled with pain and worry as he paces at the foot of the bed. "I...just thought it was time she woke up." He shrugs a shoulder, crossing his arms over his chest.

"Lie," Tristan accuses, coming up behind Ash.

"You know what? Fuck it. Sleep the day away, see if I care." He throws his hands up before stomping from the room. Ash's eyes narrow on his retreating back before he follows quickly on his heels.

I frown as I look to Tristan. "He was lying about wanting me to wake up, or lying about why he woke me up?" I try to wrap my tired brain around everything that just happened twenty seconds into waking up.

Tristan shakes his head with a sad smile. He crosses the room to the bed, coming over to give me a hug. As he pulls away, he puts his face right in front of mine. "The real question is why he feels the need to lie to us in the first place."

∼

Ash

That's it. I've had it with this shit. "Remington!" I bark out angrily. Jace pauses ahead of me, turning to send a nasty glare in my direction. "That's right, you little fucker, house meeting time. Whatever's going on with you ends today."

He sneers at me. "You can't make me do anything, Ash. It's my business; why don't you mind your own."

"Your business *is* my business. Or have you forgotten that, *brother*?" I growl at him. This place is fucking cursed. Everything is wrong. We're not who we used to be.

"Ash?" Rem questions, opening his bedroom door. "What's going on?"

I point an accusing finger at him. "Apparently, a fuck ton. I'm tired of this shit, Rem. Either you fix it or I'm pulling us all the hell out of here, kicking and screaming if I have to."

"God, you're such a drama queen," Jace chimes in under his breath. I snap. In two seconds I have the golden boy pinned to the floor, my fist connecting with his jaw. Shouts reverberate around us as he smirks up at me, blood coating his lips. I growl in his face before releasing him to stand. Fighting someone who isn't fighting back irritates me, and he knows it.

"You need to calm down," Tristan tells me calmly, his palms out. I flick him off as I pull a face.

"I'm as calm as I'm gonna get. Now get your asses in the living room for a meeting before I *put* your asses there," I throw out as I stomp the rest of the way to the living room. They have three fucking seconds before I really lose my shit.

Luckily for them, they pull the remaining guys together and find places around the room quickly. "Where's Kitten?" I ask.

"She wanted a shower to help her wake up," Logan replies.

"Depending on what this is about, that may be a good thing. I'm grateful we've finally managed to get everyone together, but I'm not sure why theatrics were necessary. Someone better start talking," Remy tells us.

I snort in disgust. "Talk to the duke's son."

Remy looks to Jace, taking in his appearance and defensive stance. He sighs. "We'll get to that. Kitten and I were going to have a discussion with him about what's been bothering him. Obviously, you have some things you'd like to get off your chest first, though," he says to me.

"How about we start with why the three of you were going to have a conversation that concerns us all? Or about why it took so long for the eight of us to sit down together? Better yet, let's talk about how we're all so busy with nonsense tasks that we forgot how to be a FUCKING FAMILY!" I shout in his face.

"We knew there would be changes when we agreed to come here..." he starts.

"Yeah, we agreed to help a pack of dipshits get their act together enough to deserve our girl."

"Uhh, dude, I don't know where you got that idea from, but that's not what we agreed to," Reed chimes, sounding confused.

"I don't know what the rest of you had in your heads, but I was under the impression shit was fucked up here and we were going to show them how to live as we do. Instead, here we are, acting like them. Following their rules. Tell me, Reed, when's the last time you picked up a paintbrush? And Remington, tell me how it is that you've gone from millionaire architect to a fucking laborer?"

"Live as we do?" Finn asks for clarification.

"Yeah. Peace, togetherness, harmony. We had our issues, but we handled them. What we couldn't handle ourselves, we trusted our Alpha to settle. Now, we pass by each other like strangers. Tristen is in the kitchens with one set of wolves, Remy's building houses like that solves shit or something, Finn is a ten-time Harvard grad teaching algebra. Logan is a personal shopper, Kellan treats colds and fleas, and who the hell knows what Jace even does! All you do all day is shop online. Congrats, you're a Real Housewife of Wolf County."

"I didn't know you felt this way," Remy says as he thinks it over.

I turn and punch the wall, making a hole in the plaster. I'm beyond frustrated. "Me feeling this way isn't the problem. I can handle it. What I can't handle, and what I can't understand, is why the rest of you *don't* feel this way."

I turn to Rem, the fight leaving me. "I know Kitten getting kidnapped messed with your head, and I've tried to be patient. I've been waiting for you to pull your shit together and fix this.

Don't you see how close we are to losing everything that we've built?"

His eyes flash in anger. "What would you have me do, Ash? Hmm? We built our own pack from scratch. We chose our own members, made our own rules, created our own history, and lived our lives how we wanted. How's that supposed to work here? Half of these people I wouldn't spit on if they were on fire. That army you train is a fucking joke no matter how you slice it, these people will never make enough money or food to support themselves, and I've got a pregnant mate that I hardly ever see outside of a bedroom! So, tell me, great wise one, what the fuck do you want me to do!"

There's a long pause that follows his outburst. Understandable, considering shit must be bad if Remington feels lost. Yep, this place is cursed.

"I've been working on that," Finn says quietly. He squirms in place when we all turn to look at him. "It's not a perfect plan, and I haven't figured everything out yet, but it could be a long-term solution. I'd like to work on it more before we really get into it, but what Remy said was true. This pack isn't really a pack. It's a bunch of scared wolves that don't know any other way. What I have in mind is a complete reboot, a break the system kind of thing, if you will."

"Thank you, Finn. I look forward to hearing all about it. When you're ready, of course," Remy manages much more calmly. "If we're done with the yelling portion of our meeting, I'd really like to take time and have a proper discussion as a family. I think we should all catch up with one another and air any griefs or feelings we've got going on. Lord knows if our normally silent and broody brother had that much to say, then there's sure to be plenty from the rest of us," he jokes, lightening the mood.

I roll my eyes at the nickname. Just because I'm not a blabbermouth like some of the other guys doesn't mean I brood. I *don't* brood.

I break the awkward silence that follows, nobody else knowing where to start. "This declaration of war on us has been a joke so far. They've sent scouts and small tactical teams, but nothing that couldn't be handled easily. It makes me wonder if they're waiting for something to make a real show of force, or if *war* means something else entirely around here."

"I've met with both Marcus and Albert about this briefly, but they seem more concerned with making sure the army is ready for a fight. Albert has suggested that we use Kitten to reach out on the political front, due to all of us being changed wolves. In his opinion, that's what all of this is about—us opening our doors for other changed wolves. To other packs it might seem like we're attempting to build an indestructible army," Remington explains with an eyeroll.

Reed sits forward, ticking items off on his fingers. "One, Kitten doesn't even know about the war. Two, we *are* an indestructible army, just the eight of us. Three, we've made no move toward any other pack, aggressive or otherwise. I don't even know why they fight each other. This isn't the old days where everyone fought for territory."

"I think we should hold off on telling Kitten still. She's in the beginning of her pregnancy, a fragile time for her," Kellan adds his opinion.

Remy nods in agreement. "Have you gotten a chance to examine her yet? Make sure both she and the baby are healthy?"

Kellan frowns hard. "No, not yet. There's a virus going around the pack that's been keeping me busy, and I don't really want to bring her into that cesspool until it clears up. From everything I can see without the use of an ultrasound, everything seems to be going normally. A lot of tests I would run for a human female wouldn't apply to Kitten, so I'm going to need time to speak with some of the midwives who have dealt with wolf pregnancies before."

"We also need time to sit down and go over a budget. I don't think anyone realizes how fast the funds are draining, now that the entire pack is being cared for," Jace points out.

Remy scrubs a hand down his face. "I think we're going to have to make a schedule for everyone, including Kitten. I'll start one after we're done here, so you guys will have to let me know any times you want blocked off. But this reminds me of something else I've been meaning to bring up..." He trails off, thinking carefully how to word what he wants to say.

"Everyone answers at once, first thing that comes to your mind. Who is the Alpha?" he asks, grey eyes scanning the room.

"Of the pack?" Kellan replies, everyone else waiting for the answer before replying.

"Fuck," Rem groans, leaning his head back against the wall. "Same as Kitten. Okay, so, raise your hand if you don't want to be an Alpha to the Ivaskov pack," he instructs.

Immediately, six hands shoot into the air. Turning to me, he raises an eyebrow. I give him a *duh* look. I'd rather chew off my own arm than play political puppet and get bugged repeatedly about dipshit matters. Leadership has always been Remington's thing. When someone needs their head smashed in or to be taught a lesson...well, that's my thing.

"The reason I ask, is because it was brought to my attention that this pack could use stability, and that it somehow involves only answering to one Alpha. That being said, I was also informed that Kitten is Alpha material herself, though she sees me as her Alpha."

"What the fuck does any of that actually mean?" Logan asks.

Before Remy can reply, Finn steps in. "This might be a good time to restructure and install a new form of government. A key to instilling a sense of real change, and breaking away from how things have been done in the past."

"What do you suggest?" Remy crosses his arms, waiting.

Finn looks uncomfortable with all the attention on him again, but shakes it off. "I think removing all responsibilities from the rest of us at this point would make us appear weak, but I agree with having one Alpha. Honestly, every time someone said Alpha, I would look around for you."

"For Kitten's part," he continues, "I, too, think that she was born to lead. No matter if it's a pack of wolves or a playground sandbox. However, I think her title needs a different name. Not only do all born wolves think of a male at the term Alpha, but a separate title would help differentiate between the two of you as well. Think in terms of kings and queens; sometimes they ruled together, sometimes a king, sometimes a queen, but the power of either title garnered the right amount of respect and labeled them as leaders."

"I could see that. I'm good with it. What would we call her?" I ask.

"Oh, oh, I know! Let's call her the Mistress of Wolves. Scratch that, how about Lady Badass, Kicker of Shins, Taker of Names," Logan chirps excitedly. Without looking, Tristan reaches behind Kellan to smack him upside the head.

"What about Luna?" Jace suggests quietly. A small smile plays on his lips as he inspects his nails. Something tells me he didn't just pull that term from his ass. I still want to know what that little shit is hiding.

"Goddess of the moon. Yes, I like it. Kitten is definitely goddess-like, and it's fitting, all things considered." Finn nods.

"And you all could be ranked Betas. That way it's still clear that they can come to you with issues as well as Kitten and myself," Remy adds.

"Um, can I not have a title, though?" Reed asks.

"Me, too. I just want to help people as I always have. I'm content having you and Kitten lead. I'm still a changed wolf and Kitten's mate, so it's not like anyone is going to give me trouble over it," Kellan says.

Remy sighs heavily. "Fine. I already know which of you are going to ask the same thing, but you will still have the title of advisor because you have always been advisors to me, and I want no wolf underestimating your importance. So, as it stands I will be the only Alpha, and Kitten will be Luna. Ash and Jace will be Betas, with everyone else being advisors. That said, Albert will remain Omega, a title that now represents the personal advisor to the Luna."

"I don't want to be Beta," Jace scoffs.

"Too damn bad. You're good at it, and I need you. Ash will have full reign to punish and defend, while you will have full reign to attend matters in my stead. It makes sense."

I smirk at the golden boy as he huffs a "fine" in acceptance. Good, now if anyone bothers me with shit I don't want to deal with I'll just send them Jace's way.

For a good hour, we vent about all the things we've dealt with since arriving. Some of it is actually entertaining. I don't spend a lot of time in the house like some of the others, but they tell me that ever since Kitten's possessive display, the other females around practically run from them if seen in the halls or kitchens.

We also talk about things we hope to accomplish, such as me wanting to form an elite group of enforcers instead of playing human soldiers, training for human-style fighting. Mostly, though, we talk about Kitten and the baby. How we're lucky to have her, how she's adjusting, and what it'll be like to be fathers. We've never openly discussed it before, but I'm pretty sure that no matter whose scent the pup carries it won't make a difference to us. We've been sharing everything for decades, and centuries for some of us. We all just want the experience of raising a child. On my part, I feel lucky to have seven other guys around to help protect our child. They can teach him things I don't know myself, and be there when I can't be. Not to mention, the more people around the less diaper changing for yours truly.

"We should probably go check on Kitten. Either she's taking the longest shower known to mankind, or she went back to bed. She needs to eat some breakfast," Tristan suggests.

"How's that going by the way? Will she eat things that you don't cook yet?" Reed asks him.

"Yeah, some." Tristan nods slowly. "She still won't eat anything even close to resembling a sandwich or on a silver plate, but she'll eat fruits, breads and snacks that I don't make. I think I might see if she's up to eating takeout soon. She still eats better when someone actually feeds her, though I think that has to do with her seeing how happy it makes us."

"Is she craving anything yet?" Kellan asks.

Tristan frowns. "Not that I can tell. She has a new affinity for popsicles, but that's because she didn't know about them until the boys asked for some. She'll scarf down food every now and again, but she doesn't eat like she used to. Like she pecks for most of the day, but seems unable to stomach a full meal a lot of the time."

Kellan nods. "That's fairly normal. Don't worry, though. As the pregnancy progresses, that will change. Just keep an eye on it and remember that she doesn't know much about proper nutrition, pregnant or not. She's relied on her wolf's healing abilities most of her life."

Reed returns, informing us that Kitten must have wandered off with Mikey. Looking like everyone is about to head off, I call attention to what started all this. "Jace, I still wanna know what's going on, man. I gave you time to bring it up yourself, but you haven't."

He sits back in his chair, looking for the world like a rock truck is weighing him down. A hand slides through his hair, messing it up. Whatever it is must be pretty bad for pretty boy to not notice his hair is out of place. "I don't even know what to say. I've spoken to Albert about it, about why and how it's happening, but I don't even know if it's real."

"If what's real?" I ask.

For the first time in a very, very long time I see Jace's insecurity peek out. It took a long time for us to get him to understand that he can tell us anything. He used to have a real issue letting anyone know anything about himself that was less than perfect. He spent three decades pretending to be too concerned with his hair to swim with us when, really, he was just terrified of drowning and didn't know how to swim.

"Brother, I thought we were past this." I shake my head, calling him brother to remind him that we'll always have his back.

He meets my eyes, the vulnerability still there, but determination rising through. "I think...I think I see Kitten's dreams. That's why I haven't been sleeping much, and when I do it's when she's awake," he admits.

Finn pulls a face. "Kitten doesn't dream."

"What do you mean she doesn't dream? Everyone dreams," Logan calls him out, looking at him like he's crazy.

Finn puts his hands up in "*I don't know*" gesture. "She just doesn't. If you haven't noticed, she's not like everyone else. Even her photographic memory isn't a photographic memory. It's different than any other case study ever done, though Eidetic memory has never been proven. While her mind stores the information like a file cabinet in her head and can be pulled up whenever she needs information, she can't access it whenever she likes. I think it has to do with her being able to access her wolf abilities in human form. Much like her wolf helped her survive long before she ever turned, it may have been a coping mechanism for her lack of formal education. It seems her wolf always filled in the gaps that her human side couldn't fill on its own. So, her not being able to dream isn't that big of a shocker when you take into account she's pulled off a feat that no other wolf or human has done in history."

"If I'm not simply going insane, then she does dream," Jace states worriedly.

"They're probably not dreams, just moving pictures she has stored in her mind. Like movies. Or memories," Finn says gently.

Jace nods. "That makes sense, seeing as they're all of her at a younger age. I kind of hope that I'm just going crazy, though. If those are her memories, then I don't understand how she isn't crying in a corner twenty-four-seven."

"Why? What do you see?" Reed asks, nearly falling off his seat as he scoots closer to hear.

"Horrible, horrible things. This morning I woke her up because some pervert had drawn her to a secluded area after she waited a week at a park by herself for some man to return with food. She was also a very literal child, believing if she stepped on a crack she'd break some kid's mother's back. A mother who thought she was a monster and hit her with a broom. Idiot humans. Though because I can't see her in these dreams unless she walks past something shiny, it makes me wonder if any of her wolf features ever shifted, or if she was just so unkempt as a child, as no one ever cared for her. My guess is the latter. I can just picture a tiny waif in tattered clothing; no shoes, the palest of blonde hair knotted and stuck to her head like a stray dog, covered in dirt." He shakes his head, eyes lost to recollection and tearing up. Jace never fucking cries, and it's making me uncomfortable.

"In that book we found of Ivaskov histories, there was

mention of bonds so strong that certain abilities were formed," Finn tells us.

"What abilities?" I ask.

"In the book it said it was based on levels of domination. I'd have to read it again to remember the other gifts that were mentioned, but I'm pretty sure the ability to thought-share was in there, and that was for mates on or near the same domination level. Like I said, I'd have to look again," he explains.

"If you have time, do that today. It's bothering Jace, and I'm sure we're all curious now," Rem instructs Finn before turning to Jace. "You're going to have to talk to Kitten about this. For one, you can ask her if they truly are memories from her past and get reassurance you're not crazy. And two, because this is a whole new level of privacy invasion and she deserves to know, and if it goes both ways, so she can be prepared for it to happen to her," Remy instructs.

Jace groans. "I don't know how to tell her."

"You'd better figure it out. She thinks you're avoiding her, which you are. You might want to think about what that means to Kitten. We recently found out she's pregnant, and she formally adopted Michael without asking our permission first. More than likely, she thinks you're mad at her for either of those things or you've lost interest. It's hurting her," he tells Jace sternly.

Jace's head rocks back at the revelation. He probably didn't even realize how she could misinterpret his actions.

"Is anyone else up for Mikey calling us Dad, or Daddy, or Father or some shit? It's weird if he calls her Mom then straight up calls me Logan like I'm some unwilling stepdad caught up with her baggage." Logan makes a disgusted face.

I nod my head, grunting in approval. "His biological dad deserves to rot in hell for what he did to him. I'm all for being a team of dads who actually give a shit about him and look out for him." A round of approving statements and head nods go around the room.

"We'll have Kitten inform him that it's okay for him to call us that if he wants. We should let it happen naturally after that, though. I don't want to push the idea onto him. He's known Kitten for a longer time, and already thought of her like a mom, so it may take some time, if it happens at all," Kellan speaks up.

"I bet he calls me Dad before he calls you Dad," Logan quietly challenges Tristan. He shakes his head with a smirk, but takes on the bet anyway.

I roll my eyes at the two tricksters of our little family. Of course they'd make a bet on something like this. I used to wish that they'd grow up and mature, but their antics have grown on me over the years. Not that I'd ever tell them that.

"We should go eat and find Kitten. We talked about a lot today that she should hear and get a say on. I for one feel a lot better now that we've talked some things out and there's a tentative plan to move forward. Let's keep in mind that we need communication among ourselves now more than ever." Remy wraps up our chat, the other guys filing past on their way to the kitchen.

He takes up a spot near me, leaning against the opposite wall. "That goes for you, too, you know? I know I've been different since everything happened with Kitten, and honestly, I'm still trying to find my way back from that. Having her taken from me like that…it's hard to recover from. I should have seen it coming, should've been stronger or smarter about it. But don't ever feel like you can't tell me what's going on with you. Even if it's about me being a shithead and needing to pull myself together. We've lived lifetimes together; I'll always care about what you have to say." He clasps me on the shoulder roughly.

I grunt, smirking at him. "I know. I was just giving you time. I get that it's harder with her. I don't lead this merry bunch of idiots, but I do protect us. Trying to balance being soft enough to love her and hard enough to be strong for her is a challenge. Just know that I get it."

We have a moment, both showing how serious we are and that all is forgiven. "Let's go eat before Logan does something awful to our food," I joke, bringing him in for a manly hug before shoving him roughly into the wall. His laughter booms in the hallway before he quickly catches up to me, a foot going out to trip me. If Logan and Tristan only knew they weren't the original tricksters of the group. I shake my head. Too bad we never show them this side of ourselves.

~

Kitten

My tail swishes through the snow yet again as I stare at nothing. I had gotten out of the shower only to find that my mates were enjoying some much-needed time to themselves. I was just slipping down the hallway, trying to not interrupt their moment, when I heard it.

War.

War was declared against us, and they didn't tell me? They didn't *want* to tell me. I hadn't meant to overhear their conversation, but it's hard not to when your name gets mentioned. I don't know how to take this. Should I confront them? Act like I didn't hear them? I should have stayed and listened to what else they were hiding from me. Do they think I'm weak and can't handle things? I guess I am weak compared to them. I don't know if I'm angry, or just really sad.

Howling out my frustration makes me feel slightly better. Within moments several other howls echo back to me, creating the most beautiful song my ears have ever heard. I howl again, this time losing the sadness and letting my excitement show through. My tails sways behind me as, once again, the other wolves around the area sing back to me.

I had shifted in a hurry so I wouldn't have to talk to anyone for a while, but howling with these wolves makes me see that there are many ways to communicate now. It's comforting to know that there are so many people out there willing to share in my feelings, even if they don't know the cause of them.

Eventually, I just listen to the rest of them as they continue. I pick up several emotions from them as well. Loneliness is the most prevalent, but anger, confusion, and heartbreak leak through, too. My poor wolves. Will we ever be able to leave the pain of the past behind, our songs joyous and happy? I may be hurt and confused at the moment, but I've had times of pure happiness along the way, especially lately. I wonder if some of these wolves have gotten to experience that.

I hear and smell them coming long before I can see them. They come from the trees, bunched together with their heads low, moving slower the closer they get to me. I huff my annoyance at this and paw the ground, hoping they know I mean it like a person would pat the seat next to them. Who knows what it means in wolf language? I don't have much experience with that. Although, I've noticed that if I stop trying to think like a human, instinct will take over.

I take time to admire their coats, noticing that all but one has a variety of shades throughout their fur. They take up spots around me, surrounding me with their larger bodies. I don't really know what they want, but I'm content with them being here. A few eventually break off to play, rolling around and biting at each other. I cross my paws and lay my head on them, feeling as if I could sleep in the sun's warm rays.

When I wake, it's to a short bark from Albert's wolf as he nudges the sleeping wolves who have managed to enclose me in a wolf pile while I slept. They mostly pay him no mind, but shift tails and legs out of the way so he can reach me. He squeezes in beside me, turning his neck so the top of his head can rub against my back just once. I look over to him, wondering what that was about. He pants happily as his eyes scan our surroundings. It takes a moment for the sleepiness to wear off, but once it does I remember why I'm out here in the first place, and know without a doubt that Albert knows about the war and didn't tell me either.

With a sigh I find my feet, taking a short moment to stretch. The other wolves stand, too, looking like they're ready to go wherever I am. I shake my head at them, hating how their tails tuck and heads bend in sadness. I nip at a few ears and rub my head against a few of them, trying to lessen the blow and let them know I'm not purposely leaving them, and that I've enjoyed our time together. It seems to be the right thing.

Albert, however, follows me anyway. He bites at my tail playfully as I trot along and I turn to growl at him. He lied to me, too, and now he wants to play? Nope. No way. Instantly his belly is on the ground, ears pulled back. I bare my teeth at him before resuming my return to the house.

I feel the shift in the air just before his human voice calls out for me. "Princess, wait!"

I ignore him, sprinting toward the back doors of the house. Once I get there I decide I'm still not ready to go in and face any of my mates, but I'd like to shift back. The problem is, I don't know how to get clothes without going in. A young soldier passes me, bowing as he does so. I follow him and he stops, looking to me. I tilt my head as I try to think how to tell him what I want.

Slowly, I move forward and grasp his pants between my teeth, giving a small tug. "Uh, Princess?" he asks, confused. I huff and do the same to his shirt. "You want me to...follow you?" He guesses.

I shake my head.

"Uh, you want me to undress?" My head rears back and I bark a resounding *no*.

"She wants you to get her clothes, you idiot," Albert chides as he comes up behind the man. Somehow, he managed to find a pair of black sweatpants. "I'll get you something to wear, Princess. Then you might tell me what has you so upset with me." He jogs into the house quickly.

"Oh, thank God!" The soldier sighs in dramatic relief. "I didn't really want to die today. The Alphas would have torn me limb from limb if we were to...you know. I mean, you're beautiful, both as a woman and as a wolf, and it'd be an honor, but...I was hoping to meet my own mate one day, and I'd never get that chance if I was a headless corpse," the younger man rambles.

I'm not sure what he's even talking about so I just sit, tilting my head and blinking at him until Albert returns with a bundle of clothing. He drops the clothes in front of me, unfolding a sheet and tossing another one to the soldier. "Hold this up, will you? The princess needs to get changed."

The younger man makes a face. "What does the sheet have to do with it?" he questions, even though he does what he's told.

"She wasn't raised in a pack, as you should know. She still holds on to her human modesty," Albert explains.

"Oh. Right, I got you." He nods, turning his face away from me as he holds out the blanket.

I ignore the both of them as I quickly shift, stepping into the yoga pants sans panties and slipping on a cami and covering it with a thick green sweater. The soldier watches me closely as I untuck my hair from my clothing, running my hands through it. It never ceases to amaze me how, after every shift, my hair is softer and shinier than it has ever been. As an added bonus, it's never tangled either. It's actually easier to shift than to brush it out.

He swallows thickly, his lips parting and tongue reaching out to wet them. "I...should go now. Yeah, I should definitely go," he mumbles, balling the sheet up and turning away from us quickly.

I turn to Albert. "He's an odd one."

Albert chuckles. "Don't hold it against him. He hasn't had the opportunity to meet many females, let alone a beautiful, young, royal one."

I shrug a shoulder. "I don't know why that would make him act so odd, but there are more females here now than ever before. And even if I don't like some of them, they're all very pretty. It makes me wonder if people think I'm beautiful *because* I'm a royal or whatever. Either way, I think most people are pretty and many things are beautiful, but I've always failed to see how that changes anything."

"That's not what makes you beautiful, dear girl. But that's yet another reason you shouldn't be running around by yourself," he says, pressing his lips together in disapproval.

I narrow my eyes at him. "It seems we're all doing things we shouldn't, aren't we?" I glance around, looking for a direction to head in.

"Right. Would you mind telling what I did wrong now, please?" he asks.

"If you walk with me. I don't want to be around the house," I tell him, already walking away.

I head towards the dormant orchards, figuring no one else would be around. We walk in silence, giving me time to form rational thoughts and plan out what exactly I want to do about what I know. Albert strolls beside me, hands behind his back. I can tell he has to get used to my pace, since my legs are so much shorter than his. The trees are all bare, stick-looking things, but I still think they look pretty, all lined up in neat rows with equal spaces between them.

After the twentieth row, Albert finally presses me. "Please say something, Princess."

I sigh. "When it's just us, can you please just call me Kitten? I hear my name so rarely these days I've nearly forgotten it."

"I...will try, Princess Kitten," he responds, making me roll my eyes. Maybe it's the most he's capable of?

"I'm mad at you because I know you know about the war everyone is hiding from me." I jump right in.

He splutters out nonsense in shock. "How did you..."

"It doesn't matter how I know," I interrupt. "What matters is that you and the others thought it was okay to lie to me and keep things from me. Do you all think I'm weak?" I turn to him, asking him earnestly.

"What? No! No one thinks that of you," he tells me vehemently.

"Then why?" I almost whine.

Albert takes his time answering, giving a deep sigh before he speaks again. "Because men are stupid?" he asks more than states a real reason. A sad smile crosses his lips. "Your mates and your grandfather will always want to protect you. At first, they thought you were acting strange and needed time to adjust. Then they found out you're pregnant and...I think they didn't want to stress you, giving you time to be happy about the baby. Also, in my opinion they think that, as long as you don't know about the dangers in your life, they can't harm you."

"But that's so very wrong. Not knowing is always worse than knowing," I scoff.

"I think your mates are used to handling problems a certain way, and none of them know how to handle them when it comes to you," he adds.

"What's your excuse, then? You're not my mate, and the

other day you claimed to be loyal to me only. Yet, you kept this from me," I accuse.

He sighs again. "Princess..." I shoot him a glare. "...Kitten. If I asked how many conversations we've had alone, what would you tell me?"

"Including this one? Two. Or not really, I guess, since everyone was present for the last one, just standing back."

"Exactly." He nods. "My place is on your right, standing slightly behind you. Not because of tradition or rank. But because it is the natural way of things. I exist to advise and protect the Alpha of this pack. If you had given me the opportunity to do what I'm supposed to, I would have told you."

I make a face. "You're saying it's my fault? I don't know the natural order of things, Albert! I fell into all of this. And just because you tell me you're supposed to advise me doesn't mean I know what that means, or how to have you beside me, when I've barely had friends in my life to begin with!" I shout at him.

"I understand that," he says gently. "I'm not saying you've done anything wrong. Your trust in me will take time. I just ask that you might speak with me every now and again, and maybe give me tasks so that I might start earning your trust in me to accomplish them."

A large boulder sits off to the side of a row of apple trees. I take a seat on it, able to kick my legs against it as I think. Albert sits beside me, leaving plenty of room between us.

"I have a task for you then," I tell him, our eyes connecting. "I want to know how to contact all the pack leaders. And I don't want you to say a word of this to anyone," I say seriously.

His eyes widen momentarily, his throat constricting as he swallows. He nods his head deeply, standing and turning from me. I can tell he slightly regrets the conversation now, but he wanted to earn my trust, right? This will be one heck of a way to do that.

CHAPTER FIVE

Avoiding people might be fine if you're not a wolf, living with other wolves. Eventually, it was my traitorous scent that gave me away, as Jace found me going over multiplication flashcards with Mikey. At first he simply entered Mikey's room, where we'd been hiding, and observed as Mikey rattled off answers for each new card shown. He's really good at these, only struggling with times nines and twelves. He's already on to division, but he struggles with the same numbers so we had come back to this. Finn told me his favorite math was actually geometry, he just didn't want to move forward without Mikey having a solid foundation first. Only, Finn doesn't know that we each get a gummy bear when Mikey answers correctly when we do flash cards.

I eyeball Jace, wondering if he's going to tattle on us. I had thought that once I saw one of them, the anger towards them would rise to the surface. But it hasn't. Instead, it fizzled out completely. All I'm left with is sadness. Plain and simple, I feel hurt and left out. But until Albert gets me what I asked for, I don't plan on revealing what I know. In my mind, they started it.

"Hey," Jace says softly. I realize I've been staring at him for a while now.

"Hi," I respond. We stare at each other. Neither one of us breaks eye contact.

I hear plastic crinkling and I snap my head to Mikey, who has a mouthful of gummy bears and a multicolored smile as he gets caught. "Hey! You cheated; you didn't answer any questions first!" I point at him.

"And you!" I swing to point at Jace. "You helped him; you can see him and you didn't say anything," I accuse, a smile breaking over my face at their antics.

"I have no idea what you speak of, oh beautiful lady of mine," Jace says with his most refined accent, a hand over his heart as he bends to kiss me. His trademark smirk is in place as he pulls away.

"You're lucky you're so charming. You just cost me several candies, blondie." I narrow my eyes playfully.

Jace laughs. "You realize you're a blonde, too, right?"

"Oh, is blondie an insult?" I ask, tilting my head. I've been called that several times, so I hope not.

He laughs harder, reaching down to pick me up off the floor and drape me over his lap in one smooth move. "No, not really. Just the way you said it made it sound like that."

He brushes my hair away from my face with a finger. "Besides, you love my blonde hair. I catch you looking at it all the time," he says confidently, making my cheeks heat. How he still manages that, I'll never know.

"If you guys are going to get weird, can I go play?" Mikey asks, already shuffling the cards not in my hand.

"Ah, you'll be weird one of these days, too, my boy. I don't mind if you want to go play, you have to ask your mum, though," Jace tells him, making the boy look to me. I smile and wave him off. Morris had gotten a set of Matchbox cars to add to his collection and I know Mikey has been wanting to get a peek all day.

I turn my head back to Jace once the door closes behind Mikey. "Mum, huh? Don't you mean mom?"

"Nope," he responds, flicking my nose. "I'm English, babe. Get used to it," he says, making me giggle. He leans forward, kissing me deeply until we both need air. I sigh in contentment, moving my face into his shoulder. When was the last time I had a moment like this with Jace? Too long ago, that's for sure.

"I came to see if you'd like to spend the evening with me," he says softly, holding me to him and stroking my hair idly.

"Like sleep in your room tonight?" I ask for clarification.

"If you'd like to. Though I was asking you to a proper date with me. It's not safe to go out, but I've arranged something we can do here. So, Kitten Ivaskov, would you accompany me this evening?" He raises my hand to his lips, kissing the back of it.

Oh, how Jace can make my heart melt with one flash of those golden eyes. "I'd love to," I tell him breathlessly.

"Good," he says as he stands, my feet touching the floor as he takes my hand, opening the door for me. "Then get your pretty tush down to Logan so he can help you get ready." He ends with a swat to my butt to get me moving. He passes me, going down the hallway to the stairs. He glances over his shoulder once, long enough to send me a wink and a wicked grin. He's just so dang...*good* at this kind of stuff.

"I look like a flower," I say in awe, standing in front of the floor-length mirror.

Logan comes up behind me, a satisfied smile on his lips. "Do you like it?" he asks.

I nod my head vigorously. "I do. I feel so pretty," I exclaim as I swish my hips, making the soft pink knee-length dress sway side to side. The silk material is layered at the bottom and shaped to resemble that of a flower. While the bottom is flowy, the top is form-fitting. The barely-there cap sleeves and bodice are lined with lace in a cream color, matching the strappy heels Logan helped me into.

Logan takes out two small blue boxes, opening them to reveal a silver necklace that sits at my throat with a teardrop pendant that dangles when I move. Taking my wrist, he opens the other box and places around it a thin silver bracelet with shiny crystals or diamonds.

"That should do it. You look stunning and delicate, just as I wanted you to," Logan tells me as his hand fixes a few flyaways in my hair that he curled and brushed out, making it look wavy. He checks the silver comb at the back, making sure it'll hold its place.

"The bastard won't know what hit him," he adds with a smirk.

"Thank you, Logan. I appreciate you taking time to do this. I'm nervous about the date, though. What do people do on dates?" I ask, biting my lip.

Logan laughs, swatting my butt. "It's Jace. You already know him. Date is just another word to describe spending time together, which you've done countless times. He's a flashy bastard, so I know you'll have fun," he reassures me.

Oh, well that's not too bad then, is it? We both turn when there's a knock on the door. Logan places a warming hand at the small of my back, guiding me to the door. Tristan pops in before we reach it, giving me a slow whistle and a wink, leaving the door open and taking a stance very close to Logan. The two share a look.

Before I can ask, Jace appears in the doorway, looking as handsome as ever. He's wearing a light grey suit, tailored just for him, complete with a matching vest and a white shirt with black buttons. It's the not the first time I've seen him in a suit, but this one seems to showcase every fine feature of his lean and tall frame. His gold eyes contrast nicely, and his hair holds a wave to it, every strand perfectly in place. I wonder if his hair even knows *how* to misbehave?

"Good evening, young man. What are your intentions with our Kitten?" Logan says in a deeper voice than is natural for him. I look to the side, seeing he has put his arm around Logan's shoulder, both their faces set in stone.

"Yeah. You better have her home by eleven or I'll release the hounds and hunt you down, boy," Logan adds dramatically.

Jace peels his eyes away from me to shake his head at them. "You guys are idiots." He sighs, but can't hide his amused smile. The two others crack up then, high-fiving each other.

Jace takes a step forward, offering me his arm. I smile softly as I take it, placing my hand in the crook of his arm and letting him lead me down the hall. "You look as lovely as ever, Kitten," he tells me.

"You're quite beautiful yourself tonight, Jace," I tell him honestly.

He smiles brightly at me, revealing those perfect pearly-white teeth that belong in a toothpaste commercial. "I don't know if I've ever been called beautiful before."

"Well, you are." He totally is.

"Wait, wait!" Reed stops us as he jogs out of his room. "Let me take some pictures."

"Yay!" I exclaim. I love the idea of adding pictures of the guys to my collection. Reed snaps away as Jace positions us for different poses. Just when I think we're done he bends down to kiss my lips softly, only it's been so long since I've had a taste of him that I can't resist. His exotic and expensive scent invades my senses and I get lost in his soft lips momentarily. He pulls away first, not even out of breath. On the other hand, I'm sure my face matches my pink dress, and I'm nearly panting.

"That will do," Reed chirps as steps back into his room and

closes the door. Out of the corner of my eye I see Jace exhale slowly through his mouth. Hmm, maybe I affect him more than he lets on.

Jace leads me past Mikey's room and further down the hall on our floor to an unused room near the end. My jaw drops as soon as the door opens. I step inside, hands flying to my mouth as I take in the transformation. "Jace! What have you done? It looks like an old English ballroom. I mean, it's smaller, of course, but it's like stepping back in time!" I breathe out. I'm shocked and so very excited. "How did you do this so fast?"

When I feel like my eyes can't handle any more details I turn back to Jace, who has taken to leaning against the doorframe. His eyes are on me, not the room, and I realize he was watching my reaction the whole time.

"I wanted to dance with you. So, I made a ballroom," he states simply.

"I don't know how to dance," I tell him sadly, feeling like I've let him down after he went to such great lengths.

He smiles then, stepping away from the wall to join me in the center of the room. He traces my jawline with a lean, manicured finger. "Everyone can dance, but I thought you might to learn to dance the waltz. I will teach you."

"Is it English night in the Ivaskov house?" I tease him, excited to get to learn something new.

He laughs, placing a hand around my waist and pulling me close. We sway together, even though there's no music yet. "The waltz isn't a dance style native to England though, at one point, we did make it our own. You Americans got that from us. Though we could have never predicted *soccer*." He shudders dramatically and laughs at his own joke.

I laugh, too. "Funny. Finn told me that the term soccer actually originated in Britain as a way to distinguish association football, where the term comes from, versus the other types of football. Like Rugby football."

Jace rolls his eyes. "It's not true if I choose to ignore it."

A pang of recognition hits me square in the heart. Is that what I'm doing when it comes to being hurt that the guys lied to me? Choosing to ignore the betrayal so nothing has to change between us?

Before I can decide one or the other Tristan and Finn enter the room, each carrying a tray high above their heads and Mikey trailing behind them with a bucket. They walk straight to the two-person dining set situated against the wall, in front of the open window. They set the table with glasses, silverware, and plates of steaming food. Tristan helps Mikey to place the bucket full of ice and an opened bottle of Champagne off to the side. They wave shortly before making their exit. I stand back, amused.

Jace takes my hand in his. "Dinner, my lady?"

"Of course, my...Jace." I fail at returning his banter. I don't know how people spoke in England. Much less during the time period Jace was born. At least my attempt got a chuckle out of him.

He pulls my chair out for me, timing perfectly when to scoot the chair in before taking his own seat across from me. He fills each of our glasses halfway, encouraging me to take a sip. It's bubbly, like soda, and less sweet than it smells. It may not be something I'd drink all the time, but I do enjoy the light flavor on my tongue. I also have a glass filled with water, I imagine for if I didn't like the Champagne.

"Is this all English food?" I ask, my eyes raking over the unique dishes set before me.

Jace tilts his head to the side with a slight shrug. "Food in England is more regional than anything, really. Though some things are universal, but cooked differently. Much like the

Southeastern U.S. with their barbeque. Someone in Texas might not prepare pork ribs in the same manner as someone from Louisiana, but they are still pork ribs, and most people throughout the entire country eat them, even in the North."

"With our dinner Tristan has made some staples from England, but he always puts his own spin on his food. Like our black pudding here; I'm sure he sweetened it up more than someone who lives in England would prefer it, because your palate is used to more sweetness."

"I didn't eat sweets a lot before meeting you guys," I tell him, confused.

He shakes his head. "No, not like that. Most foods made for Americans is made sweeter than anywhere else. Even if you don't realize it. Pastas and breads, cereals and processed meats. Basically, anything that doesn't come straight from the dirt is artificially sweetened," he explains.

I chew my food, thinking it over. How interesting. "It's not like this in other places?" I ask.

He dabs at his mouth with the cloth napkin. "Nope, it's unique to here. While almost everyone enjoys sweets in some way, they don't prefer it in everything they consume. That's the biggest difference in "American food", since this country never really had its own staples and foods. If you look at the top fast food restaurants you have hamburgers, which originated in Hamburg, Germany. Tacos, which of course are a Mexican dish. Pizza, which is Italian, and Chinese food which, naturally, is Chinese."

"Do you not consider yourself an American?" I ask.

He makes a noncommittal sound. "I don't know what I consider myself. I look like a human, but I'm not like most humans. I'm a wolf, but not a wolf. I've lived in parts of this country that weren't part of this country at the time..." He shrugs. "But I was born in England, and it's still part of England today, so it's just easier to say I'm English. It's how I was brought up, mannerisms that are ingrained and with a palate that is a hard thing to change fully," he explains.

"I guess I'm an American. You know, since I was born in this country and I've never left it. But, I mean, it's not I've ever felt like I truly belonged to any place in particular," I declare.

He nods, finishing up his meal. "I can se that. Though, my opinion would be that feeling that you belong to a place doesn't necessarily mean that a place feels like home to you. More like if a place feels like it belongs to you, that's what makes it feel like home, or where you're from. If that makes sense. England will always feel like home to me because it's a part of me that I'll never forget, even if it's named something else in the future."

"I like that. Maybe that's why you and the others feel like home to me, then," I say with a smile.

Jace shifts uncomfortably in his seat, taking a moment to respond. "That's the reason I wanted to do all of this tonight. I know I don't have much to offer you like the others do. Not like Ash's fierce protection or Finn's knowledge. All I have to offer you is myself, and I guess I wanted you to see a little of where I came from, as it's still important to me. My family...I could do without remembering, but other things, like the tastes and country parties in the summers. Trying to stand out in a sea of people wanting to stand out...those things I'll never forget."

I scoot my chair back, rounding the table to go to him. He slides back, but I put a hand on his shoulder to stop him from getting up. "Jace, if all you have to offer me is you, then I'll never want for anything. You are all I'll ever need from, well, you." I giggle, hearing how that sounded.

He reaches for my waist, guiding me to drape my legs over his. Then kisses me. Hard and deep and full of passion, just like him.

Then...we dance. Or, I try to, at least. While we're both

having fun, I think I may have stepped on Jace's toes a few too many times. I've never heard him laugh quite so much at one time, and I'm quickly becoming addicted to the sound. Jace may be one of my more refined mates, and I love that about him to no end, but it's nice to see him open up and let loose like he's doing now. I learned that the waltz is his favorite dance of all time and makes him feel powerful to perform it. Trying to dance makes me feel silly, but I like this. Any chance I get to stare into his golden, fascinating eyes, I'm going to take it.

After what feels like both forever and only a moment, I find myself wrapped in Jace's arms, slightly swaying to the soft instrumental music with my head pressed to his chest, my eyes closed. I hate to break the spell of the moment, but I feel as though if I don't ask now, I may never know.

"Jace?"

"Hmm?" he answers.

"Why have you been avoiding me? I love what you've done for me tonight, and I will always cherish spending time with you, but...you've barely been in the same room as me lately. Have I done something?" I bite my lip as I wait for his answer. I almost want to have done something wrong, so I'd know how to fix it.

He sighs deeply, pulling back and lifting my face to his. "You haven't done anything, Fun-size. I was just dealing with something. I *am* dealing with something. Which is another reason why I wanted this date before I had to tell you."

"Tell me what?" I ask, now more worried than ever.

"Come with me. I'll tell you in the bath," he says, offering me his arm and walking us back to his room.

He sits on the bed, sliding off his shoes and lining them up neatly. Unhooking the silver cufflinks at his wrists looks challenging, so I help him, placing them on top of his dresser. I unbuckle the straps of my shoes, setting them down beside his.

The silence continues as we undress, looks shared between us. A bath has already been drawn for us, the water smelling of roses and full of fluffy bubbles and light pink rose petals. Jace climbs into the oversized tub first, reaching a hand back to help me step in without slipping. He takes a seat, stopping me from following him down into the pleasantly hot water. "What?" I break the silence.

He shakes his head with a soft smile, starring at my tummy. My eyes follow his. There's a slight bump, nothing too obvious unless you're looking and knew what my tummy looked like before.

"You're starting to show," he whispers, head leaning forward to lie against it.

I run my fingers through his hair. My other hand traces over his strong shoulders. "It's crazy, isn't it?" I smile down at him. "You know what else is crazy? You not telling me what's going on with you," I joke, but I'm kind of serious.

Placing a sweet kiss to my tummy he pulls away, helping me to sit between his legs, my back to him. I sigh in contentment as the heat surrounds me, the heavy scent of the water filling the space pleasantly. "I don't want you to get mad. I've enjoyed our night so much. I don't want to ruin it," he mumbles behind me.

"You'll feel better once you tell me," I say. Is this it? Is this the moment when one of them cracks and tells me about the war and how they hid it from me? Did Jace want to tell me, but avoided me because he felt guilty?

"I see your dreams." His low whisper takes a minute to register as my imagination spirals out of control.

"What!" I shriek, turning around so fast that water sloshes over the side of the tub.

He cringes, rubbing at his ear. "Calm down. This won't be any easier if I'm deaf." He pulls me back around into his arms, now holding me securely. "I didn't know what they were at first. I just thought they were crazy dreams, like being attacked by a lion even though I'm nowhere near a lion and shouldn't be afraid of that."

I remain silent, just listening. "Then I realized that it wasn't normal to remember everything from dreams, and they were always of you. You at different ages and different places. It freaked me out, and eventually I went to Albert about it. He had said before that he was with your father for all the research he used to do, so I wondered if he ever came across anything like that. He had, but he needed to find the book where it was mentioned."

"Where what was mentioned?" I frown, not following. I'm more hung up on the fact that this is strike two for Albert not telling me things he should have told me.

"Dreamsharing. That's what it's called. There are a few texts that mention side effects of mating bonds. Dreamsharing is one of them. Basically, I dream the same dream you're dreaming," he explains.

"What did the texts say? And why can't I see your dreams? I don't even dream, I just replay memories." I try to get out of the bath, my mind too cluttered with unanswered questions to be able to relax. Jace tugs me back to him, shushing me.

"I didn't read them myself. Finn said he'd take a look. He's better at research than either of us, so just try to relax. I'm not ready to let you go yet," he pleads.

Since Jace never pleads, I let myself relax back onto him, chewing my lip in thought. "You've seen the dreams recently?"

"I have. They haunt me even when I'm awake. I thought if I slept at opposite times of you, it would help, but there's too many people around here. Too much noise to sleep during the day."

"Ah, I get it. You tried to show me something from your past, because you thought you owed it to me. Because you've been seeing mine. And you woke me up the other morning because you thought it was going to a bad place." I nod, now understanding.

"Uh, now that you say it like that, I suppose that was what I was trying to do. You're not angry that I've been invading your dreams?" He brings his hand up, turning my head so he can see my expression.

"No, I have no right to be angry about that. It's not as if you're trying to do it, or that you even enjoy it. I don't know why you wouldn't just tell me, though."

"I thought I was crazy. I didn't want you or the others to think I was crazy, too."

"Can you see in my head any other times?" I ask.

He shakes his head slowly in thought. "No, and it's not every time I sleep, or you sleep. It just happens randomly."

I flip myself around, resituating myself so my knees are on the outside of his and my arms are lightly draped over his shoulders. I try not to get distracted at the intimate position this puts us in. "Have you tried?" My voice is deeper than I intended it to be. I clear my throat and shake my head slightly to focus.

"Tried...what?" he mumbles, his hands slicking over my thighs and the gold in his eyes starting to swirl with heat.

I groan, backing away from him to sit on the other side of the tub. "See, this why you shouldn't have avoided me. We can't even have a conversation without wanting to...well, I'd say tear each other's clothes off, but we're already naked," I giggle.

Jace laughs as well. He takes a deep breath, a hand running through his hair, making me wet. *It* wet. Making *his hair* wet! "So, you want to know if I've tried to get in your head at other times? Like when you're awake?"

"Yes!" I reply too quickly, and probably too loudly. I lower my voice and add more calmly, "That's what we were talking about."

He looks at me oddly before his expression changes, giving

me a knowing look. "I know what you're thinking right now," he teases.

Oh, I highly doubt he knows just how badly I want to crawl on top of him and ride him until my legs are shaking, my wet hands slicking up his lean chest and into his gorgeous, perfect hair, messing it up. The image of just what that would look like flashes through my mind.

Jace gasps, his mouth hanging open as his whole body jerks. "Holy shit," he breathes.

"What?" I ask, alarmed at his sudden change in behavior.

"I saw that. What you just thought...I saw it. That was hot, by the way. Is it always like that in your head?" he asks me.

"I didn't say anything out loud...I don't think." Or, at least, I hope not.

He sits up on his knees quickly, leaning toward me and sloshing water over the side of the bath. "You didn't. I was looking at your lips. Quick, try it again," he demands.

I wasn't trying in the first place. Honestly, I don't know if I want Jace to hear my thoughts, or see them, however it works. What if I'm thinking of the other guys, like the other day when I had three of them. I can't help the grin that forms on my face as I remember pleasing Logan so well he passed out right after.

"Oh, nope. Not that, I don't want to see that. Ever!" Jace covers his eyes, shaking his head as if to remove the image from his brain.

I reach my hand out to him, apologizing profusely. "Jace! I'm so sorry. I was trying to not picture anything like that and I guess it made me focus on it." I instantly try to picture anything else. A favorite park of mine as a child, the library in their old house with books on shelves everywhere, a pretty yellow flower I once saw that fascinated me. "Does that help any? Those things are better, right?" I ask.

He huffs out a breath, trying to relax. Sitting back how he

was, I look on, worried. "What things? What are you talking about?" he replies.

I pull up the three images quickly. A park, the library, and a flower.

Jace blinks a few times. "Yes, those are better. Did you think of them a minute ago, too?" I nod quickly. "Hmm, maybe I can't see what's in your head if you're touching me? Come here, let's test this."

I move back to my position on top of him. Before I can stop myself, the intimate image from before assaults me as I accidentally brush against him on my most sensitive spot. Jace growls hotly, his hands coming up to grip the backs of my thighs. "Nope, I saw that, too," he tells me.

"Hmm, maybe you just blocked me out before, because you saw something you didn't like and were afraid to see more," I supply.

"Possibly. But you were right before. It's been too long and, as much as I want to figure this out, I'm not going to be able to focus until I've had you. I want you, Kitten. I need you. I promise we'll figure this out, but I need to be inside you. Right now," he says harshly, eyes heated and pleading.

I don't need to be asked twice. I lift myself slightly, Jace positioning himself where we both need him. I slide down carefully, making us both groan out our pleasure. I hold on to his shoulders in a firm grip and repeat the process, adding in a grind at the base of him to add more friction on my sensitive button. Arching my back, I thrust my chest toward him, imagining his hot mouth suckling at my nipples.

Jace thrusts up into me, hard. "As you wish, Princess." Only then do I realize he must have seen what I thought. This could come in handy.

His hands caress my back, up over my shoulders, and he uses the new position to pull me down harder onto him. My breath escapes me faster, loving the feel of him inside and all over me. I think this might be my new favorite.

As my pleasure builds, I fulfil my fantasy and get my hands into all that brilliant golden hair, ruining the perfection and presenting myself with a hot, sex-mussed version of Jace. The new look sends a jolt straight to my core, squeezing tightly around him. I rock my hips faster at his groan. I wish I could see his thoughts like he can see mine.

And…just like that…I could. Only Jace's thoughts were in words, not images like mine.

"Lord, I hope she comes soon. This feels too good. I won't last much longer," I hear from him. I'm far too worked up to have a conversation right now, explaining that I can apparently hear him, too, so I just tuck this away for now. I come to a stop, taking a moment to reposition us both, with him slid down a bit in the tub, causing him to recline slightly and giving my knees more room. I sit up straight, my hands flat on his chest, nails slightly digging in. I ride him. Ride him like my life depends on it, getting lost in everything but the sensations around me. The sight of Jace as he pants and groans out his pleasure, the smell of roses mixed with Jace's expensive-man scent, and the friction and heat between my legs all work to send me crashing like a tsunami into a state of bliss.

My head is still in an after-pleasure haze but I'm able to catch, *"Fuck yes, pretty girl. Now my turn."* Jace moves so suddenly the world is a blur. In a split second I'm pressed up against the tile of the shower, my legs spread wide as strong arms pin them harshly to the wall, water cascading off of us both. Jace's mouth presses into a hard line as he thrusts aggressively into me, lost in his own pleasure. It doesn't take long at this pace for him to find his release. With a final thrust of his hips and an involuntary shout from him, I feel the warmth of his seed enter me.

Jace crashes his lips to mine in a demanding kiss full of

possession while wrapping my shaking legs around his narrow hips. On shaky legs himself, he steps out of the tub, grabbing an oversized fluffy white towel to drape around me, and carries me out of the bathroom. Once we reach his bed, he tosses back the covers and collapses with me on my back, his leg thrown over both of mine and his face pressed to my chest. Within ten seconds, he's asleep.

My entire body feels like jelly, but I manage to reach for the blankets to cover us both as best I can before closing my eyes and replaying everything that just happened. Picking out my favorite parts to save for when I want to remember them. I wonder if this new development between us really is a gift, or if it will be a curse.

∽

Jace

I wake slowly, aware that I'm alone in my bed. Kitten must have snuck off sometime earlier this morning. I sit, scooting up till my back hits the headboard. I make a face at the still-damp sheets, but follow it with a satisfied smirk. While I may not be able to stand damp bedding, the reason behind it makes me quite pleased with myself. I only wish the lovely blonde was still here, lying naked beside me.

Stretching my lazy limbs, my muscles pull in all the right places after a night gone well. Last night was the best sleep I've had in forever. Shocking, really, since I was able have the conversation with my mate that was responsible for keeping me awake most nights. She took the news better than I could have expected. Though, there's yet another addition to our bond that we've uncovered.

Food.

I need food.

I contemplate staying in bed a tad longer, but my stomach gives an angered growl of disapproval and the wet linens nag at me. I wrap the sheet around my waist and make my way to the bathroom, brushing my teeth and drying the floor as the bathtub drains from last night. I have to keep fishing out the rose petals that threaten to clog the drain. I had intended for the bath to be for Kitten only, but the circumstances changed and it only felt right to join her. I'm sure I'll catch hell from the guys for smelling like flowers, but it was worth it. So very worth it.

Stalking from my room, grumbling about leaving my favorite hair pomade in Logan's bath, I shoot a glare his way as we pass in the hall. He chooses to follow me. "I left it in your room again," I say, idly opening his door and strolling in.

"I'll help you with it again, if you want me to. I was thinking of changing my hair. What do you think?" he asks, jumping up to sit on the sink counter.

I raise a brow at him, handing over the container of specialized, imported hair product. It may cost a small fortune, but they donate to charity and it makes my hair look amazing.

"That depends. How crazy are we talking? Not pink again, I hope. Also, keep in mind that we have a woman now, and Kitten quite fancies your hair. She may not like if you go changing it."

"First off, I've already done the pink thing, and you're an asshole for bringing that up. It was the '90s! We all did things we regret." He pauses, then shudders.

I smirk back at him in the mirror as he starts applying product to my hair with a comb. "You just thought about Ash and Remy during their grunge period, didn't you?"

He nods solemnly. "I did. It still haunts me. All that fucking flannel. Yikes."

"I hear it's making a comeback," I inform him.

"Not in this fucking house, it's not. Anyway, I was looking

through *Vogue Paris* and I noticed that some of the trendier 1920s styles were coming back for those who are able to pull them off. You know, I always regretted wearing hats back then. I told Remy that going sans hat in public wasn't a damn fad," he rants.

"You're not talking about that atrocious helmet-head, part down the middle thing?" I ask with a horrified expression. "While it may have worked for Lucky Luciano, everyone else looked like they'd dipped their head in a toilet."

Logan laughs, nearly dropping my comb in the process and leaving a weird wave in my hair. I take it from him, fixing it before it has time to dry that way. "No, man, I was thinking of leaving it mostly like it is, but shorter on the sides and slicked back up top, using product like your pomade. I'd need an inch or two taken off up top. Besides, Kitten caught me watching reruns of *Boardwalk Empire* and she liked that Jimmy guy's hair," he explains, moving a few last strands until they lined up perfectly.

I tilt my head side to the side. Yep, I look damn fine if I do say so myself. The dark blue knit sweater I'm wearing with a white colored shirt underneath and gold crest accent my eyes and hair nicely. Hmm, maybe I need to change out my watch to something smaller, as it seems to distract from the sweater.

Logan snaps his fingers in my face.

"Oh, right. I think you could pull it off. It might help showcase your high cheekbones, too. Will you keep that streak of blue?"

He shakes his head, twisting his lips in thought. "Nah, I was thinking a more classic look, but keeping it moveable enough to keep it soft and not greasy. She hid it well, but Kitten's pulse went apeshit every time a strand of Jimmy's hair fell forward. She's not allowed to watch that show anymore, by the way. I lied and said it was filmed a long time ago and that dude's probably ancient by now. I'll be damned if she finds out he's still young and hot."

I have to laugh at this. "Really? You lied to her about that? What did you think she would do, leave us and go find that actor?" I shake my head in amusement.

"Don't be a shit. If you haven't noticed, our girl is hot as hell and could get anyone she wanted. So, I don't want her wanting anyone but us," he states seriously. I choose not to argue with him, though I think he's being an idiot.

"You want my help with your hair? I know you can manage the cutting on your own, but I can get the clippers and make sure it's even on the sides and back," I offer.

"Shit-yeah, my dude, you know I trust no one else." He claps his hands together, excited about the new hairdo.

I roll my eyes at him as I browse through his collection of hair products, looking for the one that'll help wash out that blue. "I hate how you pick up slang, Logan. Why does it always have to be slang that annoys me?"

He nudges me out of the way with an elbow, finding the right bottle and setting it off to the side. I go to the closet and pull out a hand-towel, handing it to him. He pulls his shirt off, placing the small towel around his neck, starting the water in the sink and getting it to temperature.

"I do it *because* it annoys you," he jokes. "Besides, it's how Reed talks all the time. I'm still glad he found himself as a surfer-slash-artist back in the day," he adds.

I pull out a shampoo and conditioner set that I know both Logan and Kitten like, and gesture for him to stick his head under. I'll need to use the color remover first, then the others. "I do as well. Before that, he was a tortured and misunderstood artist, either brooding in front of a canvas or brooding everywhere else. I don't miss getting sunburnt in Hawaii and California every damn day, but that time period really changed him for the better. He's happier now. I know he misses the waves and water, though," I add with a frown. Maybe we can find time for him, Kellan, and Ash to surf.

"Yeah, I think everyone but us misses the beach life. They don't understand our skin tones. They've come a long way with sunblock, though. If it wasn't for this large pack thing, I might even suggest we go back. The Hawaiians will always welcome us, even if they know about us. Their culture welcomes the supernatural."

I finish washing his hair in silence. Thinking to myself about what it would be like to escape from here and live near a beach, with Kitten in a bikini most of the time. It's tempting. More tempting than it should be. After our family talk the other day, it made me realize that I'm not the only one feeling stuck and useless here. Something needs to change, that's obvious. Maybe we will end up near the water again—who knows what's possible anymore.

Over the next few days, Kitten and I try to work out this newfound connection between us. All Finn was able to find out in his research was that only strong bonds formed between mates of equal domination levels could produce this side-effect. That's it. We're on own figuring out how it works and the best ways to use it.

So far, we've figured out that the push and pull on both ends must be open for us to communicate. If I'm not pulling from my side, then it doesn't matter if Kitten is pushing on hers. I won't get the message. We've also learned that Kitten is able to hear me as if I'm speaking to her in her head, which drowns out anyone else around her, while I am able to see scenes playing in her mind like a movie.

Finn's estimated guess on this is that some people think in words while others think in images, and the two of us are just going to have to figure out how the other one thinks. Which is easier said than done, since whenever Kitten sends me an image I'm blind to everything else. I almost fell down the stairs once when she imagined herself floating high in the sky on a cloud, the ground far below her. I was so scared, I'm fairly certain I almost had a heart attack. I have to keep reminding myself that not everything I see from her is reality. Kitten's imagination is vast and detailed. She may not be able to dream in R.E.M. sleep, but she can create worlds while awake if she wishes. I can see now why she's such a great budding artist. With help from Reed, she might even surpass his abilities.

The only thing I can't quite figure out is why Kitten completely blocks me whenever she spends time with Albert. We've both slipped up many times, not realizing we were either pushing or pulling, but her mind is a fortress whenever she's with him. Which seems to be more and more often lately. When I asked her about it, she said they're working on their own dynamics in their new roles for the pack. They have to learn to work together, and that's as much as she's shared. I didn't press her, but I'm determined to get to the bottom of it. She can't hide from me forever.

CHAPTER SIX

Kitten

Keeping my thoughts to myself is harder than I ever thought it would be. I mean, thoughts are supposed to be private, and I've spent my entire life thinking what I wanted, when I wanted. I'll admit that it's nice to know what Jace is thinking sometimes. He's one of the harder ones to read for me. That blank and bored expression of his is so ingrained, I don't think he knows he's doing it most of the time. Alas, it's my fault I'm struggling so hard with this. If I wasn't keeping secrets from them it wouldn't be a problem.

I'm beginning to feel guilty about hiding what Albert and I are up to. Weren't secrets and lies what started all this in the first place? Will the guys be just as hurt by my actions as I was by theirs?

"Princess Kitten, we have another call in three minutes. Are you ready?" Albert asks, breaking me out of my inner ramblings. Maybe I should tell them. Yes. I decide I have to tell them. Just not right now.

"I'm ready. I don't know why the South African pack

requested a video call. Everyone else was fine with the phone. It will be harder to look at my notes and keep my face from reacting, like you said." I bite my lip nervously.

"It was the only way they agreed to speak with us. They don't want to be caught in the middle of a war. Alpha Jabulani will have his mate, Lindiwe, present as well. It's considered disrespectful for a male to speak with a mated female privately in their pack. Also, remember that if you want to show appreciation, you can bow your head slightly, but don't divert your eyes. They'll see it as a sign of weakness."

"Are they different from us?" I ask curiously.

Albert sniffs. "From us, *when*? We've had many cultural changes throughout our history, customs that have come and gone. I imagine it's been the same for any other pack out there. This Alpha in particular I met once upon a time, with your father. I'm not sure if these examples are a cultural thing or a *him* thing, but he is very respected and considered to be a fair ruler."

A ringing starts from the laptop and I suck in a breath for courage. Albert clicks on the accept box and a couple appears on the screen, two men holding long spears standing behind them. "Hello?" I answer automatically, before remembering that I'm supposed to greet them more formally.

My *faux pas* makes the Alpha smile. "Good day, white wolf. Forgive me if I had to see you for myself. These are trying times in our world, are they not?"

I nod my head, trying not to get distracted by his dark blue eyes that stand out like jewels against his dark skin. He's so beautiful. "They are. Which is why I wanted to reach out to you and your pack. I would like to ensure peace between us. To be friends."

His expression changes immediately to something less friendly. "You have the eyes of your father, which is the only reason I have not exited this call. My sympathies are with you at his loss. He was a good man. However, my pack has remained outside of the Ivaskov reach since the beginning of time. Your father was only permitted here as a guest. I have no wish to do your bidding," he finishes sternly.

I blink back my shock at his brush-off. "I don't wish for you to do my bidding either. My only goal is to bring the wolf world closer together. Peacefully. We may have to hide, but we don't have to hide alone. Knowledge, culture, and wolves should be able to pass throughout any territory freely and willingly. Do you not agree?" I challenge him.

He looks to his very pretty mate a moment before responding. "You speak so highly of peace, but your pack is the only one under threat of war. How can you come to me with peace, with claws at your throat?"

My own expression hardens and I narrow my eyes at him. "Do you see claws at my throat? Do you see me cowering from the big, bad wolf?" Albert clears his throat, trying to get my attention. I refuse to look away from this Alpha, though.

Alpha Jabulani laughs harshly in response, leaning forward in his seat. "Is that the heart of the Ivaskov I see? Your pride blinding you as your false sense of safety in larger numbers makes you have faith you are stronger than anyone else."

"I don't have faith that I am stronger," I reply, Albert coughing louder now.

I wave my hand at him to be quiet. "What I have faith in is my pack's willingness to adapt, to change for the better. I have faith that my mates and I will not falter in this endeavor. I'm not speaking of the past; I'm speaking of the want and need to make changes right now, for our future. For all our futures. My pride lies in what is mine, and right now what is mine is broken and in need of healing."

I pause to let that sink in for him. "I'm reaching out to you, to all the Alphas, in hopes that together we can give our wolves something better. A world where all wolves can attend school together, where they all meet to see if their mates are out there, no matter where they reside. A world where if one pack struggles the other packs help them." I'm nearly shouting by this point.

"You'd throw that all away...for what? Because you're afraid I might ask you for a favor? Well, guess what? I *am* asking you for something. I'm asking you to put aside whatever holds you back and help me pull our world together once again."

I breathe heavily as I stare at the screen. Tears of frustration burn the backs of my eyelids, but I refuse to let them fall.

Before me, Jabulani's eyes are wide, even if his mouth is set in a tight grimace. Beside him, Lindiwe's expression has turned almost peaceful and soft as she peers at me through the screen.

The silence drags on uncomfortably until the Alpha finally speaks. Instead of yelling back at me like I thought he would his voice is quieter than before, more curious than anything. "You'd let one of my men mate one of your females, even if they chose to live on my lands and not yours?"

"Of course," I'm quick to reply, putting as much sincerity into my voice as possible. "What I want more than anything is to make them happy. I know I can't give everyone everything they will always need, and that I won't always make every wolf happy with everything I do, but I can start by doing what is right. And what is right is to open the doors that have been closed to them for far too long."

"I have wolves here who have never left pack lands. I have females here who have been forced to bond with men they were not meant for. Wolves starved and shunned just because they were competition for higher-ranking males. I won't be a part of that. I never was, and will never be. Now, I'm doing everything I know how to do to help them. Will you help me with I do not know, Alpha Jabulani?"

"He will, young Princess Ivaskov," Lindiwe responds with a bow of her head and authority in her voice.

Jabulani shoots her a sharp look but she merely returns it, raising an eyebrow. With an added quick poke to the ribs the Alpha turns back to the screen, lacing his fingers through his mate's on the table before them. Their show of unity gives me hope.

"We will offer ourselves in any way you need. Our pack has seen our own struggles in recent years. The humans have spread nearly everywhere, hunting us and driving us further off of our lands. We also struggle with feeding ourselves when our crops fail, and making enough money to purchase human items," he reveals.

I bow my head in appreciation for sharing something he didn't have to. None of the other Alphas have responded to my request in such an open way. "This is an issue I hope to solve for my pack as well. One of my mates is currently working on a solution. If one is found, I'll make sure to share that information with you at once. The next step is for my pack to resolve the issue with the Australian pack, but I'm hoping a meeting of the minds can take place and that you are both able to attend. In the meantime, is there anything I can do to help ease your burden?"

I can tell he's about to refuse my offer but one of the men with a spear in the back leans forward, whispering in his ear. The Alpha nods firmly, meeting Lindiwe's eyes before speaking. "There have been severe droughts, combined with flooding in other areas. Both of which has left us with a small amount of drinkable water. We're dealing with the issues as best we can, but I would not refuse some help if you see fit."

"I'll send something right away. After all, that's what friends are for, right?" I give them a wide smile, happy they're letting me help.

"We are honored to call you our friend, Princess Ivaskov. I would wish you luck with the other packs, but seeing your diplomacy firsthand I do not doubt you will accomplish your goal without the aid of luck. On our end, we will spread the word of your generosity and kind heart. May we meet again soon." They bow their heads goodbye, and I do the same. Albert comes to disconnect the call.

"You had me worried for a second there," he tells me with an amused smile.

I collapse back into my chair, feeling like I've aged a few years. "I was worried, too. I'm glad we worked it out, though now I have another problem."

He raises an eyebrow. "What's that?"

"How exactly do I make a large delivery to Africa without my guys noticing?" I pout.

"Perhaps it's time to tell them what you've been up to," he suggests.

I nod my head quietly. Thinking. "I was going to anyway. I don't like all this sneaking around and feeling guilty about it afterward. But..."

"But, what?" he asks warily.

"Is the Australian Alpha still refusing to take our calls?"

"Yes..." He draws out the word.

"Then I think I know how to tell them." I turn my head to the side to meet his eyes. "And I'm going to need a plane."

Albert visibly deflates in front of me, covering his face with both hands and groaning loudly. "You're going to get me killed, aren't you?"

I don't answer him. Mostly because I don't have an answer. I just might get us both killed. One thing is for sure, my mates are going to be *maaad*...

Later that night all ten of us, including Mikey, sit around the table as we eat a very nice dinner of fried chicken, mashed potatoes and gravy, and cornbread. It's one of Mikey's favorites, and quickly becoming a top five of my own. I'm just glad no one thought it odd that I requested we all spend the whole evening together. The guilt of what I'm about to do weighs heavily on me, and I wonder if I didn't set this up so I'd force myself to tell them everything. But I can't. Not yet. I just have to do this one last thing and then it will all be over.

A note will be waiting for them in the morning, explaining how I had overheard them and everything I've been up to since. To be honest, I'm not even sure why I'm keeping things from them anymore. Will they be mad? Most likely. But I also know that this is what they want, and they'll be happy with what I've accomplished so far. Earlier, I had planned to end this secretive nonsense, but that was before I decided to trek across the globe and take on the Australian wolf pack myself. If I tell them now, they'll never let me go through with it.

It will be okay, though. It will all be okay, I chant over and over again in my head.

"Kitten, I'm taking the day off tomorrow and will have plenty of free time. What do you say you and I spend some time checking out our little one? I still think it would be better not to have you around the makeshift clinic, but I can bring the equipment I'll need upstairs to one of those empty rooms." Kellan suggests excitedly.

A hot pang of grief stabs me right in the soul as I realize I'm going to have to lie to him. I don't lie, it's just something I don't believe in ever doing. Somehow, with all my sneaking around, I've not had to do it. Not even once.

Reed's fork clatters clumsily to the table, hitting a plate in the process, and drawing everyone's attention to him as he rubs at his chest, his expression set in confusion and hurt.

And aimed right at me.

His gaze is so intense that I have to turn away from him before his ever-changing eyes can see too far into me. Jace, who sits next to him, checks that he's okay before they both go back to their dinner.

Reed's distraction gave me the moment I needed to form my response to Kellan carefully. With Tristan at the table as well, it's not a good idea to attempt a lie anyway. So, I opt for the truth. "That sounds like a wonderful idea, Kellan," I tell him softly, trying not to let my sadness at not being able to spend time with him show.

Out of all my mates, Kellan has been one of the busiest since we arrived here. Now he's willing and wanting to take a day away from where he's needed and I won't be around for it. I feel like a really bad person.

Reed shoots me questioning looks throughout the rest of dinner, his mood seemingly changing from content to silently brooding. He pushes his food around his plate, same as me, neither of us hungry any longer. It reminds me of my first meal with the guys. When we had eaten breakfast together. Reed had looked much the same in a long-sleeved white shirt, his cheeks pinkening when he introduced himself. The thought lifts my heart, even as Jace sighs and grumbles about me flashing things through his head. I give my golden boy a sheepish smile. I hadn't meant to push that, just like he hadn't meant to be pulling at the time. He narrows his eyes at me, but the grin playing on his lips lets me know he's not really mad at me.

"Perhaps we should watch a movie after dinner. A few of you look too tired for much else," Remy suggests.

"I'm not tired!" Mikey exclaims with a frown, as if calling him tired is an insult.

I chuckle at him. "You're never tired. I don't know where you get your energy from, but I'd like to get some of it."

"It's the pregnancy hormones. Creating life takes a lot of energy. All your resting is a good thing," Kellan explains, approval clear in his tone.

"We should watch a Clint Eastwood movie. I could be in the mood for that," Ash says as he piles up his plate with seconds.

"Like *American Sniper*, or *Heartbreak Ridge*?" Finn asks.

Ash shakes his head. "Didn't mean one he directed."

Logan's hand shoots up into the air, waving wildly. "Oh, I know! *Trouble with the Curve*," he tosses out happily. "He's in that one and it's about baseball. I fuckin' love me some baseball."

I raise an eyebrow at him. "You do?" I didn't know that.

He nods his head. "Oh yeah, Yankees all the way."

"They have too many unfair advantages as opposed to other teams," Finn and Kellan chime in, in unison. Okay, that was *awesome*.

Remy sighs. "Some things never change," he grumbles under his breath. "That is precisely why we're not watching that movie. I don't want to hear this argument yet again."

"Besides, you'd just get jealous once Kitten started fawning over Justin Timberlake," Jace adds with a smirk. Logan sticks his tongue out at him, making a disgusted face.

"I was thinking something older like *A Fistful of Dollars* or *The Outlaw Josey Wales*," Ash explains.

"He directed that last one," Finn informs him. Ash glares down the table at him. "What? He did. Just saying."

"This is why we never get to watch movies," Tristan says sadly, pouting.

I can't help it. I laugh. Not because anything said was particularly funny, but because I have so missed how they interact with each other. And probably because of the hormones. I'll blame it on them. "This is why I love all of you," I say with a giddy smile, swiping tears of laughter from under my eyes.

"Love ya back, little Luna." Logan winks at me.

"Luna?" I narrow my eyes at him, rage bubbling up as I wonder why he's called me by someone else's name. My skin ripples, my wolf fighting to surface.

"Oh, shit!" His eyes widen in horror as he realizes his mistake. "Fuck, someone explain before she tries to kill me with that fork!"

"Explain *what*?" I growl lowly through clenched teeth.

"Calm down, Kitten. Logan was referring to a conversation we've not yet shared with you. He hasn't mistaken your name, he merely forgot that you haven't been apprised of the conversation," Remington says cautiously.

I turn my head to him, tilting my head and baring my elongated canines. "Who is Luna?"

"You are," he states, silver eyes boring into me. If my mind wasn't so clouded with anger, I'd swear he was getting turned on at my show of dominance and possessiveness.

"Remy spoke to us about your conversation with Albert. About the two of you being an alpha pair," Tristan adds in that calming voice of his. "We concluded that Remington should remain Alpha of the pack, and you should take on the title of Luna." He stresses the name.

My wolf backs down slightly, enough to allow me to be able to speak clearly. "So, no more 'princess'?"

"You'll always be an Ivaskov princess. Born wolves love a good monarchy, but you can be called whatever you wish. We thought a new title and hierarchy would drive home our declaration of a new order," Remy explains.

"Luna is often used as the personification of the moon. A night goddess. Goddess of the moon," Finn enlightens me.

"Oh. So, I could simply be called Luna? Not Luna Ivaskov or Princess Luna, or any of that? Just Luna?" I ask.

"If that's what you want. I'd simply be Alpha, Jace and Ash Beta, and the rest are our advisors," Remy explains.

My teeth retract, my wolf settling completely. I look to each of my mates. "You're all okay with this? This change will help us and the pack?"

They all nod.

"I couldn't stand being called Alpha," Jace states.

"Us neither," Kellan adds seriously, pointing to include his twin in the statement.

I purse my lips. "That means you're not all equal anymore."

Reed laughs softly. "We never were, sweetie. Our dynamic has always worked for us. We're happy to return to how we were before we got here. We're still your mates, equal when it comes to you, and higher in the pecking order than the rest of the pack."

"Except Albert. He's your personal advisor, but he's still the Omega. His duty is to look out for your interests, as it always has been, but he'll gain the title of your advisor as well. I have no need of him. I have Ash and Jace at my side, as always," Remy clarifies.

They give me time to process as we finish up our meal. I suppose nothing really changes, other than the responsibilities of my mates divvying up differently. Something that they clearly want and already discussed.

"So glad you no longer look like you're going to stab me," Logan quips, breaking the silence.

That comment gets the rest of the room laughing. I blow him a kiss, giggling when he pretends to catch it.

They finally decided on a movie, Tristan and Logan grabbing snacks from the kitchen and everyone else getting pillows and blankets to make a pile in front of the couch. Yay! I guess we're snuggling!

Mikey and I were told to go get comfy, and I wait for him until he pops out of his room wearing his favorite hockey emoji sleep set. On our way to the living room on our floor I stop at

Reed's room, grabbing one of his long-sleeved white t-shirts and throwing it over my black cami. The shirt lands slightly past my pink and white stripped shorts, so I grab a hair tie as well, tying the shirt up in the back. I wiggle my toes in my black toe-socks that have grips on the bottom to look like paws and come up to my knees.

"Those things freak me out," Mikey says with a grimace as he looks at my socks.

"They're just socks." I shrug.

"They look like gloves for your feet. It's weird." He shudders.

I laugh, putting an arm around his shoulders and strolling into the living room.

Everything looks set for the movie so Mikey finds an open spot near Jace, who sits close to an end table dipping a cookie into a glass of milk. As for me, I happily slip between the twins who have chosen to lie on their sides, heads propped up on their hands.

Finn lays in front of me, wearing a grey t-shirt and green and black checkered pajama bottoms. He rolls onto his back and scoots closer to me so I can wrap my arm around his stomach and use his chest as a pillow. Behind me, Kellan cuddles up to my back, throwing a leg over mine and placing his hand on my hip.

The other guys settle in around us. Logan, Tristan, and Reed sit with their backs to the couch, legs stretched out, sharing a bowl of popcorn. Remy stretches out on his side on the couch, occasionally stealing a handful of the buttery goodness for himself. Ash lays closest to the television. His silky black basketball shorts are the only stitch of clothing on him as he lies flat on his stomach, propped up on his elbows. I can smell the Skittles he's munching on and I'm half tempted to switch positions, but I'm quite comfortable with my twin sandwich at the moment and someone has already started the movie.

It's not too long before Mikey nods off, cookie crumbs still outlining his mouth. Jace follows my line of sight and smiles down at the adorable boy. He places a spare blanket around him and picks him up, carrying him to bed. My heart swells at the sight.

A pillow hits me square in the face and I blink my eyes at Reed, who threw it. "Stop that," he tells me lightly.

"Stop what?" I ask, confused.

"Fawning all over Jace. I can...feel it, and it makes me feel weird," he explains.

I chew on my lip in thought. "You can feel it? You mean you can see it?" I ask for clarification.

"Nope. I can feel what you feel sometimes. And, I think, the baby. But it's all new and weird and it's hard to tell," he says with a shrug.

Our conversation gets everyone else's attention as well. Especially Kellan's. He pops up and stares at Reed open-mouthed. "You can *feel* the baby?"

Reed scratches at the back of his neck, face turning a little pink. "I think so. I felt from Kitten that she was tired doing yoga the other day, but I also felt from someone not her, and not me, that certain poses were fun but also made them nauseated and want milk." He shrugs awkwardly. "It's very confusing to read. So much so that it doesn't seem worth mentioning most of the time."

"That's so fucking awesome!" Logan chirps. "What else? Does the baby like fashion or video games or what? Tell me *everything*," he demands.

"What's awesome?" Jace asks, coming back in. Logan quickly runs through what he missed.

Reed, and everyone else in the room for that matter, looks at Logan like he's a lunatic. Reed is nice about it, though. "Uh, the baby can't see, so...I'm pretty sure it doesn't have an opinion on either of those things. To be honest, I don't think it knows what it likes. There's always a lot of different emotions when it's awake."

"I know it likes our voices, though," he adds. "It will pause whatever it was doing or thinking to listen to Kitten talk, and gets excited when Ash yells for some reason."

"Why didn't you tell us?" I ask softly, rubbing my stomach at the thought of the baby listening to us right now.

"I was going to, I just wanted to figure out how the whole thing worked first. And, like I said, the baby can be really hard to read. It's almost as if…"

"You can feel Kitten's emotions, though, right? Like I can see her thoughts?" Jace interrupts him.

Reed nods. "Yeah, Kitten is pretty easy to read, though I don't always know what she's feeling. It just goes in and out."

"That could come in handy if she's ever scared or hurt," Ash chimes in, looking satisfied with this development.

"It makes me wonder what else will surface. I mean, will all of us share some extra connection like this? Or do you think it's all temporary due to high levels of hormones caused by the pregnancy?" Finn asks no one in particular.

"It's hard to know," Remy says with a yawn. "All we can do is take it one day at a time. We need to be able to communicate everything going on better than we do now. For those of us who don't have a sixth sense, it will be harder to understand what's going on with those who do. I know we're busy most of the time, but we need to stick together and talk openly, guys."

A round of agreement sounds around the room, myself included. I try my best not to feel anything at all. Mostly the guilt. With Jace knowing my thoughts and now Reed knowing my feelings, it's hard not think that my secrecy is the cause of all of this. Maybe if I was more open, these things wouldn't have developed. Not that I would take them back, because I like being able to hear Jace's thoughts, and I hope I'll get to feel what Reed feels, too. I just hope any new developments hold off until after tomorrow.

With that in mind, I suggest we get back to the movie. I can't exactly sneak out if they're all still awake. My suggestion gets me a couple of confused looks, but they settle back in. This time Kellan snuggles closer to me, his hand rubbing over my belly, like he's trying to be closer to the baby. It makes me smile, and I find myself watching his hand a lot more than the movie. As the second movie is put on I feel myself drifting in and out, my eyes staying closed longer and longer as I blink. Maybe I'll just rest them for a minute or two.

The next thing I know, I'm being carried and hearing hushed whispers. My overtired mind barely acknowledges any of it. I must have fallen back asleep, because I jerk awake to the sight of a very dimly-lit bedroom not much bigger than the bed itself.

As the room does a quick bounce, I realize that I was carried onto the plane. A plane that is very high in the sky, taking me farther and farther away from my mates. Oh, God... what have I *done*? Tears streak hotly down my cheeks and a sob is wrenched from me. I cry and shake uncontrollably, knowing that they'll never forgive me. Knowing that my actions will hurt them.

The tiny door slides open, light pouring through, but I'm sure it's Albert since no one else knew of my plan. "Albert, we have to go back! They're going to hate me and they're going to leave me. I can't do this. Please, we have to go back!" I choke out through a sob, covering my face with my hands and screaming silently into them.

Arms wrap around me, pulling me into a hard chest. It's an awkward hug and takes me a minute to realize that Albert would never be so familiar with me. Slowly, I raise my gaze to see steely gold ones looking back at me. My heart lurches in relief at first, but that quickly fades as I take in his ticking jaw and expectant expression.

"I'm s-sorry," I hiccup, my face crumpling once again when his eyes narrow before he turns his face away completely.

Jace's arms fall away from me as gets up from the bed, pacing in the too-small space between it and the door. "You're sorry you got caught, not sorry you lied and went behind our backs in the first place," he says coldly.

I shake my head, but it doesn't matter. He doesn't believe me. As a new pain settles into my bones, I go back to crying uncontrollably. Jace eventually leaves when his phone rings and I curl into myself, crying until I pass out from it.

When I awake next it's to a leathery-feeling, snot-covered face, and itchy eyes. A long time passes as I just lie there. I don't want to move, or think, or breathe. I've made a monumental mistake and now I don't know how to live with it. Eventually, I get to the point where I either have to get up or pee myself. I guess bodily functions don't understand the need to wallow in self-pity.

I find the tiny bathroom near the bedroom at the back of the plane. Inside, there's a sink and counter with an outfit supplied for me to change into. I go through the motions numbly—brushing out my hair, brushing my teeth, washing my face.

I end up in nicer clothing than I normally wear. If it wasn't for the bloodshot eyes and distraught expression, the cream-colored, wide-legged slacks and soft blue sweater I'm wearing might even make me look a little fancy. I opt to forgo the nude sling-back sandals with a low heel. I'll put those on when I'm forced to. After staring at myself in the mirror for what seems like forever, I realize I'm stalling. I don't want to face Jace, but I'm going to have to at some point.

I find him in the main area, sitting stiffly with an ankle crossed over one knee, a cup of steaming tea on the table beside him and a newspaper held up in front of his face. Alberts sits a few seats away, nearer to the front. He also wears a suit, like Jace, though his is black with a white shirt and green tie. Jace is in a light grey one with white pinstripes, also wearing a white shirt, paired with white shoes, his gold cuff links, and gold watch. He always dresses nicely, but this is how he used to dress when he left the house for work.

"Are you going to stand there all day, or are you thinking about going back to crying in your room?" Jace asks curtly without looking away from his paper.

I swallow hard, forcing back the emotions his cold demeanor causes in me. I cautiously take a seat opposite him, biting my lip and tucking my hands between my knees. "Hi," I rasp out.

He lowers the newspaper slightly, just enough for me to see him raise a brow. "Are you sure you chose the right seat? Or are you trying something new and choosing your mate over Albert for once?"

My eyes water, but I try to smile through it. "I didn't choose him over you, Jace," I say softly.

He folds the paper perfectly, bringing it down with a snap to the table. It makes me jump, but he ignores my reaction. "Tell me, then, what did you do? Because from this side of things, it seems like you trusted him more than you trusted me or any of your mates."

"I'm sorry," I whisper, looking at my knees instead of him. I don't know what to say, so I stay silent. I'm not used to Jace being this mad at me and it scares me. Also, it makes me unendingly sad.

Out of the corner of my eye I watch him take a sip of his tea. He holds it in one hand, the little plate in the other as he stares out the window. "I've arranged the shipment of water for your new *friends*," he informs me.

That has me looking up quickly. "Thank you."

He turns his head, glaring at me, a none-too-friendly smirk teasing his lips. "Tell me, Princess Ivaskov. Is that one of those things you thought I wouldn't, or couldn't, understand? That wolves in South Africa were in need of water, and your barbaric, cruel mates would never let you help them if they knew the truth?"

My head rears back in shock at the animosity being thrown at me. "Jace, I didn't..."

He cuts me off. "Because charity work isn't something I'm interested in or anything. It's not like I do that for a living, have done for hundreds of years. Not like I have the connections to make it happen quickly, safely, and efficiently. No, I'm just some selfish asshole who doesn't give a damn about anyone. Isn't that right, Princess?" he says with so much sarcasm it's almost palpable.

"I didn't say that. I don't think that," I tell him quickly.

When he goes to cut me off again I talk over him, louder this time. "I didn't mean for this to happen. You guys were keeping secrets from me. I heard you talking about a war. In that same conversation I heard it mentioned that some of the other packs wanted to speak to me. So, that's what I did. I spoke to them. One thing led to another, and I got it in my head to finish this stupid threat against us. I didn't even know why I was keeping it from you anymore, and I didn't realize until I woke up on this plane just how big a mistake I was making. Please, don't be mad at me anymore. I can't handle it."

I choke up at the end, covering my face with my hands to block everything out as I get my breathing under control. He doesn't want to see my tears, remaining unaffected by my obvious pain. Rightfully so, I guess, but it still hurts.

"That's what this was all about? Tit for tat?" Jace chuckles humorlessly. "We kept something from you, so you did the same to us? We did that to protect you, so what's your excuse?" He doesn't wait for a reply, just stands and walks past me to the front of the plane.

"You did it because you thought I was weak," I say to his empty seat, low enough I'm sure he didn't hear me. I blink rapidly, refusing to cry anymore right now. Maybe I am weak, look at me right now.

"I've never, not once, thought you were weak," Jace tells me, sounding tired. He walks back to me, roughly placing a finger under my chin and lifting my eyes to his.

"That's not why we didn't tell you. Maybe it was wrong on our part. That doesn't make what you did right, either. I know you're young, and I know relationships in general are new to you, but you're going to have to make a decision. Either you're the type of person who confronts an issue head on, or the type to seek justice in the form of payback. I love you more than I thought it was possible to love someone, but Kitten…I won't live with this feeling of betrayal the rest of my days. I won't live looking over my shoulder, waiting for your retribution of a perceived slight toward you. I'll never walk away from you. I don't know how. But I'll figure out how to harden my heart against you if you make me."

All the air leaves me as he walks away. I'm left with the image of his watery golden eyes and heartbroken expression as he tells me he'll find a way to not love me anymore seared into my mind to forever haunt me. It's all that I can see. Eyes open or closed, he's there with the pain I caused him in his eyes. I. Can't. Breathe.

CHAPTER SEVEN

I feel Albert's hands on my arms, shaking me, and can hear the desperation in his voice as he yells for someone. But I can't bring myself to care, to take a breath, or un-see the image running through my mind. Just as black starts to creep around the edges of my vision a pair of strong hands lift me in the air, hard lips pressing to mine. I gasp in shock, taking in much-needed oxygen, and blink my eyes rapidly.

Ash holds me in the air, away from his body, determination set on his face. "You don't get to fall apart now, not when you've caused so much trouble proving your strength. You get to learn from this, you get to come back from this and be forgiven, but you don't get to feel sorry for yourself and fall apart," he rumbles.

"You're here," I pant, catching my breath. "You're mad at me, too," I add sadly as he sets me on my feet.

He nods once. "I am. Someone had to fly the plane. And yes, I'm mad at you. Not for sneaking around, we've all done that, but because you put yourself in danger with no thought as to what that would do to the rest of us."

My shoulders sag. "I didn't really think about it."

He crosses his arms, shifting around like he wants me back in them, but at the same time doesn't. "You shouldn't have to think about it. That's what I'm for. That's why we have the family that we do, so each of us fills in the gaps where the others are lacking," he tells me sternly.

"This is a setback, but we'll figure it out," he adds in a softer tone. "We always do. Things have been hectic ever since you set foot through our door, and I don't think we've had time to truly get to know each other. So, this is me, standing in front of you and telling you that I will protect you and everyone you care about to the best of my ability. It's what I do. But I can't do that if you don't let me, so don't shut me out."

I swipe the tears from my face, looking up to meet his hard almost-black eyes. "I won't. Never again, I promise," I tell him with all the power I possess in my words.

"Then I'll let it go," he says, moving his shoulders in a small shrug. "Some of the others won't forgive so easily, but I got to you before anything bad happened. I still hate this mission you're on, but I feel better now that I'm by your side. No harm was done, as far as I'm concerned."

Ash doesn't hate me.

He's saying the others will forgive me, in time. It's what I needed to hear to be able to stitch myself back together so it doesn't feel as if my soul is being torn to shreds inside of me.

"Are they here?" I ask shyly. I don't even know what I want the answer to be. Part of me wants to apologize and make them happy with me again, and the other part is scared to death they'll be so mad they won't love me anymore. If that's the case, I never want to see it.

"Who? The others? No, they stayed back at the house. Remy said that if you felt like you needed to do this so badly, he wouldn't stand in your way. You need to talk to him. Soon. If he doesn't think you trust him to lead this family, then he won't trust himself to be able to it. That's not a wound you leave to fester," he tells me with a pointed look. "Tristan says he understands why you did it, and the others were too hurt to even comment before I left."

Time passes with the two of just standing there. "I guess I did want to make you guys mad, because you made me mad. I just didn't think..." I trail off, not knowing how to explain it.

"That it would hurt so much?" Ash supplies, bending down so we're at the same eye level. I nod my head sheepishly. "That's why I find it easy to forgive you. I know you weren't prepared for the fallout. Trust was broken here, on both sides, but it can be earned back. We all just have to want it badly enough."

"Right," I say, chewing at my lip. "I do want that, Ash. I want to be trusted again."

He opens his arms and I move faster than I thought I could, wrapping my arms around him in a tight hug. His rough hand ghosts over my hair. "You will be. This wasn't an outright betrayal, no matter what the others may think. You just have to realize that the eight of us come with our own baggage, and trust issues and abandonment are at the top of the list."

"I hurt them. I hurt all of you. I don't think I can forgive myself for that," I mumble into his chest.

"Once they calm down and get over the shock, they'll see this for what it was. You still need to make amends and learn what it means to be a part of a whole, but nothing is unfixable here. Running from your problems doesn't fix anything, Kitten. Stomping into the room after hearing our discussion and putting us in our places would have been the better move, but..." This time he trails off and groans loudly, eyes rolled to the ceiling.

"We're fucking idiots. Of course, you would run. Avoid confrontation. With how you lived that was always the answer, wasn't it?" he says more to himself than me.

"I need to get back to flying the plane, and I have a few calls I need to make. Keep your chin up and stay strong back here," he tells me, a smile finally lighting his face. I smile back, my heart speeding up a little.

Sinking into one of the plush chairs, I pull my knees up and wrap my arms around them. I've had a heck of a morning already and feel utterly exhausted. Turning my head, I stare out at the fluffy white clouds through the window. Everything is going to be okay, because I'm going to make it okay. I need to remember that.

"I'm sorry," Albert says lightly, taking the seat next to mine.

I tilt my head to look at him. He looks dejected. "Don't be. I put you in a hard position, and I shouldn't have kept this from them in the first place."

"I didn't realize when I booked this plane that it belonged to the Beta Jace, or that the pilot would be the Beta Ash. It was the only private jet company willing to work so quickly. After they confronted me, I had no choice but to tell them everything. Not only would they have killed me, but it was the right thing to do for you at that point," he explains.

I shake my head, waving a hand in dismissal. I know his position as Omega wouldn't allow him to lie to my mates for me. Not if it wasn't in my best interests. "Seriously, don't worry about it. I'm kind of relieved it's all out there now and I can start repairing the damage I've caused."

"I wish you wouldn't put it like that," he says on a sigh. "Your mates are shocked and angry, but they're also blowing this up into something bigger than it is. Much like you did when you overheard them. All of you overreact and take things too personally. The truth of it is, you haven't known each other long enough to know how the others will react to anything," he tells me casually, making the events of the day seem almost normal.

I smile sadly at him. "Ash said something similar. And it's

probably very true. Though, that doesn't make this feeling any less painful."

He pats me on the back awkwardly. "You're all passionate and stubborn, there's bound to be a few bumps and bruises. It has been a very long time since I've seen a bond burn as brightly as yours. You love as fiercely as you fight, and you're all smart enough to know it's worth holding onto."

I blink a few times, thinking it over. I meet his eyes, a genuine smile in place this time. "Thank you, Albert."

A few hours later, I finally find enough courage to call home and speak to the others. I dial Remy first, just hoping he answers. "Yeah?" His rough, gravel-like voice comes on the line.

"Hi, it's me," I begin lamely.

"I'm aware," he responds coldly.

I sigh into the phone, closing my eyes. "Are the others around? Can you put us on group chat or whatever?"

"On speaker," he corrects. "Yes, they're here. They came running when my phone rang." The sound on the other end changes, and I hear shuffling in the background.

"Look, I don't want to fight or argue with anyone. I knew what I was doing was wrong when I was doing it, but I didn't know that I would hurt you as much as I did."

Remy jumps in, trying to interrupt me, but I speak quickly before he can. "I promise to never hide things from you again, even if you're hiding things from me. All of us made mistakes here, but I promise that I'll spend the rest of my life earning back your trust and forgiveness." I pause, giving them a chance to speak.

"Kitten..." Remy starts, trailing off with a frustrated growl.

"I'm angry, and I have every right to be, but more than anything we were worried. If you could just take a step back and look at the situation from an outsider's point of view, you'd see a young woman who is currently pregnant, planning to run off in the middle of the night, not telling anyone where she's going other than into known enemy territory."

"Oh." I pause. "Well, when you put it like that it sounds really bad." I grimace at the phone.

"Yeah...*Oh*," Remy repeats hotly. "You're not in *anything* alone anymore, Kitten. Not this pack, not this pregnancy, and certainly not this family. What happens to you, happens to us. Even the decision to give you time before telling you about the declaration of war was made as a group. That little rat, Albert, was in on it as well."

"Don't take it out on Albert," I defend.

"No! You don't get to tell me what to do about him. You're my mate, not his. I'm his Alpha, and he will have to answer for his actions. Being your advisor doesn't make him above me when it comes to you or your safety. If he wants to keep his position then he'll have to learn not to follow you blindly. Our family isn't like any other he's served under. There are nine of us adults, not just one Alpha to answer to. To serve you doesn't mean to shun us," he explains his reasoning.

I have to admit, he makes a good point. Though, I'll have to make sure they aren't too hard on Albert for his part in *my* plan.

"Okay, I understand. Just don't make him suffer for the both of us, since it's harder to be mad at me. And no violence, please," I ask.

"Oh, it's not that hard to be mad at you, too," he quips.

I hear him take a long, deep breath, probably pulling himself together. "Look, Ash called a while ago and gave us all some perspective. It actually helped a lot in understanding your irrational behavior. It's easy to forget that the rest of us have had each other's backs for quite some time. Whereas you have had to handle everything on your own, with only your instincts guiding you. You came up against a situation and didn't know how to handle it like we would, so you did what you've always done. That's not hard to forgive, Love."

Warm tears track down my cheeks and I have to speak around my throat threatening to close off. "Thank you. For forgiving me, I mean. I'll get the hang of this, Remy, I promise. I'll learn not to exact tit for tat like Jace said. I just want to be included in everything you guys are. You left me out, and it made me feel weak in your eyes. It made me feel useless and powerless to help."

I hear several snorts and huffs on the other end, but it's Logan who speaks first. "Says the girl who has gotten nearly every wolf pack in the world to agree to a sit-down in a matter of weeks. Something that has never happened in the history of wolves. Who is on her way to a country she's never been to, where they could be waiting to rip her throat out, all because the assholes wouldn't answer when she called. Right, like anyone would ever think you're weak."

I shake my head, even though I'm smiling as his assessment of me. There's a long pause, making me curious as to what they're doing. Eventually, Kellan's voice floats to me from the speaker. "I know you've had a rough morning, Reed's been experiencing everything with you, and it doesn't look pretty. I need you to take care of yourself while you're gone, Kitten. We never did get to check out the baby, and while I think he or she will be as strong as their mother, stress is never good for an unborn baby, and you've had your fair share of it."

"Yeah, have you been eating? You have to eat, Pretty Girl!" Tristan shouts from further away from the phone.

I cringe inwardly. "I haven't yet, but I will. I guess I didn't think about, uh, my issues with that."

"Fuck it. I'm meeting them at their next stop. Logan, pack me a bag," Tristan responds immediately.

"Calm down. Don't rush into shit, Chef Boyardee," Logan quips.

"I resent the hell out of that, and you know it!" Tristan accuses.

"Ravioli does sound good," Finn states conversationally.

Remy groans loudly. "Boys, can you please act like the grown men you really are for ten fucking minutes? Kitten, maybe you can try some of the packaged food that's on the plane. If you're able to eat it, then try to stick with that for the rest of your very, very short trip. If you can't, I'll have Tristan on a plane first thing."

"Okay, I can do that," I tell them. I wait a beat, picking imaginary lint off the comforter beneath me. I figured I could use as much privacy as possible when I called, and chose the little bedroom. "Are we...okay, then?"

Silence greets me from the other end of the line, then Remy comes on again. "We're okay, Kitten. We're family. We fight, but we always stick together. I love you. Be safe." His parting words are echoed by the others as well. I tell them all how much I love them and miss them already, eventually ending the call with a heavy heart. Though not as heavy as it was before I made the call.

Making my way to the front of the plane again, I knock lightly on the door that leads to the control room. Jace slides the door open for me, his eyes raking me from head to toe. I'm sure I look a mess with all the crying I've done today.

"Hi," I say shyly, not knowing how to act around him now.

"Hey," he replies. Well, at least he didn't call me Princess Ivaskov again. Baby steps.

In that moment, I realize that Jace is always going to be the one who makes me work for it. That's okay, though. I'm willing to work as hard as I have to, as long as I get to keep him in my life.

Ash sits behind a control board filled with levers and switches. Huge headphones cover his ears and a complicated-looking seatbelt straps him into his chair. Even in a plane, he looks too big to be comfortable behind the wheel. Once he spots me, he flips one side of the headphones away from his ear and turns his chair to face me.

"Hey, baby. You look like shit," he tells me before motioning me forward.

I happily step into him, his large hands going to my waist, pulling me between his spread legs. "I'll take another shower soon. Tristan told me to eat some packaged food, so I'm going to do that first. I just wanted to come thank you for talking to the others earlier."

He searches my face, his thumbs making small circles on my hips underneath my shirt. "You talked to them then? To Rem?" he asks.

I nod my head, a sheepish grin forming on my face. "Yeah, I just got off the phone with them. I think we're going to be okay."

"We will be. This is just a little speedbump. We'll get this trip knocked out and go back and work on our family. Shit will settle down then," he tells me, letting go of me to unhook the seatbelt straps. Once free he leans forward, his hands grasping the back of my thighs, head resting on my chest.

I put one arm around his shoulders, my other hand going to the back of his head, holding him to me. We stay like that for a while, neither one of us having anything more to say. His hands have me distracted, the electric tingles from the bond making it impossible not to notice them. My body warms, making me hungry for something other than food. I subconsciously move my legs a little further apart, making Ash chuckle knowingly at me.

"Needing a little relationship reassurance, are we?" He grins up at me, dark eyes sparkling with humor.

I tilt my head to the side. "I don't know what that means."

He chuckles again. "That's okay, I could use some myself," he responds, confusing me further. He pulls me toward him by my hips, stripping my slacks down my legs and off me faster than I thought possible. In moments, I'm placed on his lap, my thighs to either side of his.

"Sorry, baby. We need to be quick. I don't want to leave the plane on autopilot for too long," he says, reaching under me and adjusting himself.

"I don't mi.... oohh." I trail off as he pushes into me, forgetting everything except the sensations wracking my body.

Ash keeps one hand on my hip, guiding me to take more of him while his other hand finds my neck, bringing me forward to crash my lips against his. I moan deeply into the kiss, opening to let his tongue in to plunder my mouth. He nips at my bottom lip before lifting the hem of my shirt and bra in one fluid motion. I laugh as they get tangled in my hair, causing him to grunt with impatience. I reach back and help, freeing my hair and flinging the clothes to the floor.

Leaning back with my hands on his knees gives him more room to thrust up into me, something Ash takes full advantage of. My head tilts back and eyes flutter closed. I feel his strong hand trail up my side, over my ribcage, taking the path between my breasts until he can cup the side of my face. I lean into it, my head turning to kiss his palm. His thumb rubs over my lips, and my eyes slit open to see him watching the action intently. My lips part, his finger seeking entrance and massaging my tongue as I lightly suck.

Ash grunts, biting his lip and thrusting harder as my hips move to match his, both of us chasing the addicting release we can only find with each other. He pulls his thumb free of my mouth, bringing it down between my legs, toying with that bundle of nerves that drives me insane. His dark eyes never leave mine, waiting, wanting, asking me to crash over the edge and show him how good he makes me feel. It doesn't take long, my arms nearly going out from under me as my whole body turns to a mushy lump of sensation and electric sparks.

I feel him pulse inside me and know he's close. Before my brain can catch up I'm being spun around, my hands finding purchase on the windshield, bent at the waist with my hips thrust backwards. Ash wraps the end of my hair around his wrist and hand before gripping my shoulder, his other hand at my waist, slightly lifting me to make up for the height difference. My feet don't even touch the floor anymore.

With a long groan and a hiss of pleasure, he slides himself back into me in a hard push that has me yelping in both unimaginable pleasure and just a pinch of pain. He doesn't hold back now, chasing his own release and using my body like a tool to get him there. The display of strength and power fills me with primal pride and an overwhelming urge to please him. I want him to explode inside me. I need it. I need to be filled by him so badly.

As sweat coats my skin I let my head loll forward, begging him to come inside me, his mate. At some point I think I downright demand it, and claim that it's mine and he has to give it to me. Honestly, I lost the ability to think clearly a while ago, giving myself over fully to the lust and need this man creates in me.

With a roar, Ash finally allows himself fall over the edge. His hips lose their rhythm, shoving himself into me as deep as he can go, but still pushing deeper as he expands and pulses, a hot flood spilling inside me.

Ash wraps his arms around me, gathering me to him. My too-heavy head rolls back to lean over his shoulder as I pant in satisfaction. He sits heavily in his chair, my body draped over his like a blanket, even as we remain attached in the center. We learned before that after being so full and stretched around

Ash's length I end up feeling empty and sad when he withdraws too quickly. I'm glad he's able to remember that fact in this moment, as right now I feel like I would burst into tears.

"Maybe we should fight more often," Ash rumbles into my ear as his hands caress my splayed-out body. He sounds a little breathless, if I do say so myself. Exhausting a wolf is no easy task, and I find myself immensely pleased and satisfied that I was able to steal such strength from my strongest mate.

"Why's that?" I slur.

"I've never seen you like that. Hearing you beg me for me to fill you was the hottest thing I've ever witnessed. You were like this lust-filled, sex-creature that only wanted *me*. It was hot, baby. Beautiful. That's why I did it twice," he adds playfully.

I smack his arm. "That's why you took so long. I thought I was going to die of need. Though, now that I can actually *think*, that seems ludicrous."

He laughs, making us both hiss in surprise as the action pulls him out of me. "I like knowing I can make you lose yourself."

"I kind of liked it, too," I giggle.

Ash laughs, his wide smile and perfect teeth making an appearance before he turns more serious and sighs. "As much as I want to stare at your gorgeous naked body all day and watch you fall asleep, I really should get back to piloting this tin can."

"Can't the autopilot thingy fly the plane?" I almost whine. He's so comfy and I don't want to move.

He cups my chin, bringing my face around so can place sweet kisses all over it. The kiss to my lips is light but filled with appreciation, tenderness, and love. My heart swells. "It can, but I don't trust it for long periods of time. Not with you and the baby on board. Besides, you should go shower and eat something before you sleep again."

With those words, resolve seems to come over him and he

helps me to my feet, helping me into my sweater and slacks. He doesn't bother with the rest, knowing I'm going to shower anyway.

Before I leave Ash presses his face into my tummy, letting me stroke his hair as he promises the baby that I'll give it some food real soon. I smirk down at him, shaking my head. He doesn't baby talk like some of the others. He speaks to it like it's a tiny adult. I find it charming.

With great reluctance and a pleasantly sore body, I find myself in my second shower of the day. Albert had looked quite flustered when I had walked through, keeping his eyes to the window the whole time. Jace hadn't paid me any attention. Instead, he chose to glare at Albert with his arms crossed. I didn't have the attention span or mental capacity to ask what that was all about, so I had just quickly walked through. Now, I let the hot water soak into my skin, hopefully washing away all signs of my earlier distress. Oddly, it makes me feel stronger. I'll have to keep that in mind for the future.

When I return to the bedroom wrapped in a towel, it's to find another set of clothes laid out for me. This time it's a tight pair of black leggings, soft as a peach. Yet another thick sweater and cami set are present, this time in a pale pink, matching the lace panties and bra. I forego the bra, figuring the sweater will hide anything worth hiding. I'm only sitting around and probably sleeping soon.

Returning to the small bathroom, I brush out my wet hair and blow it dry. I braid it to either side of my head, tying them off with ribbons I found on soap boxes under the cabinet. If I had been awake when we left I could have packed my own bag, and I definitely would've remembered hair ties. Though, I do like these white ribbons.

Albert is waiting for me outside the door. "The Beta Ash has told me you'd like to try some packaged food. I wasn't sure what that meant, exactly, but I've set a few things out." He gestures for me to walk ahead of him into the cabin area.

On one of the tables is an odd assortment of frozen meals that heat up in the microwave, cracker and cookie boxes, canned vegetables and fruits, and two different types of sliced bread. "Oh...ummm." I look over everything, hoping I'll be able to eat some of it, knowing Tristan didn't have anything to do with it.

"There is peanut butter and bread. I could make you sandwich," Albert offers.

"No!" I shout, my heartrate spiking instantly.

Soldiers standing against the walls. Gilded framed paintings. Hot breath at my ear. The knife. Concrete floor. So cold. "If you eat, I get to touch you."

"I'll handle this, Albert. Why don't you go grab a shower and a change of clothes?" Jace says calmly as he slips in from the control room, closing the door shut behind himself. My eyes connect with his as I try to stop my shaking. I use him as my anchor, keeping me firmly *here*. Not in that dining room. Not that in house.

Albert doesn't argue, just bows in my direction and heads to the back of the plane. Jace studies the table momentarily, circling around me to take a seat at a different set of table and chairs. "You didn't think this through very well," he comments casually as he inspects his nails.

I blow out a breath. "Yeah, well, we can't all be logistical wizards like you," I grumble unhappily. He saw what flashed in my head. Does he really not care?

He smiles like the cat that ate the canary. "No, but you *are* mated to me. I could have helped you with this problem if you would have let me. I could have had Tristan prepare enough meals to last you for this trip, but...here we are."

My nails dig into my palms as I squeeze my fists tightly. "You're here, aren't you? Right now, you're here with me. I have eight mates, Jace. Any one of them would have came with me, but it was you and Ash that I woke up to. No one is forcing you to stay with me. If you want to be mad at me, fine. Go be mad at me somewhere else. Right now, I'm hungry and I need to find a way to eat."

He stands to his feet, rebuttoning his suit jacket. "I'm here because I'm the best at diplomacy and negotiation, not to mention a "logistical wizard", as you so eloquently put it. Believe it or not I'm actually good at a few things, Princess Ivaskov."

I throw my hands up, frustration taking over. "What do you want from me, Jace? I apologized. I'm sorry, okay? Nothing I did had anything to do with your ego. I know very little of what you actually do, but I have no doubt that you're the best at it. It's just who you are. You work hard at everything you do. You can keep up with Finn when he spouts scientific babble, you're just as knowledgeable as Reed with art and artists, you're a good sparring partner for Ash, advise Remington, assist Kellan when he needs help…I get it. You're good at what you do. I never said you weren't!"

He steps close to me, invading my space and forcing my head back to maintain eye contact. Stupid tall people. "You implied it when you left me out of the loop. Like I wasn't good enough to help the fierce and mighty Kitten take the wolf world by storm. Don't get me wrong, I'm proud of what you've accomplished. I just expected to be by your side when it happened."

"You are!" I scream at him.

I shove at his chest. He doesn't move an inch. "You're here! What don't you get about that? All I've done without you is make a few phone calls. Even then, I spoke to those people like I was one of nine members of a team. Promises I made included things only you and the others could accomplish. Because, Jace, what I accomplish, you accomplish, I can't do anything without all of you. Do you truly believe that I was never going to tell you any of it?"

"You would've had to at some point. When was that going to be, though? When we were breaking bread with the Alphas of the world?" he scoffs.

I scrub a hand down my face. "No, Jace," I say quietly, all the fight leaving me. "It would have ended this morning, either way. I should have woken up squeezed between the twins, but someone carried me onto a plane. I know it wasn't Albert, as he wouldn't have dared. I'm not his. But even if I had walked onto the plane myself, a note was left, explaining everything. More importantly, when I *did* wake up today I was ready to turn this plane around and head back to all of you, because I finally realized my mistake. So, hate me if you want, but don't go making things up in your head just so you can stay angry."

He scoffs. "You think that's what I'm doing?"

I step around him, only looking back to shake my head sadly. "I think you're hurt, and I think you've put me in the category with everyone else who has ever hurt you. But you're mine, Jace. Mine now and forever. I won't let you walk away from me or harden your heart against me. I'll love you even if you hate me. If it takes hundreds of years to earn back your trust, then it will be worth every moment. Because you're worth it. To me, you're worth anything."

I fail at holding back the never-ceasing tears, but I manage to hold back the painful sobs until I close the door on the tiny bedroom. Fine. Not crying isn't an option, it seems. But I refuse to let them see me cry anymore. Especially Jace.

Later that night I'm partially awoken from a dream to something being set on the bed beside me. It's a silver tray, filled with a few packaged food items and a note. The note simply reads: "These are things Tristan doesn't make by hand, that you eat all the time. Fresh fruits and vegetables should also be fine."

I stare at the little slip of paper, wondering who wrote it. Albert is my guess, and I'm just thankful he didn't make me a sandwich.

I'm able to force down quite a bit of what's offered. The crazy dream I was having begins replaying in my head over and over again.

"Get out here, boy!" Father's shouts can be heard from every corner of the estate. Servants scurry past me on their way to anywhere but near him. If only I could run away as well.

"Yes, Father?" I ask woodenly, entering the sitting room where my mother lies in a crying heap at my father's feet.

"Don't you "yes, Father" me, boy! Did you, or did you not, reject the invitation to the princess' ball?" he bellows, swaying slightly on his feet in his drunken state.

I swallow thickly, lifting my chin. "I did."

Swearing profusely, my father's dirt-brown eyes glare daggers at me. With a sickening smile, he reaches down for my mother. Back-handing her harder than I've ever seen him hit her, he points to me. "I may not be able to hit you and get away with it, but I'll take it out on this filth if you upset me again," he threatens.

"You're going to send a reply to the princess, informing her that you were mistaken before and that you will be attending her ball." His tone brooks no argument. "That little twat has been after your hand since she could babble. Your refusal to offer her father a contract is getting old, boy. I'll see myself in that castle before year's end, or so help me I'll kill your mother and burn this whole place down to the nothing you deserve!" As if I'd ever want to step into his role as a duke.

I watch helplessly as he shakes my mother like a ragdoll before tossing her to the side like she's nothing. "I'll send a messenger this evening," I reluctantly agree.

Now satisfied his will will be carried out, he leaves us, sending for his man to help him undress. I rush to my mother, helping her onto the settee. "Forgive me, Mother. I know not why he takes his anger out on you. I will end your suffering one day soon," I promise her with all the strength I have in me.

Her delicate hand reaches up to stroke my face. "I have every faith in you, my dear boy. Don't fret over me. Tell me, how was the square this evening?" Her dull gold eyes, a shadow of their former brilliant glory, implore me to let this go. Just like all the other times I've witnessed him beating her.

She knows not what she asks of me. How much longer do I have stand aside, watching the sham of their marriage play out before he eventually kills her? He would've killed her long ago if it wasn't for me, I know it. He hates her. Knowing that her heart belongs to another, a woman, in fact, has been slowly driving him mad for years. Only the birth of his heir saved her. Not so much for the other woman. He held out hope that my mother would come to love him, save him the embarrassment and shame of her actions. That's never happened, and now I fear he has given up hope of it ever happening. It puts her in more danger than she knows.

God help me, but I can't do this anymore.

It isn't one of my own memories, I know that. It's Jace's. Feeling his helplessness first-hand is crushing. I don't know if he's sleeping and slipped up, allowing me to see a glimpse of his past, or if he pushed it at me on purpose. If so, I can't figure out what he was hoping I'd learn from it.

Yes, no doubt it was an accident. A rare peek at what haunts Jace behind that perfect façade of his. I really hope my actions didn't bring this on for him.

I feel better now that I have food in my stomach. I'm sure the baby is happy about it, too. Shoving the tray aside, I curl up with the spare pillows. I wish it was one of my mates, but Ash has to fly the plane and Jace…Jace hates me. It's a been a long time since I've felt this alone.

CHAPTER EIGHT

Stepping off the plane is an experience in and of itself. The sun is blindingly bright, the dry heat washing over me like when you open an oven door too quickly. And... we're in a desert.

Don't get me wrong, I knew Australia had a large stretch of desert in the center, but almost all the people seem to live around the lush edges, which is where I thought we were going. Oh, and the half-wolf/half-humans surrounding us with guns and spears is a new experience as well.

Ash stands firmly in front of me, his body tense as his eyes scan the threat around us. I feel Jace and Albert behind me, Jace's hand tightly gripping my arm as if he wants to pull me back into the safety of the plane. The half-shifted wolves stand their ground silently, neither retreating nor moving in for the kill.

They're waiting. It only takes a few minutes to find out what for. I can feel the power rolling off the very large, yet very different-looking Alpha wolf weaving a path to the front of the crowd. His stance is predatory, lips pulled back in a rumbling warning growl, teeth bared.

I sigh heavily. Well, this isn't going how I wanted it to. And we've only been here for mere minutes. I put my hand on Ash's shoulder, leaning around his large frame. I smile brightly at the angry wolf, waving cheerily. "Hello, Alpha Kendrick! You wouldn't answer our calls, so we thought we'd stop by on our way...around the world? I don't know, we're here, so, nice to meet you," I chirp awkwardly.

He barks viciously in our direction, the wolves around him bending their knees, readying to pounce. I slip by Ash, moving in front of him. He grunts in disapproval, but I stay close enough that he can reach me, so he allows the move.

Pressing my lips together in a frown, I place my hands on my hips. "This is no way to greet your future allies. This is my first trip anywhere and I won't have it ruined by a stubborn Alpha. We're going to talk, and we're going to find a way to be friends. We get it, you're scary and we're outnumbered. Point made. Though, I do have six other mates back home who won't hesitate to finish off the rest of you if any harm comes to us." I add the warning at the end with a pleasant smile on my face, like I don't have a care in the world.

The Alpha shifts in an instant and I keep my eyes trained on his face. "The *rest* of us?" he asks with scorn.

I bob my head. "Oh, yes. I'm sure the two Betas with me will end quite a few of your lives before you manage to subdue us all."

"Kitten, chill," Jace whispers harshly, now standing closely behind Ash.

I turn my head to whisper back. "No, he's a bully and this this how you deal with them."

Jace glares at me. "This isn't your typical human bully. This one can kill you."

Our argument is cut short as the Alpha gestures the armed

wolves forward with a flick of his wrist. "You dare come to my lands, unannounced, to threaten me?"

I put one hand out in a stopping motion. "No, I came here to talk with you. To make peace. If I wanted to fight you, I would have brought a whole fleet of planes. You're the one too busy to answer a phone, or else we've would have been announced."

I quickly turn back to Jace. "Is a group of planes called a fleet? Or is that just boats?" I whisper quietly.

"For the love of god, Kitten. Focus!" he demands.

I huff my annoyance, turning around to face the Alpha again. If Finn were here, he would have answered me.

Kendrick now paces below the steps, his eyes narrowed in thought. He takes his time, clearly thinking his next move through carefully. I grow impatient, stepping down a few more stairs, lowering my voice to a normal volume.

"I really do wish to simply speak with you. I don't know what this war is about, or why you declared it in the first place. If nothing else, am I not owed an explanation?"

Kendrick comes to a halt, blinking big eyes at me. He appears stunned. He studies me, coming to some conclusion as he releases a harsh laugh. He stands with hands on his hips as he addresses me. "You honestly don't have a clue, do you? How is that even possible?"

I don't know if he's speaking to himself or to me, so I shrug my shoulders. "Maybe we can figure that out together once we sit down and talk." I smile sweetly at him.

To my relief he laughs again, less harsh this time. "You know what? Fuck it, let's have a chat, little princess." He turns abruptly, clearing a path through his men and gesturing for us to follow.

I twist around to smile happily at the guys, seeing them already making their way down the steps. Ash still seems wary, and Albert flustered, but Jace actually looks impressed. That makes me smile wider.

My mates take positions on either side of me, Albert trailing behind us. I meet the eyes of all those we pass, smiling to them as well and nodding to those who do the same to me. We walk for what feels like forever, the Australian wolves flanking us, many still half-shifted and meeting our pace. Alpha Kendrick is way ahead of us, his stride quick and sure.

I watch as he enters a very tall rock formation through an arched opening. The rock is the same reddish color of the sandy dirt that stretches as far as the eye can see. I would call the cluster of them mountains due to their size but I feel that would be the wrong word, as they seem to be free-standing, almost like they were placed here by a giant in the middle of a flat desert. I find it enchanting. Magical, almost. My excitement skyrockets as we approach the entrance, which I now can see is a tunnel carved through, and I can't wait to see what awaits inside.

Ash moves to take the lead as we step through the dimly-lit tunnel. It only takes a moment for my eyes to adjust after being under the bright sun for so long. The shade is blissful, but short-lived as we step out of the other side of the tunnel into the center of the rock formations. I gasp in awe at what I see. On every surface inside of the mountainous rocks are more tunnels, arched caverns and bridges connecting them all. In the center is a large, circular home built with large beams and sitting on a raised platform over a deep-looking pool of water.

"It's not as fancy as your castles and whatnot, but it's home." A sneering voice makes me close my open mouth and leaves me blinking dumbfounded at the Alpha.

"What do you mean? This place is amazing. It's simply gorgeous. Now we *have* to be friends because I want to come here all the time. Remy and Finn are going to just love it, too. Can I take pictures to show them?" I gush, speaking too quickly in my excitement.

His face scrunches up. "What? No! So you can do recon? I

don't think so. You'd never be able to guess our true numbers from the photos anyway."

I roll my eyes dramatically. "Oh, give it up. No one wants to fight you, Kendrick. You're seriously going to need to get over it already."

A feminine laugh gets our attention and we turn toward the sound. An absolutely stunning woman with silky orange hair, dressed in a one-shoulder white dress that falls to her knees, glides down the ramp leading from the round home. She's model tall, barefoot, and all smiles as she makes her way to our little group. Her arm snakes around one of Kendrick's as she cuddles up to him, presenting her cheek for a kiss.

"That's wonderful to hear, Princess Ivaskov. Care to join us for some tea?" She doesn't wait for a response, already pulling the Alpha up the platform along with her as she heads back inside.

"They are enemies, they shouldn't get tea," Kendrick grumbles.

"They are guests, so they will get tea and that's that," she replies firmly.

I giggle at their quiet banter as Ash places a large hand on the small of my back to get me moving. We follow them up the ramp, ignoring the weight of the stares we're receiving from those who have gathered on the bridges and platforms around us.

We're seated at a heavy-looking table that could probably seat thirty people, with cushioned chairs scattered about. A silver tray has been placed in the center of it, laden with a matching teapot, cups and tiny plates, and other small containers with lids. It's a full-on tea set and I want one just like it. A gaze around me shows an open room with a high ceiling, showing off those large beams overhead. The whole place is done in what I think Logan would call simple elegance, but it feels lived in, warm, like a home should. I swallow thickly, having no idea why I'm getting emotional over the thought.

A soft hand lands on top of mine in a gentle pat, getting my attention. My eyes land on the very pretty woman. "Are you all right, dear?" she asks kindly.

I turn my body to face hers, gripping her hand with both of mine. "It's just...your home." I smile and shake my head, trying to find the right words. "It's so home-like. I love it. Maybe your Alpha will have to fight me after all, to make me leave," I joke, trying to chase away my emotional overreaction.

She laughs, a warm, rich sound that makes me smile, even if Kendrick grunts in disapproval. "I'm honored, thank you. I'm Anna by the way, Princess." She winks at me, setting about pouring the tea.

"Please, call me Kitten," I tell her. She raises an eyebrow at that, but doesn't agree or disagree.

"If you don't mind, I'd like your invasion of my pack lands to be short and to the point," Kendrick starts.

"Same," Ash rumbles. For some reason my gaze finds Anna's again, and we both roll our eyes.

"Why don't you start by telling me why you declared war on my pack? It seems as good a place as any," I tell him.

He huffs, sitting back in his chair, sipping from his cup. Placing it down, he stares at the table in front of him. "That's quite a long story in itself."

"What's the abbreviated version then?" I push.

He plays with his cup some more, spinning it around on the little plate. "Beyond our history with the Ivaskov pack and its Alphas, there's an even longer, more sordid history with changed wolves. When we got word that the Ivaskovs were under a new reign, with not one but eight changed wolves in power, opening their gates to any other changed wolf who wanted to join them, well, war was the only option."

Well, that explained nothing other than the fact that he doesn't like Ivaskovs or changed wolves. "I'm afraid that version is a little too abbreviated to be able to follow," I state, my confusion clear in my tone.

"You might as well tell her everything. Either the two of you can work out your differences or they decide to fight back and will learn our secrets for themselves," Anna tells the Alpha sternly.

He grunts, his eyes flashing to her in warning. Anna just glares right back. "Changed wolves are a plague on our society. They take our women as mates for themselves, even though we have so few of them. They are immoral, creating immortal children. Because they were once human they try to stay in the human world, living as they once did, blending the two to the point of exposure. Each and every one of them risks the lives of all born wolves and wolf society as a whole. You worry about the war against you now, but have you forgotten the countless wars changed wolves have raged in the past?" he asks me accusingly.

I shake my head no. "I haven't forgotten, because I never knew of them. Are you forgetting that changed wolves don't come into existence on their own? Humans can't become wolves unless bitten. You blame them for something that they didn't ask for," I remind him, holding back my temper at his blatant hatred of my mates.

"Figures they wouldn't teach you the parts of history that truly matter. That's Ivaskovs for you, erasing history and rewriting it until it suits them," he scoffs.

My eye twitches in repressed anger. "*They*? As in my mother and father? I never met either one of them. My uncle, the former Alpha? I had him killed after kidnapping me. Who are *they*, Kendrick? The only Ivaskov I've ever met is my grandfather, who was living away from the pack before my mates found him, and he doesn't speak openly about the past. I've read every book with any kind of history in it, and I have to tell you it's not much and reads like a bunch of fairytales.

"If there's something you think I need to know, then just tell me. Don't sit here insulting my mates, who have raged no wars and stolen no women from you, nor exposed anyone, and expect me to read your mind. If you truly have people watching us and gathering information for you, then you should know that it's been months, mere *months* since I've been in power, and just slightly over that since I've even known that wolves exist!"

Kendrick's whole body turns to stone, his head slowly turning to me, eyes flashing with anger unmatched by any other. *"What?"*

He growls out the word so fiercely that, in an instant, my chair is slid back with me still in it and Ash is in his face. "That's the last time you're gonna growl at my mate. Is that clear? Alpha or no Alpha, I will tear your head from your body and mount it on a fucking spike for the world to see," Ash threatens, muscles rippling in warning of his wolf coming out.

Kendrick stands slowly, accepting the challenge Ash throws at him.

Oh no, this isn't going to end well.

"Stop this," I say quietly into the silence. My tone is more of a request than a command, as I think both men have been worked up enough already. "*What* about what?" I ask Kendrick, my voice as soothing as I can make it. A quick glance at Jace tells me that he's prepared to get me out of here quickly if the two men come to blows. His eyes implore me as he makes a barely noticeable gesture with his hand to continue what I'm doing. "I kind of said a lot there, so which part would you like for me to clarify?"

Alpha Kendrick comes out of it first, blinking at me before turning back to Ash. "My anger was not directed at your princess. I suggest you back down. This is not a challenge you want to issue."

Ash turns toward me, seeking approval. I nod my head quickly, not having taken offense in the first place. I take a moment to calm myself as I scoot my chair back to the table. I've never before been afraid of Ash, but his show of raw power makes me understand why everyone else is scared of him. I take a little more time examining him, making sure he's okay. His body is still stiff, even after he reclaims the chair next to me. His dark eyes find mine and my heart squeezes just a little. He's on edge being in this place. Having his pregnant mate threatened right in front of him is his worst nightmare, and his pain is reflected in his eyes.

I lean up to kiss his cheek, reassuring him that we're all okay and thanking him for being my strength. He visibly relaxes, as much as Ash relaxes in the first place. Jace nods his head imperceptibly, a show that he's all right and I did a good thing. Poor Albert just looks like he'd rather be anywhere but here.

Finally, I resume my silent process with Anna, to see that, like me, she's a bit shaken, but no harm done, and Kendrick is warier than he was before. I think he realizes just how close to death he was a moment before.

"Something I said angered you before," I begin again, hopefully moving us past the intense incident. "If your anger isn't with me, then who is it with?"

Kendrick's voice is steady and strong when he speaks. "Most of the men I have keeping watch on your pack are just observing your movements. I know you are training your soldiers more than you have in the past. I want to be aware when they move. Only a few scouts were sent to collect data. What they've gathered...what they've told me is that you were under the protection of your Uncle Marcus, kept away from the pack by him to be the future ruler of the Ivaskov pack. You then turned his men against him, having him executed and taking eight changed wolves as mates as a show of power. You then collected all of your women and assets and promised to redistribute them under a new ranking system. Before you deny it, know that we captured two prominent wolves that managed to escape your pack, seeking refuge elsewhere."

When he finishes, the room is stale with the heavy silence. My jaw literally feels like it has become unhinged as it hangs open. I don't even know where to start responding to that statement. Apparently neither does Ash, because he just starts laughing and doesn't stop. Jace follows shortly after and I smirk at the two. Tears form in the corners of their eyes, Ash's fist pounding on the table in an attempt to calm himself. Jace attempts to apologize for his behavior through his laughter, but I can barely understand it.

I turn back to Kendrick and Anna, giving them a sad smile. "You have it all wrong. Like, everything you said was so outside the lines that I don't even know where to start correcting you. With that kind of information I can see why you were quick to declare against me, but I realize now that we're both going to have to start from the beginning."

"I think that would be wise," Anna interjects, with Kendrick nodding in agreement.

My mates finally calm themselves, chugging tea and busying themselves with refilling their cups as a distraction. I start from the very beginning.

"I was found in a dumpster when I was a baby. A woman with mental issues thought I was a cat and attempted to raise me as such. I shouldn't be alive, to be honest with you, but somehow I survived my early years and was able to eventually wander away from her, and thus began my life living like a nomad of the streets. I won't go into detail of what it was like or how I managed it, because one of my other mates and I are still looking into how I could have had my wolf senses since before I was turned into a wolf. There's a lot that we don't understand about that time, though I remember every second of it. I was saved by Ash," I point to him, "and another of my mates one night when I was trying to escape an attacker."

I swallow thickly in an attempt keep my voice steady as images of that night flash across my vision. "They took me home with them. They didn't know what I was at the time, only stating later that I smelled different to them. I stayed with them and they showed me what a family was like for the first time in my life. It was during that time that I found out about wolves. My uncle had me kidnapped from them, almost killing two of them. He kept me a hostage in his basement, along with someone named Adam Vanderson. They kept me naked, only offered food for inappropriate touches, which I refused, so I starved. I nearly lost my mind in that place, and they had a plan to harvest my eggs, which was only stopped because my mates had found my grandfather, and together they launched an attack on my uncle's compound."

Ash rubs my back, trying to soothe me as my voice becomes strained with emotion.

"So, you see, I wasn't brought up with Marcus, and I wasn't under his protection. Adam Vanderson was his spy. A boy I thought was just some hockey player at a place I worked at, who apparently was keeping an eye on me. Adam wanted me for himself, and my uncle was going to let him have me after he got what he wanted from me. He was going to sell my harvested eggs to the highest bidders. In the process he almost killed me, or I did die. No one knows for sure in the chaos of that day, but one of my mates was able to get his blood into my system and I was able to heal. In the aftermath Marcus was executed in front of the pack he terrorized, giving both me and them closure. The urge to claim my eight mates took place, followed by my full transition into a wolf. My grandfather claimed that the pack needed me, that I was its rightful ruler until I have an Alpha son. I wouldn't go without my mates, so that's how we came into power. None of us asked for it, and all nine of us would have been content to live out our lives in the relative peace we had in their home, away from all other wolves."

I pause, not knowing which issue to address next. There were slivers of truth in what Kendrick accused me of, but it was all twisted, and painted in the worst light imaginable.

"The bastard did it," Kendrick mumbles to himself, glaring at Albert, who nods sadly.

"I think he did," Albert confirms.

"Did what?" Jace asks the question on the tip of my tongue. My eyes narrow as the two men share a knowing look.

Alpha Kendrick shakes his head. "That's a different story for another time. I assume you have evidence to support your claim of being a street rat and not under the care of your uncle?"

Anna reaches out and slaps him. Hard. "Watch it!" she growls at him.

"Just because your scouts got it all wrong doesn't mean that you will take it out on her. Can you even imagine a wolf growing up like that? A pup left all alone to fend for itself, a female one at that. Have some compassion," she chides, swiping a stray tear from her cheek.

"You forget that I have witnesses. Even if you were a street rat, that doesn't explain your actions once you came into power," he challenges.

"I don't know who you have and why they spun such a tale for you, but I would never do such things to my pack, or to anyone. When I arrived on Ivaskov lands I was appalled by what I saw. So, yes, I demanded change right away. Do you know how most of my pack lived, Alpha Kendrick?" I question.

He shakes his head warily.

"I hope not, because I hope you're the kind of person who would've declared war on their behalf if you did. *That* would have been a worthy cause to start a war." I eye him pointedly.

"They lived like dogs out there! Most of them didn't even own clothing. They didn't receive any kind of education. They stayed in their wolf form most of the time so they didn't freeze to death during the long winters. They worked fields and orchards, but weren't given enough food to live on, nor were they paid. They lived in shacks and under tarps. While, on the other hand, a select few pack members lived like kings and held females as hostages to get what they wanted. They even forced a few bonds in order to mate. So, yeah, I took all the earnings and assets of the pack, including everything I inherited from my uncle, and threw it into a theoretical pot to be used for the entirety of the pack, not just the few jerks who horded it. I opened every door of the pack house and invited all the wolves in from the cold. I fed them, clothed them, and started teaching them. The women who came to the house came of their own accord. I didn't force them to do anything. They wanted protection and protection for their children. I never promised women or money to anyone, and the only ranking system that has changed is that of my mates and me.

"That's what *we* did, my mates and I. Ash trains our soldiers, because they should have the ability to protect themselves. I gave an out to anyone who wanted an out. Told them they were free to leave if they didn't like it there. I wasn't going to continue to let a few thrive off the backs of the many," I finish.

"My guess would be that the men you have in custody and are getting your false information from are part of the group that chose to leave when they saw Kitten wasn't going to be a tyrant like Marcus," Jace supplies.

Kendrick rubs a hand over his head, sighing deeply. "You can see the position I'm in, can't you? How do you expect to know the truth when both parties could be lying or spinning the story in their favor? One side has you playing the Ivaskov villain, and the other has a righteous hero."

"I'm neither of those things. I'm just a girl that got caught up in a mess and is trying to do right by everyone. Maybe I am the villain to those who lost their way of life, and maybe I am the hero of someone who used to starve to death in the cold." I shrug.

"But facts are facts. I did some things and said some things. I didn't do some things and didn't say other things. There are plenty of people who can answer any questions you have. You're welcome to speak to anyone in my pack. You're also welcome to visit the library I practically lived in when I was a street rat, and the ice rink where I worked at. I can give you a whole list of people who can lay my life out for you like a book. Honestly, I don't care what you do, but I came here to make peace with you and I'm not leaving until I do. So I'd work quickly if I were you," I huff, and sit back in my chair with my arms crossed.

Kendrick snorts. "You're really mad that I don't believe you just because you told me your version of the truth?"

"I can help you with the list if you'd like, my Luna," Albert offers helpfully.

"You've given the Alpha quite a bit to think about and some homework to finish. Why don't we go back to the plane until he gets all he needs?" Jace suggests.

My stomach feels like a swirling pit filled with something thick, like tar. Is this how it's always going to be? Having to give speeches with fake confidence and bravado, spilling my emotions like an open wound for the untrusting and doubtful? I can't imagine a life filled with only that. It makes me sad and it make me angry and it makes me feel hopeless.

Ash's hand lands on my back once again, a thick finger going under my chin, pulling my face to look at him. "What's wrong?" he asks, dark eyes searching.

I close my eyes, fighting back tears of frustration. My body sags in defeat. "Why am I always having to prove myself to people? In my opinion, you trust who you decide to trust and put faith in what you believe in. It's like everyone I meet wants me to do all the work for them. Every conversation I have lately is me laying myself bare and waiting to see if the other person picks up all the pieces or not. I'm starting to ask myself if any of it is worth it, Ash. And that scares me."

"You know what? We should have lunch. Yes, lunch sounds like a good plan," Anna throws out, forced cheer in her voice.

"I would, but I only eat food prepared by a mate of mine who isn't here. A side-effect from my made-up captivity," I reply with a bored-sounding sigh. "The Betas and Omega will join you, though. Maybe you all can discuss my untrustworthiness together. I'll find my own way back." I stand abruptly, keeping my eyes cast down as I make my exit.

Right now, I couldn't care less if any of them choose to follow me. I want to be alone. I don't feel like crying, I don't feel like screaming or kicking anyone. I just feel tired on a level I've never understood before. Not the sleeping kind of tired, but the why-bother-with-anything kind.

I make the trek back to the plane without incident, a few half-shifted wolves following far behind me and stopping to turn back once they seem satisfied I'll make it there on my own. Once inside, I go to the small bedroom and fall back on the bed, my feet and legs dangling off the end. I stare at the ceiling for a long time, listening to my steady heartbeat and even breathing. Why do I feel like my life just snuck up on me and I've ended up in a place I don't want to be? I really, honestly, don't want any of this. I want what I've always wanted. A family, a home filled with love, warmth, and happiness. I have a family now, sure. But do I really have the other things when having this family comes with so many strings that I feel like I'm tied up within its web?

I had everything I wanted once. For that brief amount of time with the guys at their house. Before Marcus went and messed it all up. That time was beautiful. Perfect in every way. I was getting to know the guys, falling more in love with them every day. I was just figuring out who I was when I wasn't struggling to just live.

Now, so much has changed and I feel like it was forced on me. On all of us. There are two mes now. The me from before and the me now. I feel like there is no in between, no gradual, natural shift from one to the other. I don't want to go back to being the me from before. I would never give up being with the guys and having Mikey, Maksim, and even Albert in my life. Though, I can't help but miss the simplicity and freedom of my life before. Life was pretty simple when my only focus was on my next meal and where to sleep at night. It wasn't pretty, but it was simple. While I will always cherish the relationships I've managed to build with the many people in my life, they require a certain delicate balance of time, energy, and effort that I just can't seem to get right, no matter how hard I try.

This new me is constantly messing up, saying and doing the wrong thing at the wrong time. Being questioned and picked apart piece by piece. Why did I go here? Why did I speak to that person? Why am I running down the hall? Why don't I know this or that?

Constant questions about everything I do, but no answers for *me* when I'm the one asking. For a person capable of knowing all the things, as Finn suggests I am, there sure is a lot of information I don't know.

The question I want an answer to the most is when will I be able to just live my life with my family? I mean, do all families have to worry about so many outside influences? Do they always share their time with so many others, to the point that they hardly see each other?

Maybe if I knew it was normal and that I'd get used to it, I could cope better. Right now, I just see a life I came from that I don't want to go back to, and a life ahead of me that I don't see me ever wanting.

CHAPTER NINE

From behind the screen over the small window I can see that the sun is setting, the day almost done. I imagine that the three others with me are giving me space after my little show earlier. That's probably best, as I don't know what to say to them anyway.

Eventually I take out my phone, scrolling through all the apps, seeing if anything catches my interest. I don't want to listen to music, or research on the internet, or look through the hundreds of photos I've taken with the thing.

I keep coming back to the contacts app that looks like a little notebook. I decide to open it, scrolling through the names even though I know the order of everyone listed. I close it, only to repeat the process. Remington's name shines out at me over and over again.

Against my better judgment, and with nothing to say, I press the call button.

He answers on the second ring. "Hello?" he answers groggily.

I chew on my lip for a moment, finally answering with a lame, "Hi."

The line is silent for a while. Remy eventually asks, "Is everything okay?"

"Yeah." I go back to chewing on my lip, though now it's to try to stop from crying yet again. I don't even know why I feel like this.

Remy doesn't push for the reason I called him. He simply waits me out. I can hear his breathing and when he shifts around in his bed or wherever he's sitting.

"I don't know why I called," I tell him after a while. I don't feel like hanging up, though.

"That's okay," he tells me. "I like when you call me."

Silence reigns again as I go back to staring at the ceiling, warm tears leaking from my eyes and tracking down to my hair. "I don't know why I'm crying," I tell him, for some reason hoping he can tell me. It's dumb, but true.

"I wish you wouldn't cry, Love. Are you sad?" he asks.

I shrug. "I don't know."

"Are you…angry about something?" he guesses.

"Probably," I consider.

A long time passes before he asks his next question. "Are you lonely?" He says it so softly I almost miss it.

A sob escapes me, unbidden. I cry harder, eventually pulling the phone away from my face to curl up on my side. I don't know what I feel, but lonely sounds like an accurate description to me. In a sense, I *am* lonely. Not for lack of people around me, but the lack of people who seem to understand me. Even *I* don't understand me.

After some time, I pick up the phone and check if Remy if still there. Of course, he is. "Sorry." I sniffle into the phone.

"You don't have to be sorry. I'll stay here as long as you need me to," he answers sweetly.

"Thanks."

More time passes and I'm eventually able to start a real

conversation with him. "I don't know who I am. Sometimes I wonder if I ever knew. It's like I'm lost and I don't like who everyone is trying to make me."

"Those are some deep thoughts, Love. Can I ask what brought this on?" His concern is evident in his tone. I almost regret bringing it up.

I blow out a breath. "I think it's been building up, but Kendrick wanting to literally fact- check everything I shared with him today was the last straw. I don't know who I am, what I'm doing, or why I'm even doing it anymore."

Remy makes a "hmm" sound. "I'm no Finn, but I'm thinking this is all part of a delayed reaction to the changes you've gone through these past few months. You've been through a lot lately. Things a lot of people would struggle with; you've always bounced back quickly, but maybe it's time you slow down a bit to process."

"Are you sure you're not Finn?" I tease. Remy laughs, the sound making me smile. I love his laugh.

"Maybe you're right, but I'm not sure where that leaves me." I sigh dejectedly.

"I don't know what to tell you, Kitten. Believe me, I wish I did. All I can tell you is that I'll be here for you and do whatever I can to help you. We all will. Whether that means giving you space, sitting on the other end of a phone while nobody speaks, or holding you when you cry out your frustrations. We're here for that, Love. Ups, downs, and every twist in between."

"I know that. I mean, I've heard it and I even believe it. Doesn't mean that I understand it. I've been trying to, I really have. Sometimes I even think I've figured it out, but I always end up lost all over again," I try to explain.

"You don't have figure out everything right now. Knowing yourself, knowing others…it takes time, and sometimes things change anyway. Life isn't a quiz where there's a right answer to every question. No one is testing you and waiting for you to fail," he tells me.

"It feels like that, though. I'm always being told that I'm thinking wrongly, or I'm acting wrongly. That I don't know what I should know, and I don't do what I should do. If I say something, then it should be trusted to be true. If I do something, then I should be allowed to do it. I'm always having to prove myself to someone, and I guess I just don't know the why of it." I vent my earlier thoughts.

Remy sighs deeply. "This includes me and the rest of your mates, I take it. There's a difference between being true to yourself, and doing whatever you feel like while everyone around you falls in line.

"That's relationships for you. Sometimes even the people closest to you are capable of disappointing you and hurting your feelings. It happens. People make mistakes. Learn from them and move on. Love isn't all or nothing, Kitten. You can love someone and be disappointed in them at the same time. We'll learn who you are as you learn that yourself, and you'll learn who we are. The same holds true for Mike, your grandfather, and even our future child. You're going to struggle with this a little more than most, because you didn't have healthy relationships throughout your formative years. It doesn't make you less, it just makes you unique."

I nod as I think it over. "I guess that makes sense. I've never thought about it like that before."

"As for everyone else? Yes, they will expect you to prove yourself to them. You're young, a female wolf in an all-male Alpha world, and you weren't raised in wolf society. But you know what, Kitten? Just because they expect you to, doesn't mean that you have to. If Kendrick is having a hard time believing something you told him, that's his trust issues not yours. Either the man wants peace and he's willing to put his own shit aside and try, or he wants war and no matter what you do he'll chase after it. That's his choice."

Some of the weight I've felt pressing down on me lifts as he speaks. It's new insight from a source of great wisdom. "Thank you, Remy. I needed that."

"Anytime, Love. I meant every word of it. Do me a favor?" he asks.

"Anything," I answer quickly. It's the least I could do after holding him hostage on the phone until he made me feel better.

Remy chuckles darkly. "Careful with that," he warns playfully.

"Promise me that you won't sit around alone? Jace can be cold as ice when he's hurt, but he cares about you. And Ash just wants to be wherever you are. He'll turn into a snarling beast if you shut him out for too long."

I giggle at that, knowing it's true. "Okay, I promise."

"I miss you," I add on a tired sigh.

"Now you know I'm just a call away. I miss you, too, beautiful. Hurry home to me," my Alpha almost whines.

I laugh again. "I will. I love you, Remington."

"Love you, too." I hear the smile in his voice as he ends the call.

I feel infinitely better after my call with Remy. While I know nothing has changed and I still feel as lost as ever, I now feel as if I'm not lost *alone*. Maybe we're all lost, and maybe we can turn this all around to be some kind of adventure. Or, maybe I'm just really tired and I should get some sleep to keep the crazy at bay.

CHAPTER TEN

I jerk awake at the alien feeling inside my tummy. It almost felt like... there it is again! I'm being kicked... From the inside.

Pulling up my sweater I watch in horror and terror as a lumpy mass pushes against my insides, making me look deformed. Then it kicks me again, and I think I might pee myself. With a shriek I hurry to the bathroom, quickly doing my business and washing my hands without drying them before practically running to find Ash.

Both of my mates are seated at one of the tables with Albert, already dressed and ready for the day, Jace's hair still wet from a recent shower. I shift uncomfortably on my feet as I stop next to Ash, tapping his shoulder until he removes the headphones over his ears.

One look at my face has his body freezing and his eyes scanning the plane. "What's wrong?" he asks once he scans around for the threat, coming up empty.

I lift my sweater again, pointing to my belly. "I think the baby is trying to escape!" I explain hysterically.

Ash's head rears back like I've slapped him and he makes a face. "Uh, what?"

Why is he not panicking, too? "The baby...it keeps kicking me and pushing on me like it's looking for an exit. What do I do?"

Before I even finish speaking the baby is back at it, doing the lumpy ball thing that makes it looks like I have a baseball rolling around under my skin. I feel queasy as I watch.

Ash's eyes double in size, his mouth parting as his tongue slips out to wet his lips. His hands come up, one landing on my hip with a slight shake, the other spreading out over my bare stomach. The baseball reacts violently, kicking at his hand repeatedly. Ash swallows thickly, his eyes closing momentarily. Just when I think he's starting to understand why I'm freaking out, he opens his dark eyes and stares at me with tears in the corners and the happiest smile I have ever seen grace his face.

I. Do. Not. Understand.

I seek out Jace, wondering if he will help me, but he too is wearing a sappy smile as he stares at my belly. I drop my sweater as I place both hands in my hair, slightly pulling it. "Guys, why are you happy? Don't you understand that this is bad? It's trying to get out when it's supposed to stay in, and it's angry and trying to hurt me."

Jace makes a squeaking sound, but when I glance at him again his lips are pressed firmly together and his eyes are on Ash, not me. If I didn't know any better I'd swear he was trying to hold in laughter. But this situation isn't funny.

Ash leans his head down and starts whispering to the baseball. "I know you're having fun in there, but I need you to relax, little one. You're scaring your mama. Don't worry, we'll explain everything to her and then she'll calm down."

"Explain? Explain *what*?" I ask.

Jace holds out a hand to me. I take it instinctively and he tugs me around the side of the table to stand in front of him, the same way I had Ash. "This is normal, Kitten. The baby has probably been moving around for a while, but only recently has become big enough for you to be able to notice. He's not trying to escape. Trust me, he wants to stay in there for as long as possible and get big and healthy." A small smile plays on his lips, his gold eyes shining as his fingertips play lightly over my skin. The baseball seems to follow his movements.

"Then why is it so angry and violent? You don't kick someone unless you're mad," I question. Though the baseball is making me out to be a liar right now, as it seems calmer than it was before.

"I don't think he's kicking you because he's angry, Doll," Jace says smoothly.

"Do babies even get angry? Do they know how?" Ash asks, but it's not as if I know the answer to that.

"Let's call the guys and ask. Reed might know if the baby is angry or not," Jace suggests.

Ash has his phone out in a heartbeat, putting it on group chat or whatever it is when everyone can hear it.

"Hey, Rem, I have you on speaker." Oh, right, speaker phone." "Can you call the other guys to you? There's been a new development."

"Is everyone all right?" Remy rumbles out.

"It's a good thing, not a bad one," Jace tosses out with eyes on me. I stick my tongue out at him. He doesn't know how weird it feels, even if it *is* a good thing.

"Give a few and I'll call you back once I have everyone," he tells us before the call ends.

I'm snacking on crackers, sitting in Ash's lap with his hand under my sweater when the phone rings. Ash quickly swipes the screen, not bothering to say hello before he launches his first question. "Do babies get angry?"

There are a few snickers from the other end and a shushing sound before Finn speaks. "Most people believe that fetuses have no feelings or emotions of their own. However, more recent studies have proven that they can sense whatever the mother is feeling, as hormones are released with emotions, and the fetus will receive the same surge of hormones as the mother. Keep in mind all of these studies were on humans, and our baby will not be a human child."

"Now that that odd question is out of the way, what new development were you speaking of earlier?" Remy asks.

"The baseball tried to escape earlier, and they tried to tell me it was normal that it was so violent and that it *wasn't* trying to escape," I explain quickly, polishing off the last of the crackers and wishing there were more.

Ash and Jace roll their eyes dramatically as the other end is dead silent. From farther away from the phone I hear Logan ask, "Did she just say a baseball tried to escape?"

Followed by Kellan's quiet answer of, "It's ungodly hot there this time of year. Maybe she's having a heat stroke."

"The baby started moving around today and it freaked Kitten out. She thinks he was angry at her and wanted out. I'm pretty sure she's referring to the baby as a baseball because it sort of looks like that when he pushes against her stomach," Ash explains.

"Oh." Several relieved sighs sound at once.

"I want to see it! Make a video and send it to me. So not fair you assholes got to feel it move before I did," Logan pouts.

"I'm feeling it right now," Ash replies smugly.

"You know what? I think I'm going to go through your closet today. You know...to *brighten* up your wardrobe," Logan threatens in a sickly-sweet voice.

Ash frowns deeply. "You wouldn't dare," he growls. I would

laugh, but my belly starts moving around frantically at that moment, making me feel uneasy again.

Reed chuckles from the phone in front of me. "We might have a problem. Our little guy seems to really like it when Ash is pissed off."

I stare down at my tummy in confusion, even though I can't see it through my sweater and Ash's hand. "Remy, tell it to stop," I whine.

"It really makes you that uncomfortable?" Kellan hedges.

I shrug. "I don't know. Kind of. Something is moving around inside me that isn't me, but kind of is me. It's just...strange, I guess," I answer.

"It's not something, baby. It's our tiny little guy and he likes to play around in there. Watch, if I move my hand over here he'll kick it," Ash tells me, showing me what he means. That time I think I actually saw the shape of a foot or a hand. "You try it," Ash encourages, lifting my shirt for me.

I poke at my belly, making something both kick my insides and push the same spot I poked. The inside kicks are really uncomfortable.

Reed laughs again. "You startled him with whatever you did. But he's excited at the same time." He adds with a sigh, "I think he's going to have multiple personalities or something; he rarely settles on one emotion at a time."

"Well, he's coming to life. I'm sure it takes time to learn emotions and all that. Just look at Ash. He's *ancient*, and barely understands emotions," Tristan jokes, followed by what I know to be the sound of a high-five with Logan.

"Tell Kitten that he's not angry and trying to escape," Jace demands. "That should put her mind at ease and maybe she'll warm up to him."

I blink at Jace. "It's not that I don't like the baby. I do; I love it already, actually. It's just that seeing and feeling it move is different than just knowing it's in there. Picture a baby, then imagine it's in your stomach, living in there, moving around, doing whatever babies do. Tell me that doesn't freak you out a bit."

"Of course, it does. I'm a man. That would never happen," he states simply. I roll my eyes. Maybe they can't understand.

"He's not angry, Kitten. The only time I pick up any negativity is at night, when he's awake and no one is speaking. He likes our voices and misses them when he can't hear them. Though, he is hungry, very much so. Have you been eating?" Reed asks.

There's a shocked gasp on the other end of line. "My baby is hungry?" Tristan asks sadly, a little bit of panic slipping through his tone. "Feed her! What the hell is your malfunction, you assholes? There better be a mountain of food in front of that girl in two minutes or I will hunt you down and beat you to within an inch of your lives, I swear to God." He continues his shouting as he's obviously being dragged away from the phone and being told to calm down.

My eyes are bugging out of my head. I've never heard Tristan so upset before. He's usually the calm and collected one, with a voice like warm butter.

Mmm...warm butter on fresh bread. Yum.

"What did you just do?" Reed asks curiously as everyone else remains silent.

"Nothing. I haven't moved," I respond, wondering if he was talking to me or someone else.

"Weird," he says.

"We should go see what's happening with Tristan and the others. It's been a long time since I've seen him that worked up, and it never ends well. Eat something, Love. Call whenever you want. I know Kellan had a lot he wanted to talk about before he had to go. Try to call him, please."

"Okay, Remy. I love you and I love anyone else still in the room, too," I add.

"Love you too, sweetheart," Reed replies amusedly.

"Love you," Remy responds. "Guys, keep her safe. Take care of yourselves as well," he finishes before the call ends.

"Great, now Tristan is going to try to poison us from now on," Jace grumbles.

"We'll be lucky if that's all he does," Ash says with a shudder.

I stare up at him, tilting my head. "You're afraid of Tristan?" I ask with a smirk.

Ash raises his brows, looking down at me with a serious expression. "Tristan can be one scary mother fucker when he feels like it. Don't let the mellow vibes he gives off fool you. He chooses to be that way now, but that wasn't always the case."

Tristan? *My* Tristan? I have a hard time believing that, but Ash would know better than I would. It's an interesting fact to keep in mind. I feel bad that he's so upset, though. It's my fault I haven't been eating, not the guys'. He should know that. I kind of feel like the baby just tattled on me through Reed.

Looking at my tummy again, I lift my shirt to address the baby. "Next time you're hungry, tell me first, okay?" The small kick I get in return is response enough for me. I'm glad we understand each other. At least on that issue. I might be satisfied with crackers, but it seems the baby won't be, so I decide to make more of an effort.

∾

Tristan

"No! I will *not* calm down. I finally have a child and it's starving before it's even born? I don't fucking think so. We have money, we have food, and yet we have a hungry baby? What part of this is making sense to you?" I shout at the room as I stalk back and forth in front of them. How can they sit at a time like this?

"Reed didn't say he was starving, just that he was hungry. For all we know, he's constantly hungry. Kitten will eat when she feels like eating," Kellan placates.

"Will she, though? Her own emotions have been all over the place, and so far, every time she's thought one of us was mad at her, she's punished herself. Since eating without me around is an issue for her in the first place, I can only imagine that's how she's choosing to punish herself this time."

My heart literally aches, knowing my mate and child are starving to death while I sit around and do nothing about it.

"It's all in your head, Tristan. You're not thinking clearly," Finn chimes in.

I kick at the coffee table, ensuring it flies across the room and smacks into the wall. That felt fucking amazing. Stepping over to an unoccupied chair I stomp on the arm of it, a satisfying crack igniting my blood. It takes me only moments to shred that fucker and tear the frame apart. It's not enough, I want more. More destruction, more pain.

I *need* it.

Just as I'm looking for something to put up a bit more fight than a piece of furniture, Remy strides in, followed by Reed. I meet his steely eyes and sad expression, with desperation showing on my face for him to see. "I can't take this anymore, Remington. She needs me. They need me. I've tried, but I can't... I can't do it." I choke up, my nails biting into my palms, causing me to bleed all over the carpet. A slight relief goes through me, but it's not enough.

I was convinced to stay behind and allow Jace and Ash to escort Kitten to Australia. I didn't like it, but I agreed that too many of us would send the wrong message. They assured me that she'd be taken care of. They *promised* that they'd remind her to eat. I told them this would happen. I fucking knew it! You can take the girl out of the streets, but you can't the streets out of the girl. She eats when we eat now, but if left to her own devices she reverts back to old habits. The worst habit being forgetting to eat unless she's starving.

The only real change to this habit since being with us is the fact that she can't stomach just any food she comes across when she *does* realize she's hungry. Not like when she was living on the streets. I've worked my ass off to fix the damage Marcus and Adam caused. Who knows if my not being around to care for her is causing a setback? Why did I agree to this? What the fuck have I *done*!

Remy watches me with a resigned expression. My other brothers know what's coming. It makes them sad, especially Reed. I wish I wasn't like this, wish I didn't cause them so much pain every time the need is too much to bear. It's how I control it, though. The darkness that is a continual rage inside me. Either I tear apart everything and everyone around me, delighting in the pain and destruction to feed that darkness. Or, I need to be in pain. To have that darkness literally beaten back.

"We can go to her. Right, Rem?" Reed practically begs, his eyes shifting into a haunted blue, already turning watery.

"We can," Remy says carefully, his eyes never leaving me.

"See, Tris? We'll go. You'll do your thing and everyone will be fine. No need for...you know," he pleads, hopeful. Too hopeful. I'm not strong enough to fight this. More guilt piles up, knowing my weakness is hurting him, too.

I grind my teeth, closing my eyes to try to calm myself, thinking of getting to my girl. It doesn't work, it just makes me angrier. In my mind she's skinnier than ever before, her movements stiff and slow due to no energy. The baby, my baby, cries silently from inside his mother as he starves to death before he's even given a chance.

I slap at the side of my head, attempting to knock the image from my mind. I push the image away as hard as I can, but it's quickly replaced by another. Then another. Memories assault me like a sick and twisted show.

Silk.

Lace.

Thick fingers wrapping around tiny wrists.

Ribcages exposed through ill-fitting finery created to tease and entice.

Eyes. Always the fucking *eyes*! Sunken sockets surrounded by gaunt faces and painted lips. "No! Fucking no, no, no, no!"

It's enough to set me off. The last thing I remember is an ear-shattering growl and my point of view changing as I'm forced to shift, throwing myself at Remington, going for his throat.

∼

Remy

The five of us converge as one, moving quickly to subdue the sand-colored wolf that snaps and snarls at us. Reed had turned away, shutting himself in his room, dealing with his own pain over the situation. We fight and struggle with Tristan as we move him to a room we had to set up here that Kitten doesn't yet know about.

Logan takes a swipe to the face, Tristan's claws leaving deep gouges and nearly missing his left eye. Throwing him in and shutting the door quickly, I thank the others as I mentally prepare myself for what I have to do. The door shakes behind me as the unhinged wolf throws himself at it, trying to break free.

"I'll be ready," Kellan tells me softly, clapping me on the shoulder in a show of support. This isn't easy for him either. It isn't easy for any of us. He and Finn help Logan navigate as they go to patch him up.

Damn, I had hoped this all would have come to an end. It's been so long since the last time...*fuck!* I scrub a hand roughly down my face and blow out a breath. How am I supposed to explain this to her? How could she ever understand? She'll hate me, I just know it. I'll fail her, again.

Feeling like I'm slitting my own wrists, I slip through the door and meet the broken eyes of my brother. I feel the same right now. I have to. It's what *he* needs from me. I won't leave him to deal with this himself.

With hackles raised and teeth bared, he stalks the other end of the room. Waiting. Tristan is the most observant of us all, and he gets that from his wolf. And maybe a little from his human life. His wolf is smart, always looking for that little tick of vulnerability, an opening. I have half a mind to give him one and let his ass get in trouble with Kitten instead of me. Though, even as I think it, my own wolf bristles inside of me at the thought of losing a fight. Once he's out, there will be none of that. Besides, Tristan isn't himself. He's out for blood. He'd shred me to pieces if I let him. His wolf wouldn't be satisfied with a simple defeat; he'd want the kill.

Making a pile of my clothing in the corner I eye the feral wolf once more, knowing that as soon as I shift, he'll attack. I won't have even a split second to reorient myself before he's on me.

Right. Let's do this.

~

Kitten

I wake feeling sad. Cornered, frustrated, and anxious as well.

But mostly sad. I've been lying here for a long time, not wanting to move, not knowing what my next step is when I do. I don't know what I was thinking coming here. What did I really think I was going to do about this war they declared on us? How do I make them see that we should all be friends?

"You worry too much," Jace grumbles from above my head, sounding more asleep than awake.

"I'd say sorry, but I wouldn't mean it. I can't help but worry. I want this over and to go back home with the others," I tell him quietly, trying not to wake Ash lying next to us.

"You miss them." It's not a question.

"I don't feel right being away from them this long. Like I'm not whole," I try to explain.

"You're getting homesick, Doll," Jace sighs.

"Maybe. I've never been homesick before," I admit. "I'm also worried that I'll leave here having accomplished nothing. I feel like getting these people on our side is the final piece of a very long puzzle, but no matter which way I twist and turn it I can't get it to fit."

"You're going to have to get out of bed before you can do anything. That's your first step. Your next step will be to eat something and get dressed. Then, you're going to have face them again," Ash's deep voice tells me. His eyes are still closed, but I guess he was awake the whole time.

Taking Ash's advice, I'm dressed, once again in an over-sized sweater in a cream color, and black slacks with low heels. I've discovered I have a new-found love of cheese crackers with peanut butter spread inside them. I'm disappointed that I ate all of them in one go.

God, I miss Tristan. He's spoiled me and now I don't know how to function without him.

Outside, my two mates and I let our eyes adjust to the bright sunshine that Australia never seems to be lacking in. If I concentrate my sight on the far-off boulders that make up their pack home, I can see the Australian wolf pack relaying the message that we've left our sanctuary.

Within moments, there's movement towards our plane. A few moments later the Alpha and his entourage are in front of us, redressing and encircling us.

"So, it seems you're done pouting. Is today the day you leave then?" Kendrick says with amusement lilting his tone.

I laugh. Long and deep. *This* is how he wants to start the day? "Really, Kendrick?" I say once I get myself under control. I throw my hands out to my sides. "Maybe I gave you too much credit. I thought, here's this strong Alpha out here, surviving where little else can survive. No, scratch that. Your pack is thriving out here. I've been in contact with a lot of packs. Almost none of them are as well off as yours. Yet, here you are...letting your hatred rule you like a little bitch."

Logan would be so proud of me.

Snarling ensues, as expected. Also as expected, my mates meet the threats with their own. However, I continue as if I heard none of it. "What is you want from me? I've been honest, vulnerable, open to your side of things, and more than willing to work with you. All that's left is a show of force.

"You might want to take time and *really* think hard about that, Kendrick. You started this war because of the threat my mates and the other changed wolves I have in my pack pose to you and yours. Your fear of their raw power and overwhelming strength speaks for itself. You're afraid to fight us, yet you seem determined to push me to do just that."

Kendrick's lip curls in disgust. "You think I'm afraid of the four of you? On my lands, with my entire pack just one order away from ending you?" he scoffs.

I press on as if he hadn't just interrupted me. "Not to mention I now have several other packs that would come to my defense with one phone call. I want you as an ally but, make no mistake, I do not *need* you. I could take you out and replace you with someone willing to work with me. I could also end your entire pack right here and now. I *choose* not to do that. That's the Luna *I* am," I growl, my skin rippling as I work to repress my wolf. That part of me wants to rip him in half and call it a day.

Kendrick is obviously having the same problem as he replies, "What I *want* is for you and yours to leave here and never return. I want nothing to do with you."

I laugh again, though this time it sounds cold, even to my own ears. "You should have thought of that before you started a war you can't win. *You* brought *me* here. Your actions alone. Now, I *will* leave here today. I'm done with you. But I came here for an answer, for a solution. Either way, I'll have my answer. This stupid war ends today. I leave here with a friend and ally or I leave corpses to rot in the sun. The choice is yours. If a show of force is what you wish, I'll gladly oblige."

The men surrounding us have all shifted to wolves, an almost undetectable wave rippling as they fight the need to charge forward, waiting on their Alpha's order. I feel the coarse hair of Ash and Jace's wolves at my sides, their bodies taught with tension. They've shifted as well. In a split second this could go from heated conversation to bloodbath.

I'm sorry it's come down to this. I really am. Kendrick showed up today having already made his decision. I've offered friendship yet again, but it's like Remy said: It's not up to me. I won't leave this threat hanging over our heads. If he wants a fight, I'll give him one.

CHAPTER ELEVEN

My eyes never stray from Kendrick's. I've tried. I know I'll regret having to hurt him or anyone else, but I can't think of that now. He's forced my hand. His unwillingness to listen got us to this point.

He stares back, eyes dancing with emotions I have no name for. He's stuck. I know it, he knows it, we all know it. He can't back down now, but moving forward could mean the demise of them all if he's overestimated his strength. Same as me. We're both stuck.

A slow clapping sound makes its way to my ears, almost breaking our stare-off. However, the voice that follows manages to break Kendrick's first. "Bravo, young one. I couldn't agree more. Kendrick, my darling, I'd say the Luna has proved her mettle, don't you? It's clear these changed wolves don't rule her, as you thought. They were waiting for her order, not the other way around," Anna says brightly, like there's not a bunch of wolves ready to kill each other right in front of her.

It's obvious when Kendrick finally caves. I saw what she did. Anna was offering him a way out. He chose wisely and took it. His shoulders lose their tension even as his eyes never stray from my mates, who have yet to back off. Not that I'll tell them to. Contrary to what Anna just said, I don't give them orders. I never will. I think she knows that, too, but her words allowed her mate to save face in front of his pack members.

Kendrick holds out a hand for Anna. She cheerily takes it, sidling up to his side like glue. I don't miss the elbow she gives his ribs when the silence drags on a little too long. "Luna..." Kendrick clears his throat before continuing. "I will agree to attend your meeting of the minds, and to call off the war against your pack pending what transpires there," he states grudgingly.

More silence follows, along with another elbow from his mate before he drags her to the side and they converse low enough that I can't hear. Fortunately, their distraction has their members shifting toward them and prying their eyes off us. I use that moment to release the adrenaline built up inside me in the form of a slow breath, and lay my hands on the giant wolves on either side of me. I shake slightly but they both press into me, calming me. That was close.

Kendrick eventually sends away all but one other wolf to remain with him. His look tells me he expects me to do the same. I just smile sheepishly back at him. No way will Ash and Jace leave me, so I'm not even going to ask.

With an eyeroll of understanding, Kendrick moves closer to us. "We need to talk."

My brows rise in surprise. "I would have thought you'd want me to leave as soon as possible."

He nods slowly. "I do, but there are things we need to discuss if we are ever going to be allies. Things you need to know. Anna thinks you have a right to know."

"Do you? Think that I have a right to know, I mean?" I ask. It's hard to tell which one of them played the better game today. Did Kendrick really want to back down because I passed some sort of test? Or did his mate know he was about to lose a fight and offer up an excuse like a lifeline? So far, I've been the only one to give anything. They've only taken.

For the first time since meeting him, he looks a little lost. "I do, but at the same time I'm wary to tell you, in light of your chosen mates."

"Well, then, that's easy. They're mine and I'm theirs. That's not going to change, so you might as well tell me," I offer.

"It's not that simple. There's telling and then there's showing. And for that, you're going to need to come with me alone," he explains.

Ash growls deeply, stepping in front of me. I stroke his side, reminding him that I'm right here, that I'm safe. "That might be a problem."

Kendrick's expression hardens. "If you want me to trust you and yours, then you're going to have to trust me. Where we're going, they can't come. It's not for my benefit, but other's. It's a promise I won't break, and once you see you'll agree."

I blow out a breath, looking to the sky for patience I don't possess. "I need to speak to all my mates about this. I make no guarantees."

He nods. "Take all the time you need. I'm going to go check on Anna. Come find me when you're ready."

Kendrick is barely out of sight before I'm snatched up bridal-style and moved with blurring speed to the back bedroom of the plane. The door is slammed shut in Ash's face as Jace rounds on me, getting in my face. "What the actual fuck!" he yells.

"Excuse me?" I say, crossing my arms in defense.

He stalks forward, making me step back until I hit the wall. "You did it again! Un-fucking-believable. You almost got all of us killed because he insulted you. You rush in head first without thinking. What were you thinking, standing out there, pregnant as fuck—need I remind you—daring the leader of the fiercest wolf pack in the world to kill you!"

I shove at his chest. He doesn't move an inch. I rant back at him anyway. "I was thinking that I was solving the issue. We weren't getting anywhere dealing with him like we were. He showed up here, done with *us* today. I showed him that *we* decide when it's done, not him. And look! It worked. Why are you mad?"

"Mad?! Fucking mad doesn't even begin to describe what I feel right now. I am downright bloody livid, Kitten! You can't do that to us, you can't do that to *me*. I won't fucking survive without you. You don't get to decide to put yourself on a silver platter for our enemies taking. That is *not your choice!*"

"That's not what I was doing and you know it!" I shout in his face. "Why can't you trust me?"

Jace leans forward, his palms caging me in above my head, his chest brushing mine as he breathes rapidly. "What are doing to me?" he says quietly, frustrated. "Are you trying to kill me? Do you want me dead?" He pushes from the wall, brandishing a long knife from his waist and thrusting it into my hand.

When I move to drop it, he places his hand over mine, squeezing so tightly it's almost painful. He aims the point at his chest, over his heart.

"What are you doing?!" I scream, panicked. "Jace, stop!"

"No, I won't stop," he growls, pressing the blade deeper and causing himself to bleed. "Just kill me now. If you just can't help yourself and have to put your life on the line at every given chance, then just make sure I go before you. End it now so I don't have to live with that kind of grief." His voice breaks as he begs me.

"Jace, stop." My own voice ends on a sob. "You're scaring me. I don't want you dead. I'm not trying to get myself killed."

"I know. I know that, beautiful. I do. But you keep ending up in these situations anyway. I won't live like this. I don't want to live always wondering when you're going to be taken from me.

Knowing you're going to jump at the chance. You broke me, Kitten. I was fine without you, but now I can't live without you."

"Jace..." I sob, feeling every bit of his pain. Pain that I caused, once again.

Bringing my other hand up, I pry his hand away from mine. He lets me. Flinging the knife as far away from us as possible, I wrap both arms around his chest and bury my face in his neck, crying uncontrollably. "I need you, too. I'll stop, okay? I'll...I don't know...I'll stop doing whatever hurts you."

"You won't," he replies thickly. I realize he's crying, too, though he's hiding it better than me. He cries pretty. Of course, he does. He's Jace. "You don't even know you're going to do before you do it."

"I d-didn't offer myself up on a platter out there. I don't know how to make you believe me. How can I make you see things the way I see them when we're awake? I saw his eyes, Jace. Heard it in his voice. He was waiting for us, probably has been since we came back here. He was going to intimidate us into leaving. He didn't want peace; he was going to make us back down then throw his whole force at our pack. I couldn't let that happen. I trusted you and Ash to keep us safe. They fear you. You already had power over them. I picked a fight I knew we'd win because I had you and Ash."

"You didn't know that," he denies adamantly.

"I did. I saw it. Why don't you trust me?" I ask breathlessly. I close my eyes, now seeing this is the real problem here.

He pauses, just staring at me.

"Because you're a loaded gun with a faulty trigger. I never know when you're going to go off, and I can't prepare for the blowback," he growls at me, gold eyes dancing with emotion.

"Jace, I am who I am. How do I change what makes me *me*? I need you to trust me. I don't want to die. I won't leave you. But I have to fight for what I think is right. I can't live any other way. If you want me to stand back and watch others suffer when I can do something about it, then you might as well pick up that knife and end me yourself."

He grabs my shoulders roughly. "Don't ever say that again," he snarls. I get a look at his golden eyes, shining with glistening tears. On any other man they might look less than manly. On Jace? He looks like a fierce warrior-angel.

I scoff accusingly. "Yet you asked me to do the same to you. I won't survive without you either, you know? I don't need to live thousands of years to know that a world without you in it isn't worth having. I can't live without me, either. So, I don't second-guess myself. I've lived my whole life based on instinct and I don't plan on changing that. It's who I am. It led to me to you, it told me I could trust you. Listen to your own instincts, Jace. I bet they're telling you to trust me, too."

"I-you...*fuck*! You are the most infuriating person I have ever met." His lips crash to mine painfully and without warning.

I grip his hair roughly, trying to pull him away. This conversation isn't over. He growls in warning before his tongue snakes into my mouth. His hands go behind my thighs, hoisting me up against the wall, his body pressing between them, pinning me.

I groan in both frustration and pleasure. Taking control of his punishing kiss, I bite his bottom lip before sucking it into my mouth. His response is to tear the front of my sweater, using one hand to push down the cups of my bra. He rips his mouth away from me, and now *I* growl at *him*.

His hot mouth shifts to my bared breasts. My head thumps against the wall as I arch into his touch. One of hands comes up to grip my throat lightly, applying just enough pressure to keep me in place, chest and neck bared to him in submission. The heat between my legs is almost unbearable. I can feel him between our clothes. Hot. Heavy. Needy.

I rub against him, but the friction isn't enough. I grab at his shirt, my lust-filled brain not knowing if I'm pulling toward me or trying to push him away. "Jace..." I groan.

He only growls again, showing no signs of ending his feast of my hardened nipples. Drawing my legs around his, I press at the back of his knees with my heels. A surprised grunt leaves him as his hands release me to cushion our fall. Landing on top of him on the floor, I waste no time ripping his shirt open, my hands skimming his muscled chest possessively as I sink my teeth into his neck, tasting him, claiming him as mine all over again.

He curses, head falling to the side, giving me better access. I lick and suck like my life depends on it. I make the mistake of grunting in smug satisfaction as I grind my hips over his. He uses my pleasurable distraction against me.

Flipping us over, Jace pulls on my waistband until both the button and zipper break. His mouth finds its way back to mine, tongue fighting for dominance against mine. With one hand behind me, holding my hair hostage, his other hand works my pants and panties down my legs.

I reach forward, attempting to do the same to him. He releases my hair, capturing my hands and holding them above my head. I struggle against him, wanting so badly to feel his velvety, pulsing cock in my hand before placing it inside me.

He doesn't release me as he shoves his pants down just enough to free himself. I feel him brush my slick entrance and stop my struggle. This works, too.

He presses the full length of himself up and down teasingly, but holds back from entering me. I break the kiss long enough to beg. "Please..."

"Oh, no. I need you to feel me, Doll. I need you to feel how much I need you. I fucking need you more than I need air. More than I've ever needed anything. You'd take this from me? This perfect fucking body and this feeling of absolute belonging that I can only get with you now?" he spews hotly at me. Moving his hands to my biceps he grinds harder into me, his face hovering above mine the ultimate example of bliss.

With my legs wrapped around his waist, I turn us again so that I straddle him. I continue to slide over him as his hands fall to my hips. I kiss the evidence of the knife pressed to his chest reverently, the wound already healed. Leaning down, I drag my aching breast up his chest as I nip at his ear, letting my lips and breath soothe the sting as I speak. "I won't take anything from you, I promise."

His eyes show his vulnerability. He's finally letting me in. I kiss him again, passionately, giving back everything he's giving me. Reaching between us I grip the base of his cock, lining it up with my hot and ready entrance. "Except maybe this," I whisper as I sink onto him. "*This* is *mine*."

"Hell, yes. Always this. Take all the *this* you need, Doll. Fuck, take all the *this*," he responds on a groan.

I close my eyes, savoring the stretching feeling of finally having him inside me. When I reopen them, I'm on my back again. Before I can protest, he's slamming into me hard enough to make me cry out. He works my knees over his shoulders for a better angle and pounds into me as I reach out for something to grab on to, something to hold me to the here and now as he fucks me to a new plane of existence.

I crash, slam, explode, and detonate so many times that I think I forget life outside of Jace being inside of me before he finally releases his hot seed inside of me with a possessive roar of a conquering king.

I'm half-dead, or more likely half-asleep, when I hear his smug voice whispering in my ear. "I win."

I smile sleepily. I don't know about that. If the sedated pleasure I'm feeling right now is any indication, I definitely won.

I don't know how long the guys allowed me to sleep, but eventually I was awoken to shower and change once more. Now, sitting around the table with a smug Jace, a jealous Ash, and an embarrassed Albert, we listen to the line ring as we attempt to contact the others. I had tried Kellan first, but he hadn't answered. Remy's phone almost goes to mailbox or whatever it's called before we hear his signature rumble come over the line.

"Is everything okay on your end, Rem?" Ash picks up Remy's odd tone immediately.

With a deep sigh, he replies. "If that isn't a loaded question..." He trails off.

As the two men wait each other out to speak first, Albert attempts to break the tension. "Kitten was able to get the Australians' acquiescence and they've agreed to the meeting."

"Really, now? Congratulations, Kitten. I'm proud of you. Does this mean the war is over?" Remy asks.

"The war is over," I say softly.

"Thank fuck," he says, relieved. "Look, I don't have much time, but plans have changed. Once everything settles here, we'll be on our way to meet up with you. If you plan on leaving soon, give me a heads up."

"What's going on, Remington?" Ash asks again, losing patience.

"Just leave it for now, Ash. Everyone is whole and accounted for. That has to be good enough for now," Remy replies just as sternly.

"Fine. The reason we called is Kendrick is wanting to take Kitten somewhere that Jace and I can't go. Apparently, the asshole has information he needs to share with her and only her," Ash informs him.

"No," Remy says with finality.

I groan, loudly. "Come on. Why does it always come down to this?" I grumble.

"We're not risking your safety," he says flatly.

"I get that you want me safe, but why do you all act as if I'll accidentally walk off the side of a cliff if left on my own?" I respond heatedly. This is almost the exact same conversation I just had with Jace.

"If your fall and subsequent death would feed a stray dog for a day, you would," he drones.

"Exactly! Well put, Remington," Jace chimes in.

"Hush, you," I snap at my golden boy. "Remington, we are going to at least discuss this. I don't believe Kendrick will harm me. He alluded to ensuring the safety of others by us traveling alone. I want to know what he knows. He's asked for our trust, and I think it would be a good move to give it to him."

"So, you're going to run off again behind our backs if I say no?" He's furious, I can tell.

Well, so am I. "No, I won't. I told him that we would all discuss the matter. I'm just asking to have an actual discussion here. All of you will need to learn to trust my judgement and value my opinions, just as I will yours. Am I not your Luna?"

I'm met with silence. As I wait with my heart in my throat, I notice Ash's eyes assessing me. I don't have time to figure out why he's looking at me like that before Remy finally speaks again. "You are our Luna. You're correct that trust has to go both ways. Can you do me a favor, my beautiful and intelligent Luna?" He's sucking up. That doesn't bode well for me.

"Anything," I respond quickly, and a little more breathily than I'd intended. Something about how Remy called me his Luna sent delicious shivers throughout my body.

He chuckles deeply. "Careful with that, Love. I'd like Albert to escort you out of hearing range for a few moments. I'd like to get all the men together and discuss this, like you've asked."

"Why can't I be a part of the conversation?" I pout.

"We already know your opinion, and it's easier to say no, if that's our decision, when you're not pouring your heart out and using your "Kitten logic" against us," he jokes, but I know he's kind of serious at the same time.

"Fine, that seems fair. Just promise me you will really think about it," I sulk.

"I promise. Just a few minutes."

"I'll walk you out. We'll get some air." Albert offers me his arm before realizing that I'd never take it. Instead, he waits for me to pass him, then closes the exit hatch as I descend the stairs.

It's still light out, and as hot as usual around here. If I had my doubts before, I'm more than positive now that Logan didn't pack my wardrobe. Or maybe he did and this is his way of punishing me for leaving without him. He's sneaky like that.

"That was a very brave thing you did earlier, my Luna," Albert tells me as we stroll leisurely around the plane, making a big circle. He walks with his hands behind his back, as I've seen both him and Maksim do countless times. I try it myself, but instantly feel uncomfortable and drop my arms back to my sides. Maybe that's only for people with long arms.

"I assume you think I was being reckless, too." I roll my eyes.

"You know what they say when you assume." He smirks.

I pause, turning to him. "No. What do they say? And who is they?" I ask, curious.

"Uh," he splutters momentarily. "It's just a saying. Also, a play on the word's spelling. The end of the saying is, "you make an ass out of U and ME," he explains.

I give a minute and then start giggling. "That's funny. I like that."

"It's good to hear your laugh again. To answer your question bluntly, no, I don't think what you did earlier was reckless. I was around your father enough to grow used to these types of situations. He knew when he had a situation under control, and when he was beat. He was always two steps ahead of everyone around him. He had a knack for reading people and situations. I see the same in you."

I smile sadly up at him. "I wish I knew him. Plenty of people have told me how great he was, or how I compare to him. I feel like I really lost out not having met him."

"You shouldn't feel that way. It wasn't your fault you weren't able to. If he was here now, he'd be proud of the young woman you've become," he tells me softly.

I take his word for it, continuing our stroll in comfortable silence. Albert, in his full black suit, doesn't appear to be affected by this heat. I admire that, seeing as I feel like a wet blanket is trying to smother me even if the air is dry.

"Albert?" I say after a few laps around the plane.

"Yes, my Luna?" he responds immediately.

"Do you think this information Kendrick wants to share will be worth it? I mean, if my mates agree that it's in our best interests for me to go with him," I add.

He takes his time answering. "I think so. I think it has to do with you. Him wanting to take you away on your own *is* cause for alarm. However, it wasn't his words that I was paying attention to, it was how he delivered them. Anna wanted you to know whatever it is. Alpha Kendrick was reluctant. He said you have a "right to know." That seems important."

I'm already nodding before he even finishes. "That's what I got, too. How could it be about me, though? I've never been to Australia; how could he have information about me?"

"Remember what I told you before? About your father spending quite a bit of time here?" he asks gently.

An electric shock seems to burst from my chest as I turn and grip his arms, nearly shaking him. "You think it could be about my mother?"

I don't wait for his reply, already running for the stairs at full speed. I have to let them know that this could be about my mother. I can't *not* go. Not if it could mean answers to questions I've had since I can remember having questions.

Once inside, I nearly collide with the table as I stop abruptly, panting hard and bracing my arms on either side of the phone lying between my two mates.

Ash stands, his eyes scanning for threats as Jace grabs me, placing me on his lap, caging me in with his arms. I wiggle to get free, my whole body shaking with nerves. "Remy!" I call out, too loudly.

"Kitten, Love. What's wrong?" He sounds alarmed.

"No, everything's fine." I wave my hand, brushing the overprotective crap aside. "It could be my mom, Remy! I have to go, he could know my mom," I tell him hysterically.

"Who? Slow down and start from the beginning," he instructs.

"Kendrick. It was *how* he said it. The information he wants to share with me. It sounds personal. To me. The only personal information he could have for me would be about my mom. My dad was here. I might meet my mom!" I explain, albeit a tad stilted.

"Kitten..." Remy sounds wary, and sad.

"No! Remy, it makes sense. It really does. Trust me. *Please*," I beg.

It's Finn's voice that greets me on the other end of the phone. "Oh, Kitten...sweetie. Let's calm down and think clearly about this. Even if your mother were still alive, she must have...you were found in a dumpster..."

"I know, but there must have been a reason. Maybe she didn't mean to, or...or if she did, then I can just forgive her and I can have a mom. I can have a *mom*, Finn." I need him to understand how important this is to me. I've always wondered why I never had parents like other kids. I mean, I knew I must have had them, but I've never known what happened to them. Why I was left alone. I've learned what happened to my father, that he was killed by his own brother before I was even born. But no one, not even the wolf community, has been able to tell me anything about my mother. She could still be out there. Maybe here in Australia.

"Kitten…Kitten, are you with us, sweetie?" Finn calls out, probably not for the first time.

"Yeah, yes, I'm here. I was just…thinking." I snap out of my own thoughts.

"We just don't want you to get your hopes up. Kendrick didn't say this was about your mother, so it might not be," he says calmly.

"But it *could* be," I respond quickly.

"She's most likely dead, Kitten," he almost whispers.

"I know that!" I scream at him. "But we don't *know*, Finn. We don't know anything for sure."

"Don't yell at Finn, Kitten," Kellan tells me sharply.

I release a rush of air. "I know, I'm sorry, Finn," I say, deflating quickly. "I love you, and I didn't mean to scream at you. I just…I thought you of all people would understand my *need* to know the truth. To have all the information."

"I do get it," Finn tells me, no anger in his tone. I think I offended Kellan by yelling at his twin, more than I did Finn. "I don't want to see you heartbroken if you don't get the answer you want."

"Finn…" I breathe out, shutting my eyes tightly to block out the tears. I will not cry again. God, it's all I do these days. "I grew up without my mom. I've always been heartbroken."

I keep my eyes closed, knowing if I open them I'll see looks of pity. I don't want to be pitied. I just want a shot at finding out the truth. I'd like to think I'd keep my promise to them about not running off on my own anymore, but…could I really leave here not knowing?

"Kitten, I'm going to speak with the Alpha and his mate. See what all this is about. We'll come up with a plan from there. I know this isn't the answer you wanted, but it's not an outright no. We do trust you, Love. Caring about your safety and the safety of our child does not make us unreasonable ogres. As our mate, you are still a woman who can make her own decisions, whether we like it or not. Our child is just that, *our* child. Decisions regarding our baby should be made together. Does that sound fair?"

I nod, even though he can't see me. "Yes, that's fair. I can respect that."

CHAPTER TWELVE

Reed

I can't remember the last time I was this excited. Excited enough that Logan's fake enthusiasm and his running around packing for everyone isn't grating on my nerves as it usually would. I get where the dude is coming from. Trying to cheer up Tristan and pull him out of his funk, but damn can he act like a tweaker when he wants to. Don't even get me started on Remington. If I didn't know any better, I'd swear he was heading to his own execution.

"You gonna be okay, little dude?" I ask Mikey as I crouch in front of him. Reaching out, I fix the collar of his green polo shirt with the Ivaskov crest on the chest sticking up at an odd angle.

He meets my eyes, searching for the truth. He's like Kitten in that way. He's good at reading people. "Are you sure she's okay? You guys aren't acting right. You're gonna bring her back, right?"

I place my hands on his shoulders as I bring my face even with his. "Your mom's a fighter, she's always okay. Remember that. But she isn't fighting right now, she's safe. I promise. She has some things to take care of, then she'll be home."

"Then why are you guys going, too? And why can't I come with you?" he demands.

"Well, we're going because we are weak men without her." I joke halfheartedly, even though it's partly true. "And we thought your Grandpa Maksim could use some looking after. He gets grumpy left on his own." Also half true. The other half being if we put Mikey in danger, Kitten is liable to kill us all.

"You're all coming back, though? With Mom, too?" The look he gives me stabs my soul.

I gather him up in my arms, hugging him tightly. "Oh, Mikey, I promise we're not leaving you. We'll be back. You're ours, okay? We're yours, too, you know? We're family, and family stays together even when they're apart."

"Not my family. My old family," he corrects.

"Well, they suck," I joke, making the boy laugh. "We're not like that. We will be back. All of us."

"Fine." He sighs. "But I'm not drinking any tea."

I laugh with him, knowing the traditional Russian will no doubt try to convert Mikey into a tea-drinker while we're away. Honestly, I think the time together will do Maksim good. His backward thinking when it comes to bloodlines needs fixing if he's going to continue being in Kitten's life. She won't put up with him favoring the baby over Mikey, and neither will I. He may be our adopted son, but he's our son nonetheless.

"Logan laid out some outfits for you in your closet, but you don't have to wear them if you don't want to. Tristan put several meals in the fridge and freezer for you; do me a favor and eat those, okay? It'll hurt his feelings if he comes home and sees them still there. Finn didn't leave any lessons because he knows Maksim will try to teach you Russian and will skip your lessons anyway. Just go play with your friends when you need a break."

"I got it," he says with an eyeroll.

"One more thing?" I implore seriously. He nods his head, waiting. "Be safe. Don't get hurt or your mom will hurt me."

He giggles. "I know. I will."

With that, I leave to see if the others are finally ready. Before I turn the corner, I call back to him. "Hey, love you, kid."

Swallowing thickly, he responds, "Love you, too, Dad."

My heart nearly stops, but I manage a smile and a quick wave before taking two steps at a time to the lobby. Damn, that felt awesome. And scary at the same time.

Feeling like I'm flying, I come across Kellan and Finn talking quietly by the door. They stop talking as I come to stand next to them. Finn raises a brow in question. I beam at him. "Mikey called me 'Dad'."

"Yeah?" He beams back at me.

"Yeah," I say proudly. Kellan clasps my shoulder in a quick move of understanding the gravity of the boy's acceptance.

We do the "guy thing" and leave it at that as we wait quietly for the others to join us. A subdued Tristan is the first to join us, along with Logan, who talks his ear off even though Tristan isn't responding. Looking as if he's riding to battle Remy is the last to join us, striding right for the door with us following behind him.

Outside, the whole pack has congregated to see us off. It's a humbling sight. They wish us luck and safe travels, along with their wishes for our quick return. The deference never sits well with me, but this overwhelming show of support for something as simple as a trip abroad gives me hope for this pack. They came together for us today, now all we have to do now is get them to do this for each other.

Starting off on what's sure to be the most awkward trip of my life, I wave goodbye to the well-wishers and settle into the back seat for the trek to the airport.

Our pitstop in Miami is short, but not short enough. Tristan came to life long enough to go to a local market, stocking up on supplies for meals he wants to make for Kitten, and Logan dragged Finn with him to search for a variety of swimsuits for the lot of us, claiming that it would be a sin not to hit the beaches Down Under while we had the chance. That had me pretty excited, as Australia has some of the best surf in the world. I'll wait until we're there to get a board, though. If I'd thought about it, I'd have brought one of mine. Just as I'm about to ask Kellan if it's safe for pregnant women to surf, we got the call.

While I'm proud of our girl for ending this so-called war against us, I worry about her execution style. I'm convinced she enjoys giving us all panic attacks. Though, I have to admit that her steamroller antics sure do get the job done. I absolutely adore her ability to set a goal and work her ass off to achieve it. Somewhere between our debating the need for the information the Australian Alpha possesses and when we were supposed to give them an answer, Kitten's emotions flood my own, drowning me.

"Reed? What's wrong?" Kellan asks as I dive past him for the bathrooms.

I almost don't make it to the toilet before I heave my guts out, barely able to catch a breath between the puking and the sensory overload. "Something's wrong," I gasp out.

"No shit. You're experiencing flu-like symptoms or food poisoning maybe, even though we don't get those," Kellan points out unhelpfully as he presses his hand against my forehead. "Christ, you're burning up!"

He leaves me to dry-heave on my own, the contents of my stomach long gone at this point. I try to shut the door on whatever bond connects me to Kitten as I sprawl out on the floor, my body trembling. There are too many emotions coming from her. Strong ones. Hope, happiness, relief, suspicion, need, guilt, excitement, and panic all pulse from her into me in crushing waves.

Kellan returns with Remington and his bag of tricks. As he takes out a blood pressure cuff and places it around my arm, Remy slides a bag of ice under my head like a really uncomfortable pillow. Their voices blur together as they try to talk out what could be happening and assure me that I'll be fine. I concentrate on trying to unlock my locked jaw and tell them what's happening, but my muscles seem to have a mind of their own.

Remington's phone rings loudly in the background, only adding to the chaos.

"Her," I grunt out.

"What? I can't understand you, Reed," Kellan says, forcing me to try again. I close my eyes, body feeling like a taut rubber band. "Not me. Her."

The two of them pause, just staring at me, the phone going off once again. "Answer it," I grit out.

Remy rips the phone from the back pocket of his jeans, swiping the screen to connect the call. As his voice responds to the person on other end of the line, my body is released from whatever hell had taken hold of it. I can still feel her emotions, the same ones as before, but it's as if she's reined them in to be able to speak to Remington.

Kellan eyes me warily as I melt like a puddle of goo on the floor as my muscles fully relax. I can finally breathe normally and listen in to Kitten's voice. She sounds just like she feels. Erratic and frayed.

We move the call to the seating area, just as the other guys come back from their shopping. With Remy's promise to come up with a plan that will make us all happy, he ends the call and looks to me. "You okay?

"The hell if I know," I answer honestly. "I feel like I was

attacked by dragons. How the hell is it that she was able to bear that but it almost killed me?"

"She's a woman," Kellan answers simply. "They're strong in ways we will never comprehend."

There's a moment of silence where I'm pretty sure we all fear the abilities of womankind before Logan speaks up. "So, what shitstorm are we in now?"

I leave the others to fill in the blanks as I go get myself cleaned up. Tentatively, I reach for Kitten's emotions again. Feeling only guilt with a trickle of fear, I close my eyes and hang my head. *This girl.*

Joining the conversation once again, I air my thoughts. "She going to go with him, no matter what we say."

My words are met with a scowl from Remington. "She asked for our trust."

"You're right. She did. But she'll still go," I tell him. "I can feel it."

He stands to pace the aisle. "This is so infuriating. *She's* infuriating. Young or not, she has to learn what it means to be part of this pack, this family."

No one argues with him on this. "She does." I nod slowly, chewing over how to say what I want to say next. "At the same time, we have to learn what it means to have her with us."

"Well, now that you've made that clear," Logan says sarcastically, rolling his eyes.

"What I mean," I growl towards him before turning back to Remy, "is that trusting her doesn't just mean we trust her to do what we say. If we tell her she can't go, that it's too dangerous, and she goes anyway...yes, that's her breaking our trust. So is her telling us that she needs to do this and us telling her no. That's us breaking *her* trust. Who are we to tell her what she needs?"

"We're her mates, it's our right and our duty to keep her safe," Remy responds angrily.

"No," Finn jumps in calmly. "It's our wish to keep her safe, it's our duty to keep her whole. If we convince her to fight her own instincts, she won't be whole. She'll second-guess herself and look to us for answers. She'll end up a mirror, just a reflection of each of us. It's not our job to stand in her way. It's our right to stand beside her, no matter where she chooses to go."

"So, we just let her do whatever she wants no matter how it affects the rest of us? That's not how we work," Remy replies, voice strained.

"I think the point is not "anything she wants, and damn the consequences", but more that we trust her to know when to push and when to back off, just as we do each other. We don't contemplate your safety when you make work trips, Remington, or when Logan spends a month or more in Europe with half-dressed females. We know the score on both of those situations. With her, we panic and send out a search party if she spends too long in the bathroom. She's independent, just like we are. So far she's experienced what it's like to fit into our group, but we haven't given her any leeway to operate outside of that in ways that benefit us all," I try to explain.

"I think it's worth noting that Logan's time abroad hardly equates to potentially being ripped to shreds by an entire wolfpack," Kellan chimes in.

"Clearly, you've never been left alone in a room full of starving models," Logan retorts.

"I think we're getting off track, men." Remy rubs a hand over his ever-growing beard. "I think Finn and Reed have a valid opinion on the matter, and when we're all together again it's worth a discussion. However, at the heart of it all is Kitten's safety in the hands of Kendrick. I don't want to tell her she can't do this. I don't think any of us do. I just want to make sure she's safe while doing it."

"There has to be a middle ground," Finn supplies.

"Right. That's what we need to figure out. I'm going to call Kendrick and pry as much information out of him as I can. Let's see how far we can get with that route before we make any final decisions."

Kitten

The wait is almost painful. Getting sent outside again was silly in my opinion, but whatever. This time I chose to sit on the top step, in clear hearing range if I wanted. I leave them their privacy, lost in my own thoughts. This time their conversation doesn't take as long, though. Jace calls for me to enter the plane again, the phone still on speaker.

"I think we've come to an agreement we can all live with," Remy begins. "Kendrick did admit that some of what he wants to share has to do with your origins, and we all know how important this is to you. We want you to have your answers, Kitten. We never want to stand in your way, please know that."

"I do," I offer quickly.

"The plan is for the three of you to travel with Kendrick and Anna to Albany, where we will meet you. After that, we're not welcome to accompany you. Albert will travel with you to a remote community as guard. Kendrick will only take one of his own in exchange. You will have one day there, Kitten, then all bets are off and we will come for you, understand? That's all I can bear, Love. If you need more time then we can regroup and talk it out, okay?"

I'd have one day. One day to learn everything I need to know. Okay, I can work with that. And they're trusting me to go by myself! "I love you guys. So much," I squeal happily.

Remy laughs, sounding relieved. "We love you, too. We're

overprotective, but we care deeply for you. Your happiness is our happiness, Love."

Flying into Albany is an experience I'll never forget...if I could forget things, that is. There was one part where the ground was bright yellow as far as the eye could see, sitting in stark contrast to the clear, dark blue sky and snow-capped mountains in the distance. Kendrick had noticed my fascination and explained that they were canola fields. Whatever it was, it was probably the most beautiful thing in nature I've ever seen. Technically we didn't land in Albany, but a few miles away from it. Now we sit in an elaborate hotel room near the airport, waiting for Remy and the others to arrive.

"Are you going to stare out every window you come across?" Jace asks, his legs kicked up on a table as he reclines in the bedside chair, sipping some kind of alcoholic beverage with a sweet scent.

"Oh, yes. I want to see all the things. I've never really been anywhere, remember?" I tell him, not taking my eyes from the view. There isn't anything special that I can see from here, but I know I'll never it again and I want to memorize every detail.

"I remember," Jace whispers in my ear before laying his chin on the top of my head and wrapping his arms around my waist. "I can't wait to show you the world."

"I can't wait to see it. Can we go to the water before we leave? I've never seen a beach," I ask.

"I'm sure we can find time for that," he replies.

Ash grunts from the balcony on the inside of the room, which faces a courtyard-like lobby area the hotel has made to look like an old town. "Is there enough sunscreen in the world to keep your skin from burning?"

"Who, me?" I ask, not sure if he means me or Jace. We're both fairly pale compared to Ash's natural tan.

"Yes, you. With that hair and that complexion, I don't think you'd last five minutes in the Australian summer." He smirks.

"Hey! I grew up outdoors, mister. And I never had sunscreen," I remind him.

"And I bet you spent several months out of the year a nice shade of pink, too," he jokes.

"Maybe," I grumble reluctantly.

"Aww, don't let him get to you, Doll. Tanning is overrated. We'll get you a pretty parasol to keep the evil sun away from your delicate skin," Jace assures me.

Ash laughs. "And so you can hide under it with her, you pasty bastard."

"Don't be jealous that I'll be snuggled up to a bikini-clad Kitten while you frolic in the sand," Jace retorts.

"I don't frolic," Ash says disgustedly.

"Riveting conversation we're having, it seems. Is this the kind of shit my girl has had to deal with this whole time?" Logan's voice carries to me from the now open door of the suite, and I swear my heart leaps from my chest.

Moving at a speed I didn't know I was capable of, I launch myself at him and jump for him to catch me. He does, and I squeal in delight. "You're here! I've missed you so much."

"Then stop running off, you silly girl," he says before crashing his lips to mine.

"Okay," I respond when we finally come up for air.

The twins stand side by side, Finn with a strap over his chest holding his computer bag. They look deliciously disheveled and I squirm in Logan's grasp to go to them. Mint and grass-green eyes track my movements, cataloguing me from head to toe. "Hi, guys." I smile brightly at them.

"Hello, beautiful," Finn says through a smile of his own.

Kellan takes longer to reply, choosing instead to run his hands over my abdomen, feeling the bump that is significantly larger than when he last saw me. "You're showing. That's...not possible. How is that possible?" he asks, more to himself than me, before pulling me into a hug.

Remy stands by the door still, looking as if doesn't know whether he should come or go. "Rem?" I question.

"Come here, Love," he demands, arms open wide. I go to him without hesitation. Drawing in a deep breath, I take in his scent, my hands running over his strong back. Instantly, I feel calmer than I have in a long while. It's his presence, I realize, that steals some of the burden of life from my shoulders. He makes it his, just by being in the same room.

It takes me longer than it should to realize what's missing. Or rather, who is missing. "Where are Tristan and Reed?" I ask no one in particular.

"They're down in the kitchens, making you something to eat," Kellan tells me.

I frown. "They didn't have to do that. Are they even allowed to do that?"

Logan laughs loudly. "Are you kidding me? Like anyone would say no to the world-famous Chef Tristan taking up residence in their kitchen. Reed's just keeping an eye...on things. Helping."

"Oh." I guess that makes sense. "They didn't want to see me first?" I try to hide the hurt in my voice, but it's clearly there anyway.

"He didn't want to show up without food. It's a Tristan thing, Love," Remy corrects.

Okay. I guess I'll have to let that go then. Still, I hope they hurry. "Did you guys bring bags?" I change the subject.

"We have a room full of them. Come on, I want to show you what I got you," Logan tells me, taking me by the hand and pulling me down the hall.

"You got me a present?" I ask as we enter another room.

Wow, he wasn't kidding; it is a room *full* of bags. "Where are you even going to sleep?"

"Huh?" Logan says distractedly as he rummages through several bags, making a mess. "Oh. No, this room is just for stuff. We rented out the whole place. There're plenty of beds to sleep in."

My head rocks back in shock. "What? Why would you do that?"

He raises a brow at me, having found what he was looking for. "Uh, cause you're a fucking princess? Security measures and all that." He stalks toward me, fisting a scrap of green fabric. His cat-like stride does things to me.

"Besides," he uses his free hand to brush my hair away from my face, "I plan on making you scream out...repeatedly, and nobody but my brothers get to hear your sexy screams of pleasure."

"Oh." I breathe, swallowing thickly as my body heats.

"Yeah. *Oh*." He smirks, knowing full well what he just started.

There's a knock on the open door, and with a look full of promise Logan breaks eye contact. "Food's here," Ash informs us.

That means Reed and Tristan! Finally. With a bright smile, I practically skip back to my room. Reed must be able to sense me because he turns to me as soon as I enter, his own excitement written all over his face. He scoops me up under my arms, bringing my face up to his for a loud, smacking kiss. "I missed you more than you will ever know," he says through a smile. Lifting me above his head, he nuzzles my tummy with his nose. "I missed you, too, little one."

I giggle uncontrollably as he sets me down on my feet. I love this silly side of Reed. My eyes scan the room for Tristan, finding him at the table arranging platters with his back to the room. I almost call out for him, but I stop myself. He knows I'm in the room, but he hasn't so much as turned around? That's odd.

I watch him for several minutes, noticing how stiff and robotic his movements are. It's like his body is here but his mind is somewhere far, far away. "Tristan?" I call softly as I approach him slowly. He pauses, but doesn't turn around.

I eye Remington for answers. The look I receive is filled with resignation and guilt. Ah, I see. Remy's odd behavior has something to do with Tristan's. I silently wave everyone else from the room. Remy tries to escape with the others, but a hard look in his direction has him stopping in his tracks.

"Tristan?" I say again, taking another step to him. I'm close enough to reach out and touch his back, so I do. His body tenses momentarily before he sighs deeply and relaxes. Before I can pull my hand back, he spins and grips it tightly in his own.

His appearance makes me gasp. "Oh, Tris. What's wrong, my sweet man?" His eyes are sunken and rimmed in red. Not like he's been crying but as if he hasn't slept in weeks, like he's torn and raw. Bleeding out on the inside. His normally chocolatey eyes are dull, his skin pulling tightly across the hard planes of his face.

I turn to Remy accusingly. "Explain," I grit through my teeth, taking up a defensive stance in front of Tristan.

"Kitten, stop," Tristan says behind me. His usually smooth voice is as rough as he looks. The sound grates on my nerves. I don't like it. I want *my* Tristan.

"It's not for me to explain, Love. It's his. I'll answer for my part when the time comes," Remy says, resigned.

"Well, someone better start talking then, because the two of you are scaring me and that's making me angry. Why does Tristan look so broken, and why was this kept from me? Did I do this? Because I left?" My breath leaves me in short pants as the realization that my actions could have done this to such a beautiful man.

"No, Sweetie. Not you. I'm just…this is my shit, okay?" Tristan bends at the waist to say in my ear, his hands placed loosely around my hips from behind. "Don't blame Rem. He helps."

I close my eyes against the tears that want to fall. This isn't about me, this is about him. I need to be the strong one here. "What do you need help with, Tristan? Tell me what's going on, please," I beg.

"I don't know where to start with that answer." He sighs.

"Start anywhere," I implore.

"Okay." He swallows thickly. "You already know that I grew up in a wealthy family much like Jace, but that's only partly true. I was only with my human family for part of my childhood. I was taken from them, to a place I can only describe as Hell on Earth. I was stuck there for a long time. Every now and again, the memories become too much to handle. Rem helps me the only way he knows how."

Knowing that was the shortest version of events ever, I think hard about how to pry the rest of the story from him. "Where was this Hell?" I ask, feeling like this is a small detail to reach for.

He shakes his head as he buries it in my neck. "It doesn't exist anymore. It was just an old English route used for trade. It was mostly a small village that catered to travelers."

"And you were taken there," I state. Holding my breath, I ask a question I already know I don't want the answer to. "For what?"

Silence reigns for so long I'm not sure he's going to answer. After a time, he does. "At first? I was taken for a ransom. When it became clear that my father wouldn't pay—I had brothers and he had other heirs—the thieves had to find another way to make money from me."

I give him time, not interrupting.

"I was sold to a pleasure house, Kitten," he admits painfully.

Well, fuck being strong. A sob escapes me as tears crash against my eyelids and stream down my cheeks. I can just imagine a mop-headed little boy with dazzling brown eyes, scared out of his mind as he's ripped away from his family and sold to the worst kind of humans. How long did he wait for rescue before he gave up?

With an angry roar Tristan rips away from me, almost causing me to fall where I stood against him. "They forced me to do things no child should even know about. I was fair-skinned, a rarity around those parts. Most of the people didn't even speak my language. They kept us in this tiny room, left us weak with hunger and pain, and only brought us out for clients who requested us!" he shouts angrily, swiping out at a lamp and sending it crashing near Remington.

Remington moves for me but I put up a hand, holding him back. Tristan is dealing with something, but I still don't think he'd hurt me. "That's why you cook? Because you grew up hungry?" I ask softly.

Tristan laughs darkly, scrubbing a hand down his face as he starts to pace in front of the window. "Ha! No, sweetie. Not because *I* was hungry. I prayed to God every night to let me die of starvation. It would have been better than what I had to deal with during the days. It was *them*. The other whores who stared at me day after day, night after night. With their smeared, painted faces and torn dresses and suits. They'd stare at me with hate and hunger and the worst...understanding."

"Understanding?" I manage to choke out.

He laughs again, doubling over with the effort as his own tears break free. His mind is definitely not in this room with us. "I was rare. I got special treatment. Clients fucking *loved* me. I mean, how often do you get the chance to fuck a member of the gentry? Some lord pisses you off? Here, take it out on this boy who looks just like him," he scoffs.

He turns then, heading straight for me. Taking my shoulders roughly in his large hands, he shoves me back until I hit the wall. "I learned to play their game, Kitten. I took advantage of them as much as they took advantage of me. I made demands of my own. Jewels, food, anything my little whore-heart wanted. So, they stared. Stared at the whore making a fool of himself as he ate aplenty and sat decked out in fine clothing and gold in front of them as they fucking *starved to death*!" he roars in my face, canines elongating.

"That's enough, Tristan!" Remy barks, once again trying to come between us. I stop him again, even as Tristan's hands feel like they're crushing my shoulders, nails digging in painfully. I know he doesn't want to hurt me, he wants to hurt *himself* by hurting me. If I let it show that he's succeeding, he'll really break.

"That wasn't your fault, Tristan," I say shakily.

"Wasn't it? I could have shared, you know. Why didn't I fucking *share*!" He uses his full weight to press against me, his teeth scraping dangerously close to my carotid artery.

"You were a scared kid. You didn't know any better. They made you that way. You weren't a whore, Tristan, you were a victim." My eyes connect with Remington's across the room. His body shakes with the need to pull this unhinged version of Tristan away from me. He won't let it continue for much longer.

"Tristan, look at me," I demand, making my voice as hard as I can.

He raises his head, eyes pleading for me to punish him. I bring my hands up to his cheeks. "That wasn't *you*. Not the *you* I know. You were a kid put into an awful situation. There was no right and wrong in a place like that. Only survival. You got out, you're not there anymore. You do good for others now. You fed me when I had no food, remember? You don't need to punish yourself over this, Tristan. You deserve a medal for surviving that kind of Hell, and for not killing every last one of those bastards!" My own anger at his situation gets the better of me.

His laugh is breathy this time as his body sags against mine. My hands come up to help hold him to me. "I did. A wolf visited our little establishment once. Not to partake, mind you, but to shut it down. He took me into one of the bedrooms and asked what I desired most. I asked for rubies and emeralds, but he told me he knew that wasn't what I truly wanted. He asked and asked until I finally broke and told him. I told him I wanted every bastard who frequented the place to burn."

My eyes connect with Remington's once again over Tristan's shoulder. I don't know how I know, but I know that wolf was Remington. His eyes hold no apology, no remorse, and I suddenly know the end to this story. "You turned him, then," I say, not a question.

Remy nods. "I did."

"You wanted him to?" I ask Tristan.

"I did. I *so* did. I wanted to make them pay so badly, I'd have given anything. My life as a human was a small price." His hands begin to roam over my body. His hips press into me, his state of arousal clear. I take a moment to shake off the lust he creates, reminding myself he's not *my* Tristan right now.

"So, you tracked them all down?" I ask.

"They kept a log, just as all inns at that time did. We used it to find every one them we could. Took us years," Remy answers.

"You should have seen the looks on their faces, Kitten. The fear I caused in them the way they caused in us whores. It was euphoric. I took my time ripping them apart piece by piece. Their screams! Oh, God, the screams," he says throatily as he rubs himself against me. It's the bloodlust, I realize with trepidation. The bloodlust is turning him on.

I seek out Remington, asking with a look for him to help me now. He nods once before coming closer to grip Tristan's shoulder. "Come on, man. You need a cold shower."

"No. I need her," Tristan growls, inhaling my scent deeply. "Can you believe she's mine, Rem? She's ours. After everything, we have *her* now," he says dreamily.

"I know, but if we want to keep her you need to go shower. She needs to eat, remember, Tris?" Remy placates.

Tristan reacts like a bucket of ice water was thrown on him. "Right. Kitten needs to eat." He pulls away from me, albeit on shaky legs. He takes my hand in his, leading me back to the table laden with food. He proudly points out all the things he's made for me. So much about Tristan is instantly made clear, even if his calm nature is more of a mystery now more than ever.

I pile my plate high with every food I can reach, just to make him happy. After he watches me eat a few bites appreciatively, he allows Remy to lead him to the bathroom on the other end of the suite. He waits to hear the water turn on before making his way back to me. He looks relived to have Tristan locked behind the door.

"Don't fear him, Love. He gets this way after he gets what he wants from me. He punishes himself with drugs and alcohol to block out the memories. I won't let him take it too far with you."

"Remy," I sigh. "We can't let this happen anymore."

He nods. "I know. This has been going on for longer than you can imagine. Believe it or not, this is the best way we know how to handle it," he tells me.

I shake my head. "No, I mean we *can't* let this happen anymore." I place a hand over my stomach for emphasis. "We're having a baby. Hopefully, Mikey was nowhere near this at the house. We have children, Remy. Drugs, alcohol, aggression? There's no place for that near our kids."

"I know, okay?" he says defensively.

I place a hand over his. "You're not hearing me. You allow this to happen. Tristan punishes himself, but so do you. It's pretty obvious now that I know the story. He feels guilty for the others going hungry, and you feel guilty for turning him into a monster who craves blood. Am I right?"

"What? No!" He stands and stares at me with hurt in his eyes.

I nod calmly at him. "You're afraid you awoke a beast within him. That's why he's so calm usually, isn't it? You and the others worked to get him that way because he was so violent when he turned."

"We did, but..." He trails off, sounding unsure for once.

"And you still feel guilty about it. Remy, you have to know that he was violent before he ever met you. You didn't create that in him. *They* did. Neither of you should feel guilty here. You let him punish himself to keep the "*violent beast*" at bay, but also so you can assuage your own guilt. When he hurts, you hurt. Both of you think that you need to hurt. You don't. Sorry to burst your bubble, but this system you have going on isn't quite working. He's on drugs right now."

"I'm glad this is so easy for you to fix, your first go 'round. I've only been dealing with this shitstorm for hundreds of years," he mocks angrily.

"Remy, I'm not condemning you for how you've handled anything. You helped him, he said so himself. Whatever you do helps him deal with something that he can't deal with himself. You saved him. I love you right now more than I ever have. I don't have any answers about how to handle this going forward, I'm just giving you an outsider's perspective. This is what I see happening here," I explain myself.

"I know, it's just...and the baby... I just wish he could forget all that shit and see the man that the rest of us see, the damn good man that he's become. I don't know how to make that happen," he says impatiently.

"To quote you here, you're not alone in this anymore. You don't have to bear the weight of every decision on your own. I know you have Ash, and I know the others would follow you over a cliff. I'm also starting to see why you can't show weakness, to anyone. That your strength is intertwined with your ability to lead others without indecision. What I was saying, Remington, is that *we* cannot allow this to happen anymore. You and me. Together. You'll always be my Alpha, and I'll never, not once, see you as weak. It's an impossibility. You're mine, and I'm yours, and together we will lead our family *and* this pack."

He stares at me. Hard. Like I just blew his mind wide open. I don't know what I said to gain such a reaction. We've spoken at length about this. Maybe he just didn't believe it possible until now. I think a part of him had planned on holding back from me as much as possible. Like, at any moment, I could lose my love and respect for him. He should know that will never happen. I'll just have to prove it to him over time, I guess.

"I don't deserve you," Remy says, voice strained.

I stand from my chair, coming to stand in front of him, my neck craned back to meet his eyes. "You deserve only the best from this world. You and Tristan, and all the others as well. You guys seem to think I'm it so, yes, you do. I always knew that being with you guys meant that I'd have to contend with your pasts, but I've heard that I'm very stubborn, and I'm up for the challenge. My mates are worth it. You're worth everything. We'll figure everything out, I promise. Now, kiss me while I'm still feeling all smart and bossy." I smile up at him.

I don't expect the gentleness in his kiss, but I'm profoundly grateful for it. Something about this man makes me feel powerful and weak all at once.

By the time Tristan drags himself from the shower, the guys

and I have depleted most of the amazing food in front of us. I had set aside a plate for Tristan and demand that he eats every bit of it. I already asked Ash to search through everything he had brought with him and throw out any drugs he may have gotten his paws on. I also asked Kellan to hide his medical bag, just in case there was something Tristan could use in there. We all agreed not to let him out of our sight for even a moment. Beyond that, I'm not sure we have a plan so much as a general goal of letting all the venom built up inside of Tristan *out*, instead of just suppressing it.

"We're losing daylight if we're heading to the beach," Logan announces, providing us a much-needed distraction.

"Yeah, we can head out after everyone changes," Remy says as he starts to clear away dishes.

With that, we all disperse to change into our swimsuits.

Standing in front of the bathroom mirror, I check myself out in the two-piece suit Logan picked out for me. It's less revealing than I've seen some people wear, but cute and feminine at the same time. The top is a hunter-green, off the shoulder ruffle that stops just under my breasts. My midriff is bare, showing off my rounding tummy, but I like the idea of showing off my baby. The shorts are the same color and material, though they hug my shape like a second skin and have a gold buckle in the front, giving the illusion of wearing a belt. Leaving my hair down I place the oversized, floppy hat over my head and grab the sunglasses Logan gifted me.

My heels clack against the hardwood flooring as I make my way to the guys. Apparently, it took me longer to change than any of them. Because I'm staring at my toes and wondering if I painted my nails, would my wolf have painted nails when I shift, I don't catch that the room is completely silent. I look up with a frown. "What now?"

"Oh, nothing. I've just stunned them with your beauty once

again," Logan answers smugly. "But this sexy as hell addition is all you," he says as he skims his fingertips from my ribs to my hip. A shiver of awareness runs along my skin. He's such a tease.

"You mean you like seeing my belly get bigger?" I ask for clarification.

"Oh, baby. You have no idea the possessive pride your pregnant body evokes in us," Ash rumbles darkly.

"Here." Kellan offers me a light piece of fabric that fits like a loose dress to shrug into. "This will keep you covered up until we get to the beach." He helps me into the white dress, taking time to run his hands over my tummy too.

A bright flash has me blinking rapidly. I look to where it came from, only to see Reed smiling sheepishly at me from behind a camera. I beam at him for being so thoughtful. Now we can take pictures of our time here. He snaps another one of me smiling and I giggle.

The trip to the beach was more fun than a car ride had any right to be. I sat in the back between Reed and Finn, pointing out things to take pictures of and Finn interjecting historical facts about the area from time to time. Kellan, who was driving, rolled all the windows down while Logan hooked up his phone to the radio and played his "get hyped" playlist. I didn't know the words to sing along with the guys, but I had fun dancing inside the restraints of my seatbelt. I was almost sad when we stopped at a surf shop near the beach. The guys' enthusiasm quickly wiped away that feeling, and we posed for silly pictures outside the shop while we waited for the others to pull in and pay for parking.

Inside was filled with some of the most interesting things on the planet. They had a whole section of what Finn called snow globes. They're simply fascinating. I spent a long time examining each one while the guys talked with the shop employees about getting surfboards. I was wandering around on my own when I came across a clothing section intended for tourists. On the wall with t-shirts, swimsuits and towels, were tiny bodysuits meant for babies. The smallest of them all was only slightly bigger than my hand. Beside those were little hats and stuffed kangaroos, and sharks with big eyes.

That's where Remington and Jace found me, just staring at the baby items in the store. "Do you want to get one for the pup?" Jace asks, fingering a bright shirt reading "mum's 'lil Aussie" on the front.

"I, uh...I want this," I say as I hold up the best snow globe I could find. "And I wanted to get Mikey a shirt but..." I wave a hand at the baby stuff, panic starting to claw up my throat.

"Kitten, focus," Remy says, taking my shoulders and turning me to face him.

My lip trembles as I try to explain my thoughts that are spinning out of control. "We don't have anything. For the baby, I mean. It should have things, right? And where will we put it? Do we get it a baby-cage thing or like, a puppy bed? There's so much I have to learn and do and stuff to get. Babies need lots of stuff, Remy! I've seen it. Moms walk around with big bags of stuff for just short trips, I can only imagine what their homes look like."

"Ah, shit. Don't cry, Love. You have to know that our baby will want for nothing. We'll get everything he needs. What's the real problem here?" Remy asks as he pulls me to him and rubs a hand up and down my back.

"I don't know the stuff, Remy. I'm supposed to know what stuff a baby needs," I admit. I don't feel prepared at all, that's the problem.

"Hey," Jace says, getting my attention. "You have us for that. Whenever you want to we'll go baby shopping, and when we get home we can get started on the nursery if you want."

"There's time, Kitten. No reason to panic," Remy adds.

"What's going on over here?" Logan asks as he and Tristan join us.

"Kitten was having a moment, that's all. She saw baby things and was concerned that we don't yet have any for our pup," Jace fills him in.

"Oh, thank the fucking heavens! My girl is ready to shop. Finally!" he spews dramatically as he drops to his knees and raises his hands in the air.

"You truly are too much at times." Remy shakes his head at Logan.

"She's starting to nest," Tristan says, a small smile lighting his face.

"Nah, that's when females go insane with preparing and cleaning and shit. Kitten's just freaking out because she doesn't know *what* our baby needs."

"Thanks, Logan," I say sarcastically.

"What? I didn't mean it in a bad way. Look, I don't either. We'll just get everything, and if he needs it, he'll have it." He shrugs a lean shoulder.

I can't help but laugh. He makes it sound so simple. Maybe it is, I don't know.

"Let's pick out a shirt for Mike, hmm? I think Ash and the others are already loading the boards." Jace takes my hand and peruses the t-shirts in Mikey's size. "Just for future reference, the baby-cage things are called cribs," he tells me after we picked out a light blue shirt with a shark eating a surfboard and head to the checkout.

"What's that?" Jace asks as I set my finds on the counter to be purchased.

I follow his finger to the stuffed shark with big, friendly eyes. "Oh, I wanted it."

"You're getting our baby a *shark* to cuddle with?" he says with an indulgent smirk.

"Sure, for the baby." My cheeks color but I try to hide it with my hair.

Jace laughs loudly. "You want it, don't you?"

"Maybe," I mumble. "I'll share," I add defensively. He just laughs again, leaning down to kiss my head.

Waves are some of the most incredible, mesmerizing things. It's almost scary how hard it is *not* to watch them crash over and over again. I ditch my shoes first thing, leaving them in the car. I'm handed a beach bag full of towels to carry while the guys grab various things from the cars, including their newly-bought, brightly-colored surfboards. Not all of them got one, some enjoying the sport more than others. As we find a spot on the soft sand to spread out, Jace sets up three large umbrellas and digs them into the sand, creating shade.

"I'll take those," Logan tells me, plucking the bag of towels from my hand and spreading them out in the shade.

I'm distracted from watching Logan as Ash, Reed, Remy, and Kellan strip down to nothing but their shorts and run for the water, each with a surfboard under their arm. Watching the muscles in their backs contract with their movements is even more mesmerizing than the ocean. A flood of heat travels through my body that has nothing to do with the sun. In synchronicity all four of them dive onto the boards, strong arms pushing through the water, boards cutting through the waves like butter.

"You're drooling," Logan jokes.

"I'm allowed," I shoot back, shaking off my hormones.

Finn rubs me down with an extraordinary amount of sunblock, both front and back...twice, before he lets me do the same to him. I'm disappointed that I'm not allowed to get right into the water, more than ready to cool off. Apparently, it takes time for sunblock to sink in or something.

The five of us spread out lazily over the towels. I sit between

Tristan's knees as he feeds me snacks from his own bag, my back against his chest, my hair draped over his shoulder. We watch the guys out on the water, sometimes snapping pictures. They mostly sit out past where the waves crash, chatting with one another as they wait for a wave. Every now and again one or two of them will paddle hard to chase the raging water, get to a standing position, and cruise up to the beach riding a wave. I clap and squeal every time they do. It's an amazing sight.

Eventually, the rest of us are allowed to brave the sun. I grab my hat and sunglasses, dragging Finn and Tristan with me by the hands. I bite my lip as I inch my toes in to meet the water where it drowns the sand. Feeling brave I take a few steps closer, laughing as the water takes the sand out from under my feet as it recedes. I look to Tristan, only to find him watching me already. He's smiling, enjoying himself, too. Logan circles us, snapping away with the camera.

The others, seeing us in the water, make their way to the beach to join us. We play in the surf for a while, seeking broken seashells and smooth rocks. I don't know why we want these, but it seems important at the moment.

After some time, most of the guys break off to swim in the water in front of me, cooling off. I chew my lip, watching them dive under the waves and attempt to drown one another.

"Want to go in?" Ash asks next to me, watching as Reed backflips over a wave, daring Logan to do the same.

I shake my head sadly. "I don't know how to swim."

"I've got you. Come on, we won't go far." He bends down for me jump onto his back, his hands holding me under my thighs. "I won't let you go," he promises as he walks us into the water, and my body tenses slightly.

As we get a little over waist-deep, Ash's waist, not mine, Reed pops up from the water out of nowhere, making me jump. "I swear you're part fish," I tell him jokingly, splashing water at his face.

He laughs happily, taking the compliment for what it is. "Give me time, and I'll make you into a beach bunny yet. You'll be swimming by my side in no time." He winks before diving under the water to torment his brothers some more.

I relax my hold on Ash, choosing instead to drape my arms loosely around his neck. I rest my head on his, sighing in contentment.

Sometime later I find myself back on the beach, propped up on Jace with my fingers playing with Kellan's hair as he naps on my lap. The others are still out in the water, either surfing or playing around. As I let my eyes roam the beach, my brow creases. The guys are drawing quite a crowd of attractive women. A game of volleyball that had started further down now nearly blocks my view. There's plenty of room in the water, but where my guys tread water it almost looks crowded. I huff in annoyance, ready to shoo them all away.

Jace chuckles behind me. "You just noticed the surge, did you?"

"Yes. They need to leave. They're *mine*," I state firmly.

"Oh, let them look. The guys don't even care or notice them," he tells me lightly.

"Well, it's rude. They aren't here for them to ogle." I pout, suddenly wishing they were wearing more clothes.

"You don't think you draw the same kind of attention?" Jace whispers in my ear. "Take pride in having others crave what's yours. Let them dream of what only you get to have. The guys won't let them touch them, or probably even speak to them."

I snort. "That's such a Jace thing to say."

He bites my earlobe, his tongue snaking out to soothe the small sting. "They are yours. Don't let jealousy ruin our day. Feel this?" He trails his fingertips down my arm, sparking the bond electricity to life. "They know who they belong to."

I raise an eyebrow, or at least I try to. "They?"

He smirks his signature cocky smirk. "We," he corrects.

I sigh, watching the crowding females a moment longer before letting it go and sinking back into my golden mate for a nap in the summer heat. Jace is right, sort of. I shouldn't get jealous every time one of my guys turns someone else's head. If I did that, I'd always be jealous. I can't imagine a place or time every one of them wouldn't draw attention. They definitely get *my* attention.

I don't know what wakes me sharply out of my peaceful slumber first. The sense that something isn't right, Jace's body tensing underneath me, or the multiple low growls surrounding me. Blinking my eyes to adjust to the lowering sun now hitting me directly, I take in my mates who have come to surround me.

"What's going on?" I ask through a yawn.

"Wolves," Tristan answers on a growl.

"We should have sensed them earlier. They're just staring at you. More are gathering," Jace explains.

"I say we get her out of here," Ash tells Remy, arms flexing as he stares at the strangers head on.

"Well, what do they want?" I ask, not understanding the problem. *We're* wolves. Why are we scared of them being in the same place?

"Don't know, don't care. They aren't getting near you," Remy replies.

"Don't be ridiculous. Why don't you go ask if they want something, or if they're just being rude?" I roll my eyes. There's plenty of attractive women on this beach, some of them in next to nothing, so I don't think this has anything to do with me.

"You don't seem to understand," Remy says as he helps me to my feet, shoving the cover-up over my head urgently. "They're changed wolves, like us. Right now they outnumber us. Our advantage is lost here." Half of our bags and the surfboards are left abandoned on the beach as I'm rushed to the cars, encircled by my guys.

I look back, seeing through a gap between Reed and Ash that one of the strangers has broken away from the pack and jogs warily in our direction. The guys must sense him coming, because they stop and face the newcomer.

"If you want to leave with your head attached, you'll stop where you are," Ash states menacingly.

The young guy stops in his tracks, jaw ticking at the threat. His mismatched eyes seek me out. One dark blue, the other a bright brown. "I… We weren't trying to intrude, even if this is *our* territory. I was just surprised to see her. Especially an *expecting* her."

"How do you know who she is?" Tristan demands, stalking forward and circling him. Logan grips my hand subtly and I know the plan is for my fastest mate to get me out of here as soon as he gets the order from Remy.

The guy blinks rapidly, his jaw hanging open. "You serious, mate? Word travels, you know. The Ivaskov princess has taken up residence Down Under. Did you think that would go unnoticed? Every pack from here to Norway has been talking about her."

"And what's being said?" Remy demands.

He smiles at me through my fence of bodies. "Just that she's gonna start a revolution." He bows dramatically, winking for added effect.

"Cheeky bastard, isn't he?" Jace grumbles from behind me somewhere.

"Why were you gathering?" Remy asks. "If your purpose is to take her from us or harm her in any way, I can guarantee you won't be walking away with your life."

"Ah, right," the guy says, scratching the back of his neck as his eyes find his friends down the beach before flicking back to me. "We were wonderin', ya know...if your call to arms was just for your territory, or if anyone could join you."

"Call to arms?" I ask out loud.

"For made wolves, like us. We heard your pack was looking for recruits," he explains.

I shake my head, looking to Remy. "Does he mean when we opened our pack for changed wolves?"

Remy nods. "Yeah, I think that's what he's getting at," he answers me before turning to the guy. "Look, we aren't recruiting anyone. Our Luna here has opened our ranks to allow any wolf to join us. Not to join our army specifically, but so that anyone, no matter their origin, who wants to be part of a pack can have one. We've had several changed wolves join us already."

"For protection, most likely," the guy agrees. "The days of being hunted down by natural wolves is almost at an end, yeah? So, what do we have to do to join your pack?"

Do? What does that mean? Is there an acceptance process that I don't know about? I eye the guy critically as he continues to speak to Remington. Then I turn my eyes to his friends. They're all young-looking, much as my mates and I are. His friends are tense, not knowing if this is going to end badly for them. They also appear anxious. From the looks of them, they've been traveling for some time now. Dirt-covered, disheveled, and days-worth of growth on some of their faces speaks to that theory. Oh. I blink with the realization. They've been looking for us.

"Why do want to join us?" I interrupt whatever conversation was taking place.

"Other than becoming an Ivaskov and not fighting for my life on a daily basis?" he replies sarcastically.

"Yes. Other than that," I state.

He scratches his neck again, nervous. "I guess we just want to be on the ground floor when things change. No Alpha has ever offered sanctuary for made wolves before. It seems only a fair and righteous leader would lead the charge on such a thing. That's an Alpha we could get behind. We'd give our lives for it. If you need soldiers or doormen, we're in."

Silence reigns for a time as we take in his words. Frankly, I'm stunned. These people half a world away believe in what we're trying to accomplish. They'd risk their eternal lives to support us. The knowledge is humbling, to say the least.

"We'll need a minute," Remy dismisses the guy back to his friends. We continue to the vehicles, Logan and Ash going back for the things we left. Once our stuff is stored away, we gather at the open back of the SUV.

"This shit is crazy," Logan starts.

"They took a big risk, approaching us in this way," Ash acknowledges.

Remy looks to me for my opinion. I give it without having to think. "When I offered sanctuary, I meant everyone. If the pack accepts them, then I will."

"I don't like how they were looking at her. How do we know they don't have some misguided idea that they could also be her mates?" Jace states. That garners growls all around.

I slap him on the chest. "Even if they did, it's not like I'm willing to bond with anyone else, so the point is moot."

"I'm more concerned about how other Alphas will see this. It was one thing to take in changed wolves from our own territory. Accepting them could send the message that we're building an army of immortals, just like they feared," Remy points out.

I shrug. "Let them fear it. They already think we're doing it anyway. We know we're not, and it's not our fault that they refuse to allow them into their own packs. They've always had the option, if not the responsibility, to have them join them."

"Would serve them right, too. They hunted us and killed us off like a disease, even though they created us. They *should* be wary," Finn adds passionately.

I shrug again, meeting Remy's eyes. "We lead our pack. We set the rules. What the other packs do or fear isn't our concern."

Remy smiles widely, leaning down to kiss me quickly. "I agree. Just had to make sure we were on the same page."

Calling over the nervous group, Jace takes the lead. "Are you all able to get yourselves to Colorado? That's where our pack house is and I assume you'd need a place to live."

The one who spoke earlier speaks up again. "We kinda just live off the land, mate. Hard to hold a job when assassins are after you, you know?"

Jace nods. "Yeah, we do know." He turns his attention to Remy. With a slight nod, Remy gives him permission to proceed. "Is this the lot of you?" Jace asks.

"There's a few more of us that hasn't made it here yet. Why'd you ask?"

"We'll have a spare plane flying back within a few days. If you can get all of your documentation together and anything you'd want to bring, you can catch a lift," Jace explains.

"Really? You mean we're in? Just like that?" the guy chirps excitedly.

I narrow my eyes on him. "The pack as a whole has to accept you as well. I won't put anyone out by moving you in. We don't have many rules, but everyone contributes and everyone looks out for everyone else. You'd have to find your places within the pack, see where you'd be most happy and most helpful. If you can do that then, yes, you're in."

"Of course, my princess." He bows again, which I have to admit looks downright silly in shorts and a tank top.

"My title is Luna," I correct him gently.

Remy tells them where to meet us, which is a lie because we

arrived at a different airport, but I don't question his motives. We part ways and make our way back to our hotel.

With the sun setting behind us I know our mini-vacation is over, and tomorrow brings with it a whole new set of things to deal with.

After dinner, I snuggle up to Tristan and Kellan as we watch a movie before bed. I hate to leave him with the new knowledge of what's going on with him, but I have every faith that the guys will keep Tristan safe and drug-free while I'm gone.

CHAPTER THIRTEEN

Morning comes entirely too early, as most mornings seem to. After a quick breakfast, and Jace finally explaining why my wardrobe here has consisted of oversized sweaters and pants (because we don't want the world to know that I'm pregnant, apparently), we set off for the day.

Remington and Ash had explained last night that the phony airport was given to the other wolf pack so that they could scout for any threats and make sure they are who they say they are. Once they've seen just how many more wolves show up, and if they determine that their intentions are good, they'll load them up on a van and transport them to the correct airport. That's where Albert and I will meet up with them to start heading home.

Sitting in the back of a limo with Albert, Anna, Kendrick, and one of their guards in complete and total silence is beyond uncomfortable. The windows are completely blacked out both ways, so I can't even watch the scenery pass by on the way to who knows where. I can't help but think something has changed since the last time we were together. I can't put my finger on it, but something definitely feels off. Even Anna won't make eye contact with me.

The car comes to a stop on a dead-end street lined with overgrown trees and shrubbery. We're still near the water; I can smell it on the air as we exit the car. Albert sticks to my side as the car pulls away. Kendrick leads the way through an opening in the trees, the rest of us following after him. I scan my thumb over my palm, tempted to press the emergency button Finn and Kellan inserted under my skin earlier. They told me to keep it a secret, only pressing it if something happens unexpectedly so they can find me. According to Finn, it should be undetectable. I wouldn't even know it was there if I hadn't seen them insert it. I certainly hadn't expected to exit the car in such a remote area, but I resist pressing it just yet. So far I've gained not a word of information from Kendrick, and I'm determined to know what he has to show me.

"We'll shift and run from here. Try to keep up," Kendrick informs us briskly as Albert and I push through the last of the foliage.

I wait to shift last, placing my clothing on top of the others' and shoving it under a low-hanging tree. Albert runs in front of me, leaving me open to attack from behind, but making sure he would see any threats ahead of us first. It's funny how, not long ago, I wouldn't even have these kinds of thoughts. Now, danger is my first thought.

We run towards the edge of the ocean, taking a sharp turn to run parallel to it. We run for quite some time, the sun getting lower in the sky as the terrain climbs higher and higher. We're definitely going up a mountain. As we reach the summit, Kendrick's wolf pauses and releases a howl. Oddly enough, I feel no instinct to reply to it. After a moment, we hear a responding howl in the distance and set off in that direction.

Our destination lies in a natural bowl-like valley between

two mountains. Only one side remains open, facing the ocean. I can imagine this would be a very difficult place to access by vehicle or plane. Now I know why we were running.

As we get closer to the valley floor, I scent both humans and wolves...and something *other*. I can't pinpoint what the smell is. It's oddly familiar, made even more odd by the fact that I can't place it. I search my mind for any memory containing the scent, but come up empty. But how do I remember it, then? I'm so distracted by trying to place something I can't find a name for that I almost crash into the wolves who have halted in front of me.

Kendrick is shifting back to human already, the others doing the same. I hesitate, knowing full well that they'll notice my pregnant belly once I shift. So much for the big sweaters. I decide to stay as I am. No one said I had to be in my human form to take this tour. I'm given odd looks as two women approach us, carrying clothing and greeting the Alpha. I tilt my head as I listen to them, fighting my wolf to pay attention when all I really want to do is nap on the warm sand surrounding the beautiful water. I have an overwhelming desire to roll in it.

The pair speaks in hushed tones, taking turns eyeing my wolf. I yawn at them, not caring one bit for the secrecy when I was brought here for answers. I get bored of them and stalk past to seek out the scent from earlier. I have to know what it is. Approaching a squat, wooden building, I'm instantly surrounded by growling wolves. I growl back, snapping at those daring to come too close. They attempt to circle me but I manage to back them against the building, Albert keeping watch behind me.

"Easy there, Ivaskov. They're just doing their job," a feminine voice tells me, none too nicely.

I turn my head to growl at her in warning to watch her tone.

Her head tilts slightly back and away, submitting to me against her will. Good. That will do.

"I have clothing for you," the other woman informs me. I eye the fabric in her hand before looking to Albert, hoping he understands that I need to change in private.

"My Luna would like to dress in private," he lets them know, already donning a pair of dark sweatpants himself.

"A wolf with modesty? An odd guest you bring us, Alpha," the rude woman sneers. I bare my teeth at her. Luckily, the other one points to a small clearing in the trees that should provide enough privacy. I only need a moment.

I dress quickly, throwing on the pink sweatpants and large t-shirt. I stalk from the trees, pointing at the building. "What's in there?" I demand.

"It's one of our housing units," the mean one replies.

"Luna. You will address me as Luna when speaking to me. I don't know what problem you have with me, but you will respect me while I'm here," I inform her.

"Of course, Luna," she replies, somehow making my title sound like a dirty word while still attempting compliance.

"Sybil," the other woman warns her. She holds out a hand to me. "I'm Lacy. Welcome to our home, Luna."

"These women will accompany us and show you around," Anna tells me as she gestures for me to join her and Kendrick. I walk beside them, hoping he'll finally speak, letting the scent drift from my mind, for now.

Albert places himself behind me and between the two women who follow as we near what I now see is the heart of a small village. I take in all the modern amenities alongside what look like buildings from a time long past. What strikes me the most is the abundance of females. Albert and Kendrick look severely out of place as we pass women of every age huddled in groups, pointing at us and standing in doorways.

There's also a lot of children. Like, *a lot* of them. The middle of the town is designed specifically for them, it seems. A larger than life playground sits squarely in the middle of the town, facing a row of small shops selling toys, children's clothing, and an open-air restaurant featuring tiny picnic tables and table and chair sets with tea setups. The children are all ushered away from us, making me frown. Maybe it's because of the males with me? I don't think so, though, considering all the women here eye me with fear or derision.

"You might want to start talking now, Kendrick. This is pissing me off," I growl at the Alpha.

"Well, for starters, this place is where you came from," he states bluntly. "This village is protected by my pack and a few others."

"But why? What is it?" I ask.

"You're looking at the last changeable female population," he tells me.

My head rocks back and I look again at those still out and about. "You mean they all live here? But the children...how?" I ask breathlessly.

"They've always been here. The disease that plagued our women never reached here. The only reason your father was granted access is because he boasted of a vaccine to protect them from ever becoming infected."

"That's impossible. If he made a vaccine, wouldn't that mean that he also made an antidote?" I question.

"It would stand to reason that he did. If so, I wasn't privy to it," he responds.

Anna drops back to walk with Albert, leaving me with her mate. I stare accusingly at the Alpha. "He wouldn't have kept that to himself. From all that I've heard of him, it was his life's mission to cure the illness that took his mother and sisters."

"I suppose we'll never know. What we *do* know is that he

found a way to get around the bonding process that protects our females from unwanted matings. It was quite an accident on his part. The females who reside here had agreed to help him search for answers to help our race procreate. He took a liking to one woman in particular. A woman I believe was your mother," he informs me.

I swallow thickly. "Is she here?" I ask, my heart in my throat.

He shakes his head. "Sadly, no. We don't know what became of her."

My stomach plummets. Of course not. That would have been too easy, wouldn't it? "If he found a way to help our people, then why isn't this information shared? Why do these women hide here instead of trying to find mates?"

Kendrick stops at the entrance to a graveyard. It's surrounded by a low wrought-iron fence, the gravestones simple carvings on rounded rocks. "Can you imagine the fallout if his so-called cure got out? Look before you. Most of these graves were filled *after* your father visited here."

"He... Are you implying that my father killed all these people? All these women?" I ask, getting in his face.

"In a way, yes. Not all of the women who volunteered for Mikel's experiments were from here. Most of them were found in hospitals, already dying. He had them brought here, injected them with his serum, and waited for the results. He was trying to save them while attempting to find a way to change human women into wolves."

I let the information sink in. I've read countless journals and texts, but none of them mention anything about this. Surely, he documented everything he did. He was a scientist. I don't allow myself to suss out how I feel about all of this yet. I'll do that when I'm not being monitored by strangers. I have so many questions that I don't know where to start. I wish Finn was with me right now. He'd tell me to slow down, take in the details, and work backwards.

Taking a deep breath, composing myself and forcing my mind to slow down, I list the facts. One: my father was here, doing experiments to increase fertility. Two: he was successful in that he unlocked the bond usually necessary to mate and procreate. Three: there are children here. Lots of them.

"The children. If there are kids here, then these women aren't hiding from *everyone*." I look at Kendrick to gauge his reaction.

"In exchange for protection, some of the women here chose to mate with members of the packs that protect them," he tells me carefully.

"In my experience, sex in exchange for something else equals prostitution," I state. "Are you telling me your pack and others treat these women as your own personal prostitutes?"

"Never!" he replies vehemently. "They came to *us*. Sought *us* out, and they set the rules."

I'm already shaking my head. "That doesn't make sense. Why would they do that?"

"Because news of your father's trials got out and your changed wolf filth descended like the mongrels they are. They were being taken and abused left and right after your father disappeared." It was subtle, but a quick flash of his eyes in Anna's direction gives away the fact that he just slipped and told me something he hadn't planned on revealing.

This all happened after my father left. Not while he was here. Something had to have happened. "Why would my father disappear? You mean he was taken, or did he leave?" I ask, watching him carefully.

Kendrick splutters before finally settling on changing the subject. "We're heading off topic. I brought you here today to inform you of this colony and make you realize the importance of keeping their secrecy. If we're to be allies, you should be informed of this project that is near to my heart."

I don't fall for it. "Why did my father leave, Kendrick? I can only imagine this place was under *his* protection while he was here. Why would he willingly leave them to fend for themselves?"

"That's not my information to share," he says, voice full of steel.

I match his tone with my own. "Then whose the fuck is it? Just point me in the right direction and I'll get the information out of them myself. Do you dare tell me I don't have a right to know?"

"You're missing the point," he tries.

"No, *you're* missing the point. You brought me here, alone, without my mates, so that when I started asking questions about how your pack seems to have more children than any other, I'd think of these *poor women* who fell under attack. Probably by something you caused!" I scream in his face.

"She doesn't know what the hell she's talking about," Sibyl sneers quietly, but not quietly enough.

I turn my attention to her, stalking closer slowly. "You. Answer me. Why did my father leave here, leaving you all alone?"

"What? I... It's not my..." she stammers.

"Finish that sentence and I swear you'll find out what it's like to lose a limb," I threaten. I'm so sick of hearing that statement. If it's not their story to tell, then whose the hell is it? My father's? My mother's? Because they're both dead. It can't be mine, because I sure as hell don't know it.

Sibyl's face goes a nasty shade of red, ready to explode, even as her friend warns her to stay calm. "He chased that whore of a mother of yours out of here. That's why he left. When that cunt fled her own people, he left without a word or a care what would happen to the rest of us!" she shouts in derision.

Without thinking, I reach out and slap her with the back of my hand. She falls to the ground in a heap. Holding the side of her face, her eyes spew venom at me. If looks could kill, I'd be a goner. "You wanna know the real story? Huh, do you?"

"Sibyl, stop it! Alpha, do something," Lacy says, panicked.

"No, Sibyl, please continue. Kendrick, if you interfere Anna will be the one to lose a limb," I warn, eyeing Albert and nodding toward the Alpha's mate.

Without warning, Albert moves to grip Anna from behind, awaiting my order. I press down on the button in my hand. No matter how this ends now, there will be no alliance between Kendrick and myself. Not after I threatened his mate.

Our group has caused quite a scene at this point, crowds gathering in windows and doorways. Sibyl looks for an escape, eyes darting around for help that won't come. Not for her anyway, but my help is already near. I wait for them to gather behind me, already taking in the scene. I know they don't know what's going on, but they'll have to wait.

"Oh, Sibyl. Sibyl, Sibyl, Sibyl..." I *tsk*, stalking around her threateningly. "You got quiet. No need to be shy, these are just my...what did you call them, Kendrick? Mongrels? That's it. My mongrel mates. All eight of them. Don't worry, though, my dear Sibyl, they won't lay a hand on you. Well..." I trail off, leaning in to whisper venomously in her ear. "Unless I ask them to," I finish.

She shivers in fear, words spilling from her lips. "Your mother ran..." she starts.

"Yes, but why did she run?" I ask sweetly, flicking her hair from her shoulder, exposing her vulnerable neck.

"I don't know," she says through gritted teeth.

"Liar," I whisper in her ear again, this time from behind. I force my teeth to shift, my canines elongating to sharp points. Without warning, I tear into her shoulder. She screams and tries to flee. I hold her to me with her hands behind her back.

When I raise my head, I ask her again. "Why did she run?"

"Please...stop. You're going to kill me no matter what I say!" Her anger takes control of her again.

"At this point? Probably, but how painful it is depends on you telling me the truth. See the sandy-haired tall one with the pretty eyes?" I ask her, pointing out Tristan. "Well, he's like a walking lie detector. If you tell a lie, you bleed. My blood can heal you, over and over again. So, you see, I can hurt you and make you bleed as much as I want," I say in a sickeningly-sweet tone, scaring even myself.

"She was his favorite! She got closer to him than anyone else. It was disgusting! She wasn't here for the vaccine, she wanted *him*. She was a disgrace to our race; a traitor!" she spews.

"Then she got pregnant. She went on and on about how she was going to mate the Ivaskov Alpha. She let it slip that Mikel found the cure. Her pregnancy was proof of that," she continues.

I look to Tristan, who nods. She's telling the truth so far. "What happened after that?" I question, pushing her to her knees, no longer able to stand having her so close to me.

Tears stream down her face even as her hateful eyes glare up at me. "You have to understand! We never wanted him to find a cure. We're humans and want to stay that way. All we wanted was the vaccine for the disease that was killing us. Instead, he brought other wolves with him to aid his research. Our community was ripe with disgusting relationships, including your parents'."

I laugh at the ridiculousness of her words. "You're talking over yourself, Sibyl. If there were relationships forming, then not everyone wanted only the vaccine. Did your group inform my father what you wanted? Or did you try to play him to get what you wanted?"

"Like he would've helped us otherwise," she responds.

I shrug. "Maybe not, but that's a choice you made, wasn't it? He wanted to help his people, and thought you lot were the key. Sounds like he didn't do anything you didn't ask for."

"He ruined our community! He brought in change that we didn't want. With his cure, the rest of your kind would have preyed on us like the predators you are. Those other women were weak. Your father's wolves took advantage of their weakness."

I look to Tristan again. He shrugs. "She believes it's true. It's her opinion."

I huff. "What happened to my mother?" I ask the question I really want the answer to.

She hangs her head, not in shame but in the knowledge that I won't like what she has to say. "We held a meeting. We confronted her about her abomination of a child. We gave her a choice: end it herself, or we'd end it for her."

"You fucking bitch," I force through my teeth. Gripping the back of her neck, I slam her head to the ground until blood gushes from her face in several places. To appease the rage boiling inside of me, I do it again.

"Kitten, she can't talk if she's dead," Remy speaks up, his voice careful.

I throw the bloody mess of a woman away from me. "So? There's plenty more around here that I can make talk," I say as I eye the onlookers with disgust. They cower away.

"True. Shall I fetch us a fresh one?" Tristan offers with a smile that would make grown men piss themselves in fear.

"Not yet. I promised this one pain," I answer him, the darkness taking over me reveling in the answering darkness we sense in him.

Sibyl manages to get to her knees. With a look, she starts talking again. "She fought us. That demon baby of hers made her stronger. We didn't expect that. She ran, and we chased her across the globe for weeks. She was trying to get to your father, but he was already dead."

"How did you know he was already dead and she didn't?" I tilt my head. Something isn't adding up here.

"We went to your uncle. He was more than happy to dispose of his brother. We didn't tell him why, we just gave him the opening he needed. Your father rarely had security forces here," she explains.

My whole body shakes from the sheer hatred I feel in this moment. I close my eyes, forcing myself not to shift and rip her apart. "Finish it," I grit out.

She sobs uncontrollably now, knowing without a doubt her life is forfeit. "We tracked her to the States. When we found her, she was already giving birth. An elder was supposed to have taken care of you while we ended your mother. It was only recently that we learned of her betrayal."

"And let me guess, she's dead now as well?" I ask.

Sibyl only nods.

"What was her name?" I ask.

"Who, the elder?" she responds, confused.

"No, you idiot. My mother. What was her name?"

"Riley," she whispers.

"Do you have children?" I ask her.

"No," she replies quickly.

I look to Tristan. "Truth," he tells me.

I turn to Remington, pleading for understanding from him. I hate myself in this moment, more than I've ever hated anything or anyone, even more than I hate Sibyl. But that doesn't change what I have to do.

I walk to Sibyl, helping her to her feet and turning her to

face those brave enough to still be eavesdropping. "For the lives you took and all the pain you've caused, Sibyl, I, Luna of the Ivaskov pack, daughter of the brutally murdered Alpha Mikel and the open-hearted Riley, sentence you to death."

Without hesitation, I snap her neck, watching as her knees buckle. With my eyes pinned on the crowd I rip her head from her body and toss it at them, screaming at the top of my lungs in rage and pain.

Screams and cries sound around the village square. Some run, thinking they're next. Part of me wants to end them all. Sibyl didn't act alone, after all. One woman gets my attention. She stands tall, not quivering or sniveling. She stares at me without any emotion at all. I motion for her to come forward.

She's an older woman, maybe fifty or so. Probably one of the elders Sibyl spoke of. "After my parents were killed, what happened then?" I demand of her, my throat raw and aching.

"We destroyed your father's research. We burned everything he worked for to the ground. Only after did we realize that he'd broken the bonds. We were able to procreate with whoever we wanted to, bond or no bond. Your uncle didn't care about what happened to us. We sought out Alpha Kendrick and explained what happened to him. We agreed that those who were willing to mate with wolves would mate with his pack, and eventually the other packs he brought around. The Alpha is a traditionalist, and only allowed those with full bonds to mate and have children. In exchange, he protected our village," she explains.

I look over to see a pale Kendrick. Turning back to the older woman, I ask bluntly, "Was Kendrick aware of what happened to my mother and father?"

"Yes," she responds simply.

"Truth," Tristan informs me.

"You didn't think I'd find out," I say to Kendrick. "You brought me here and didn't think anyone would tell me."

"No," he growls. "Your refusal to spill blood on my lands made me think you didn't have it in you. You were supposed to see a village of women who needed your help."

I scrunch my face up. "They don't even want my help, Kendrick. You were just covering your own ass, hoping I'd stop by for a quick tour and dismiss this place, because I'd start asking questions eventually."

"What are you going to do with him?" Anna asks through a sob.

What a good question. Stepping back to the older woman, I look in her eyes. "Did Kendrick or any of his wolves ever force bonds or mating on anyone here?" I ask.

She looks over my shoulder at Tristan. "No." She frowns. Well, he has that going for him. I eye Remington, looking for guidance. I don't think death is warranted, but he should be punished.

He nods in agreement, giving me free rein to make a judgement call. I turn to the Alpha. "Kendrick, you will release all members of your pack. The Australia pack will cease to exist, starting today. I revoke your title as Alpha, as you have abused its power and used those weaker than yourself for your own gain."

"Who are you to revoke my title? A title I was born with and earned!" he shouts, indignant.

I pounce on him, knocking him to the ground and using my elbow on his throat to keep him down. Spit flies from my mouth as I shout back in his face. "I'm Kitten Fucking Ivaskov and I'll revoke any damn thing I want. There're enough shitty leaders in this world without adding you to the mix. You failed your people, get over it. Lose you title or lose your life."

"Kendrick, please," Anna begs him.

"I'll tell you what. I'll release the two of you, right here, right now. You go back and release your pack, or you go back and lead them to their deaths if you choose to war with me instead," I offer.

I turn to his guard. "You'll swear an oath to me?" I ask. He nods reluctantly. "Go back, tell them all the truth of what happened here. Tell them all who your Alpha truly is. That way, if they choose to stand with him, they do so having all the information."

"I swear it, Luna," he tells me.

"Truth," Tristan confirms.

"Then the three of you get out of here. I'm done with you. And Kendrick? If you so much as try to lead a horse to water, I'll be coming for you. Understood?"

"Understood," he grumbles, catching Anna as Albert releases her. The two of them shift and are out of sight in seconds.

Their guard turns back, stopping before the trees. "You should probably know that Kendrick put out a hit on your new friends. They probably won't make it to the airport to meet you. He had surveillance on you the whole time." With those lovely parting words, he shifts and runs after his former Alpha.

"Shit, we have to get to them," Logan says on a sigh.

"Agreed. What do you want to do about this village, Kitten?" Remington asks.

I turn to face the now-abandoned town square. "I don't know." I meet his steel-grey eyes. "I honestly want them all dead," I tell him truthfully.

"I know you do, Love. But could you live with yourself with that much blood on your hands? What about the children?" he adds.

I raise my hands, looking at the literal blood coating them, and begin to shake. "No, I couldn't," I whisper.

"You could speak to the other packs. Make it to where no one protects them any longer. They'd have to fend for themselves for once. Maybe if they leave this seclusion, they'd gain a different perspective," he offers.

"I don't want them. They aren't welcome with us," I plead with him. I won't cuddle up with my parents' killers. Not even I have that much forgiveness. The only thing saving them now is the children and the few innocents. "The children can, when they're older, and if they're not poisoned by their mothers."

"I understand that. Why don't you get cleaned up and I'll deal with them? I'll inform them of their new, unprotected status," he suggests.

"We could burn down all their buildings," Tristan chimes in. "That would force them to move. Make them start from scratch."

"Yes. That." I nod in agreement, pointing at Tristan.

Remy sighs. "You don't mean that, Kitten. I wish we could punish them in some significant way, but there's no way to do that without punishing the innocent and breeding a new generation of hate. You don't want to do that to children."

With the pain of my parents' deaths still fresh in my veins, I kind of do want that. Why should these kids be allowed to have what I wasn't given a chance to? If the world was a just place, I'd have them all thrown in dumpsters and see which of them survives.

But I know that's the pain talking. I know, just like me, these children haven't done anything to deserve such a fate. If I was clear-headed, I'd agree with Remy that nothing more can be done. Hopefully, these women stop behaving selfishly and change their ways. "Okay, Remy. Let's just go. I can't forgive them right now, maybe never, but I refuse to care about them in this moment. I want to go home."

"That's right, Love. Let's go home." He takes my hand, placing it in the crook of his arm, not caring that I'm smearing Sibyl's blood on his white shirt.

My guys gather around me as I'm undressed and led into the

water. They help me get the blood off and out of my hair. I'm given Ash's black button-down, which fits me like a dress. We walk into the woods, pausing in a clearing for Remy to run back and warn the village not to seek protection with any other wolf packs.

Walking is much slower going than running, but I don't trust myself yet not turn back and slaughter them all if I let my wolf loose.

When the sun finally sets on this horrifying day, we choose to run the rest of the way. Concern for the changed wolves we met the day before overrides my need for vengeance. We get as close to the airport as we can in wolf form before shifting and finding clothes. We probably look odd sans shoes, but no one seems to notice.

The airport Remy sent them to is a small one, nearly abandoned at this hour. The stray pack is clearly trying to keep a low profile as they stand vigilant in a secluded part of the airport, keeping watch. There's only a few more of them than yesterday, as they said there would be. They look as haggard as we are.

"Thank fuck. We thought you weren't going to show. We had to fight our way here, and then you didn't show," the talkative one relays as soon as he sees us.

"We've had out own shit to deal with. We're glad to see you all made it whole," Ash tells him, shaking his hand.

The men eye me, taking in my vacant state. I don't currently give a damn what they think of me. They seem to pick up on this and direct their questions to the guys. Jace eventually places a call to the other airport and has the planes delivered here. He also has the hotel send a carrier with our bags. Apparently, they never got the chance to get out of the hotel before my button went off. Finn explained that when I ran as a wolf every step I took pressed it, constantly sending my location out to them. They were worried at first, thinking something majorly wrong had happened. It had, but before all of that went down they were able to catch up to us, able to run faster than the Australian, natural wolves. They stayed back until I pressed the button on purpose. That explained how they got there as fast as they did.

The baggage arrives before our planes do. Jace and Logan sift through clothing, finding what they think will fit the new guys. They shower, shave and change, looking even younger than before. If I didn't know any better I'd swear one guy was only thirteen, tops. Looks don't mean anything when it comes to changed wolves, though. That thirteen-year-old could be eighty or two-hundred years old.

I'm given my own clothes to dress in, a comfortable pair of sleep pants, a cami and sweater set, and colorful toe-socks. When I exit the restroom, all the guys seem to be busy talking or on their phones, so I seek out a quiet corner to relax in, well within eyesight of my mates.

After a time, I sense a new presence near me. By this point I've stretched out over several seats, under the unmovable arm bars. I continue to trace the mini figure-eights in the carpeting with a finger, ignoring whoever it is.

"You're different today," the person finally speaks up.

"What's your name?" I ask lazily.

"Quinn, Princess," he responds.

I snort. "It's Luna. I never was a princess. And Quinn? I'm almost never the same person day to day anymore." I don't know why I'm admitting anything to a stranger, but it feels good to say it out loud.

He whistles. "Sounds like some heavy thoughts you're having there."

I smirk. You think? "Your voice sounds like music," I say instead.

He laughs. "You think so? Want me to sing you a tune?"

I giggle lightly. "You sing?"

"From time to time," he tells me. "It's one of the jobs that's easier to keep, believe it or not. Stage name, nomad lifestyle, paid in cash...it makes life easier at times."

"Yeah, I used to feel that way about the diner I worked at. I didn't have a stage name, but everyone assumes Kitten is a nickname, anyway." I shrug awkwardly from my prone position.

"You worked at a diner?" Quinn asks in disbelief.

"Yep, and an ice rink, and a hotel laundry facility. All this?" I wave my hand around wildly. "It's new to me. I was a street rat until fairly recently."

"That explains a lot, actually," he says thoughtfully.

"Does it?" I raise a brow, turning to look at him for the first time. He's an attractive guy, one might say. His brown hair hangs past broad shoulders, sky-blue eyes full of pain and mischief. A scar cuts through one dark eyebrow, adding mystery to the young-looking man.

"Forgive me if I'm crass, but it's easier to believe a street rat could take on the world, as you have, rather than some princess raised in a castle," he tells me.

I shake my head. "I don't know why you keep saying I'm taking on the world and all that. I've made a few phone calls and one disastrous trip to Australia."

"Why was your trip here a disaster?" he deflects.

"Oh, you know...I killed some people and dethroned an Alpha. I came here to end a war and gave them a reason to fight one instead. All a day's work for a rogue princess."

He whistles again. "Imagine what you could do with a week," he jokes. We both laugh. Deep, side-stitch laughter even though nothing is funny. I think we both just need it.

My laughter tapers off to tears. I shove them away, over the damn things. I turn to lie on my back, staring at the ceiling. I calm myself with a deep sigh. Quinn moves so that his back is leaning on the seats I'm lying on. We sit in silence for a while, each lost in our own thoughts.

"Sometimes you have to concentrate on the good things," he says, low enough that I have to strain to hear him. "Even if all you have to hold on to is a few moments of peace that you can barely remember. You have to take it in both hands and hold on for dear life, because the good things are what make the rest of it worth it."

"I have a kid. He's a good thing," I tell him. "I kind of stole him," I admit.

He chuckles. "Of course, you did. You don't do anything half-assed, do you?"

I shrug. "I always thought I was a nice, decent person. I'm only starting to see that I may also be a stubborn, homicidal wolf with rage issues."

He's silent again, probably figuring out how to get away from me as quickly as possible. I wouldn't blame him. You should definitely run from anyone admitting to being homicidal.

"You know how everyone else describes you?" he asks eventually.

"Do I wanna know?" I cringe.

"It might help. They say you're like an avenging angel. Righteous beyond belief. You're not concerned with politics. You storm in, Ivaskov eyes blazing, and get things done. So, where you see a homicidal wolf with rage issues, the oppressed wolves of the world see hope."

"I don't know if I can look at it that way," I tell him.

"Maybe not. There's a saying, you know? That a reluctant leader is usually best suited for the job."

"That's a weird saying," I say through a yawn.

"Look, I know you have your mates and probably lots of people you can talk to, but if you ever need another friend, I'm here, okay?" he offers.

I blink at the back of his head. "I don't think I've really been friends with anyone. I'm probably bad at it."

He laughs quietly, shoulders shaking. Turning, he meets my eyes. "Then I'll be your first one. Friends get to tell other friends when they're being homicidal wolves with rage issues. I'll help you figure that out, if you want," he jokes. At least, I think he's joking.

I smile. "Okay, then. Friends it is." I hold my hand out for him to shake. I don't know if that's right, but it seems the same as making a deal.

He takes my hand, shaking it. "Friends."

CHAPTER FOURTEEN

Being carried onto planes while asleep is apparently a hobby of mine. This time, I'm able to come to life enough to brush my teeth and climb into bed myself. Sliding in between Ash and Reed, I try to get comfortable. I can't.

"Come here," Ash exhales, sliding an arm under my neck and the other gripping my hip, pulling me into him. He throws a heavy leg over mine, trapping me. "You're not evil for what you did today. I promise." Reading me correctly, as always, my shadow goes out of his way to reassure me.

"Even what I did to Tristan? I fed his crazy with my own today. No way did that help him with his issues." My guilt eats away at me.

"Tristan had those issues way before he met you. If anything, I think you connected with him on a level no one else has been able to reach him on. Now that he knows you share in that kind of darkness with him he's more apt to listen to you than he is us."

Reed turns so that I can see his hazel eyes. They're sad, as expected, but he's not pulling away from me. He's here, and that's something.

"She said, *'She was his favorite'*. What do you think that means?" I ask out of nowhere. I can't get those words out of my head.

"I don't know," Reed answers, thinking I was talking to him since I'm staring at him.

"It's what she said first. It's odd, don't you think? When I forced her to tell me about my mother, the first thing that came out of her mouth was *'she was his favorite'*. Almost like she was jealous," I continue on.

"Does it matter?" Reed asks gently.

I huff. "It all matters, Reed. It matters to me."

"You'll drive yourself insane with thoughts like that. Isn't it better to focus on finally having your answers? Now you know that your parents were in love. They both wanted you, and didn't want to leave you."

"Somehow, that makes it worse," I tell him.

"She fought for you," Ash rumbles behind me. "You thought she threw you away, but she fought for you. I know that's important to you."

"It is," I say quietly.

"They never bonded," I point out. Something about this seems important. "If they loved each other, and she was in danger, then why didn't he change her and bond them together? She would have been stronger."

"She said the baby, you, made your mother stronger than they expected. Maybe your father thought that would be enough to protect her. Or he didn't know she was in danger at all," Reed guesses.

"He was an Alpha and she was pregnant with his only heir. You don't think he'd do everything he could to keep her safe?" I mean, really.

As I continue to think about it, I start to giggle. "Oh my God. I'm an idiot," I say as I jerk the covers away and dash for the main cabin.

Most of the guys are asleep, reclined in seats and sprawled out where there's room. Kellan and Finn sit side by side, arms and legs crossed identically as their heads lean into each other. They're almost too cute to wake.

I shake them both anyway. "Wake up, wake up!" I giggle excitedly.

"Kitten?" Kellan asks groggily.

"Yep. Me. I have the best news ever!" I squeal.

Finn looks at me warily, probably wondering how I went from depressed to unnaturally excited in the span of an hour. In fact, he probably assumes I've lost my mind. Maybe I have, but that's why I have these two. One twin to diagnose me, the other to find a way to fix me.

"They never bonded!" I tell them with a big smile.

"Who?" Kellan asks.

"My parents. They weren't bonded. Odd, right? Also odd... why would my father not give the cure to his own pack members?" I ask, not really looking for an answer.

"He only gave it to the women at the village," Finn says, drawing it out. I think he's starting to put it together, too.

"Right. A village that was still secluded, instead of doing his research on his own pack lands? If they were cured then why was he still working in secret, not dosing his own female population with the cure?" I say skeptically.

"You think he didn't have it?" Finn asks.

"I think he figured out that changeable females, unbonded, were still fertile and able to bear human babies. Whatever he gave them wasn't a cure for them...it was a cure for their offspring," I theorize.

Finn's eyes light up. "Most wolves would bond before trying

to make babies. Bonded females were at the mercy of the disease, probably carried by their mates and transferred in the bonding process. Bonded wolves equal wolf pregnancy resulting in a pup. Wolf plus unbonded changeable female equals what? A human pregnancy resulting in a changeable male or female baby?"

"Or...a human child already carrying their wolf inside them, needing to bond to change? Like me. I don't think those women were given a cure, I think I was the cure my mother bragged about. If my father had a cure, he'd have shared it. I know he would. But my mother got it from somewhere that he found the cure, most likely him telling her so after she became pregnant."

"That would mean that all his work wasn't lost. Whatever he gave them, gave your mother, would still be in your DNA. We could reverse engineer it and find out what it was." Finn says quickly, excited.

"That would work for the infertile females...maybe. But what Kitten's saying could mean that she and the other children at the village might be the cure itself. We could possibly use her blood to cure females of infertility and also protect any female wolves at birth from the disease itself," Kellan states to his brother.

Then it clicks. "The scent! The scent at the village. It was familiar, but I couldn't place it. I don't forget things, but I couldn't remember where I've smelled it before. Because it smelled like me. Like the blanket I was found with in the dumpster. I didn't pick up on it because I smelled everything else, I didn't think to find my own scent on the blanket. Tell me we brought my treasure chest with us when we moved."

"We did," Finn confirms.

"Yes! Then I can test my theory. If I'm correct, that would mean that all those kids at the village carry the cure with them, too. That's the only reason they'd smell like me, right?"

"Right. Your parents were killed right at your birth, and those children were younger; they can't be siblings," Finn states.

"That would also explain why those women still agreed to mate with wolves when they seem to hate us so much. They must have known that any children they had with wolves would be protected from the virus. Those made with human men would have been susceptible, perhaps. Either that, or they weren't willing to risk it," Kellan theorizes.

"We'll need to put together a lab as soon as possible," Finn says as he reaches for his laptop.

"You think we're right? That we really might solve this after all?" I ask.

"You did, smart girl. You put the pieces together." Finn says sweetly, kissing me loud and wet on the cheek. I don't know if I've ever seen him so excited.

"Your father would be very proud of you, Kitten," Remy says from behind me, causing me to jump out of my skin.

My other mates are all awake now, having watched the three of us silently, letting us work through our thoughts. "You think so?" I ask through a smile.

"He would," Albert confirms. He knew the man, so I guess he would know.

"Good came out of this trip after all?" I question.

"It did," Remy confirms. I smile like an idiot, swiping happy tears from my face with the back of my sweater.

Ash picks me up, carrying me back to bed and wrapping me up in the blanket, burrito-style. "Get some sleep, baby. You need to relax and I'm tired. Do me a favor? Don't move until I get up. I don't want you out of my sight for a while."

"Okay," I promise.

Reed climbs back into bed a while later, snuggling into my side and dozing off quickly. My mind is working too hard to sleep, but I stay still and let them get some rest. Eventually I drift off in a fitful sleep, too.

We arrive home to cheers and applause from the gathered pack on the front lawn. I don't know why they're cheering, but I love their enthusiasm. It's infectious. The crowd parts as we make our way through them to the house. Only a few reach out to the guys, people they know, but each one has a kind word to say about our return. Whatever this is, it's nice.

Only a few murmurs and rumblings take place as Quinn and his friends follow behind us. Then again, my pack is fairly used to changed wolves by this point.

Mikey and my grandfather wait for us just inside the door. I'm shocked as Mikey launches his little body at me, hugging me around the waist. "Miss me?" I ask with a laugh.

"Maybe," he grumbles, but smiles back at me.

"Well, I missed you," I tell him, running my fingers through his hair. "Were you good?"

"Never!" he says proudly.

I laugh, hugging him. "That's my boy." I toss a wink at my grandfather to let him know I'm joking. I really hope Mikey didn't cause him too much trouble while I was away. For some reason, the kid has a knack for seeking out trouble.

"Don't let him lie to you, he was an angel," Maksim tells me, patting my cheek. Now who's lying?

I wave Quinn forward as everyone else makes their way into the house. "Mikey, this is Quinn and his friends. Quinn, this is my son. The one I was telling you about."

Mikey looks up at me with a confused look on his face. "You go away and bring me back an Australian?"

That has us all laughing. "He's not for you, you little weirdo. He's my friend; I just thought you should meet."

"And I'm not Australian, mate. I'm from New Zealand," Quinn adds, flicking his ear.

Albert takes over showing our new members where they can stay, while the rest of us head upstairs. I make a face at the third floor as a whole. You would think after being away I'd feel relieved to be back, but this place still doesn't feel like home.

I take a quick shower, not wanting to dawdle. Mikey has discovered something called the *Marvel Universe*, and we decide to make a night of watching as many movies as we can before falling asleep. So, with a bowl full of popcorn, I sit wrapped in a blanket on the floor. Logan sits behind me, drying my hair as the first movie begins.

Hours later I'm staring at screen intently, trying to decide if I love Loki or hate him. Mikey is beside me, face covered in chocolate from way too many brownie bites. Ash is the only one keeping up with us. Actually, I think he's more into this than me and Mikey. We've already discussed our favorites. Mikey is a loyal Iron Man fan, Ash favors the Hulk (naturally), and I'm crushing hard on Thor. But Hawkeye is so freaking cool and mysterious that I like him, too. I'm determined to get my hands on a bow as soon as I can. I'm positive that I can get Finn to design some arrows that explode on contact for me. I tried to wake up Jace and ask him to get me a bow, but he just looked at me like I was insane and promptly went back to sleep.

I'm pretty sure the sun has already come up, and I'm sure this is a prime example of bad parenting. On the other hand, thoroughly researching a subject matter isn't a bad thing. Besides, I missed the little guy. I'm glad we found something we can share, even if it's just movies. Completely awesome movies, but still.

During the slower parts, Mikey talks to me. He tells me about his refusal to learn another language and his total dislike of tea. He was able to break Maksim down until he let him enjoy sweet iced tea with him instead of the traditional stuff. I suppose that's proof that the old Alpha just enjoys having the company.

He also let Mikey ride on him for a run with some of the other pack members. It warms my heart to hear that he wasn't left out while I was gone. The two seem to really have gotten along.

When Mikey starts yawning more than not, I decide to call it a night. I help him wash his face before we brush our teeth together, competing over who can hold the mouthwash the longest before it burns too much. I totally let him win that one. Tucking him in is an easy task with him being as tired as he is. I nearly break my ankle on the mess that is his floor, though. Seriously, the guys may have gone a bit overboard on toys. Which only makes me think again about not being prepared for the baby.

Not yet feeling sleepy myself, I snag Jace's computer out of his room and settle in behind Remy's legs on the couch. A general search for "what babies need" pulls up several websites with checklists. Many of the lists are much the same, the only variance being if a hospital checklist is attached. I'm only somewhat satisfied with my find. It's good to know that babies don't need as many things as I first thought; it turns they sleep more than anything. But I'm not having a normal human baby. There's no checklist for my baby, and that frustrates me.

Sending several saved files to the printer, I click on a link for a baby registry. It's like a fun game where you collect all the things you want and list them for other people to buy. I use it to mark several items I want to remember, along with a few themes that I think are awesome. I'll have to ask the guys' opinions, though. It would also be easier if we knew whether we're having a boy or a girl. Almost all baby stuff is categorized by gender; including gender neutral, which translates into the boring stuff.

Curiosity gets the better of me and I spend the next hour or so researching wolf pregnancies and births. Some of what I learn makes me nauseated. Like seriously, I'm *not* going to be eating any placenta or licking my baby once it comes from *there*.

Other things, like the whole making a den thing, sounds like a good idea. I wonder if that translates into a nursery for the baby, but maybe not. I do like the idea of creating a space not just for the baby, but for all of us. I open Jace's email and write down my thoughts, sending it to Logan. I figure I can ask either of them for it later.

I must fall asleep mid-browse, because the next thing I know I'm awoken to the smell of bacon. My mouth watering, I open my eyes to see all of my mates gathered around the laptop I was using. By the time they figure out I've woken up, half the plate of bacon has disappeared into my stomach.

"Hey!" Logan laughs, pointing at me. "That was for everyone."

I shrug. "You were neglecting it. I was giving it a proper home." I pat my belly proudly.

"It's good to see your appetite has returned in the presence of Tristan," Ash notes.

I nod, shoving another crisp slice in my mouth. "His food is magic."

"Thanks, sweetie. You're adorable with bacon grease all over your face, you know?" he tells me playfully, leaning in to lick at my lips. Well, hell. That shouldn't be hot, but it *so* is.

"How late did you stay up?" Kellan asks, frowning at me in disapproval.

"Uh, well, Mikey and I made it all the way through most of the first *Avengers* movie. I put him to bed, then looked things up on the internet."

"We can see that. Interesting topics you were researching there, Kitten." Jace smirks. "You know, we have a few females here who have given birth. You could ask them what it's like to give birth to a pup," he suggests.

I nod, attempting to bat Logan's hand away as he tries to steal my bacon. He's too quick, though, and manages a handful that he shares with Reed. "I thought of that as well. I plan on asking them for advice. My grandfather, too."

"Speaking of him, he's asked to take Mike and his friends to an arcade and ice cream shop in town. Would that be okay with you? I figured we could all ride together, and we'll hit up a few shops and pick up things for the nursery. How does that sound?" Remy asks.

I'm on my feet in a flash, already running to change out of my pajamas. "Oh, wait! The lists." I turn back to the guys. "I printed lists," I tell them.

They laugh at my excitement. "We'll bring your lists. Go get ready, crazy girl," Logan tells me as he shoos me away.

I stick my tongue out at him playfully before bouncing all the way to my room.

Remy honks the horn as Maksim's vehicle makes a turn, heading for the arcade, and our cars continue toward the shopping center in town. I wave to Mikey and the other kids as they pull away. They were over the moon about the trip out of the house. To be cautious, Ash sent a few of his best soldiers with them to keep watch. Quinn volunteered to supervise, but I think he just wanted to go play, too. I don't blame him, as it does sound like fun.

Although, my guys and I are going to have our own fun. Pulling into the parking garage of the sprawling shopping center, I barely wait until the car's in park before shrugging out of my seatbelt. Reed holds me back from jumping out too soon.

"Calm down, little lady. We have the whole day. No need to rush." He chuckles, helping me out.

We enter a very large store first. It has all kinds of things, not just baby stuff. I read the overhead signs, looking for directions to the right section. I recognize the name of the store and squeal excitedly. "Hey! I have a registry here. Did you bring the printout of the list?" I ask no one in particular.

"Yes, yes, we know. That's why we came here first. We brought your precious list," Logan teases.

"They had a really cool baby cage on the website. It was round and had a veil thing on it. It was cooler than the rectangle ones," I explain.

Ash chuckles. "You really have to stop calling it a baby cage, baby. It just doesn't sound right."

"Well, it cages a baby in, doesn't it?" I ask.

"Yes, but let's call it a crib anyway," he says uncomfortably.

"Fine," I sigh. "They had a really cool *crib* here." I draw the word out, rolling my eyes.

Ash picks me up by the hips from behind, making me yelp in surprise as he nips at my neck. "Don't be difficult," he jokes.

I laugh with the rest of the guys as he carefully places me back on my feet. We find the right section; a few styles of cribs already put together line one wall, along with car seats, rocking chairs, and bouncy chairs. I'm disappointed that the one I liked is decorated differently here than the picture on the website. This one is made up in some children's character, whereas the one online was done in pink and white checkers with ruffles and the veil hanging from the ceiling.

"It doesn't look the same," I tell them, biting my lip as I circle around it. This one is also white, whereas the one I wanted was a dark wood.

"This is just the one they put together so people can see what it looks like. Look over here." Jace points out a stack of boxes showing a small picture of the crib in different finishes. "Which one did you like?"

I point at the right one. "This one, but it's all plain-looking." I make a face at it.

"Everything is sold separately, Kitten. We can put together any look you want. I'm sure they sell everything they advertised on the internet," Logan explains.

"Oh, okay. I liked the pink set," I tell them, my eyes searching for where they keep the decorations.

"You think we're having a girl?" Remy asks, sounding slightly horrified.

I shrug. "There's a fifty-percent chance."

"Baby, I hope your heart isn't set on having a girl. Females are still very rare in our world," Ash says gently. Well, as gently as Ash's deep voice allows.

"So, no pink?" I hedge.

"I don't know how our son will feel about pink," Remy says.

"You never know, our baby might like pink no matter the gender," I supply. I know *I* like pink. And he'll be a baby, so he won't care. I'm the one who has to look at all his stuff.

"Maybe, but I was thinking we could look outside the gender box and go with something that would suit a boy or girl," Reed chimes in.

I make a face. "You mean that boring yellow or pea-green?"

He laughs. "No. More like fire-engine red, or forest green. Orange is gender-neutral, in my opinion. Not that I ever thought genders could claim colors. If you're dead-set on pink, I'm sure there's a way we could make it masculine enough for a boy."

"I'm not set on anything really. I just liked the way the crib looked on the computer. I guess we could do dark green and gold, like the Ivaskov insignia? He'll most likely be Alpha one day, after all. Or at least, that's what everyone is hoping for," I suggest.

"What about green and silver? Those go together really well, too. We could do silver silk sheets, green bedding and trim, with a silver curtain in matching silk," Logan states, eyes far away as he imagines it in his head.

"Yeah, we could do a mural on one wall. A forest maybe. Put it on the side facing the window and let the light play over it. I could add in some metallic paint, make it sparkle like a true forest," Reed adds.

I smile, the mental picture becoming clear in my mind. "I like it." I turn to the others, gauging their reactions. We all seem satisfied with this idea.

"Did you guys see my email?" I ask.

"I wasn't aware you had an email address," Finn says with a brow raised.

I shake my head. "I sent it from Jace to Logan last night."

"Oh, yeah. I saw it. I thought it was from Jace and, honestly, it was just a jumble of thoughts," Logan says sheepishly.

"Well, I was thinking we could knock down a wall between two of the rooms. Like have an archway or something between them so that we can have an area for us in the nursery. Remember those big cushion things in the library at the old house? We could have some of those, maybe a low bookshelf where we put books we can read to him, and a few rocking chairs or a bed for napping with him? I don't know, it was just a thought," I explain. I guess it isn't really thought out.

"Like a den," Kellan adds, getting it right off. "You did quite a bit of research on them last night. You want to make a den for all of us to spend time with the baby?"

I bite my lip. "Yeah, kind of. There's a lot of us, and we're spread out a lot. I thought it might be nice to have a centralized area where the baby will be most of the time. Where we can all stop by and hang out whenever we have time. Does that make sense?"

"It makes perfect sense, Kitten. It's a lovely idea," Logan says softly, coming to kiss my forehead. He steps back, looking around the store. "All right. Fuck this store, we'll make everything custom. Let's go look at clothes already," he says, clapping his hands with a bright smile.

"I'll make the bed," Ash tosses out. "Rem, you can help me

with the plans. Kitten, how about we keep the circle crib idea, but we lower it so our pup can get in it himself when he's in wolf form? We'll keep part of it open with cushions under the opening, so he'll never fall out."

I smile widely at him. "That sounds amazing. Can we still do the dark wood?" I point at the box with the finish I like.

"We could." Ash nods.

"Do you like that, or this better?" Logan shoves his phone in front of me, showing me pictures of a pale, almost grey, wood.

"Oooh, I like this. It would go really well with all the silver, right?" I ask.

"I think so. I'd have to see it for myself. We'll order samples and see which works best."

We leave the furniture area after picking out several car seats. We don't get them, but Jace takes a picture of the ones we want to order online later. I don't really have an opinion on those. Remy and Ash debate over which ones are safer, and we choose those ones. Logan swears he'll fabricate custom cushions for those as well.

I'm a little disappointed that we don't get much to bring home, but knowing that the guys are going to take the time to make our baby everything with their own hands makes me love them more than I thought I could. We do, however, get lots of tiny little clothes, bottles, and a breast pump. We aren't very clear if I have to stay in wolf form until the baby will be done with milk, or if I'll be able to switch back and forth. I think the guys are hoping for the latter, so that they can take turns feeding it.

We also collected an unreasonable number of blankets, towels, and tiny robes. Mostly because those were so cute and everyone had an opinion on which was softer, warmer, or best for wrapping a baby up in. From the large selection of them, I've learned that babies seem to like dangly things. So, we also got dangly things for over the bed, the car seats, the stroller, and some we can manually dangle above his head. By the time we finish shopping, I'm in desperate need for food and a nap. Who knew shopping could be so exhausting?

Ash, Remy, Logan, and Reed split from the rest of us as we head home. They said they have a few more places to go before they meet us at the house. I cuddle up to Tristan on the way home. I know who feeds me. He whispers sweet nothings about macaroni and cheese and ham the whole way there. I don't think he means for it to come across as seductive, but it sounds that way to me in my state of hunger.

I sit on the counter, close to the cooking food, as I watch my sweetest mate move about the kitchen like he owns it. I suppose he does, but it never fails to turn me on watching him command the room. He really enjoys what he does, and it makes me happy to see it. I pull him to me as we wait for the ham to warm in the oven.

Tristan leans back against the counter, between my thighs with his back to my chest. He's still taller than me but I rest my cheek on his shoulder, my hands splayed over his chest. "I love you," I say, just because I feel like saying it.

He brings a hand up to rest over mine. "I'll never get tired of hearing those words coming from your lips." He turns his head to smile his perfect Tristan smile at me. God, this boy is beautiful.

I urge him to turn to me, running my fingertips over his jawline as I stare into his chocolate eyes. He leans in, kissing my lips gently. His hands slide up and down the outside of my thighs, heating me up in more ways than one. I deepen the kiss, needing to taste him. To my delight, he groans. I love the sounds I evoke from all my mates.

After a while, Tristan breaks the kiss to lean his head against mine. We stay that way until the oven beeps. With a smacking kiss to my nose, he moves to get the food ready to take upstairs. If he was anyone else, I'd knock the food from his hand and take him right here on the floor. Being that this is Tristan, I know he'll make me wait until after I've eaten enough for four people. By the very Logan-like smirk on his face, I know he knows where my head is at.

Reluctantly, I shake off the lust and follow him upstairs to eat on the balcony off his room. He watches my mouth as I eat and sip from the Champagne glass filled with sparkling cranberry juice. We talk about the day, about looking forward to the spring and the orchard coming to life, about missing each other when I was away, and about our time at the beach. Lunch one on one with Tristan is pleasant and relaxing, much like the man himself.

When it's clear that I couldn't eat another bite if I tried Tristan stands, offering me his hand. Leading me back into his room he stops us beside the bed, leaning his tall frame down to gently suck at my lips. I grip his shirt, ready to tear it free, but he stops me.

"Slower," he pants. "I want to savor you. I don't want to hurt you."

"You won't hurt me, Tristan," I respond.

"I just... Let me love you, baby." He gives me no time to respond, his lips covering mine, distracting me.

I slowly unbutton his shirt, dragging the fabric down his arms. Backing me to the bed Tristan strips me down to my red panties, leaving those on. With a gentle shove to my shoulders, I fall back. My eyes close, feeling the palms of his hands skim up the sides of my legs. Electricity sparks at his touch, hypnotizing me.

"Give me those eyes, sweet girl," he demands.

I look to him, seeing his passion swirl within them. Parting my legs, eyes locked on my face, he leans in, inhaling my scent, growling in satisfaction. Holding back is taking a toll on him, as well as me. With a long finger he slides the scrap of fabric covering me out of his way, exposing me to him. A long, needy lick at my core is all it takes to set me off.

Tristan plunges two fingers into me, driving my climax higher and higher. While I ride out the heavy bliss that follows an explosion, he laps up my juices like his own personal reward. Time and time again he pushes me over the cliff of satisfaction, each time growing more desperate, his ministrations harsher, deeper, more all-consuming. No matter how many times I crash, he never lets me out of the haze of lust he creates in me. I chase more, always more. I claw at him, his back, his shoulders, pulling at his hair and grinding my hips to his face.

At some point I realize I'm screaming, my throat raw with my efforts. I don't know what I'm saying, don't know if it's even English or if it matters at all. All I know is that I need this. I need him. Like if he stops, so will my reason to exist.

By the time he finally mounts me, I'm a complete and utter mess. He slides in to the hilt, moaning at the tight fit. I don't realize I've been crying until he brings a hand up to wipe away my tears with the pad of his thumb. He kisses me sweetly, reverently. The strokes of his hips are strong, deep, filled with meaning. He fills me. Every part of me, with every part of himself. He takes from me as much as he gives.

Panting, slick with sweat, and filled to bursting with love and Tristan, I can't help but think the darkness that lives within us is no match for the kind of light we create when we come together.

CHAPTER FIFTEEN

Ash

Demo is always fun. There's something so satisfying about using brute force to tear down something that once was, but no longer is. Or maybe I just like hitting things. If it were up to me we'd be doing all the demo today, but considering Remy's new plan is to completely remodel the entire top floor that might mean a total collapse. At first I'd thought he was nuts, but I'd forgotten how one had to be careful what they said around him. You never know what's going to trigger his next project. In this case, it was all the talk of the pup's room. I blame Kitten.

After our talk of building the room to suit our own unique needs Rem has been restless, awake at all hours, doing God knows what. When he showed us the blueprints he'd been creating, it made sense. We all sense that Kitten isn't thrilled with our living arrangements. At first, we had thought that she'd adjust or change things around until she was satisfied, but she simply doesn't like being here. Remington decided to do something about that. I have to give it to him—his plan is genius. And I get to do demo.

"Are you sure we'll have this completed before she gives birth?" Logan asks, twisting and turning one of the blueprints like he knows how to read it.

Remy shrugs, carefully removing the paper from his hands. "It's not like we know when that's to take place. Her pregnancy appears to move at its own odd pace."

"True dat," Logan responds, making me cringe.

I point at him in warning. "No." I'm not listening to his past-its-time fad speech. Took him forever to stop saying "whaaasssuuup" because of a dumb movie he went to see.

"With construction mostly finished on the neighborhoods we created here, we should be able to dedicate most of our time to finishing this as soon as possible. Starting on the side with all the unused bedrooms will make it easier. We'll get the basics out of the way before starting on Tristan's new kitchen. The plumbing is going to be the real bitch," Rem continues.

"We'll get it done, man. Don't worry." I clap him on the shoulder before attacking the wall again.

"Where is our girl, by the way?" Logan asks, finally returning to his task of tearing up old carpeting.

"Finn and Kellan took her to the bookstore. I don't anticipate them returning anytime soon," Rem tells him with an amused smile. Yeah, Finn and Kitten in a bookstore. They'll be there until someone kicks them out. Hopefully she won't be upset with the mess we're making. I feel like maybe we should have warned her, but when Remy showed us the plan it seemed like a good idea at the time to just get started.

I don't know why I'd worried. Kitten is beyond ecstatic as we fill her in. I'm not usually jealous of my brothers, but the smile she gifts Remy almost pushes me to it. Damn, she's gorgeous when she's happy.

Over the next several weeks, we form a pattern that works for us. With Remy at the helm as general contractor, and Jace and Logan as project managers, everything runs as smooth as silk. Coordination always was our strong suit. With the rest of us acting as sub-contractors, we take the opportunity to add in our own bits and pieces.

Personally, I focus on adding additional security. With the new setup focusing around a centralized kitchen and living area, and a continuous hallway following all the way around, that leaves the bedrooms on the north and south sides exposed to the exterior, and the offices on the east and creative spaces and playrooms on the west side. After running it by Rem, we agreed on implementing false walls throughout the closets in the bedrooms leading to an escape tunnel. A hatch will be added to the floors in the playrooms, leading to the same tunnels. My plan for bulletproof windows was out-voted, but we agreed to only one balcony off of our new shared bedroom. We'll all still have our own rooms, for when we want them, but with the pup coming and with Kitten enjoying us all together it was a good call on Remington's part to include a larger room to accommodate us all. I highly doubt Kitten will ever be alone in that area where a threat from the balcony will be an issue.

Finn has wanted to implement smart home technologies for a while now, and works closely with Logan to add in all of the electrical components he'll need while not interfering with the overall design. He's why I let the bulletproof windows go. With his help, we decided that a perimeter security system that allowed me or my security force to be notified when windows were opened or anything passed through doorways would suffice. I especially like his idea of tech bracelets that trigger access to our floor. Without a bracelet, the doors won't even open. You can go out, but not in.

Keeping Kitten busy proves to be the hardest task, as she's

chomping at the bit to help in any way she can. Wolf pregnancy or not, none of us are willing to put her in harm's way or let her do any heavy lifting. We take turns distracting her with food, sex, or getting her input on design elements. It was actually her idea to place our shared bedroom in the center of the south wall. That way a connecting nursery could take one side, and leave room for bedrooms for older children on the other side of our room. When the children get older, they could take rooms on the north side of the house, further away from our bedroom, giving them and us a bit more privacy. We had to move Reed and Kitten's art studio from the original plans, but we worked it out. Their corner studio will feature glass exterior walls, which most certainly *are* bulletproof. I put my foot down on that one.

Kitten has really done well reaching out to other pack members since we began renovations. I know she started out just trying to stay out of the way and letting us focus, but it's good to see her discovering friendship. As much as I hate that most of her new friends are male, I'd never want her to feel like we're all she has. I think she's a little too young and possessive of us to develop relationships with the other females in the pack just yet, but she's made a real effort to spend time with them and get their advice. Once she gets her bearings and feels secure, I'm sure she'll be more open to them. As of now, she's wary of them. It doesn't help that most wolf females are spoiled rotten. That's not something Kitten can relate to. She's too independent. Besides, any male wolf stupid enough to make a move on my girl knows he's setting himself up for a world of hurt. While the guys and I are content to keep our inner circle mostly closed to others, since we have each other for friendship and comradery, Kitten likes being accepted by others. She likes listening to them and hearing their stories. Her constant need to gather information drives her to seek out as many people as possible. I'd never deny her that. It's just one more thing to admire about her.

By the time we begin moving in furniture, Kitten's stomach looks ready to explode. I've noticed her growing ever more self-conscious about her growing body, but I don't think I'll ever be able to describe how beautiful pregnancy makes her to me. I just don't have the words. She sleeps more throughout the day than before, often napping in Mike's room while he plays video games or does something quietly to let her rest. He's a good kid like that. He knows she's getting anxious about letting him out of her sight, and instead of rebelling against it he seems to enjoy all the fuss she makes over him.

The two of them also like spending time out in the orchard, seeing the world around them coming to life as the snow melts and things bloom. Kitten and Reed sometimes paint out there, Mike content to watch them or doodle in his coloring books. Watching her attempt yoga in her state is entertaining for us all. She glares at us when she catches us watching her do her Reed-approved pregnant poses, but it's worth it. With her hips widening to accommodate childbirth, there's only more to drool over now. A fact I take full advantage of when taking her from behind in bed. Her growing belly keeps me from having her under me and possessing her as I normally would, but something could be said about bending her over any soft surface available and letting my hands roam her full breasts and pup-filled stomach. Male pride only enhances the experience, if you ask me. That pregnant woman? Yeah, she's mine. I did that. Probably.

"What is this thing?" I ask, finally getting the table part of this contraption together and going for the three-panel mirror that apparently sits atop it.

Logan peers around an over-stuffed chair he's angling through the doorway. Seeing what I'm pointing at, he snorts in amusement. "That's Jace's new obsession, I'm sure. He got her a vanity table so he could watch her primp. I think the ass forgot that she doesn't primp, but he's holding out hope."

I raise an eyebrow. "She'll brush her hair here?" I ask, trying not to sound as interested in the answer as I am.

Logan must pick something up in my tone because he pauses his task to stare at me. "Ah, I see. Jace isn't the only one who likes to watch," he teases me.

I shrug, unashamed. I'll have to remember to thank the golden dandy next time I see him. No more hiding behind a door while she tames all that glorious pale hair.

"Come help me with this," Logan grunts as he tries to haul the massive mattress onto the frame. He had to make it in this room, as it'd never fit through any door. Remy and Reed designed and put together the frame, while I hand-carved the detailing.

I help lift the awkward pallet, sliding it into the base. I grunt in approval at the perfect fit. The bed itself is low to the floor, a flat base for the custom mattress to rest on. Corner posts rise several feet in the air, slimming down and curving to meet in the middle. Supporting beams rest between them, allowing for fabric to drape over them, creating a canopy. I imagine it will feel as if we're in own little world once it's finished.

"Hey." Kellan pops his head around the door. "We've got countertops," he informs me.

"You got this?" I ask Logan, wiping my brow with the back of my hand. How is it possible that tearing down an entire level and rebuilding it is easier than decorating?

"Yeah, I'm good, homie. Send someone back to help if you can. I know Tristan's been waiting on those countertops for fucking ever. Don't make him wait," he responds as he starts pulling out new pillows from their packaging and tossing them at the bed.

I find Tristan, Reed, and Rem already maneuvering the first

piece up the second-story stairs. The solid granite is heavy, but no real issue for the four of us. The real problem is getting it angled correctly to walk it into our personal kitchen. Peeking through a gap in the covering, I take a moment to admire the shiny black material. It's a good choice. This kitchen will be a bit darker, done in red and black with cream cabinetry, but the skylights and track lighting should brighten it up quite well.

As we lift the countertop into place, Reed jerks away, almost causing it to slip from my grip. "What the fuck?" I ask angrily. "If we drop this, it'll be another three weeks before we can get a new one out here."

His only response is a groan. The rest of us get it situated atop the lower cabinets before I'm able to see what's going on with him. He's bent at the waist, holding his stomach like he's been shot. We're on him in seconds, prying his hands away to check the wound. When we see nothing bleeding, Remy calls for Kellan.

"Just hang in there, man. Kell will be here in a minute," I assure him, patting his back awkwardly. I'd try to get him to tell me what's going on, but his jaw is locked tight and I don't want to frustrate him when he'd try to answer. Sweat breaks out on his forehead as he's left panting through the pain.

As soon as Kellan and Finn round the corner both of them freeze, faces draining of all color. "Oh, shit."

I scowl at them. "What the hell, Kellan? Get over here and help him."

Finn shakes his head slowly before eying his brother with a gulp. "It's not him, it's Kitten."

It takes me longer than it should to process those words. As Kellan finally snaps out of his trance and moves to instruct Reed to rein in his connection to Kitten and breathe, I'm out the door and down the steps, needing to get to her.

How could this happen? I know she didn't leave the grounds

today. Did someone manage to get to her here? On our lands? Is she shot? Stabbed? Oh, God…is the pup okay? My mind spirals out of control as my wolf takes over and sniffs the air for her scent. It's all over the place. Tracking her through the house is nearly impossible, but once it leads me to a door, I crash through it and am able to pick up a stronger, newer scent leading to one of the houses in one of the communities we built.

Kitten is already on her way back to the house when I find her. She's in wolf form, whining on the ground, surrounded by other wolves nudging and licking at her in solidarity. She pants hard as I run for her. Tipping her head back, she howls loud enough for anyone on or near the property to hear her cry for help.

A resounding chorus springs up in aid of their Luna. Every wolf, in every corner of this place, sings as one, no doubt barreling straight for her.

Releasing my own howl, letting them know I've got her, I quickly shift, gathering her in my arms. I don't see or smell any blood, so I don't waste time running her back to Kellan. She pants and whimpers in my arms, taking turns burying her snout against my neck and nipping at my arm nervously. I ignore the pain, knowing she doesn't mean anything by it. She's in pain and scared. I can smell the fear coming off her coat. The remaining wolves form a guard around us all the way back to the house, joined by any others that were out here.

The guys are waiting for us at the back door, already prepared to move her upstairs. The place is a madhouse, pack members gathering both inside and out. I bypass them all, following my brothers up the flights of stairs and into the room Kellan directs me toward. My brow furrows as I notice which room it is.

"What? I…oh." Realization dawns on me and I look to the

white wolf in my arms in horror. "Oh. Fuck. Oh!" I stare at her stupidly.

"Put her down on the blankets, Ash. She'll be more comfortable," Kellan instructs. I do as he says, placing her down gently in the middle of the bazillion blankets Kitten has been dragging here for the past few days. No one knew exactly why she was doing it, but we've had our suspicions. It's just a large, empty closet with no windows. I think Logan had planned to use it as an overflow closet or something. Along with the blankets, Kitten has gathered quite a bit of odds and ends in here, all shoved up against the wall haphazardly. We let it go, not questioning the crazy, hormonal pregnant woman. It's still kind of crazy that she prepared a den, but most likely she was working off instinct as usual.

As I step back to give Kellan room to do whatever it is that Kellan does, I'm handed a pair of sweatpants. Stepping into them, I seek out Reed. I toss an arm over his shoulder, my eyes not leaving my mate. "Sorry for yelling at you, man. You all right now?"

"Yeah. I closed the door on the connection for now. I'm not sure my body or brain could understand what she's going through at the moment," he says hollowly, watching the scene as well.

There's barely enough room for all of us in this closet but we give Kellan as much room as we can as he adjusts Kitten on her side, elevating her head. He starts giving orders to us all, making room for Finn to assist him when the time comes. Tristan fetches a pot of hot water and Kellan's bag for him, while Logan goes for the washcloths and warming blankets for the pup. Remy heads downstairs to tell Maksim and Albert what's going on, having them spread the word that the Luna is just fine and giving birth. Jace heads for the medical equipment Kellan asks for. Reed and I mostly try to stay out of the way, too stunned to do much.

Everything happens so fast, yet also seems to be moving in slow motion. Heart in my throat I keep my eyes trained on Kitten, knowing that in a short time I'm going to be a father.

~

Kitten

Why did I ever allow this to happen? Seriously, why do people do this? It's insane, absolutely absurd. I'm never letting one of those assholes touch me again. Nope. Never again. Not if this is the result. The overwhelming pain ebbs again, letting me pant for much-needed air. Kellan praises me for breathing while trying to remind me to do it even when the pain returns. Easier said than done. I try not to snap at him or Finn when they move too close. I don't want to hurt them, but I kind of do at the same time. Mostly, I just want to bite something. Actually, I'd really love a drink right now. I don't know how long this is supposed to last, but the closer the contractions get the more I feel like I'm going to pass out or die. I'm hot, I'm cold, I'm nervous and excited. It's all too much on top of the pain.

"She's thirsty," Reed tells Tristan, who goes flying from the room, no doubt getting me a drink. If I was in any other situation, the guys' behavior would have me giggling hysterically. Their panicked expressions and worried faces put me on edge at first, but I'm starting to realize that they're just as scared of this baby as I am. Even Kellan is a little tense. Finn tells him more than once that they've got this, reminding him that he's here to assist him.

I thirstily lap up the water placed in front of me. I have mere moments before yet another contraction rocks my body, every muscle in me rebelling, working to squeeze this baby out of me. They get closer together until I can't tell if there's any break between them at all. I'm a snarling, clawing mess, howling with everything in me for someone to put a stop to this. I can't even hear Kellan's instructions anymore.

What I can only assume is hours later Tristan moves into my line of sight, lowering himself down to rest on his heels, hands out in front of him. He speaks, low and soft, trying to calm me. While his voice does soothe me, as always, it does nothing to calm the body-wracking pain. Stroking my head, he eyes me sympathetically before moving against the wall with the others. The more time that goes by the more worried they get. Kellan reminds them frequently that this is a process and that I'm built to handle it. I don't know for sure if that last part is true. It sure doesn't feel that way.

Eventually a new, terrible feeling takes place between my hind legs. The pressure intensifies as the squeezing in my abdomen hits a whole new level. It hurts so much that I forget to howl. Something is definitely coming out of me down there.

The guys all crouch down, leaning forward to get a closer look as Kellan does something I can't see, but feels like he's washing me off. Finn instructs Remy to lay a soft towel over his outstretched arms, turning his body to face his brother's. He takes a deep breath before smiling over at me, telling me I'm doing a good job. I push with all the strength I have left, and the pain between my legs ebbs immediately.

The guys move into action instantly, but I don't watch what they're doing. Instead, I take a moment to catch my breath and rest my eyes. I hear whoops and cheers as the guys celebrate, as overly-emotional as I am.

Opening my eyes I scent the air, finding the new scent immediately. It smells of me, yet not fully. I also smell the twins. Not one of them or the other; the scent a combination of both, yet neither. My eyes land on a too-tiny-to-cause-that-much-pain ball of fur held aloft in Finn's arms. Closing his eyes, he drags his nose over the pup's head before sharing a conspiratorial smile with Kellan, who's beaming back at him with a smile brighter than I've ever seen it.

Casting my eyes around the room, all I see is smiles and a few teary eyes. There's no disappointment like I was afraid of. Finn hands the pup up to Remy, who reverently cradles him to his chest as Ash and Logan close in on either side of him to get a better look.

Reed gives me an odd look just before a shooting pain ricochets through my abdomen again. "So, I was right then," I hear him murmur before turning his frantic eyes away from me and darting them to the others. "We're going to need more blankets."

Everyone freaks out at once. Mostly me. With them talking over each other, they've forgotten that I have no voice to ask what the hell is going on. By the time they start paying attention to me again I'm lost to the pain once more, unable to hear any sound over my own pounding heartbeat and panting breaths.

Sometime later, I give birth to a blonde bundle of fur that seems to purr when cuddled. He smells of Reed and sunshine. The guys pass the pups around, each taking turns holding them and nuzzling their heads. No doubt memorizing their scents and just taking them in. This time, everyone looks to Reed to see if it's all over.

Sadly for me, but joyously for us all, it's not. Another round of pain brings another ball of fur; this time an orangey-red one with pure white fur on his paws, making him look like he's wearing socks. Even without the scent I'd know he was Remy's, that bright, fiery hair giving him away.

Next comes the biggest surprise of them all. A little girl. She's the smallest of them all, with a glossy black coat and white-tipped ears. She cries the quietest cry I've ever heard until her twin is born. He comes out fighting mad, and growling until he's brought close enough to smell all of his siblings. Once he does, he grunts and curls up for a nap. The guys chuckle and laugh at his attitude. A resounding "Alpha" choruses from their lips as one. Smelling of fire, charred wood, and smoke, Ash's pups stun the hell out of their father. He falls to his knees with a groan of "cruel gods" when our girl was born, and has been staring wide-eyed at his son since he was born.

I check in quickly with Remy to see if it upsets him that Ash ended up spawning the next Alpha and not him. I don't know if it's the joy of being a father to not one but five pups that make him a shining ray of joy, but Remy seems like he couldn't care less. All of them are overjoyed with the babies, none of them claiming their own offspring for themselves but excited and happy for each one of our children.

Finally getting the all-clear from Reed, who explains that he doesn't sense any emotions but mine coming from me, I'm cleaned up and lifted so that the blankets under me can be changed out for clean ones. Tired as I am, I greedily accept all the affection my mates shower me with. I wish I could shift so I could hug and kiss them back, but I can't find the energy to do so. When the pups start whining, they're reluctantly put down so that they can nurse from me.

The guys seem content to hang out with me and our pups in this small room, sprawling out where they can and basking in the afterglow of childbirth like they did something. I'd roll my eyes at them if I could. Playfully, of course, because now that the pain has receded I'm able to remember why I love them all so much. I'm happy that they're happy.

As the pups finish nursing they try to snuggle up under me, but the guys can't seem to help themselves and quickly snatch them up, wrapping them in blankets to keep them warm. I don't mind a bit, as I'm finally able to doze off.

Reed

Five pups. Hard to believe, and yet the simplest explanation all along. I had an inkling, but I was scared to mention it or to believe it myself. I had to be content with only ever having one pup. We all did. We may never get another, as children are so rare for our kind. If I had mentioned my suspicions to anyone else, I might have gotten their hopes up and taken away from the birth of our first child. It seemed impossible, so I had let it go. Thinking back, maybe that wasn't the wisest decision. Hard to feel bad about it, though. The others' faces were absolutely priceless.

Kitten finally gets some rest, eyeballing her pups safely in their fathers' care one last time before huffing and closing her eyes. I couldn't be prouder of my girl. She's been through a lot today, experiencing a mostly human birth and all the pain and waiting associated with it, while physically giving birth to wolf pups. I know it took a lot out of her.

Remy quietly goes to retrieve Mikey and to let Maksim know the good news. I watch everyone else, trying to remember this image the way Kitten does. Logan plays with our only female pup, teasing Ash as much as he can. "You're not going to wear all black like your daddy Ash, are you? No, of course not. Nothing but bright pinks and yellows and glitter for my little one. Lace and frills and ruffle socks, and every other girlie thing I can think of, huh? Yeah, you're going to love it," he jokes in a baby voice, though I know he's not joking at all. God help her, she's going to be the embodiment of all things female.

Currently, I snuggle our firstborn to my neck, the pup seeking out heat. He's an oddball for sure. Not one of us can tell whether he's Kellan's or Finn's. I suppose it doesn't matter, but I wonder if that will happen to those of us who aren't twins? Maybe it's because they share the same exact DNA or something. Either way they all smell of Kitten, and even though one came from me and smells of me I don't find myself placing him above the others. I love them all so much that I hardly know what to do with myself.

Remy returns with Mikey, letting him meet his brothers and sister, and letting the pups scent him as well. He doesn't stay long, letting his mom sleep as he reports back to Maksim how everything in here is going. We take our cue from the kid, reluctantly letting the pups snuggle up with each other and their mom to bond. Sneaking out of the closet and down the hall a ways, we form a plan for the night.

"We still have a lot to do to get this place pup-proof," Logan is explaining.

The rest of us agree, figuring out what we can get done without making too much noise. We don't know when Kitten will feel like leaving her makeshift den, but she'll need somewhere to go when she does. Our shared bedroom is practically ready, but I know she'll never sleep in there with the pups. She'll want to take them to the nursery.

Turns out we hadn't needed to rush around getting the house together. Kitten and the pups haven't left their little closet for nearly an entire week now. They mostly eat and sleep. Lots and lots of sleeping. Those of us who aren't busy usually sit or nap with them, or bring in visitors. Besides Maksim, Albert, and Mikey, Kitten only allows those in wolf form to approach our pups. Maksim had explained that the pack would all want to take turns taking care of them, but so far Kitten only allows others to exchange scents and sometimes find a spot to curl up in the room with them. Mikey usually reads them stories, though I can tell it makes him sad that Kitten can't communicate with him. He wants her back, and I don't blame him; I do as well. We've all explained that this is just temporary and what the pups need right now to nurse and grow strong. I'm pretty sure he and Remy have accidentally named the copper-coated pup. He's awake a lot more than his siblings, daring to venture further away from his mother than the others. He and Mikey have really bonded during those times, the pup always up for searching his older brother for snacks and something to chew on. Once Remy had witnessed this a few times he laughed, calling him his little Raider. The two of them have been calling him that ever since. We'll have to see what Kitten makes of the name, but I quite like it. It's fitting for the little guy. Makes we wonder what we'll name the others.

Kitten

I love my babies, I really do, but I'm not sure how much longer I can stay in this room. Grandfather had told me that I'd need to stay a wolf for several weeks, but after just one I think I'm losing my mind. I miss my mates and Mikey. Having actual conversations and eating with a fork. My only entertainment is when other wolves stop by, or when the pups are awake and wreaking havoc.

Okay, so maybe scooting their little bodies around the room isn't pure chaos, but it makes me a mess of nerves. I've had a lot of time to think, and I can't fathom a way in which I don't accidentally lose one of them or forget to feed one or something. Five is too many to ever look after properly. What happens when they start exploring more than this room? There are a million places they could hide and get lost. They're little enough to get stepped on if people aren't careful. Waking up this morning—at least I think it's morning—I've come to realize that we can never leave this room. It's just too dangerous. Shaking my head, I think back to the time I was worried about being a new mom to just one baby and messing it up.

Mikey pauses in his telling of *Harry Potter* as my red ball of fur finds a loose string in his pocket after practically climbing in, and pulls at it until he ends up rolling off his brother's leg. He yips at the string like it's the string's fault he fell before he attacks it again. My all-black pup watches him momentarily before shooting an unamused look in his direction and balling himself up for a nap. My girl tries to go play with him but her Alpha brother places a paw on her back to keep her in place, causing her to whine in protest. The little blonde's ears perk up at his sister's whine, making him think she's cold, as her smaller body usually is, and he pulls himself away from my neck to go snuggle with her. The tiny grey Alpha doesn't appreciate the newcomer, and growls, but blondie puts a paw over his brother's face to quiet him before dozing off happily next to their sister. I've come to note that he doesn't really care what the others think; he does what he wants to, and nothing and no one can ruin his mood.

Mikey, having enough of his pocket lining getting tugged on, gently picks up Raider and moves him away, much to the little guy's distress. Once that one sets his sights on something to play with, he's relentless. Pulling a hard candy from his other pocket he unwraps it and puts it in front of Raider, letting him lick at the sugary treat. Satisfied he didn't hurt his brother's feelings, he gives us all a wave goodbye and leaves.

As soon as he leaves, I realize his mistake. As does the haughty little future Alpha. Almost like he was waiting for it the ball of fur makes his way to Mikey's book, sniffing at the edges and pawing the cover. Getting the book open, he moves to stand on the open pages before I see his hind leg lift.

Snapping into motion, I move to save Mikey's book. I don't

realize I've shifted back to human until I see my hand reaching out for the naughty furball. Two things happen at once. One: five human babies appear in the place of wolf pups. Two: my tiny troublemaker pees all over me. Luckily, the book is saved. Not so much for me or the blankets we were lying on.

"Oh, you little..." I huff. "I don't know if you're mean or just far too territorial." I shake my head at the slightly-tanned little boy with dark fuzz for hair and big dark eyes staring up at me in shock.

The shock wears off and five extremely loud cries explode throughout the room. It startles me, having grown used to the tiny sounds of pups. These babies have extremely healthy lungs, it seems. Thankfully, my mates are always close by these days. Bursting through the door like the house is on fire, Jace and Logan's faces are as shocked as mine.

"What happened?" Jace asks, his eyebrows nearly hitting his hairline.

I point at the baby still lying atop a book. "He peed on me," I accuse.

Logan snickers, though he tries to hide it. "And that shifted the pups, how?"

I shrug my very human shoulder. "I don't know, but I really need a shower," I say over all the crying babies.

I reach out for my little Alpha, cradling him in my arms, letting him know I'm not actually mad at him. Babies make you weird, I've come to realize. Only they can literally pee on you and you still find it adorable. Logan picks up our girl in one arm and the redhead in the other. Jace grabs the other two, heading out into the hallway. My heart rate spikes as I lose sight of the babies, so I quickly move to follow him.

Jace has already handed off a baby to Tristan when I join them in our new living room. The only ones missing are Finn and Kellan. They busy themselves fawning over their first looks at the babies as I stand uncomfortably naked and covered in pee. I huff, handing the baby I'm holding to Remy before stalking away in search of a shower.

It only dawns on me later that I felt completely at ease leaving my pups in the care of their fathers. Standing under the hottest water I can handle I stretch my unused muscles, taking as much time as I want washing myself. Near the end of my blissful cleansing, Jace comes in to keep me company. I have to love Logan just a little harder for his design of this bathroom. With the spacious shower that rains water down from every direction to a tub that could pass for a small swimming pool, open to the room with plush benches and heated floors, it's a level of luxury I could have never imagined.

Sitting on one of the benches, Jace bounces a green-eyed, black-haired baby on his lap as he watches me finish up. I admire his perfectly coifed hair, and long torso and arms clad in a white dress shirt. His happy expression makes him appear young and carefree as his gold eyes bounce between me and the baby. "I've missed you," he tells me idly.

I smile over at him, toweling off. "I've missed you, too."

I dress in a pair of light pink sweatpants and a cream cami, topped with an oversized knit sweater in dark grey. I move behind him, wrapping my arms around his shoulders and burying my nose in his neck.

Bringing my chin up to rest on his shoulder, I look over my baby boy in a footed-pajama set trimmed in red. He's adorable. His tiny fingers are quite possibly the cutest thing I've ever seen. His big green eyes stare back at me, probably taking in my human features as much as I am his. He has a full head of shiny black hair, unlike the fuzz of our other dark-haired boy.

"They need names," I say to Jace, my eyes still on the baby.

"They do," Jace replies, turning his head to kiss my cheek. He stands, gathering the baby in his matching red blanket, then drapes an arm around my waist and ushers me from the bathroom.

Out in our new bedroom, my eyes track all the progress that's been made in here since the babies were born. The bed has been put together, the pillows and blankets added, along with a spacious sitting area and small dining area in front of the balcony doors. That's all I'm able to take in as my attention snags on the very large, very comfortable-looking bed with my entire family lounging on it.

My guys sit barefoot and relaxed around the group of babies who coo and gurgle happily in the center of them all. Mikey tickles the toes of one of his brothers as Logan looks to be struggling to get a pink onesie on my wiggly little girl.

I lean against a bedpost as Jace joins them on the bed, placing the baby down on a free pillow to prop him up. This, right here…is perfection. I could watch this for the rest of my life. I don't realize I'm crying until Kellan comes to stand next to me, a long finger swiping happy tears from my cheeks.

"Hey now, none of that," he whispers.

Tilting my head up to accommodate his tall form, I meet his eyes. "I'm just so happy," I tell him through a wide smile.

He smiles back. "I know. It's a little overwhelming, isn't it?"

I nod my head, reaching up on my tiptoes to kiss his pouty lips. "It is."

He guides me over to a short bench against one wall that sits in front of a beautiful table with mirrors. "Take your time brushing your hair and whatnot, we've got the little ones." With a kiss to the top of my head he joins the others, leaving me to stare at myself in the mirror.

The table holds all manner of things. I reach for some lotion that smells like crisp red apples and start applying it to my face and arms. I find a bright blue comb, using it to untangle my wet hair as I watch the guys behind me through the mirror. I can't keep the smile from my face. Meeting my own eyes in the mirror, I shake my head. What have I done to deserve all this? I can't imagine being happier. Despite Kellan's words I rush through brushing my hair out, leaving it to air dry.

Joining the guys on the bed, I squeeze between Reed and Finn, leaning into one and holding hands with the other. My eyes rake over each baby, noticing that each outfit has a matching blanket and socks. They eat up all the attention they're receiving, eyes flitting from each person to the next. Only the blonde is being held, but I knew he would be. He's a snuggler, that's for sure. Held in Reed's arms he faces out at me, his shocking eyes making me smile even more. One eye is a mix between green and blue, the other a light brown that turns darker depending on the light. It's stunning. He smiles when he sees me admiring him. I smile back, leaning in to kiss his little light blonde head.

"It still amazes me that they look like three-month-olds. That's going to make tracking their growth rates near impossible," Kellan muses.

"It should be fine. We'll measure and track them for future reference, but we'll have to keep in mind not to compare them with typical charts," Finn responds. He turns his head to look at me. "How are you feeling? I trust the shift back allowed you to heal nicely?"

I nod. "Yeah, I guess so. It definitely doesn't feel like I squeezed out five babies. My boobs are weird, though," I tell him as I cup my breasts, inspecting them again.

"How so?" Kellan asks.

I make a face. "I don't know. They're not sore really. More like heavier and feel too full. Like pressure is building in them," I try to explain.

"Ah, that's normal then," he responds absently as his gaze drifts over the babies, who look to be falling asleep now. "They don't appear to be hungry at the moment. Would you like to try to pump? That should relieve the pressure."

"You mean go milk myself like a cow?" I cringe.

Logan laughs. "You're the prettiest cow I ever did see." He leans toward me, kissing my lips, eyes shining with mirth.

"Come here." Kellan holds out a hand, helping me off the bed and wrapping an arm around my shoulders as he leads me to a door on the side of our room. "I won't pretend to know what it feels like to go through the changes of motherhood, or where your head has been for the last week as you cared for our young on your own."

"You guys took care of us, too," I'm quick to interrupt.

"We did what we could." He smiles lightly, pushing open the door I thought was a closet but actually leads to the nursery. "I'm trying to say that we know a lot of things will be on you when it comes to the pups, but there are ways we can help you." He guides me to a set of padded glider chairs, urging me to take a seat in one of them. From a compartment in the table between the chairs he pulls out a machine, setting it on top of the table.

"One of which is helping with the feedings," he continues as he pulls out tubing and other pieces, hooking them all up. Pointing at a counter with a changing station and sink with dark cabinets underneath he explains, "There's a small fridge and freezer over there, along with a bottle warmer on the counter. Trying to feed five human babies with only two breasts would be quite a challenge. However, if you try to pump when you're in human form, the guys and I could take over some of those duties. It would allow you to spend more time as you, and less time as your wolf. Besides, as a human, your breasts will become engorged if you allow the milk you're producing to build up."

"Won't milking me make it so that I don't have any milk left when the babies go to eat from me?" I ask, now curious. I mean, if I pump out all the milk, that means they'll never nurse from me, right? That doesn't seem right.

Kellan chuckles lightly, slipping the straps of my cami down my arms. "Not at all. The female body is a marvelous thing. You are capable of producing as much breast milk as you want, given that you remain hydrated and nourished properly. The more you take from your body, the more you will produce. Almost like a failsafe to ensure infants never go hungry."

"Just to be clear, I can pump out milk and still breastfeed our babies?" I ask.

"Of course," he responds, kissing my lips.

I watch as he inserts a bottle into either cup, flipping on the machine that mimics a sucking motion. Handing them over to me, I fumble to get the right angle needed. Seeing my frustration Kellan takes one suction cup from me, gently lifting my breast to fit properly. He seems content to help me hold that one while I follow his lead with the other. It's an odd feeling, a machine sucking at my nipples, stealing milk meant for my babies. When the pups were nursing from my wolf, I had the advantage of my animal's mindset. It was natural, necessary, and never gave me pause. Sitting here with Kellan and the machine I wonder if the act should feel sexual in nature, but it doesn't.

"This feels weird," I tell him after the silence gets to me.

"It's new, but you're doing great, Kitten. You can always choose not to breastfeed at all. We could supplement with formula if you'd like. It's your choice," he informs me.

I shake my head immediately. "It's not that. It's just the machine."

"You're doing us all a favor by pumping milk for future use. You'll be able to rest, or do other things on occasion when the babies want to eat. Feeding them will also give us men time to bond with the little ones and make us feel useful, as well," he tells me.

"You guys don't feel useful?" I frown.

He laughs. "Not really. We had to watch you suffer through the births, nurse them, and keep them safe and warm. All we did was feed you and change some blankets."

"That's not true. You all took care of Mikey, and you finished the renovations so our home would be ready for our babies. You also provided us a safe environment to hole up in that room. That's not nothing, Kellan," I tell him softly.

A peaceful quietness settles over us, only the occasional swapping out of bottles as they become filled distracting us. When my breasts begin to hurt from the pumping and the milk seems to run out, Kellan hands me a warm washcloth from the cabinet and I clean myself up. Thankfully, the odd pressure I was feeling earlier is gone.

"Hold on, I'll be back," he tells me as I recline back in the glider. It's quite a bit more comfortable than I expected.

Looking around the finished nursery, I'm beyond pleased with how it turned out. The guys have made obvious changes in here, making adjustments for the unexpected quintuplets. The low crib Ash originally made is gone, replaced by a much larger one with five rounded curves to appear as though there are five separate cribs; but really, it's a just one long one. Carved into the dark wood are depictions of regal wolves and playful pups chasing the moon. It's stunning, really. He must have worked so hard to get this completed so soon. Hanging over each rounded section is a flowing curtain draping over the back of the crib. The ends are the same vibrant green most of the room is decorated in, the inner sections a soft silver, with the very center done in a soft, creamy pink. Just like I described when we visited the store. Of course, Logan would perfectly match what I had in my head. He's brilliant like that. And a good deal sweeter than what he pretends to be.

Next to the crib, built into the alcove, is a square box-like mat filled with oversized pillows to lie on with random blankets strewn about. Hanging above the pen-like lounging area are bookshelves already filled with children's books. I can just picture all of us lounging in there, the pups crawling all over us as we listen to Finn read to us.

"What's that smile for?" Kellan asks as he returns with our son, who smells of him and his twin. The baby is asleep, wrapped tightly in a fluffy blue blanket with satin edges. Only one small hand peeks out from his wrapping, clasping at his father's shirt.

"I was just picturing our life in here," I tell him softly.

His grass-green eyes dance with unspoken emotion as he smiles softly at me. "It's a good smile. You should do it more often," he tells me as he takes a seat in the other glider.

I watch him as he stares at the baby, gently rocking in the chair and rubbing his pouty lips over the baby's head like he can't stop kissing him. I understand that compulsion; their heads smell so damn good.

"What about Killian?" he asks, eyes still on our son.

"Hmm?"

"For a name. The guys and I have spoken about names for them many times. We didn't want to do anything without you, of course, but we're comfortable naming the ones that take after us. Finn and I like the name Killian. It denotes our Irish heritage, yet is modern enough as well. What do you think?"

"Killian...hmm. I rather like it. Just as long as no one shortens it to Kill; that doesn't seem right for a child," I joke.

Kellan laughs softly so as not to wake the baby. "What do you think, little man? You want to be Killian, Prince of the Ivaskov pack? Hmm?" The little hand gripping his shirt reaches up for Kellan's face, brushing over his cheek. "I'll take that as a yes." He smirks down at Killian.

"So, we have a redheaded Raider and a green-eyed Killian," I state.

"Yep. Sounds almost poetic." He smirks.

"It does," I agree, closing my eyes. Concentrating on the soft breaths and pattering hearts of my two men in the room, I drift off.

When I open my eyes next it's to see my mates piled up in the alcove with Mikey, apparently deciding to nap with me and the babies, who lie soundly in their handmade crib. Seeing all my men together piled up like puppies, I really wish I had a camera. On second look, one is missing.

Tristan.

Having no doubt as to where I'll find my world-renowned chef, I head straight for the kitchen. I take up leaning against the archway, watching as he moves quietly throughout the room. I don't think I'll ever tire of seeing him command and control his surroundings like he was born to it.

"Are you going to stand there watching me, little wolf?" he asks amusedly, without even looking in my direction.

I smile. "It's a pretty good view."

Turning to me with a devilish grin, he gestures me forward. "It's better from over here," he tells me, gripping my hips and setting me up on the countertop.

Staring into his chocolatey eyes, I sigh. "You're right, it is."

With a step forward he presses between my knees, hands going to the outside of my thighs. "I thought you'd be resting."

I shrug. "I was, now I'm not. Everyone else is still in there, though. Why are you out here?"

"Figured I'd get started on dinner. I didn't wake you, did I?" he asks.

"No. I didn't hear you in here. You know I almost never use my wolf hearing." I smirk.

He smirks back. "Yeah, I know." He leans his tall frame down to gently nip at my throat. I giggle.

"Tristan?" I hedge.

"Yes, my dear Luna?" he responds playfully.

"Are you...okay?" I all but blurt out.

His dark eyes are on mine in a second, searching. "What do you mean? Of course, I'm okay. I'm not always...like *that*, Kitten," he says a little defensively.

I shake my head. "I didn't mean it like that. I just mean that... I know you, and I wonder if you think not fathering one of the kids is some sort of cosmic punishment. I want to know if you're okay with all that," I try to explain.

He closes his eyes, body starting to shake. I grip his shoulders, panicked that I've upset him. Then he starts laughing. Loud, carefree, and happy laughter. "Sorry, baby. You just couldn't be more wrong," he says once he's somewhat gotten himself under control again.

"How so?" I ask as he wraps me up in his long arms and rocks me back and forth.

He bends down so that his face is level with mine. "For one, I *am* a father." He flicks my nose lightly. "Don't ever underestimate my bond with my brothers. Those kids are *ours*. Not one of us would have ever thought differently, even if circumstances were different."

I nod, swallowing thickly. Sometimes I forget how close these men truly are. They've been sharing a life way before I came into the picture. I make a mental note to never forget that again.

"Secondly, I don't feel as if I'm being punished, sweet girl," he continues. "I can't describe what happened to me when we were in that room when you were giving birth. Something happened to me, something changed. It was like the chains that bind me were finally broken. Or something. Like I said, I can't describe it. For the first time ever, I felt blessed. It was only in that moment that I was able to believe that I wasn't a monster, that something so *cosmically right* could happen to me. Remy and the others, and now you, have tried to tell me I deserve to be happy. But I didn't believe it until that moment. Do you understand what I'm trying to say?" he asks me almost desperately, like he needs me to really get it.

"I think I do," I respond honestly.

"Good." He kisses my head. "So, don't worry about me, or Logan and Jace for that matter, feeling like we're left out. We don't see it that way, Kitten. We never looked at you as our first and only opportunity, and we'll never look at those children as anything other than family. We wouldn't want to do any of this without each other. Not even if it was possible to have our own mates and children. That's why you're so perfect for us. Why all of this is so perfect. That's how I know that everything happening now was fated."

"I understand, Tristan. I get it," I tell him, feeling like I really do get it.

He nods, still staring into my eyes. "Then I need you believe that I now think I'm going to be okay. That we're all going to be okay. Also understand that I can't have you in my kitchen without feeding you," he jokes. Well, kind of jokes, because I know he's dead serious.

"Hmm, I suppose I'd allow you to feed me...under one condition," I tease, pretending to think it over.

"Oh, yeah?" His voice drops into that silky-smooth tone he usually saves for the bedroom. I almost forget what the hell I was going to say. The sexy devil.

"You have to kiss me," I whisper huskily.

"You drive a hard bargain," he chuckles in my ear, practically lighting my body on fire.

Tristan's smooth lips take mine before I can form another

thought. He kisses me softly and passionately, the way only he can. The taste and feel of him never ceases to drive me insane.

Reluctantly, we break apart so he can find something for me to eat. I feel beyond spoiled by this man as he feeds me directly from his fingers—all while he prepares dinner, too. When memories of going so hungry that it caused pain try to surface, it feels surreal. I know without a doubt that this amazing mate of mine will never allow that to happen again. Even if we didn't have money, or weren't wolves, he would make it his mission to take care of me. I don't know who to thank for men like him existing.

CHAPTER SIXTEEN

"Are you sure this isn't too soon, my Luna?" Albert asks as he joins us in the conference room.

"It's just a phone call. It shouldn't take that long. Thank you for your concern, though." I smile at my Omega.

"Getting all the Alphas to agree to a meeting place and date could take a while. It's better that we get the ball rolling now, in case Kendrick and the Australians raise any hell," Remy adds.

And thus begins the seemingly endless series of calls. We start alphabetically, the irony of this not lost on me. Seriously? How do the humans get anything done on a global level? It's hard enough to contact as many wolf packs as there are, let alone if we had to contact as many countries there are in the world now.

Wolf territory is an odd affair, drawing their own lines, while still using human territory names. Such as the Prussian pack. I find all the territory issues ridiculous, but it gives me another idea to bring up in our future meeting. As our last call wraps up, it becomes apparent that getting everyone on the same page will be harder than I first thought.

"Well, this was a waste of time," Jace sighs, unbuttoning his jacket and relaxing in that polished, rich boy way of his.

"Not necessarily. If anything, we've learned which packs have issues with each other. That could be useful information," Finn replies.

Logan snorts. "If we were information-gathering, maybe. Who knew grown-ass wolves could act so childish? Petty bastards make more demands than a cheer captain attending her first prom."

Jace shakes his head. "I wasn't complaining for the sake of it. I'd like to take a different approach, if you're all in agreement."

"Let's hear it," Remy states.

"I know this began as a friendly meeting between Alphas, but we could make it more than that. I suggest we announce a place and date for attendance to a United Nations of sorts, for wolfkind. Those who show will obviously be open to new ideas and changes that affect us all. Those who don't will eventually feel left out, meaning they would eventually be left behind, or agree to get with the program," Jace explains.

Finn and Kellan share a look before Kellan speaks up. "If that's the case, then we wouldn't actually need every pack there. We'd just need a majority, or those with the most influence and territory."

I'm shaking my head before he's even done speaking. "Wouldn't that mean there would then be an option to get left behind? The United Nations settles disputes and is basically a worldwide government. We don't really have a need to form one of those. My original purpose for the meeting was to form friendships so education could be shared and universal knowledge gained, potential mates can meet each other, and resources can be shared in case someone is struggling. Leaving anyone out of that seems almost cruel, does it not?"

"I get that, I really do, but you can't force friendship, Kitten.

Some packs clearly don't want to interact with us or others," Remy tells me.

"I understand that," I agree, meeting his liquid silver eyes so he knows how serious I am. "But shouldn't they want to learn what we're offering, at least, before turning it down?"

He nods slowly. "They *should*, yes."

"Then it's our responsibility to get them there. If, after hearing what's being discussed, the plan doesn't suit them, then they can leave and do what they want. They should all be there to have their voices heard and have input. I don't see what benefit it will have on the rest of us if there's still information missing, potential mates lost, and people suffering when they don't have to," I tell him.

"Then we need an incentive for them to attend. Something that affects all of them, that they can't refuse," Jace tosses out.

I frown in confusion. "Isn't a once in a lifetime meeting to solve problems on a world scale enough incentive?"

He smirks at me. "One would think, but not to some."

"We could just kidnap all the Alphas and make them listen," Ash suggests with a shrug. The way he says it, like it's the simplest way to get things done, and he can make it happen by Thursday, makes me realize why other people are so scared of him. I just blink in his direction, having no words for his suggestion.

"We could throw the biggest, most badass party those little shits have ever seen. Only losers wouldn't want to attend," Logan suggests.

"We already have an incentive," Finn says quietly, almost to himself.

The rest of us pause, looking to him, waiting for him to gather his thoughts.

"I'm not sure of the execution, but we have a starting point on the cure for infertile females. Possibly a way to ensure more females are born, meaning more mates. That's an incentive not one wolf would pass up to hear about. Let alone an Alpha. We've also experienced a miracle with the first ever known wolf litter being born," Finn tells us, unsure.

"I'm not so sure we should advertise Kitten's high fertility," Ash rumbles.

"Agreed." Tristan scowls.

"Is it Kitten, though? Or is it whatever Mikel was able to do to her? There's no threat to her if we can make it happen for other females," Finn questions.

"Can we, though?" Logan asks him.

Finn shrugs. "As of right now? No. It's a possibility, and that's enough to get others to listen. It's hope. Something most wolves haven't had in a long time, if ever. Incredible things are done in the name of hope."

"So, there's our plan. Set the place and date, inform them all of the key points we want to cover, including our intentions to research the cure. If we wanted, that in itself is an excuse to draw together every pack's best and brightest. Common ground and all that," Jace states lazily.

Remy stares at the golden boy with a pleased expression. "Why did you give up marketing and advertising again?"

Jace smirks, his eyes dancing with humor. "Too easy."

Remy laughs. "Right, I remember." My head tilts, eyes bouncing between the two, but it must be some kind of inside joke I wasn't around for.

"Having help would make the research easier, especially if Kellan and I hit a wall," Finn adds.

"I'll draw up some invitations." Jace looks to Logan, who nods, presumably agreeing to help with that effort.

With the how to get people to show up thing behind us, I turn to Grandfather and Albert. "I have a question."

Grandfather smiles at me softly. "You'll have to ask it before we know if I have an answer."

I giggle. "Right. Well, it's about the territories. Some are so large and impossible to defend in their entirety. How attached to them do you think the other packs are? Do you think if I brought up only claiming what each pack could defend, and leaving the rest as open territory for other packs to roam at will, it would go over well?"

He takes his time finding his answer, brow furrowed and lips pinched. "As all wolves, we like having a large territory. Born wolves are no different. However, with the rapid decline in our populations, it's possible some Alphas would see the move as a godsend. I feel it would also help with your quest to let people mingle."

"So, you think it's worth bringing up at the meeting?" I ask, knowing he has more insight into the matter than any of the rest of us.

"I can't promise all Alphas would welcome the idea, but some might. It's worth the discussion, if that's what you're asking. If you want them to take you seriously, you'll have to give up territory first. If not, they might refuse any changes you propose, feeling as though you're trying to limit them for your own personal gain," he instructs.

"We don't need the whole United States," Remy says drolly. "I have no interest in defending the whole damn country and punishing those who simply wish to visit and vacation."

Grandfather waves a hand at Remington. "My point. Most Alphas see the issue for what it is. One should only take what one can hold. Just keep in mind that all other Alphas live much shorter lives than you do. They'll have different expectations and perspectives than changed wolves. They very much feel their mortality."

I tilt my head at him. "You make it sound like you don't intend to join us at the meeting."

"I don't. Unless you feel the absolute need for my presence, I was planning on remaining here with the princes and princess. I have faith that you and your mates will do well on your own. Albert can offer insight into the mind of born wolves, should you need it," he replies.

I frown fully at him now. "I value your opinion, Grandfather. You make it seem as if I don't have need for you. If you feel that way, please know that was never my intention," I apologize.

He chuckles, standing from his chair so he can kiss the top of head. "You have nothing to apologize for, child. You've made me more welcome than I've earned. I just have no plans on influencing you. You crave change, will seek it out at all costs. I'm a product of a different generation, and my opinions will only hold you back. My guidance and knowledge are always yours when you have need of them, but this is your time. It's up to you and those of your generation to better the world for the next generation." He meets my eyes, his own shining with what I could only describe as pride and encouragement. It's a different feeling from him, humbling and making me feel special, than it is from the guys, where a look that like makes me feel empowered and indestructible.

"Thank you," I choke out past a closing throat. I swallow hard, feeling for the first time the weight of parental expectations. I'm pretty sure only an elder in your immediate family can make you feel like you can do anything you can dream of as easily as blinking.

Grandfather takes his leave, leaving the rest of us to finish up discussing how the calls went and what we hope to gain out of the meeting. It doesn't take long, all of us more than ready to get back to the babies.

CHAPTER SEVENTEEN

The first real day of Spring has excitement and restlessness settling over the pack. Remy decides to do a morning pack run following a big morning feast. Everyone I speak with is in good spirits, super friendly, and completely enamored with the five little fuzzballs running amuck. We discovered last week, by accident, that I could control when they shift. It happened when I was once again getting peed on by one of the boys. I swear, they aim for people whenever they can. Changing their diapers has left me feeling like I'm on a timer to diffuse a bomb. So, as I sensed the ornery little one was about to let loose, I accidently forced him to shift to wolf, turning all five at once. If I'm able to shift them individually, I haven't figured that out yet. When I'm in a separate form from them I feel a pull to shift as well, but today is fine, knowing I'll be shifting later.

Currently the pups are soaking up all the attention they're garnering, sniffing out any food that has gotten dropped. All except for Cyan, who's content to stay curled in my arms, muzzle pressed to my neck as he sleeps through the whole affair.

"You're going to spoil him," Reed tells me through a smile,

patting our pup's head. Naturally, that gets his attention, now sensing someone new to get cuddles from. Big brown and blue-green eyes blink open at Reed. A cute yawn escapes him before he starts wiggling and yips for his dad to take him.

Reed chuckles, happily securing the cuddle-pup in the crook of his arm. "And here I thought you were a mama's boy," he teases with a scratch behind the ear.

"Hey, there's nothing wrong with being affectionate. Some people need it more than others. Cyan just likes being close to others," I defend my little man.

Reed leans in for a kiss. "I didn't say anything was wrong with it. He's a happy little dude. I wouldn't have it any other way."

Barking gets our attention, and we turn to see Ash's huge wolf standing off against our three black pups and our redhead. Asher, Ava, Killian, and Raider form a line in front of Ash, barking and nipping at his paws as they jump around, tails wagging. I don't know what it is they're defending until Ash fakes left before snapping right and grabbing a tiny rope toy in his giant mouth. It's a big toy to the pups, but it looks comically small in the huge black wolf's mouth. The pups give chase, Ash purposely moving slowly enough for them to catch him

I glance at Cyan, still in Reed's hold. "Do you want to go play, too?" I ask him. His bored look is enough of a response. Reed laughs, putting him down anyway.

Cyan walks closer to his brothers and sister, but doesn't join in. He just watches. It's all fun and games until Ash lets them have the rope back and Asher is quick to claim it for himself. Ava, not realizing he's done playing and wants to chew it up, makes to grab it from him and gets her ear bitten for it.

Ash sighs, getting up to reprimand the little Alpha for biting his sister yet again. Before he gets there an angry ball of blonde fluff is on the attack, tackling his brother to the ground and threatening to chomp his throat once he gets him pinned down. The two boys growl warnings, but Asher is unable to get out from under Cyan and eventually gives in. With a glare over his shoulder Cyan picks up the toy, trotting it over to Ava and laying it at her feet. As she lies down for a good chew, Cyan uses her distraction to cuddle up to her side, keeping one eye on a sulking Asher.

Ash looks to me, probably wondering if he should still do something. I shrug at him. It seems pretty handled now. I don't know who to reprimand at this point anyway. Asher finds his way to Remington, who sits at a table playing cards with several others. I know if I shifted the pups right now, he'd be crying to Remington for losing a fight. My mate must have witnessed the whole thing, because he only has to raise a brow at the pup and his ears fold back in shame. Remy picks up the little guy, nuzzling his head. Reassuring him that he's okay, he takes time to explain that bullying his siblings isn't nice.

I look for the other two, seeing them fixated on a new toy already, a plastic red cup that they pounce on and jump away from when it makes a crinkling noise. Before I even have to ask, Logan is already exchanging the plastic that they will most certainly end up trying to eat with a small soccer ball that lights up when you drop it, or is pounced on. The new toy seems to excite Killian and Raider even more. Thankfully, they don't whine at their lost cup.

"They're a handful, aren't they?" One of the few other females asks me with a knowing grin on her face. Vivian is her name, if memory serves me, which it always does.

I laugh. "They sure are. How have you been?" I ask her. She's a quieter woman, mostly keeping to the second floor with the rest of the women and children. I've heard from a few others that she likes to knit various items for fun, and spends most of her free time doing so.

"Oh, you know, the usual. We're all pretty excited for this run. The kids are disappointed your pups won't be with us this time." She laughs.

I laugh, too. "Yeah, they're still too little for that yet. Soon enough, though."

Vivian smiles. "I know. Keep them babies for as long as you can, Luna. They grow like weeds," she jokes.

We sit in comfortable silence, jus watching the children spread out here and there as they play, always being the first ones to finish eating. A larger group has formed to start a game of wolfball, the pack's invented version of football. Quinn joins them as well, his smaller, slightly different wolf standing in stark contrast to the children's. Forming two lines the wolf in the back barks once, the one in front of him tossing a hollow disk at him with a quick turn of the head. He jumps over the opposition's line before launching the disk to his teammate, who runs beside him before doing a roll and running for the marked line at the end of their makeshift field. Onlookers groan and clap as the young wolf is tackled before he can reach the line. The disk is placed down where he landed, and they line up again.

As I watch, an idea pops into my head and I excuse myself to go find Finn. I find him and Jace enjoying an after-meal cup of tea at one of the tables set up closer to the house. "Hello, Mr. Wolf," I whisper in his ear as I drape myself around his shoulders in his seated position.

Jace laughs. "I hope you never let that go, as it entertains me greatly." He smiles broadly, teasing Finn.

Finn merely arches an inky brow. "Is that so, *Little* Jace?"

Jace scowls playfully. "And now I'm bored," he says on an eyeroll, standing to come hug me. "Come find me directly after our run, beautiful Luna. We'll get some exercise of our own in, hmm?" he whispers in my ear before nipping my lobe. My heated eyes meet his as I nod, biting my lip in anticipation. Out of all of my mates, Jace enjoys the more carnal lovemaking of our wolves than the others. They all enjoy it, just as I do, but Jace *really* enjoys it.

Finn clears his throat. "Did you need something, Kitten?

I shake off my lustful thoughts and move around to take a seat in his lap. He smiles softly, his hand brushing over my calves lovingly. "Remember when we talked about the school idea?" I ask him.

"Of course. What's in that big, beautiful brain of yours?" he queries.

I kiss his pouty lips, always rewarding him for complimenting me on my intelligence. Those are my favorite compliments. From the smartest man I know, they mean the world to me. "Are you still working it out? Because I just watched an interesting game that could serve as the school's sport. Schools always have sports, right?"

He chuckles. "They do; most of the time anyway. What we talked about was more than just a school but I can always tweak the purpose of it, I suppose. We're all starting to settle in here, and my plan formed from the need to create a place we'd be happier. We could be happy here, right?"

"I think so. The renovations on our floor helped to make this place feel more like home, and restructuring our pack and titles helped take the pressure off you guys. The pack members are doing more for themselves now, also growing more comfortable now that they see they have our support in their independence."

He nods. "Agreed. It appears to be all working out at the moment. But you're still interested in my plan for a school? Honestly, I haven't had much time to put more thought into it, given all that's been going on."

"That's okay. We have all the time in the world, right?" I smirk.

He laughs outright. I love his laugh, as he's far too serious usually. "True."

"I still think a school where wolves from all over can attend and form lasting relationships is a good idea. They could be taught acceptance and tolerance of others, as well as arithmetic."

"Right, and maybe also wolf history and farming, and all kinds of other classes to help them learn to be useful in pack life," he tosses out.

"Oh, I like that idea," I tell him, excited for the possibilities.

"You know, this gives me an idea for where to hold this meeting of ours. I have several contacts throughout the academic community; we could hold the meeting in a lecture hall. That would provide us a large enough seating area and a platform for anyone who wishes to speak. It also wouldn't draw attention, as most colleges often have guest lectures and guests from around the world to attend them."

I sigh dramatically. "You are entirely too smart, Mr. Wolf," I play.

He laughs again before kissing my lips softly. "I take it you like the idea, then?"

I nod. "I do. We'll run it by the others after the run."

"Sounds good," he tells me.

Running through the trees, sun shining down in rays of glory, I don't think I've ever felt so alive. The New Year's run was different. That was about establishing order, a tentative taste of unity. This...this is the *more* we've all been craving. There's happiness and confidence in the way the pack wolves run today. Brushing up against one another, playfully racing and nipping at each other's heels, it's obvious that they're more together now than ever. We all are. While the other wolves give my guys and me a respectable bubble to run freely, they also take pride in staying by our sides and anticipating our directions. I can *feel* it. It gives me energy like I've never known.

Flanked on either side of our group by the faster, more agile changed wolves that have adapted to our ragtag pack, I respond to our Alpha's howl with my own, adding my voice to our song. With their superior strength, the changed wolves decided to add a layer of protection for the born wolves to run inside of, where all female wolves and children stay in the middle of. Except me, of course. No one stops me from bouncing back and forth from where my mates run in different spots, so I figure I'm allowed to do this. I especially like easing my way into the group of kids, feeling their excitement as their Luna joins them. They like to chase, pushing themselves harder to keep up with my slightly longer strides. We take our cues from them when it comes to setting the pace. We're only as fast as our slowest or, in this case, youngest wolf. Remy leads the pack from the end of the line, behind the children, calling out information to the front where my grandfather runs with some of our older wolves.

When the children begin to slow, getting tired during our long run, the pace slows further as we circle back for home. I'm mostly trotting now, jumping over a line of shrubbery to join our protectors on the left, running with them for a while. They dwarf me in size, making it easy to run right under them. It's fun.

As we near the house Jace's golden wolf finds me, herding me out of the line and away from everyone else. With a call for Remy to let him know we're breaking away, he challenges me to a race, taking off ahead of me and heading for the stream that feeds the crops. I push myself as hard as I can, not even coming close to keeping up.

I huff and pout when I reach him, hating that I lost. His eyes dance with amusement as he trots over to join me on a warm rock that I think I'll claim as mine. It's a good rock.

Jace nuzzles my neck, standing over me and surrounding me

with more pheromones than I know what to do with. I eventually give in to him, not able to hold a silly grudge over the lost race against my golden mate in all his maleness.

Exhausted and sated in the sunshine, I'm further impressed when Jace returns to me with a sheep with antler things on its head. We take our time feasting, loving, lazing about, and splashing in the stream until the sun begins its descent in the sky.

On the slow jog home, I decide that my guys and I need more days like today. At least every now and again. Days like these are what all the crazy, stressful days are about. What we work for.

CHAPTER EIGHTEEN

"Are you nervous?" Finn asks, standing beside me as we peek through the curtains at the back of the stage, watching as the seats in the lecture hall fill up.

"Who, me? Nope," I respond, my voice a little too high-pitched. "You?" I shoot back.

"Nope," he answers on a gulp.

I meet his mint-green eyes and we share a smile. We're both liars.

"Just so we're clear, there will be no threatening anyone today." Remy gets our attention, pulling us away from the curtains and over to the rest of them, where we're huddling apparently. He gives me a pointed glare as he says this, though I don't know why I'm being singled out.

I stick my tongue out at my Alpha as the guys go over our talking points once again. Since we called this meeting, we agreed to try to keep the peace with the other packs, our goal today to keep the conversation on track.

"Should we go take our seats now?" Reed asks.

"I don't know where we're going to sit, since there're more people in attendance than we planned for. Some packs are

Alphas only, but quite a few of them brought anyone who wanted to come. We even have more changed wolves that showed." Finn tells them what we've observed so far.

"Shit. We should get started then, before anyone has the chance to pick a fight over a seat," Jace says hurriedly. He's right, but I *really* don't want to.

"Why do I have to talk first?" I pout. When Finn talked about the lecture hall, I didn't anticipate having to stand on the stage with so many people staring down at me. I feel like they're all waiting for me to make a mistake.

Remy takes me aside as the rest of the guys leave to join the others in the hall. "Love, you're going to do wonderfully. Just be your usual confident, bulldozer self. You've already spoken to most of these people and they listened to you." He wraps his arms around me, squeezing tightly.

"You think it'll be okay?" I ask nervously, biting my lip.

His steely eyes bore into mine. "I believe in *you*, Kitten. You have this. I promise. I'll be right beside you," he tells me seriously. I lean up and quickly kiss his lips.

"Thank you. I needed that," I say with a smile, though it must come off as a grimace if his chuckle is any indication.

Stepping out onto that stage is probably the scariest thing I've ever done. As my heels click across the smooth surface to the podium all conversation ceases, eyes turning to me. I know most everyone in this room can hear my erratic heart as it attempts to beat out of my chest, but I smile nervously at them anyway.

With one last glance over to Remington, who stayed at the edge of the stage, still visible, but noticeably allowing me to lead, I begin the small speech Jace and Finn helped me with. "Thank you all for coming. I appreciate the effort everyone made to be here today, and I hope those efforts will lead to a more unified way of life for us all before you leave."

"You said you have information on a cure for our females. That's why we're here," a man shouts from somewhere near the middle of the room.

"Uh, yes. We'll get to that. The purpose of this gathering is to open discussions on matters that affect us all. Would anyone care to start us off?" I smile at the crowd, seeing a few people beginning to rise.

"Yeah, yeah. Sure, peace and shit. If you're holding back information that could save our race, then..." the same guy starts in.

I interrupt him quickly, shutting him down. "You," I point at him, leaning over the podium. "will hold your damn horses." Remy's at my side in an instant, trying to calm me down. "What? He's being rude." I frown.

"Yes, Love. I know. Diplomacy, remember?" he whispers in my ear.

"Oh, yeah? You going to make me?" Rude Guy keeps at it.

I turn from Remy, a snarl leaving my lips. "Yeah. Me and everyone else in this room who truly want change. Don't get it twisted, sir. My pack and I have plenty to offer the rest of you, but if you have a mind to take and give nothing back then you'll find yourself on the short end of my very short patience. We're here to work *together*. Anything less, and it's all for nothing."

There's some grumbling and even a few claps throughout the gathering, but either way Rude Guy sits down and shuts up. "Now," I continue. "please, let's begin the conversation." I point to the first person who stood before the drama started.

The older man clears his throat. "Yes, thank you, Princess Ivaskov. My name is Theodore Cavalli, Alpha of the Italian pack. Pleased to meet you in person." He introduces himself.

I shake my head with a smile. "You don't have to address just me, Alpha Cavalli, and it's Luna now. My pack has restructured. Would you care to join me on stage?"

He blinks at me several times, looking at a loss for words. Huh, so that's what that looks like when someone else does it. "You...you *restructured*? Just like that?" He sounds dumbfounded.

"Well, yes. Given the very dramatic shift in power my pack went through, and the new dynamic my mates and I created, we thought it best to change the rules, starting at the top," I explain.

Alpha Cavalli moves to join me at the podium. He reaches out a hand for me to shake, teeth bared in a wide smile. "That's good news to hear, Luna. Now I know you are serious about these changes you speak of. I'd like to first discuss the territory implements your invitations spoke of."

I nod and take a step back as he addresses the crowd. I make my way over to stand next to Remy as the man speaks. "While I agree with the Ivaskovs' idea that a pack should only mark off territory that they can hold and defend, I have two questions that I'd like to discuss today. The first being what happens to those of us who do not wish to give up territory? My pack is more than capable of holding our lands, and wish to hold on to them. The other issue is what happens with the proposed territories this new mandate would open up. Would that not make it easier for our enemies to rally closer in the event of an attack?"

I go to answer him but Remy holds me back, shaking his head and nodding to the crowd, who starts to respond. Their interests are now piqued. Oh, I get it. Let others interact. Right.

When the discussion turns into punishments and penalties for those who won't release any territory, Remy nudges me to join in again. "It was never our intention to force any pack to release land. Our own pack will be releasing quite a bit of land to free territory so that any wolf has a right to visit and vacation at will. The idea was so that wolves would feel free to mingle and experience other cultures and customs."

"So, you're saying we don't have to decrease the size of our territories?" a young man in the back asks for clarification.

I walk to the podium, sighing. "Look, I don't personally think it's a good idea to speak on terms of forming a ruling government over us all. I don't think that would work for us as it does the humans. It only seems reasonable to release what you don't need and what doesn't benefit you. If it does benefit you, and you need it, then don't release it. There are other ways of mingling and allowing others into your territory. I'm not looking to police anyone or change anyone's belief systems."

People sit forward, waiting for me to say more, so I do. "I think we should all ask ourselves what benefits we could gain from being connected and on friendly terms. Do we lose anything? Personally, I don't think we do. What could the Ivaskov pack gain from the rest of you? Well, knowledge for one. What if your histories don't match up with ours? Could we benefit from exploring those? Yes; yes, we could. Could some of my pack members be fated to mate with some of yours? Probably. That would mean less loneliness for my wolves, and yours. That's a benefit. As it stands now, those wolves would never have an opportunity to meet. We're too closed off from one another."

"And where would these fated mates reside? Which pack would lose a member and the other gain? Some of us don't have as much to offer as others. Would this not cause conflict when a valuable female is lost from a pack?" someone asks.

"All wolves are valuable, sir, but those are the issues I believe are personal and should only be dealt with within the group of people it affects. Making a rule or a law on this matter in a generic, all-encompassing way would only lead to many misunderstandings. If fated mates are found, then the two wolves and their Alphas should work the matter out themselves. The main focus should be that two, or more in my case, wolves don't have to live out lonely existences. Is that not worth anything that may come after it? Do you not believe it could be worked out?" I ask.

I leave the podium again, letting everyone speak up and share their opinions. Only a few people seem to be negative toward everything brought up. I know without a doubt that those people will never be satisfied with anything, but the overwhelming majority appears more than ready for some changes, and almost all seem open to at least talking it out. I jump in when I want my opinion heard, as does Remy, which leads to some of the lone wolves and changed wolves feeling comfortable enough to lend their voices to the discussion. I couldn't be happier with how this has turned out. I had thought this would be a more formal affair, and in hindsight maybe the speaking platform was unnecessary, as people speak up right from their seats. Oh well, they're still talking it all out—probably for the first time in history.

Eventually the naysayers keep quiet, getting out-voted almost every time they open their mouths. All kinds of things get brought up, things I never even thought of, or would have thought of. At one point, a ceasefire was voted on to end all ongoing conflicts, a new slate being given in light of how the Alphas plan to implement changes that would render the past irrelevant. At another point, two neighboring packs agreed to merge and pool resources. I don't know how that will work, but it sounded good, and it's their right to do so. As the talks progress, only one thing bothers me. A large majority of the crowd wants to form a ruling government. It's like any new topic always seems to circle back to that.

When the night seems to be coming to a close, I motion for Finn and Kellan to join me at the podium. I introduce them and then step aside so they can say what they have to say. Finn speaks first, laying out his idea of a school for all wolves that would also serve as a research institution. He actually gets a standing ovation when he finishes, the only person to receive one all day. For someone who doesn't like public speaking, he sure does a fine job of it. There wasn't one naysayer to what he was offering. Remarkable.

Finn's speech ends with setting up Kellan for his. Where Finn spoke of the possibilities for many research fields, Kellan focuses on targeting illnesses that affect born wolves and combatting them, initiating standard healthcare procedures once they're able to determine the causes and effects. He leads up to what we've learned from the Australians and where we hope to be with the cure in the upcoming years. He circles back to Finn's idea of having the best and brightest of us all working together at the institute to speed along the process. I feel the crowd's disappointment that we don't already have the cure, but I also feel their hope that we're so close to getting it.

Both men do an excellent job of pointing out just how much we can accomplish when we keep open minds and work together. They really bring the point home. Maybe we should have started with my twins.

"I believe that only leaves us with one last issue, Luna." My South African friends take the podium, Alpha Jubulani and his mate Lindiwe standing tall, hand and hand.

I smile at them. "Yeah? What's that?"

"A vote for a leader," the Alpha says with a wicked smile.

I roll my eyes playfully as I join him, since he seems to want to include me in this discussion personally. "As I said, I don't think we need one. I believe in the Alphas in this room. With enough practice, we'll all learn to handle any situation that may need governing."

Alpha Jubulani smirks at me before turning his attention to the crowd. "All in favor of a small panel to solve disputes and handle only issues that involve all wolves?"

A resounding "Aye" choruses from the crowd. I sigh my

disappointment. "I really don't think that's a good idea. Bossing Alphas around will only lead to rebellion and trouble."

"I guess we'll need someone strong, righteous, and morally sound sitting at the head of the table then," he says pointedly, in my direction.

My face pales and I step back on a gasp. The crowd chuckles and hoots in laughter at my reaction.

"Luckily, I know this little white wolf that's bossier and stronger in her convictions than most Alphas I know," he jokes. The crowd gets to their feet, clapping and shouting in approval, even as I shake my head in a firm no. "All in favor?" he asks them.

Instead of the "Aye, or Nay", which is weird, by the way, the room takes a knee as one, bowing in unison.

"I think, little Luna, the majority has spoken. We want *you* at the head of that table. A reluctant leader is always the best leader. Chose your panel wisely, lead us faithfully, and guide us on this path of change with your pure heart and capable mind."

I stare at him, mouth hanging open, hand pressed to my chest. My eyes roam over the crowd, still on their knees, looking to me for an answer.

Oh, God.

Oh, no.

How did *this* happen?

My eyes flick between my mates, wishing one of them would tell me the right thing to say right about now. "I... uh... I'll think about it?" I squeak out.

Clearing my throat I try again, stronger this time. "I'll take it into consideration. I'm a new mother with six children at home and a pack that needs me."

Lindiwe takes my hands in hers, speaking gently. "We understand that you already have many responsibilities. This council doesn't have to be a fulltime job. You could always delegate as well. There simply isn't another wolf that we'd rather have in this position."

"Yeah!" a man in the crowd with a European accent agrees. "It was you who reached out to all of us. You who convinced the Alphas of the world to gather here today. You handled the Australian pack, discovered your father's success with the cure, and have changed the tides for all changed wolves. Like it or not, you've been leading us already. If not you, then it is no one."

"I did none of that alone," I quickly correct.

"Exactly," another man in the crowd speaks up. "You take those around you and make them believe in you enough to follow your lead. Is that not what a great leader does?"

Well, then.

"I will consider this. I promise. I don't have an answer for you tonight, but I will think carefully on this," I press, moving back in front of the podium. I grasp the edges tightly. "I want to thank you all for coming. I think we've really made some progress here today, and we couldn't have done it without each and every one of you in attendance. Stay in touch with each other, reach out if you need anything or have any questions. I'm sure we'll meet again soon, my friends." I smile tightly, walking quickly to Remy as clapping ensues once again. We wave as people start making their way out, the rest of my mates catching up to us as we head for the back exit.

"Well, that was..." Logan starts.

"Don't," I interrupt, my heart still beating harshly in my chest. "I'm not ready to talk about what happened back there."

"She truly is a queen, isn't she?" Logan whispers to presumably Tristan or Jace.

I shake my head, pretending not to hear him.

That's just it, I'm really not.

CHAPTER NINETEEN

Finn

Kitten absolutely refuses to discuss being voted head of the council. She won't talk about the council at all, in fact. In the weeks that followed the meeting, we've all taken our shot at getting her to open up about her feelings on the matter, but I think she's content to pretend it never happened. To me, that says all there is to say about it. She never wanted to be princess to the Ivaskov pack, only somewhat comfortable being Luna, given that Remy remains Alpha and in charge. She doesn't want to lead anyone, isn't comfortable with it. I think it has to do with her being so young. I have no doubt that as she gets more years under her belt, she'll come into herself and settle into the roles she was meant for.

As it is, the other packs are not willing to give her that time. We've fielded their calls and letters, putting off any visits until she's ready, but they're getting pushy. They want her and, honestly, so do I. She's the most incorruptible person I've ever met.

Standing on the balcony in our bedroom, I watch Kitten and

Mikey as they play hide and seek with the pups. I'm sure this is just a fun game to Kitten. Little does she know that she's teaching the little ones to track by scent and, knowing her as I do, by the sound of her giggles.

"How's it going, brother?" Kellan claps me on the back before taking up a position similar to mine on the railing. His eyes immediately go the scene below, a grin overtaking his expression. "She's teaching them to track?"

"Something like that," I respond with a smirk. "Any new discoveries with her blood?" I ask, assuming that's where he's been all day.

He sighs deeply. "I wish. I don't really want to let everyone know that Alpha Mikel's only successful attempt at a cure lives in his only daughter. We've tested the women and the children from Australia, even some of the men from Kendrick's old pack. None of their blood matches Kitten's. She is the only one whose blood has the ability to reverse damage that's already been done."

I nod, already knowing this. Some of the women were made more fertile due to a serum Mikel gave them, but their blood remains that of a changeable female. A lot of the children we saw at the camp were humans with human fathers, only a few the result of wolf pairings. While the children of those unions have blood similar to Kitten's, they don't share the qualities that allow her blood to reverse damage done by the virus. Theirs only protects them from the virus, such as a vaccine. No doubt, when they have children of their own they will be born susceptible to the virus again.

"Not sure what our next move here is, brother." Kellan sighs. "Kitten is the only known cure. We can't pass out her blood to every woman and child from now until the end of time. We don't know what makes her blood different, so we can't extract what we need and replicate it."

"I know, it's frustrating," I agree with him. "If we tell her what we've found out, she'll drain herself dry trying to help others. She already wants to market a drug with her blood to help the humans, seeing how it practically brought Mikey back to life."

Kellan smiles wide. "She came to you with that idea, too, huh?" I raise my brow at him, making him laugh. "What did you tell her?"

"The truth. That it's too dangerous. I did agree to accompany her to find specific humans that she wants to save, under the agreement that those humans would have to willingly join our pack and leave the human world."

Kellan whistles low. "Damn, that's serious, Finn. How do you figure that will work?"

I tilt my head in Kitten's direction. "She's always going to need to save people. It's who she is. She can't have without sharing. To her, there will always be people who are alone like she was, who went without like she did. She'll always try to save the *Kittens* of the world. If she isn't allowed to do so, she'll fold in on herself and wither away. We'll just have to make it possible for her to do that. If it means exposing ourselves to a few humans, then it's worth it. I couldn't just tell her no."

"Yeah, she'd find a way to do it anyway." He chuckles.

I smile, too; he's right, she would. "This way, I'll be with her. Besides, those humans will most likely worship her like the rest of us do. I don't imagine they'd do anything that could cause harm to her."

"Maybe that's how we go about handing out the cure, as well. Make it so that only bonded females can receive her blood. That would cut the numbers down until we figure out how to replicate what Mikel did," my brother suggests.

I shake my head at him, meeting his eyes briefly. "It's not up to us. It's up to her. Her first goal will be to protect all the female children. She'll probably see that only handing out her blood to bonded females as a protection of sorts for them, so she might go for it. You know Kitten, though. She's unpredictable, and will probably suggest something neither one of could think of."

He laughs again and I join in. "True. She's never boring, I'll give her that."

"So, when are we going to tell her what we've found?" I question.

"I wanted to wait to drop this bomb until after she dealt with the last one that was dropped on her. I have to say, this isn't really like her. She makes decisions quickly, usually trusting her first instinct and running with it," he points out.

I shake my head again. "This isn't like that. She doesn't want it, but she recognizes that others need her to want it. It just looks like she's ignoring the situation. Her head is probably a warzone right now, stuck in a stalemate until she can work it out one way or another."

Kellen eyeballs me for a moment. "That's some deep insight, Finn. Do you think she's waiting on us to voice our opinions? Help her make the choice?"

"I think that's part of it. As far as I know not one of us has spoken for or against it, other than Logan," I answer.

"And the other part?" he prods.

I look down at the pups, giving myself a minute to find the answer I want to give. Cyan, more often than not, is first to find his mama. He won't seek her out alone, though. Always warning the others when he's found her scent, waiting for them to catch up. Killian doesn't even bother looking, just waits for Cyan's call and trots along to find their giggling mother.

She looks so happy. All smiles and girly little claps and squeals when the kids pounce on her in excitement. Her gorgeous green eyes shine with pride and love, even from here. She doesn't care that her white jacket is getting muddy, that pieces of grass and leaves cling to her long hair, or that Jace is going to take her for another manicure, now that she's ruined hers. Her heart is in the game and spending time with her children.

"The other part doesn't know if she'll lose the one thing she's always wanted. She wants them." I point to the kids. "And us. Family. She has that right now, so she's always going to be scared of losing it. Much like us. She has to figure out if she can be a mother and a mate, and still be what everyone else needs her to be."

Kellan snorts. "Of course, she can; she's her."

"I agree. Everyone knows that but her. She doesn't know how to believe in herself like she believes in others yet. She's more than capable, but she sees this opportunity as a potential threat to her family. So far, backing out of the Ivaskov pack has always been an option for us. We could disappear, live out our lives as we please wherever we want to. If she starts down this road, she'll be the most famous wolf in history. They'll literally write books about her. There's no backing out after that happens. She's right to take her time thinking about this."

"What's your opinion? Do you think she should take the position?" he asks, watching me from the corner of his eye. My brother only does that when he's on the fence about something and willing to agree with me either way.

I turn my head, meeting his eyes fully. "Yes. Only a handful of people get the opportunity to truly make a difference in this world. The position wasn't offered to her, it was created for her by her own doing. She's going to change the world, brother. I plan on being at her side when she does. Supporting her."

"I couldn't agree more," Remington surprises me by answering, breaking my stare with Kellan. He joins us at the railing, leaning on his arms as he watches our mate and pups. He looks more content than I can ever remember seeing him in our long lives. "Face it, boys. That woman down there is destined for greatness. Our only job from here on out is safeguarding what matters to her most."

"And you're okay with that?" Kellan asks him warily.

Remington laughs, a real laugh that reaches his eyes. "I'm not sure I'd have it any other way. It's not the quiet life we've always strived to achieve, sure. Life with her is sure to be eventful, even stressful and aggravating at times, but she gives me purpose. I've lived for a very long time without her, but I've never felt as alive as I have since meeting her. She's hope, simply put. Besides you guys, I'd give up my entire past for just another week with her. I'll be anything she needs me to be to keep that feeling. Don't tell me you wouldn't." He smirks at my brother.

Kellan smirks back. "I didn't say that. I only worry that the more successful she is, the greater she becomes, the more her life is at risk. I don't want to lose what we have right now. If this is as much as we ever have, I could die a happy man. It's enough for me," he explains his reluctance.

Remington tosses an arm over Kellan's shoulder, pulling him in close. "Those worries have entered my mind a time or two, also. While I know we will always be her greatest champions, we're no longer her only ones. I've met a lot of people in my time, but the loyalty she inspires in others is unmatched. I don't know what about her does that, but it doesn't matter. It's there, and our mate will never be short on people willing to lay down their lives for her."

The three of us fall silent as we watch our family play below us. Tristan eventually brings out some picnic baskets and a blanket, setting out lunch for Kitten and Mikey and handing out bottles of warm milk to the pups. We watch that, too. I'm certain that we could watch her forever.

∼

Kitten

I take yet another deep breath. There's no one left to speak to about this. The guys gave me the time I needed to figure this out on my own, and I love them so much for that. We were eventually able to talk about what this decision would mean for all of us, not just me. They spoke openly about their concerns and gave me their honest opinions, as always. Grandfather and Albert also added their opinions. I spoke with Mikey, and I spoke with Quinn. I also spoke to Vivian, and...okay, I spoke to anyone willing to speak to me.

I'm just still not sure what my answer is. I don't know what I'm going to say, even seconds before I'm supposed to make an announcement on live video chat or whatever it's called. I'll be lucky to even possess a bottom lip after all is said and done. I've nearly chewed the thing off.

When the doors open in front of me, Jace popping his head out to tell me everyone is ready and waiting, I nearly jump out of my skin. With a last glance behind me at my pile of babies crawling all over the floor, their big brother attempting to herd them to stay in a group, I take a step into the conference room.

I close the doors, keeping my back turned to the room, giving myself a moment to just breathe as I grip the handles. Another shaky inhale and deep exhale have me facing the room. My guys are lined up behind their chairs at the table, the wall of screens featuring the Alphas of other packs shining brightly, all attention aimed right at me.

I walk to the end of the table, bracing myself on my hands to keep myself upright. I bow my head, closing my eyes and sending one last prayer to any entity that may be listening. When I raise my head, I look to each of my mates.

Reed. With his love for me shining in his multicolored eyes, so much like our son's, he lets me know he'll always be here with me.

Tristan. With chocolate eyes filled with dark secrets and a warm expression on his face, he silently tells me that I'll forever have a partner through even the darkest times of my life.

Logan. With his playful blue eyes and sinful lips, he tells me that I'll never be bored, always on the brink of something fun. I only need ask.

Jace. My golden boy. Hair perfectly in place, impeccably dressed as usual, he lends me his confidence and self-conviction. A pretty wrapping covering up a fair and loyal man to the end.

Kellan. Grass-green eyes and hair as dark as night, my worrier and healer, always waiting to catch me if I should fall.

Ash. Big and strong, he tells me with just one glance that he'll always be in my corner, protecting me and having my back.

Finn. With intelligence and faith that never fails me, Finn's minty-green eyes let me know that there's no problem in the world we can't figure out together.

Remy. My Alpha. My match in every possible way, standing tall with stoic grace, my copper-haired, steely-eyed leader calms me as his look tells me that I'll never be alone again. He'll be there, every step of the way, keeping our family together at all costs. My goals are his, his are mine.

Prying my eyes away from my mates, I meet the stares of the Alphas on the screens. Soaking in all the confidence, strength, and support my guys are pushing at me, I bring myself up to my full height.

"Okay. If I'm going to do this, then we're going to do this *my* way."

The End

EPILOGUE

"Moooommmmm!" Ava screeches at the top of her lungs as Asher and Raider work together to toss her into the pool.

"Why do you kids always call for me instead of your fathers?" I ask through my laughter, watching as Ava comes up spitting mad. Her seven-year-old face set in a scowl that could set fire to a forest.

Changing tactics, her scowl turns into a wicked smirk toward Logan, who matches her look with a devilish one of his own. I don't bother to cover my interest as I watch water droplets slide down his lean, bare chest and into his bright blue swim trunks. He sends me a wink, catching me watching him openly.

"Mama! Mama! I founded a leaf wif all the colors. Seeeeeee!" Cyan chirps happily as a leaf gets shoved in my face so close that my eyes cross. Climbing in my lap, my blonde boy points out all the pretty colors that are present on his treasure. It is a pretty cool leaf, an oddity in the middle of summer.

"Found. You *found* a leaf," Finn corrects gently as he scoops Cyan out of my lap, tickling him. "That's an awesome oak leaf you've got there. Let's go show Daddy Reed."

"Yeah!" Cyan giggles, holding his prize away from himself as he squirms around from the tickling.

A loud *boom* causes me to jump before my eyes swing to the kids' playhouse. A plume of smoke drifts from the open windows, a coughing Killian leaning out of one of them.

"Damn it, Killian! What did I tell you about blowing things up? What was it this time?" Remy shouts, cursing under his breath as he and Kellan head over to check out what happened.

Kellan lifts the boy down from the window, moving his mop of dark hair out of the way to look into his green eyes. "I gave my robot a laser. You know, to make it cool and defeat the evil trolls. I forgot about the gas until it was too late," he adds sheepishly with a grimace.

"Why the bloody hell did you have gasoline in here?" Remy demands from inside the playhouse. Watching him squeeze through the tiny door is comedy at its finest.

Killian shrugs a shoulder. "A 'speriment," he replies, like it should be obvious.

"Hey, buddy, we talked about this. You don't do experiments on your own. No more lasers, and definitely nothing to do with gasoline. You got it?" Kellan tells him sternly with a disapproving look.

"Fine," Killian huffs.

"Wait, trolls? *My* trolls?" Raider tunes into the conversation. His horrified glare at his brother lasts all of three seconds before he turns to me. "Moooommmm, Kill blew up my trolls!"

I sigh. "Yes, I heard everything you just heard, Raider. I'm sure he didn't mean to, and he's going to be in trouble for causing an explosion anyway."

"Hey! I didn't mean to blow them up. I meant to melt them with the laser!" Killian defends as Raider and Ashton attack him, grabbing him by the hands and feet and dragging him over to the pool.

"We'll get you some new, horrid-looking trolls," Jace promises drolly as he adjusts his shades, lying on the lounger next to mine. With a glance in my direction, he adds, "You have your mother's horrible taste in toys."

I glare playfully at my golden mate, not able to hold it long since he looks so delicious with all that bare skin. I have to agree with him about Raider's taste in toys. Those troll things are downright creepy, made to look like the tales of old-type trolls with tusks, gruesome expressions, and boils on their faces. I swear Logan only got them for him to piss off Jace. It wouldn't surprise me one bit.

"Aren't you too hot out here?" Reed asks as he comes up behind me, kissing me chastely before kissing the top of the baby's head.

I adjust our newest little guy as he feeds from me, bringing the blanket over his head more to shield him from the sun. "Tristan went to get me some tea. Thank you. Besides, I figured I'd jump into the pool for a while after this little guy and his sister were done eating."

Reed takes a seat at the foot of my lounger, grabbing the sunscreen and starting to work more of it into my legs. He looks to the lounger next to us, seeing Jace spread out on his back, hands behind his head and a blonde-haired baby with golden eyes and matching shades lounging on his bicep. The resemblance is uncanny. "Looks like she's done already. Want me to finish feeding him?" he offers.

"That's okay. He's almost done. Aren't you, little Liam?" I coo at my little guy with his shock of light brown hair. He smiles up at me with his one green eye and one bright blue rimmed in dark lashes. Logan was right, we do make beautiful babies.

Tristan finally returns with my much-needed iced tea, our three-year-old little girl clinging happily to his side. Her chubby little legs kick as she squirms to be let down. Toddling her way over to me, she offers me a sip of her juice box. "Hi there, cuteness. I see you talked Daddy Tristan into yet another juicy."

Tristan smiles at me with his perfect Tristan smile, no remorse. "I told Mila she had to share it with Mommy. So, if she drinks it all, it's on you."

"Gee, thanks," I tell him with an eyeroll as the toddler already moves away now that she's shared a sip. We all know she won't be back until it's gone and she wants another. Tristan leans down to kiss me before following after our little girl, making sure she steers clear of the edge of the pool.

When Liam is finished eating, I pull my swim top back into place and walk him over to the baby lounger that Ash built. With a UV-proof sunshade and fans built into the sides, it does an excellent job of keeping the little ones cool while we're out here. Jace joins me, placing Jaide beside her brother. The two naturally roll toward one another, still asleep. Jace removes Jaide's sunglasses, setting them on the table.

"I was thinking Greece for our family vacation this year. They have lovely beaches, and the food is to die for," Jace tells me as he takes my hand and walks with me over to where Ash is propped up against the side of the pool.

I slide into the cool water with a pleasant sigh. It truly is hot out here today. "That sounds good. There're a lot of historical sights I'd like to see there."

Ash doesn't waste time placing me in front of him, wrapping his big arms around my waist lazily. His eyes scan all around us idly, making sure the kids are being safe in the water and no one is getting sunburned. Most of the kids have teamed up with Mikey and Logan in a water balloon fight, no doubt the result of Logan and Ava's planning.

I take them all in. My eight mates all relaxed and playing

with our amazing children. The babies sleeping away in the sunshine, our pack moving around us without a care in the world. I don't know what I ever did to deserve such happiness, but I wouldn't trade it for the world. I've found my place in this life, found my pack, kept them with me, and love them fiercely. It's everything I've always wanted.

Here's a little something to look forward to in the near future:

I'm not sure I understand this fountain. What do angels have to do with a secret werewolf school? The plaque only reads: "Where it all began". Nothing stating why it's here. I've been told enough stories about this place to know that teenage girls revere it, usually tossing in their shiniest coins and wishing for love, but I've never been told why they do it.

"Oh, shit. Sorry. I mean, excuse me," I'm told as I'm roughly shoved from behind.

I turn my head, glaring at the guy who bumped into me. His mismatched eyes distract me almost as much as much as the tower of boxes he's balancing precariously in his arms, towering over his head. Deciding he probably didn't even see me, much less push me on purpose, I shake off the angry retort on the tip of my tongue.

"It's fine," I grumble, turning back to the angel looming above me, lit up like a Christmas tree. Or, at least I think like a Christmas tree. I wouldn't know.

"Wishing for the attention of a boy?" The guy laughs softly to himself, like I'm missing something.

I arch a brow at him. "Not particularly. Weren't you going somewhere?" I ask pointedly.

"Yeah. I always stop at the fountain, though. Pay my respects and all that. It's my favorite story of theirs," he adds cryptically.

Pulling out a handful of change after setting down his tower of boxes, he sifts through the coins until he finds a shiny quarter. "Has to be the shiniest," he explains when he notices me watching.

"Why?" I ask, despite not wanting to continue the conversation.

"Because the Luna loves all things shiny." He laughs. This

dude is entirely too happy for my liking. Makes me uncomfortable.

"Makes sense," I grumble in a way that lets him know it makes no sense whatsoever.

He eyes me from the side, frowning. "You don't know the story? Everyone knows the story."

I roll my eyes, picking my bag up off the ground and tossing over my shoulder. "Like I'd want to hear a fairytale of *true and everlasting love*," I singsong before making a gag-me-now gesture.

His pale brows nearly meet his hairline. "Uh...kay..."

I walk away, not admitting to myself even the tiniest of bits that that guy was hot as hell. Nope, not even a little.

∽

Cyan

"Who the hell was that?" Raider asks me when he catches me staring after the girl I ran into.

My brow creases as I try to remember if I've met her before. "Huh," I say after a minute and coming up empty. "I have no idea."

"Seriously, what the hell's wrong with you? You haven't blinked in, like, forever," he teases me before elbowing my ribs. I grit my teeth, glaring daggers at my brother.

"Help me with these?" I nod to the stack of art supplies I'm supposed to drop off to the studios. Well, I was supposed to drop them off a few hours ago, but I got sidetracked.

"Sure." Raider shrugs, taking the top half for me.

I grab the rest, following closely behind him. "What do you think the chances are of us not already knowing a female our age?" I ask after a period of silence.

Raider laughs knowingly. "Chick really has you caught up,

huh? I admit she looked damn good walking away, but she was *walking away*, brother. Plenty of chicks chase after us, so why waste your time on the one who isn't?" he scoffs.

"She didn't know our parents' story. How's that possible?" I look back, wondering if she went back to the fountain after I left. Nope, no sign of her. Damn, I should have gotten her name at least. That would be less weird than tracking her scent to see where she went. Wait, do I even want to?

Yes.

Yes, I do. She was hot, sure, but lots of girls are. Why do I want to know more about this one? I stop dead in my tracks, realization dawning on me. I drop the boxes as I bust out laughing, having to hold my stomach.

"What the hell, weirdo?" Raider eyes me warily.

"She..." I talk through the laughter. "She didn't know their story." I wipe the tears from the corners of my eyes. "That means she probably had no clue who I was. And *she walked away*." I smile brightly at my brother before turning to stare determinedly at the fountain.

"Annnnd this makes her special why?" my brother drones.

"Not special." Not *yet*. "Different." I wonder how much her attitude will change once she learns who I am. She hasn't been taught from birth to drool all over my brothers and me, trying to trap an Ivaskov prince as soon as possible. Will she still be able to walk away once she finds out? Hmm, for some reason this curvy brunette has me all kinds of curious. Good thing it's a new school year and I have all the time in the world to find out why.

To be continued...

ABOUT THE AUTHOR

Lane Whitt likes coffee, reading, and dreaming up stories. If you've enjoyed this story and would like to know where to find Lane's upcoming works, then have no fear! The links are below.

Lane Whitt isn't a fan of social media, but can be found on Facebook (https://www.facebook.com/LaneWhittAuthor) where she often spends time reaching out to readers and posting funny cat memes.

Lane also has a website that you can visit to see what she's up to, order signed paperbacks, and contact her directly @LaneWhitt.com.

If you just want to be notified when Lane releases new books, be sure to follow her on Amazon

(https://www.amazon.com/Lane-Whitt/e/B011WR2EW6)

Printed in Great Britain
by Amazon